Dragonspawn Vengeance

Dragonspawn Vengeance

BOOK THREE OF
THE DRAGONSPAWN TRILOGY

THOMAS ROTTINGHAUS

Dragonspawn: Vengeance
Copyright © 2020 by Thomas Rottinghaus. All rights reserved.

No part of this publication may be reproduced, stored in a retrieval system or transmitted in any way by any means, electronic, mechanical, photocopy, recording or otherwise without the prior permission of the author except as provided by USA copyright law.

This novel is a work of fiction. Names, descriptions, entities, and incidents included in the story are products of the author's imagination. Any resemblance to actual persons, events, and entities is entirely coincidental.

The opinions expressed by the author are not necessarily those of URLink Print and Media.

1603 Capitol Ave., Suite 310 Cheyenne, Wyoming USA 82001
1-888-980-6523 | admin@urlinkpublishing.com

URLink Print and Media is committed to excellence in the publishing industry.

Book design copyright © 2020 by URLink Print and Media. All rights reserved.

Published in the United States of America
ISBN 978-1-64753-517-9 (Paperback)
ISBN 978-1-64753-600-8 (Digital)
04.09.20

Prologue

The once powerful nation of Norland teeters on the brink of total destruction. The *magii'ri* Wizards and Warriors empowered by the gods to enforce the rule of law known as the Code have been scattered to the winds. The architect of their destruction, Timon Blackhelm, has vanished. And now the hope of the *magii'ri* lies with the Dragonspawn, embodied by the Wizard Mathias as a youth named Jacob Grimwullf. But Jacob has become disillusioned with Mathias' deceit and is on the verge of coming completely under the influence of the Sky Rider, the invincible Dragon Slagg, who for reasons of his own wants Jacob to slay his Dragonform.

CHAPTER ONE

Jacob felt as if he were being torn in two. The Beast which had been part of him as long as he could remember was opening both pitiless eyes and staring straight into his soul. He could see the Beast in his own mind as he simultaneously saw the immense form of the Sky Rider and felt the heat that emanated from him. The Beast yawned and stretched, fully aware that he was winning the fight and soon he would be in full control. Jacob's mind was in turmoil. For some reason he wanted to please the Sky Rider, Slagg, but at the same time he knew he could not do what the Dragon asked of him even though the Beast inside him yearned for it. How could he kill a creation as marvelous as the Sky Rider? But that was exactly what the Dragon wanted him to do. Slagg stared at Jacob knowingly.

"You're joking," Jacob replied. He looked about as if he expected to see a Wizard perpetrating this colossal prank. "You *want* me to kill you?"

"You are strong enough to do it," Slagg said. "And I will show you the way. You will terminate this vessel I am bound to and release my true form."

They both heard the sound of footsteps scrabbling among the loose rocks at the same moment. Slagg's massive head jerked up and he drew in a huge breath. "The sick one and the girl."

Jacob was momentarily confused, then he saw Link and Anja. The apprentice Wizard's face was screwed into a mask of rage as he slid to a halt and nocked an arrow.

"No!" Jacob shouted. He stepped in front of Slagg, but the Sky Rider nudged him out of the way. Link drew the bow and fired, but the arrow bounced harmlessly off of Slagg's scales. Then Slagg cocked his head as if he heard a distant sound, and with one massive wingbeat he was airborne. He pumped his gigantic wings effortlessly and hurtled away towards a distant peak. Jacob watched him go, and was amazed to see another massive body gliding above the mountain top. Then Link and Anja descended upon him.

"How could you?" Link shouted. "You let him get away! Did you make plans to lead us to him, so he could ambush us?" He advanced so close that spittle from his mouth sprayed Jacob's face.

Jacob wiped his face with his sleeve while he watched Anja. Suspicion flared in her eyes. His heart sank and his belly felt suddenly hollow. The Beast in his mind leaped forward, fangs bared, eager for violence and bloodshed. Jacob struggled to maintain control.

"I know how it must have looked," Jacob said. "But you must understand. Slagg means us no harm!"

"He's the Darklord's lapdog," Link shouted, still in Jacob's face. "He'll tear us to pieces the first chance he gets."

Jacob's vision darkened and Link's outline became a red haze. "Back off," he warned quietly as he flexed his hands. Link regained some of his common sense and stepped back. Jacob's vision returned to normal.

"He didn't harm us yet," Anja said suddenly. "He could have killed us easily, if he had wanted to."

"Exactly," Jacob agreed quickly. Then he realized the only thing that could have been gliding among the peaks. "Didn't Mathias say that Slagg is the last known Dragon?"

"Of course," Link said hotly. "Don't try to change the subject."

"Then what flees from him right now?"

They all turned and strained their eyes towards the distant peak.

"Oh, no," Link whispered. "It must be a Dragoness. Slagg is probably driving her away from their eggs. Oh, no, no, no," he moaned.

Jacob shook his head. While he felt a certain kinship with Slagg, he only felt animosity towards this new arrival. The intensity of his rage at the Dragoness confused him.

"What does that mean?" Anja asked.

"After they mate, a Dragoness will try to return and eat the eggs. The bull Dragon will do anything to defend the young. Anything," Link said.

"So, they have mated, which means there will be more Dragons," Anja said.

"We have to get off this mountain," Jacob interrupted insistently. "Now. Slagg won't harm us, but the Dragoness certainly will." Anja paused and searched Jacob's face for a clue to his loyalty. "You have to trust me." Jacob said. "Please. Trust me. I'm thinking of your safety."

Anja stepped forward to join him, and his heart soared again. But Link bared his teeth in a grimace, and Jacob saw in that instant that the apprentice hated him. He wasted no time on that as they skidded down the mountain, nearly careening out of control. They burst into the cold camp and startled Michael half to death. The older man lunged for his weapons with a white face, but Link quickly stepped forward and slammed a foot home on his forearm. Michael yelped in pain, then Link released him. Both Anja and Jacob started towards the old man, then Jacob veered towards Link as anger flared up within him. Link watched with a smug smile, until Jacob's hand went to his sword hilt. Then panic registered on his handsome face.

"No," Anja stayed Jacob's sword hand. "He's not hurt." But it was obvious that Link had revealed his true character.

"We have to find a place for you to hide," Jacob explained quickly as he gathered things up in a bundle and hurriedly tied them together.

Michael glared at the young apprentice while he rubbed his forearm, but he pitched in and helped Jacob and Anja pack up the camp. Anja hurriedly explained the situation. Michael's face went two shades whiter, and he managed to keep up even with the quick pace that Jacob set.

Jacob had spied a copse of green farther up the mountain and due West from their camp. He fixed his eyes on it, and as the sun set and the stars came out he picked a bright one to guide him. It was after midnight when they finally reached the dubious shelter. All around them the land was scorched to the barren ground by Slagg's magical fire. But a few trees and some oakbrush had escaped his paranoid destruction, and now they offered a little pocket of concealment. Michael flopped down as soon as they reached the trees, and Jacob knew the old man had given his last ounce of strength. He could go no farther. He propped his peg leg up on a rock and raked a sleeve over his sweaty face.

"I'm slowing you down again," he said. "You three should go on. Without me you could make it to better shelter by daybreak, and I would divert Slagg's attention from you while you escaped."

"No," Anja said sternly. "I won't leave you."

"Neither will I," Jacob declared. "And it's not Slagg..."

"Michael has a point," Link interrupted. "He could buy us valuable time."

"We are not leaving him," Jacob replied. "If you want to cut out on your own, then go right ahead. Leave. Tonight. As a matter of fact, I think that would be best for all of us. You should be the one to leave."

Link fell silent. Jacob returned his attention to Michael. "It's not Slagg that we have to worry about, for whatever reason. It's the Dragoness."

"So, you have reached a truce with the Sky Rider?" Michael asked. "How?"

"I can't explain it," Jacob said. "We have something in common that binds us. He asked me for a favor."

"He spoke, and you understood?" Michael exclaimed. "By the Gods! Are you a Dragonlord?"

"The Dragonlords are myth," Jacob said. "But I did understand him, and he understood me."

"And they made plans to ambush us, no doubt," Link said in a surly tone. "Did he promise you treasure in return for your favor? Perhaps gold and jewels for three fine meals, such as us?" He swept his hand to indicate Anja and Michael.

Incredibly, Jacob saw doubt once again reflected in Anja's expression.

"What would you have me do, to prove myself?" Jacob growled.

"Go find Slagg and save us. Kill both of the Dragons and destroy the eggs," Link demanded.

Fury leaped to life inside Jacob at the thought of any harm coming to the Dragon's eggs. In that instant he wanted to wrap his hands around Link's throat and crush the life from him. He fought the impulse down with a supreme effort. "Maybe with my bare hands, too?" Jacob suggested in a caustic tone.

"Go to Slagg and negotiate with him," Anja said suddenly. "Agree to do the favor that he asked of you in return for safe passage."

"Yes," Michael agreed enthusiastically. "That would do it!"

"You don't know what you ask," Jacob replied.

"Whatever it is," Anja said, "if it would mean our safety you should be willing to do it."

Jacob shook his head in despair. "Slagg *wants* me to kill him."

Michael and Anja exchanged incredulous glances.

"Then do it," Anja urged. "We can't survive an attack."

"And you have no idea what manner of being might be released by the murder of Slagg's Dragonform," Jacob replied in an icy tone.

"But to appease you and to prove myself," he glanced sorrowfully at Anja. "I will try."

Anja had to stop herself from reaching out to him, to tell him that she trusted him already. Then she glanced at Michael. The old man still breathed heavily and sweat ran down his face in streams. He would not survive a run for safety.

Jacob silently stripped off all of the camp gear and checked his weapons. Then he wheeled in his tracks and started straight up the side of the mountain. *It's always the same*, he thought angrily. *Just when you begin to care for someone, they either leave or trample your feelings in the dirt. She didn't even trust him! She believed Link, of all people, before him. Damn it. Damn her. Damn them all*, he thought. *If Luke was here they would walk right up to Slagg, spit in his face and cut him down, then slay the Dragoness when she came in for the eggs.* As he climbed, sanity slowly overrode emotion. He had no desire to kill Slagg. The thought made him want to puke. Why was he thinking that way? The girl had addled his brain. But he desperately wanted her to trust him, even now. He calmed down, as much from the physical exertion as anything, and reached the decision to approach Slagg. But he could not walk up to the main entrance to Slagg's den, not with an enraged Dragoness hovering close by. So, he wound slightly around the mountain, following a dim trail at a trot until he suddenly stumbled onto a raised wooden platform on a small shelf.

He approached the structure cautiously, with his sword drawn. It appeared to be an air vent, which made sense if Slagg's lair was an abandoned dwarf mine. Jacob pried off the cover and peered inside. He could see the rungs of a ladder that disappeared into the depths. For a moment, Jacob squatted next to the yawning, black hole. Abruptly, at the campsite below him, the twinkling light of a small campfire burst into life. Shit, he thought in disgust. Were they really such helpless fools? They were in plain view of the higher reaches of the mountain, and the fire would be a direct invitation to a hungry Dragoness. Jacob slipped into the hole, determined to enlist Slagg's aid before it was too late.

The first rungs creaked in protest when he tested them with his full two hundred twenty pounds, but they held. He lowered himself gingerly down into the blackness and pulled the cover over his head. As he inched down the ladder, he began to smell something vaguely familiar. It was a hot, reptilian smell, like a nest of rattlesnakes on sunbaked sandstone. The scent tickled his memory and images of huge, dust colored shapes lying peacefully in the sun came unbidden to his mind. He paused, and the memory was like an unreachable itch in the center of his brain. It was not just a memory. He was actually there. But that was not possible. Suddenly, the rungs beneath his feet gave way with a splintering crack, and he tumbled headlong into the blackness.

The air whistled in his ears as he slowly regained his senses, and when he did, a strangled cry erupted from his throat. His flailing left hand caught one of the rotting rungs and he gasped in agony as his full weight hit it. It splintered and broke immediately and sent him reeling downwards into the pitch black. He cringed in anticipation of the impact, but had no more time to react when he landed with a splash in cold water and plunged under the surface. Down, down he went, fighting to stop the descent. Just as he thought he would be sucked underground and spat out into the sea as a rotting corpse, his feet touched solid rock and he launched himself towards the surface. He stroked furiously, fighting the impulse to suck in anything to stop the burning pain in his lungs. He broke through the surface suddenly and rose halfway out of the water with the power of his stroke. He dragged in great lungfuls of air and forced life back into his oxygen starved tissues as he treaded water. Then he began a slow search of the walls of the shaft. Nothing was visible even to his eyes in the pitch black of the mountain's interior, except a tiny speck of light at the top of the shaft. It was impossibly far above him. Then his searching hands encountered another opening, and he crawled into it.

He felt for his weapons as he regained his breath, and he realized quite suddenly that the shaft he was in was where the snake smell came from. It was stronger here, assaulting his sense of smell with a scent almost too strong to bear. Jacob leaned back against one wall to collect his wits. Where did those memories come from? Who did they belong to? Who was he?

"You're going insane," he whispered to himself. "But, as Luke would say, no sense sitting here waiting for something to happen. Get off your ass and do something."

He cautiously reached up and felt the ceiling no more than four feet above him. That meant he had to crawl to meet whatever was coming. So be it. He crawled down the shaft, and at times it grew so small his back and shoulders bumped the top. Then his searching hand sank up to the wrist in the floor of the cave, and he smelled a new, foul odor. *This just gets better and better*, he thought. *Now I get to crawl through bat shit.*

He continued on, and the passage eventually grew larger. He stood carefully, and felt something moving on his back. He ripped it off and felt something small and furry as it sank gleaming white teeth into his thumb. He flung it away with a muffled curse and pulled another and then three more off his shoulders. He lurched into the side of the passage and ground his back against it and felt several small bodies as he crushed the life out of them. Then the cave was filled with the sound of rushing wind as the roosting bats panicked and took flight. Leathery wings beat at him as he stumbled farther into the cave and threw his arms up to protect his face. Then it was over, and dead silence pressed down on him.

"Come," the parched voice called to him.

The whites of his eyes were exposed as they flew open in surprise. But it was not just the shock of the rustling voice that caught him unaware. It was the fact that the interior of the pitch black cave was simultaneously revealed to him as if it were broad daylight. As sharp as his senses had been before, they were increased tenfold now. He crossed the cavern and proceeded down another narrow passage. A soft glow lit the far end of the passage, and the serpentlike scent of the great bull Dragon wafted in on a warm draft. It was no longer unpleasant to Jacob, but it did stir up images in his subconscious that he could not explain.

He emerged from the passage into a great hall that had been hewn from the living rock in some forgotten age. Slagg was perched upon a great nest of tree branches and grass matted together with cured mud. Piles of loot from the Dragon's raids surrounded him.

The soft soughing of his breath came in time with the heaving of his great sides, and puffs of steam shot from his nostrils. The entire hall reeked of snake, but now Jacob did not even notice it. Moisture condensed on the walls and ceiling and dripped off again. Jacob raked a hand across his forehead and it came away slick with sweat.

"Yesss," Slagg hissed. "You came to me."

Jacob nodded as he let his eyes rove over the immense treasure that stretched before him. There was gold and silver and gemstones, jewel encrusted tankards and piles of coins. He saw silver helmets, some with the owner's head still firmly lodged within them, shards of armor and jeweled swords. Despite himself, he dropped to one knee and scooped up a handful of coins, then let them trickle through his fingers to the floor.

Slagg laughed. "You wish for wealth. Do as I ask and half will be yours."

Jacob forced his sluggish mind to process what Slagg had said. The poison of greed for a Dragon's treasure had taken a firm hold on his brain and held on like a wildcat. "I have a favor to ask in return."

Slagg's eyes narrowed. "What?"

"I'll do as you ask," Jacob said, surprised that the words came from his mouth. "If you protect my companions from the Dragoness."

Slagg laughed again. "Yesss. I can do that. We have an accord and you are honor bound to keep it."

Jacob nodded. Slagg's jagged teeth bared in a grin. He slithered off the nest and Jacob's mouth dropped open in astonishment. In the center of the nest lay three oblong eggs coated with a sticky, mucous like jelly.

"I intended to kill the bitch anyway," Slagg stated.

Jacob cringed. The voice inside his head had gone from dry and lifeless to blistering hot. For a moment, Jacob had a clear vision of shimmering heat waves as they danced across an open field. *If voices had appearances*, he thought, *that was Slagg's voice*. Then it was gone, and the dessicated, rustling voice returned.

"This is the means to fulfill our pact," he had snagged a leather wrapped bundle with his serrated front teeth. He dropped it at Jacob's feet. An evil smile caused his leathery lips to pull back from those razor sharp teeth as he saw Jacob staring suspiciously at the eggs. "If my gamble does not pay off and I pass from this World, I wanted more than one specimen to carry my blood."

Jacob had little time to wonder at that remark. The bundle Slagg had brought commanded his attention. He knelt at Slagg's feet and unwrapped it, and when it was visible, Slagg showed his displeasure with a loud hiss and retreated several feet. It was the Dragonkiller arrow, with a black metal shaft and vanes from a raven's wing. The arrowhead was crafted from black steel, sharper than Slagg's talons and wickedly barbed. The head flickered with a red glow. Jacob ran his hand reverently down the shaft and tested the blade with his finger, then gasped as it opened a gash on his hand. The blade seemed to be trying to draw itself deeper into his flesh when he jerked it back. He stood, hand stinging with pain as blood dripped from his palm.

"He nearly did me in with that one shot," Slagg whispered. "It missed my heart by an inch."

"Who?" Jacob asked, his heart racing.

"The one you seek," Slagg replied. "The one you call father," he added sarcastically, but that remark was lost on Jacob.

"What do you know of him?" Jacob asked.

"Not in our accord to give out information," Slagg replied as he abruptly turned and started out the main passage. "Help yourself to the treasure." He disappeared around a bend in the tunnel.

Jacob stood, dumbfounded, until Slagg was gone from sight. He studied the Dragonkiller arrow and was surprised at a tremor of fear that ran through his body. Streaks of red light flickered through the broadhead even after Slagg was gone. He held it close to his face and felt the warmth that flowed from it. Jacob stowed it carefully in his quiver, then allowed himself to succumb to the temptation of the treasure. He filled every pocket and pouch that he possessed with jewels and gold coins, then he followed Slagg's trail out of the den. It was easy enough to find. The giant worm's tail had worn a rut nearly a foot deep, he had been using that passage for so many years.

Slagg was perched at the entrance like a giant bird of prey with a majestic view of the valley below him. His reptilian head swayed in an ancient rhythm as his steel hard claws alternately gripped the solid rock beneath him and dug furrows several inches deep. An odd rumbling sound emanated from his chest and seemed to reverberate through the rock beneath him. He was well pleased with himself. After so many years, so many centuries, he was finally realizing who he really was. He would have his revenge after all. Bit by bit, he could feel himself emerging from the shell of the Sky Rider and returning to his true form. The thought pleased him.

"Slagg," the voice cut through his pleasant dreams.

"What is it now?" He asked. These humans could be so irritating.

"Why do I feel so reluctant to keep our accord?"

Slagg refused to look at him. He kept his snout pointed downhill. "You and I are bound together, Jacob. Even I do not know how it came to be." He glanced at the sound of disbelief that came from Jacob. "It's true. I've lived a double life, as two separate beings who cannot escape each other, but there are times, gaps in my memory, that I can't explain. I don't know what the other being has done during those times."

"I'm not sure I can keep my end of the accord," Jacob said haltingly. "I feel a kinship to you that I can't explain."

"We have an accord. You are honor bound to keep it. I would not have struck the accord if it wasn't what I desired. Your friend's fire draws the bitch like a beacon and now I'll keep my end of the accord. See that you do too." With that he leaped into the sky and was gone with only a whisper of wind to mark his passing.

Jacob was startled from the spell Slagg's Dragonmagic had placed on him, and he realized immediately that his companions would soon be under attack. *If they aren't already*, he thought. He plunged down the mountain towards the flickering light that marked their camp. As he ran, he listened to the obvious sounds of a savage battle being waged in the skies. There were no vocal shrieks of rage or pain, but each Dragon's thoughts were apparent to Jacob. He shared Slagg's anger and hate for the bitch, as Slagg had named her, and he hoped that she would fall lifeless from the sky. But she retreated under Slagg's assault and was soon out of sight and mind. At least Slagg was keeping his end of the accord.

He burst into camp amid a great deal of noise, or so he thought. But no one was even aware of his approach until he stood in the firelight at Link's feet. He angrily kicked dirt over the flames and stomped them out. Anja and Michael at least had the good sense to move away from the fire light. Link stood and watched Jacob insolently.

"You're a damn fool," Jacob said quietly. "You could have killed everyone, if I hadn't struck an accord with the Sky Rider."

Anja and Michael approached from their hiding places in the darkness.

"Did you say you reached an accord with Slagg?" Anja asked.

"I did," Jacob said. "The sacrifice is something none of you will ever understand. The accord we struck pains me still."

"Probably not too much," Link said sarcastically. "It looks as if you have profited quite well from this." He nodded at Jacob's bulging pockets.

Jacob was genuinely confused, but only for a moment. Then the memories of Slagg's cavern came flooding back.

"He gave me half his treasure, if I do as he asked. I'll share it equally."

"Half?" Link cried, suddenly amicable again. "Was it a lot?"

"It was awesome," Jacob replied, thinking more of the bull Dragon than the treasure.

"What exactly is the favor he asked, Jacob?" Anja interjected.

Jacob paused. "I must slay his Dragonform. He says he has been imprisoned as a Dragon for hundreds of years. The accord we reached is exactly what he demanded earlier, but I made him agree to protect you from the Dragoness."

"Dark Magic," Michael said fearfully. "It's best not to meddle in Dark Magic."

"Bullshit!" Link exclaimed. "That is greatly exaggerated."

All three turned to look at him.

"Or so I've heard," he added hastily.

"So you agreed to slay Slagg, the Dragon, and release a prisoner from within him" Anja said thoughtfully. "And he will protect us from the Dragoness?"

"That is the accord," Jacob replied.

"But what manner of being will be released by the slaying of his Dragonform? You mentioned that earlier. Did Slagg say what will be released when his Dragonform is killed?"

All were silent for a moment.

"I don't know," Jacob said truthfully. "But he already repelled the Dragoness from this camp tonight. We have to trust him. I trust him," he added.

"You're an idiot, Jacob, to trust a Dragon," Link said.

Jacob stared him down. "You and I are going to have a serious disagreement one day."

"Here now," Michael said, as he stepped between them. "We need every hand in case something goes wrong here."

"I reckon," Jacob agreed, but his sword hand refused to release his blade. "For now. We really need to keep moving, Michael, as long as you can."

"Lead the way," the older man replied bravely.

Morning found them still much too close to Slagg's den, in Jacob's opinion. But Michael could travel no faster. At first light they came to a broad expanse of broken sandstone. Great slabs of it as tall as Jacob lay strewn about. He felt her before he saw her, just a black speck on the horizon. *The bitch is back*, Jacob thought.

"Find shelter," he shouted. "She's back!"

His companions scrabbled across the rocks in confusion, but Jacob merely drew his sword and waited. The thought came unbidden to his mind. She wanted the eggs, but she would have to go through him first. His brow knitted in confusion. Why would he think such a thing? He glanced again at the sky and saw the Dragoness as she hurtled down the spine of the mountain. Then he spied a crack in the wall of the mountain and knew it was their only chance.

"Over there!" he gestured frantically.

His companions realized what he saw and started for it as one. But Michael fell behind, and Jacob saw immediately that none of them would make it. He gripped his sword tighter, and prepared to make a stand. The blade in his hand sang a song of bloodlust and made his senses soar. Unbelievably, Link circled back towards the older man. Jacob thought he intended to help him. Instead, he slammed into him with his shoulder and knocked him off his feet, then ran back towards the cave. Anja saw none of it. Then the Dragoness was upon them.

She descended upon the most helpless first, as Link had hoped. Jacob leaped from his perch just as she dropped on Michael. He clearly saw the whites of the older man's eyes just before the huge shape of the Dragoness blotted them out. Then Jacob leaped to attack. He swung the sword with such ferocity that it actually bit through the Dragoness' scales and drew a trickle of blood. She bellowed and turned on him. He parried her claws with the sword, then she knocked his feet out from under him with her tail. But he saw Anja reach the cave before he fell. Then she was gone, and Jacob struggled to his feet just as the Dragoness reached Link. He screamed in defiance and hacked at her with his sword, but she almost casually disarmed him and pushed him to the ground with her snout. Her jaws gaped wide and began to descend when Jacob attacked again. Her attention diverted, her jaws snapped shut, not on Link's body as she had intended, but on his left leg. Link screamed again as the Dragoness shook her head and severed his leg above the calf, while Jacob rained blows upon her. He leaped to her head and thrust his sword to the hilt into her right eye. Black blood coursed down the blade as the Dragoness bellowed in pain and jerked her head back. She retreated as Link's lower leg and foot dropped from her jaws to the sandstone. Jacob reached down with one hand and jerked Link to a standing position.

"Get to the cave!" he shouted.

Link took one step towards the cave and promptly fell again. He scrambled to all fours and began to crawl. Anja rushed back out to help him.

The Dragoness pawed furiously at her eye socket, and Jacob took advantage of the lull to glance at Michael. He was obviously dead, his life blood still pumped out of a fist sized hole in his chest and stained the rocks beneath him. Jacob thrust at the half blinded Dragoness again and forced it back. It hissed in rage and lunged for him. He swung his sword in a vicious arc and opened a gash across the Dragoness' cheek.

"Come on!" Jacob shouted. A crazy light danced in his eyes as he parried teeth and claws with steel. With his free hand, Jacob whipped the Dragonkiller arrow from his quiver and, as he knocked her claws aside, slammed it into the underside of the Dragoness' jaw. It sliced through flesh and bone as if he waved it in thin air. The Dragoness bellowed in agony and cast a fearful eye at the arrow Jacob held. He retreated towards the cave, following a crimson trail from Link's wound over the sandstone. The Dragoness regained her courage and attacked again, and with one final swing Jacob severed her front leg. She leaped forward with a shriek of pain and knocked him backwards into the cave.

Jacob immediately leaped to his feet and turned to go deeper into the cave. He stopped with a jolt. It was no more than fifteen feet deep. Anja was huddled against the rear wall, her face a white mask of fear. Link lay at her feet, with his eyes rolled back in his head. Jacob whirled around as the Dragoness forced her head inside the cave, but her shoulders jammed against the sides. She could not reach them. She opened her jaws and hissed, and smoke poured from her throat.

"She's going to burn us," Jacob whispered.

But before the flames could issue from her fire vent, a tremendous impact jolted the entire mountain. The Dragoness twisted her head from side to side, but did not withdraw. She bellowed again, which nearly deafened those inside the cave. Then she arched her neck as high as possible and her jaws yawned wide with a bubbling whine. A hideous crunching, tearing sound accompanied the whine, then a wave of black blood erupted from her mouth and drenched those in the cave. The Dragoness' head flopped to the floor of the cave and twitched spasmodically, then she stiffened and her one good eye rolled back in her head.

"Slagg is back," Link said. He drifted in and out of shock.

The Dragoness' carcass was abruptly pulled back, but it seemed even Slagg's immense strength was insufficient to remove her completely from the cave entrance. One nostril appeared in the opening he had created and he drank in the scent of those in the cave.

Anja screamed. Slagg drew in a great breath like he was drinking in the finest wine. When he exhaled a fine mist sprayed Jacob and his companions. Then he turned away from the cave and followed the blood trail from Link's wound back to his severed leg. Jacob shook off Anja's restraining hand to peer out past the dead Dragoness. Slagg lowered his head and came up with Link's leg in his forepaws. He looked back at the cave for a long moment, then raised the leg to his jaws and ate it. Jacob retched, then choked back the rush of bile in his throat and retreated back to Anja. The image of Slagg as he ate Link's leg was burned into his memory. Moments later they heard the rush of wind as Slagg leaped into the air and departed.

"You have to help me, Jacob," Anja cried. "If we don't stop the blood, Link will die."

Jacob hesitated. Could he have been wrong? Was Link's clumsy jostling of Michael just that, an innocent accident? Or did he push the older man down to buy himself enough time to reach the cave?

"Jacob?" Anja said in a wavering voice.

Jacob drew a slim leather strap from his belt and applied a tourniquet to Link's leg, just above the knee. Link grabbed his arm.

"How bad is it?"

"It's bad," Jacob answered. "I'll get you out of here."

Link only nodded as he realized the seriousness of his wound. Once they had slipped by the body of the Dragoness, Jacob laid Link down on a patch of clean, windswept sandstone. The bleeding had been controlled by the tourniquet for now. Anja rushed by them and dropped to her knees beside the body of her uncle. Jacob watched helplessly as she burst into tears. He felt totally inadequate to deal with a crying woman, but he approached and tentatively placed a hand on her shoulder. She rose to her feet and whirled to face him, then flung herself into his arms. She wrapped her arms around him and buried her face in his chest.

"He should never have come here," she sobbed. "But he was always thinking of me. He was the only family I ever had."

"He was a good man," Jacob said uncomfortably. He gently pulled her back so he could look into her eyes, then brushed a golden strand of hair back from her damp cheek. "I'm sorry. This is all my fault."

"No," Anja replied. "It's not your fault. No one forced us to come."

"I'll build a cairn for him, from the stones," Jacob said. "It will be a fitting resting place for a brave man."

"I'll help," Anja said. "But we must tend to the living first. With that wound, Link may die even if the bleeding stops."

Link chose that moment to become lucid again. He squinted at his legs, then at Jacob. "Dark Magic will heal me," he stated calmly.

"Link, no," Jacob replied with a vehement shake of his head.

"Are you a Healer, Jacob?" Link asked.

"You know the answer to that," Jacob replied.

"Then do as I say," Link commanded. "Before I pass out. Fill a waterskin with blood directly from the Dragoness' heart and bring it to me."

Jacob sighed. He wanted no part of a Dark Magic ritual, but he did as Link asked. He emptied a waterskin, then reached in through the massive hole in the ribcage of the Dragoness and severed her still quivering heart. He held the mouth of the skin over one valve and squeezed until the skin was filled. He carried it at arms' length back to the apprentice Wizard.

"Worry not, Jacob" Link said. "You have no part in the Dark Magic." He made several signs over the skin and mumbled off a long spell. "Now soak bandages and bind them onto my leg. Change them once a day." He instructed. "When you are done with that, tie my hands and feet and do not release me for three days. Do you understand? No matter what I do or say, wait three full days before you untie me." Then he collapsed and his head lolled limply to one side.

Jacob sliced open Link's breeches , then he and Anja did as he had instructed. They both winced at the jagged slivers of bone that protruded from the torn flesh. Then Jacob tied Link's hands and feet. He remembered how Link had knocked Michael sprawling, and he gave the knots an extra twist to make sure they were good and tight.

"It's up to the Gods now," Anja whispered.

"I reckon," Jacob said quietly. "But which ones?"

He began to gather stones for Michael's final resting place, and Anja helped. They had nearly finished when Link suddenly bolted upright. His eyes were wide and he stared blindly ahead, then a bloodcurdling shriek erupted from his throat and sent shivers down Jacob's spine. Link strained futilely against the ropes that bound him, then he abruptly relaxed. He looked straight at Jacob.

"Where's my leg?"

"The Dragoness..." Jacob began to explain.

"I know that," Link interrupted. "Where is it now, Jacob?"

Jacob ducked his head. "Slagg ate it." Anja stared, open mouthed.

"Then it seems he has broken your accord," Link replied. "What a pity. If I had my leg back, I could have reattached it. And if Slagg hadn't broken your accord, you would not feel such anger and betrayal." His voice sounded detached, like he was merely an observer. "You want to kill him now, don't you?"

"That's what *he* wants," Jacob said. But Link did not reply. He went limp again, and flopped back onto the sandstone.

"Accord or not," Anja said. "Slagg can't be trusted. He's shown that."

"I know," Jacob said miserably. "But in truth, he did protect you from the Dragoness."

Link shot upright once again. "Take it off!" he cried. "Please, take it off! It burns!" He struggled against the ropes to reach his leg, but failed.

Jacob started towards him, then stopped in confusion. "What should we do?"

"Leave it," Anja said. "He made his decision and gave himself to Dark Magic. It's too late for him. But not for us, Jacob. We must leave this place. Now."

"Do we have to take him with us?" Jacob asked, with a nod at Link.

"Of course," Anja replied, but Jacob saw the disappointment in her expression. He hesitated. Perhaps he should tell her how her uncle really died. Hell, maybe they should just leave Link where he was. *Or you can simply kill him yourself,* the Beast said. Jacob's hands twitched. He thought of Link's insolence and disrespect towards La'Nay and Luke. He remembered the uneasy feeling that came over him when he watched Link studying others with that greasy, dirty look in his eyes. There was something sick and twisted inside Link, a poison the tainted his soul. *And it would be so easy,* he thought.

"We can leave him," Jacob said. "He's naught but a murderous son of a bitch, anyway." He was surprised at the vehemence in his own voice.

Anja stared as if she guessed his thoughts. "What do you mean?"

"I might be wrong," Jacob replied. "But when the Dragoness attacked, I thought Link purposely knocked Michael down to buy himself time to get to the cave."

"I suspected it," Anja said. "If so, he got what he deserved. But to leave him would be to lower ourselves to his level. I won't do that."

Jacob shrugged. "Then we have to build a pallet to drag him on."

It only took a few minutes for them to fashion a crude travois from tree limbs and strap Link down on it. Then they started down the slope towards the plain, and, Jacob hoped, a friendly village to dump Link on. Whether he was murderous or not, he was a liability and Jacob was done with him.

Link drifted in and out of delirium. He called out to people Jacob did not know, then he begged Mathias to help him. Then the tone and demeanor of his ranting changed completely. He ordered Jacob to turn him loose or suffer greatly. Jacob listened stoically, and eventually Link began to speak in a language that was foreign to he and Anja. Then he returned to the common speech.

"I am the eldest son of Joseph!" he cried. "Ead should be mine! I am the rightful King!"

Jacob dropped the ends of the travois in astonishment. The stump of Link's leg struck a rock and he screamed, then slumped to one side. Jacob glanced at Anja, then without a word, he ripped a length of cloth from his sleeve and gagged Link. He returned to the head of the travois and continued on. They had nearly reached the foothills when he felt something amiss. He stopped again, and scanned the horizon. Nothing. But the feeling would not leave him.

"Take shelter in those rocks," he told Anja. He drug the travois into a huge pile of boulders and watched as Anja hid in a niche between two gigantic slabs of rock. Then he climbed to the top of a boulder and waited.

Slagg first appeared as a dark speck against the blue sky. Jacob watched his approach and was awed by the speed with which the Sky Rider ate up the distance between them. He bore straight down on Jacob and veered away at the last second.

"We had an accord," Jacob thought.

The sighing , molten voice returned to his head. "I'm breaking it. You may go free. The girl is mine."

"No!" Jacob shouted.

"We can make a new accord," Slagg's voice burned in Jacob's mind. "You for the girl."

"Yes," Jacob replied instantly. "Take me instead. Me for the girl!"

Anja watched in horror, silently shaking her head.

"It will be alright," Jacob reassured her. "You'll be safe this way."

"It is done," Slagg replied. "Come with me, Dragonspawn."

"I can't leave her until she is safe," Jacob said.

"Bah," Slagg's disgust was evident. "The girl makes you weak. As you wish. There's a village to the North. You can reach it in a day. Then you are mine."

"We have a new accord," Jacob agreed. "But this time you are honor bound to keep it."

"If you can find any remnants of my honor on the trail, pick them up for me," Slagg replied.

He hovered over them for a moment, then lightly touched down. His nostrils flared as he drank in and analyzed the scents wafting about the rocks. As he approached the dubious protection of Anja's hiding place, Jacob's senses were overcome with white hot rage. He ran forward and Slagg turned to regard him with one unblinking eye.

"I won't harm her," he assured Jacob.

His head thrust downward so suddenly Jacob was caught flat footed, but when Slagg withdrew it from the pile of rocks he did not have the girl. Instead, it was Link who dangled from his serrated teeth. The Sky Rider held him gently, careful not to allow his fangs to puncture the apprentice Wizard's skin.

"Slagg..." Jacob pleaded. He knew exactly what the Sky Rider was thinking.

"I agreed to spare the girl," Slagg's scorched voice seared in Jacob's brain. "But this one...this one is twisted even by my standards."

He gave his head a slight shake and Link's body whipped violently back and forth. His eyes opened and he instantly realized where he was. His gaze locked with Jacob's, but Jacob saw no fear. All he saw was hate. Slagg tossed him in the air like a cat with a mouse, caught him full in his jaws and ground his teeth together. Link's mutilated lower body below the waist dropped to the ground. Slagg chewed three times, tossed his head back and swallowed. He unfurled his great wings and leaped into the sky.

"One more day, Dragonspawn," he said as he disappeared.

Anja retched violently, her body bent double. Even Jacob felt bile rise in his throat. But he knew instinctively that Slagg was right. Something had been terribly wrong inside the apprentice Wizard. He tried not to look at Link's lower body as he gently led Anja away from the rocks. They had only gone a few hundred yards when the girl twisted free of his light touch.

"Don't touch me," she choked out. "You...you *knew* what Slagg was thinking. You knew he was going to kill Link and you did nothing to stop him."

Jacob stared in openmouthed astonishment. "Link was a murderous son of a bitch. He didn't deserve to live. If Slagg hadn't killed him, I would have. But, I saved your life," he said. "I gave the Sky Rider my own in return. If you still feel nothing but disgust for me, that's fine. I'll take you to the nearest village. Here," he offered Anja his pack with the share of the Dragon's treasure in it, but she refused to take it. He shrugged and started down the trail at a fast walk. Anja stared after him until he had gone nearly a quarter mile, then she ran to catch up. Jacob refused to acknowledge her. They walked in silence the rest of the day. Jacob set a hard pace and would not relent. It was as much to reach the village before Slagg returned, but he preferred to think it was because he couldn't wait to be away from the girl who found him repugnant. He saw the village and the villagers who came to meet them well before Anja did, and he readied his weapons. Anja watched him, her brow furrowed in fear and confusion.

"Villagers are coming," he announced. "And both of us are still bathed in Dragon blood. I really don't know how we will be received."

He needn't have worried. The villagers surrounded them, but after a sparing explanation from Anja about the fight with the Dragoness, they were quick to accept her and invited them both into the village.

"I will not put you in danger," Jacob announced. "My life is forfeit. I owe it to the Sky Rider as part of an accord to spare the girl."

That pronouncement threw the villagers into an animated discussion. Jacob took the opportunity to press a bag of gemstones into Anja's hand. She tried to withdraw her hand but Jacob closed her fingers around the bag.

"Take it," he insisted. "The villagers will be happy with the rest, but you will need money for safe passage back to your civilization."

He turned back to the villagers and threw the pack among them. It burst open and gold coins spilled out into the dust. Silence overtook the group.

"Take care of the girl," he said, "and it is yours. Harm her and I will return. With the Sky Rider," he added.

He turned and stalked away, his back ramrod straight. The villagers fell on the treasure like vultures, squabbling and bickering. But Jacob was confident they would care for Anja, especially when Slagg swept in only moments later. The Sky Rider landed near Jacob and lowered his muscular neck.

"Climb on," his voice sounded in Jacob's brain.

Jacob grinned and did as he was asked. The villagers once again fell silent and cowered to the ground. Slagg leaped into the air and rose a hundred feet with one wingbeat. Jacob marveled at the immense thrust generated by the Dragon's bunched muscles. He felt Slagg's power flowing through him and the sudden ascension only exhilarated him even more. He watched in disdain as the villagers returned to fighting over the treasure. Only one didn't join the argument. He was a young man of average height and athletic build with neatly trimmed brown hair and innocent blue eyes. He was the son of the headman, and he had been born a deaf mute. And thus he had no way of telling anyone that inside him resided the spirit of Nish, the Seventh Scribe. He watched as Jacob and the Sky Rider disappeared in the distance.

Slagg sailed through the clouds, dipping this way and that, and Jacob was so exhilarated by the unbelievable feeling of freedom he nearly forgot his own life was now forfeit. They flew over farm fields and forested mountains, quaint villages and huge, walled kingdoms. Slagg paused in midair, folded his wings and stooped. The wind whistled in Jacob's ears as they dropped from the sky, but even then he felt no real fear. Only when they landed, as softly as a butterfly, did he remember his accord with Slagg. He leaped from Slagg's back and waited. Now fear did crawl up his back, but he knew flight would be futile.

"Do what you will, Sky Rider," he said quietly. "I gave you my life freely."

"I don't want to kill you," Slagg's voice seared through his brain. "Why do you think I showed you the glory of Norland? The two of us can reign as the supreme rulers, first of Norland, then the World."

The thought seemed ludicrous to Jacob. "Rule the World? I'm nothing, Slagg.

Just an orphan. I have no lands, no servants, no army."

"You sell yourself short," Slagg replied. "Give in to the Beast, Jacob. It will set you free."

"What do you know of the Beast?" Jacob demanded.

Slagg sighed. His breath smelled like charred meat. "Bits and pieces of who I am are making themselves known to me. I feel the kinship you already confessed to. It can only be possible if we share blood."

"How can that be?" Jacob asked. "My father was Joseph Grimwullf of Ead. My mother was Elizabeth, his queen. You were not involved."

Slagg actually laughed. It was not a pleasant sound. "I was not there," he corrected. "But I was definitely involved. And I'm quite sure there was a certain Dragonwitch present as well."

"La'Nay," Jacob blurted.

"Yesss," Slagg hissed. Suddenly he could feel his talons closing around her body as he plucked her from the beach. The Dragonwitch he had entrusted with the very essence of his plan, *his* essence, had succeeded. In a rare moment of lucidity, the memories came back.

"What am I?" Jacob asked. "Why do I have something living inside me that is not even human?"

"Now you are beginning to see," Slagg said. "You are the Dragonspawn. You are a Warrior with the blood of a Dragon, my blood, coursing through your veins."

Jacob dropped to his knees. *He wasn't even human.*

"That's not possible," he whispered.

"Of course it is," Slagg insisted. "You are here. I am here. Anything is possible. Let me show you."

Slagg face bore a sly smile as he beckoned with his forearms for Jacob to come closer. With a feeling of dread, Jacob did so. But the great bull Dragon didn't tear him to pieces. Instead he pulled the youth in closer until Jacob felt he couldn't breathe. His vision grew hazy and he felt like he was flying again. Then the haze cleared and he was looking down on the World. But what a different World it was. Dragons soared in the skies and lounged in the sun. People walked freely among them. The fields were verdant and green. Well kept farmhouses dotted the landscape, and in the distance Jacob saw the towers of a great city. Dragons and men walked side by side.

"The time of the Dragonlords," Slagg's voice announced. "Men and Dragons coexisted. In fact, they shared everything equally. This was when the Dragonspawn was first created. He was revered, almost as a god. But, in time, as with all civilizations, this World fell apart. Much of the knowledge gained was lost, including how to create the Dragonspawn. Eventually, that knowledge was discovered by Dark Wizards, but they feared the Dragons so they hid the spell. A few cults sprang up to worship Dragons and eventually the knowledge was passed on to them."

"The Dragonwitches," Jacob said.

"Yes," Slagg agreed. "They worshipped us, as it should be. It can be that way again."

The World went dark. Jacob opened his eyes. He was back in the desert with Slagg. The Sky Rider's intentions were obvious. He wanted Jacob to believe they could return to the time of the

Dragonlords. But rather than clear Jacob's mind, Slagg's revelations muddled it even more.

"I see that what you've shown me is true," Jacob admitted. "But all that really means is I truly am a monster." He spoke with such despair and finality Slagg knew he had lost that gamble. But this was only the first hand in a long game.

"Bah!" the bull Dragon snorted. "You are lucky to have my blood. Enough of this. Join me. Give in to the Beast."

Jacob felt the Beast in his mind lunge forward as if summoned. How would it feel to stop fighting? To revel in the power he knew would come if his human and Beast side were joined? A surge of strength flowed through him. He could be invincible. He would be above the petty emotions and cares of humans, a supreme being who needed no one. In time, he could even defeat Slagg. He knew it. But something stopped him from giving in. He imagined Luke turning away from him in shame, and the Beast once again cowered in a corner of his mind.

"I can't," he replied.

Slagg's patience snapped. "Idiot!" he thundered. His tail lashed back and forth, smashing slabs of sandstone to bits. He rose to his full height and his fire vent smoked and glowed red. Jacob waited for the inevitable flames. But they didn't come. Instead Slagg leaped into the air, his wings beating furiously. As twigs and particles of sand stung his face from the gale force winds spawned by Slagg's wings, the Sky Rider's voice returned to molten lava in Jacob's mind.

"We have an accord! You are mine," Slagg hissed. Then he was gone.

Jacob sat alone on the rim of the canyon. He knew he couldn't return to the village. He would not walk for weeks to get back only to be rejected again. He suddenly realized that he was truly alone for the first time in his entire life. To make matters worse, since Slagg's abrupt departure he felt strangely diminished. He sat on the edge of the canyon until the sun went down and all through the night. At sunrise, with nothing better to do, Jacob started walking downhill, following the canyon.

He hadn't eaten in so long he had forgotten his last meal, and he realized with a start that he had no water either. He carried nothing but a sword and a heavy knife. As he walked he became aware of the trickling sound of water falling. It came from the bottom of the canyon, and the sound invaded his mind until he couldn't think of anything else. He abruptly started to climb down the canyon wall.

As Jacob neared the bottom of the canyon, he heard voices. The voices were not raised in alarm, nor were they directed at him. Jacob descended the rest of the way to the stream in the bottom of the canyon and drank his fill. He then crept through the undergrowth to a vantage point where he could observe the people he had overheard. It appeared to be a camp for a trading caravan. Without realizing his own reasons for doing so, Jacob stepped away from the brush into plain sight. The conversation stopped. All of the traders lunged for weapons while Jacob merely watched. In moments he was ringed with agitated men who fairly bristled with swords, knives and pikes.

"Who are you and what do you want?" One man demanded.

"My name is Jacob. I needed water and happened to come down near your camp," Jacob responded. "I mean no harm. Let me go and I'll be on my way."

"You travel alone in these times?" the speaker asked.

"I travel alone," Jacob agreed. "At all times."

"You look pretty strong," another observed. "Are you any good with those blades?"

Jacob shrugged. The traders looked about fearfully.

"I'm alone," Jacob repeated.

"Just the same," the first speaker said, "I think you better hand over your blades and stay here while we decide what to do with you."

Jacob smiled and shrugged again, but when he slid his sword from its sheath he held it at the ready.

"Take me in at my word or try to take me by force," he said. "I won't give up my weapons."

The leader suddenly laughed. He signaled his comrades to lower their weapons.

"One can't be too careful, you know," he said. He stepped forward. "I am Aric. We are traders bound for the coast."

Jacob nodded. "You have a long journey ahead of you." He looked beyond the camp. "And who is that?"

The traders all turned to look. A solitary rider on horseback picked his way down the far canyon wall. He rode with a natural ease and grace, moving in perfect balance with his horse. He wore a black duster and a black hat and his long dark hair streamed out behind him. His hat was pulled low concealing his face. The horse was coal black as well, at least the parts that were visible. Most of its body, face and legs were wrapped in what appeared to be material for a burial shroud. Jacob's eyes narrowed and his nostrils flared as the scent of death reached him. As he watched, four men clad in dust colored clothing emerged from hiding. They formed a line flanking the Rider and began swiftly walking towards the trader's camp. There was something about them, the way they moved, the resolute, irrevocable gait that ate up the distance that reminded Jacob of Luke. His eyes narrowed as they flipped back their coats and dusters to reveal their sidearms.

"Go," he told the traders. "Forget your goods. Go now!"

Suspicion showed plainly on the trader's faces.

"You set us up?" Aric cried.

"They're not with me," Jacob said. "Hurry! Get away! You're wasting time."

Inwardly, Jacob groaned at the incompetence of the traders. With a low growl he leaped from the group and ran to meet the threat. Misreading his intentions, several of the traders pursued him with their weapons ready. Jacob heard the whistle of arrows as they sped past him and also heard the solid thumping sounds they made as they were buried in living flesh. Two of the gunslingers slumped to the ground, but the other two drew and began firing. Bullets whizzed past Jacob's head and he thought the gunslingers had missed until he heard the cries of pain behind him.

Jacob weaved and ducked and covered the distance so quickly he saw the Rider's head jerk up in alarm. But then the Rider leaped from his horse and drew his own sword. Jacob struck a mighty blow, intending to finish the fight with one strike, but his blade was parried with superb skill. He struck again and heard the Rider grunt in surprise at his strength. Then Jacob made the mistake of looking at the attacker. His eyes were empty sockets in a Death's head bare of flesh. Stunned, Jacob hesitated. The Rider grinned and attacked. Jacob parried the blows and forced the Rider back. Sparks flew from their blades. Jacob forced the Rider's sword down and slashed him across the midsection. Gooey, black, tar like blood seeped from the wound. The Rider fell back in surprise as Jacob pressed his advantage. He rained blows down on the Rider forcing him to retreat even more. He knocked the Rider sprawling and raised his sword to finish the fight. But the Rider dropped his blade. His hands darted to his belt and he drew two revolvers. Jacob's eyes widened in terror as the Rider thumbed back the hammers and shot him four times in the chest. The impact flung Jacob in the air and he fell flat on his back. He couldn't breathe. He looked down in dismay at the four holes in his chest as they pumped his life blood out into the dust. Jacob reached one hand for the Rider, then all his strength left him. His World went black.

CHAPTER TWO

Jacob lay in a gauzy blanket of agony, unable to move. Over and over he saw the muzzle flashes and heard the reports of the Rider's pistols and felt the impact of the bullets. He squeezed his eyelids shut. A faint shadow appeared as an outline on the insides of his eyelids. It became more distinct and Jacob realized it was the figure of a young man. He was a handsome youth of average height, with jet black hair and a rakish smile.

"He got you good," the youth said.

Jacob tried to reply but all he could do was groan.

"Don't you recognize me?" the young man asked. "I am Talin, brother of Lynch and the pilot of the one you know as the Sky Rider."

Jacob tried to reply but could not. He tried again and felt hot blood well up in his throat and gush out of his mouth. Talin sidestepped it with an expression of disgust. Jacob rolled to his stomach and climbed to his knees while Talin watched with a bored expression. Somehow, Jacob made it to his feet and lurched to the creek where he immediately fell into a waist deep pool. The cold water of the creek quenched the burning pain in his chest. He lunged unsteadily to his feet and stood there swaying like a fir tree in a high wind.

"Bravo!" Talin clapped.

"Help me," Jacob managed to gasp.

Talin sat on a boulder. Jacob released a primal scream of agony. The Beast in his mind leaped to the forefront. Jacob ripped his shirt apart and stared in disbelief as the bluish rimmed holes left by the big lead slugs stopped bleeding and began to close. Two of the holes regurgitated the bullets that made them. He made his way towards Talin, who watched him with a bored expression.

Jacob reached the bank of the creek and collapsed on his back. His breathing slowly returned to normal and the brutal pain in his chest subsided to a dull ache. He felt strength flowing back into his extremities. The Beast stood guard in his mind, like a giant wolf guarding a kill. He turned his head to look at Talin.

"How?" he asked.

"Now you see your potential," Talin said smugly.

"Who are you?" Jacob persisted.

"I am the being who will be released when you slay Slagg's Dragonform," Talin answered. He shrugged. "I don't look all that dangerous, do I?"

Jacob tried to process that information. "You are one with the Sky Rider?"

"Yes," Talin replied. "And we are bound together as well. That's why you can see me. You, Slagg and I are one, to a point. And now you can see the advantages of having Dragon blood in your veins."

"I should be dead," Jacob realized.

Talin shook his head. "I guess I should excuse your thick headedness. This is probably the first time you've experienced regeneration. Yes, any of those wounds would have killed a mortal man. But you are not mortal. You are the Dragonspawn."

Jacob sat heavily beside Talin on the boulder. He had no argument.

"Are you a man?" he asked.

"I am spirit, an apparition in this form. Nothing more," Talin responded.

Jacob swept his arm through the young man sitting next to him. Talin's shape shimmered then returned to normal.

"You've experienced many of the benefits of being the Dragonspawn, even if you didn't know it at the time," Talin continued. "Incredibly keen eyesight, even in the dark. The physical strength, when you let yourself go, of ten men. Acutely sensitive hearing, and that little tickle you haven't yet fully explored," with that Talin looked slyly at Jacob, who merely nodded. "That is your

Dragon sense. Embrace it and let it free, and it will do the same for you, Jacob. All you have to do is let the Beast inside you take control."

Jacob lunged to his feet and turned to stare suspiciously at Talin. "Slagg! Is this just another one of your tricks?"

"This is no trick," Talin replied. "You are seeing only a tiny percentage of your power."

"Be gone," Jacob said with a dismissive wave. Talin clawed desperately for Jacob and disappeared.

Jacob wandered down the canyon, but hadn't gone far when he came upon the destruction of the traders. They were all dead. The Rider had attacked with such ferocity many were separated from their heads or limbs. But all were most certainly dead. Jacob's lip curled at the scent of blood and death. His hands ached to hold a weapon. Without warning the Beast appeared in his mind, but it didn't try to take control. It merely observed. Then a low growl came from it, and Jacob suddenly understood. The Beast could rule him and they could serve the Dark. Or they could coexist, and he would retain control. The thought intrigued him. But how did one control such a Beast?

He armed himself with the trader's weapons and followed the stream. In time he came to the mouth of the canyon. To his right lay the sea, several days away. To his left beyond the foothills was an open plain dotted with sandstone cliffs. Jacob turned left.

Jacob traveled for days, hunting when he needed meat and drinking from springs and streams. The Beast lay dormant within him, and Jacob let him sleep. His wounds healed completely leaving only small, pale scars. At all times his mind was occupied by one thought. He was the Dragonspawn. He was human, and he was Beast. But he had no idea how to control the Beast.

On the fifth day Jacob heard voices. It was dusk and Jacob had entered a canyon to hunt for meat. As he crept along a faint game trail, the voices floated up to him from the canyon floor. He froze, then took cover in a nest of sandstone slabs. The sun set and the scent of woodsmoke reached his nostrils, along with the animal stench of Beastsoldier. The glow from the fire illuminated the foreign camp almost directly below Jacob. He counted seven Beastsoldier guards and at least that many prisoners bound in chains. They had located the camp against a sheer cliff. Jacob climbed down until he was directly above the camp. Without a second thought, he leaped from the cliff.

Jacob slid his sword free as he fell. He landed in a group of three guards, knocking two of them sprawling. He brought the grip of his sword down on one guard's cannonball head and slashed one on the ground. Another recovered from his surprise enough to attack, but Jacob broke his sword with one blow and impaled him. As he withdrew the blade, he backpedaled. His calves connected with something soft but not yielding and he fell backwards. The remaining guards fell upon him, biting, punching and kicking. One sank his fangs into Jacob's upper arm and began to whip his head back and forth. Jacob growled in response. The Beast came forward, wresting control from Jacob. His eyes glowed yellow in the firelight and he flung all of the Beastsoldiers into the air. He stood before them and howled his challenge. All of the Beastsoldiers froze. Jacob heard a slight sound behind him, then someone slammed something down on the top of his head. Dazed, he fell forward. One of the Beastsoldiers jumped in and swung one rock hard fist down in a long, looping blow squarely on the top of Jacob's head. He fell into a black pit of unconsciousness.

When he awoke, Jacob's ankles and wrists were securely bound in chains. His wrist chains were fastened to another prisoner to his left. The prisoner he was attached to looked at him out of the corner of his eye.

"You had a chance," he said. "But you can't trust anyone. That little bastard who tripped you has been trying to buy favor from the guards the whole trip."

"Shut up," one of the guards growled.

"Sure thing, Limm,' the prisoner said.

"He's awake," Limm announced. "Time to go."

Jacob clambered to his feet. His hands automatically went to his belt.

"You want this, don't you?" Limm said. He twirled Jacob's foot long knife in front of his face. "You won't be needing it. We lost a prisoner a while back," Limm added as the other guards hooted maniacal laughter. "You get to take his place." Limm looked about at his comrades. "We have the right count again. No whips for us tonight, boys! Let's go!"

The prisoners were all rousted to their feet. The man Jacob was paired with had a hard face that was all lean planes and angles. He matched Jacob in height but was much heavier through the chest and shoulders. The guards carefully avoided him. Once, he made a quick lunge towards one guard, cleverly acting like he had stumbled. The guard tripped over his own feet in his haste to avoid the prisoner. Then the guard's expression turned to fury as urine puddled in the dust at his feet.

"Scared the piss outta him," the man laughed. The other guards advanced, clubs and swords ready. "Oh, sorry about that," the man said. "Clumsy of me. I stumbled and poor old Meatball thought I was coming for him."

"Walk on," Limm ordered.

"Sure thing," the prisoner agreed. "Don't wanna hold up the party."

They walked in silence for some time. The prisoner studied him carefully as they walked. Finally, Jacob turned to look him squarely in the eye. Jacob nearly panicked. The prisoner's eyes were almost totally black. He thought he was looking into the eyes of a Demon.

"You're either very brave or very stupid," the prisoner remarked. "I'm trying to decide which one."

Jacob shrugged.

"Try to keep up," the prisoner said. "I don't want to drag your ass all the way to the Tower."

Again, Jacob made no reply.

"Head's a little fuzzy, right?" the prisoner said. "That happens when those things hit you. Man, are they ever strong. Not as strong as me, you understand, but a Hell of a lot stronger than a regular Beastsoldier. Skinner breeds them, crossing orcs with Beastsoldiers. I've killed a few. That's why they're scared of me."

"Who are you?" Jacob managed to ask.

"My name's Kelsey, but some call me Mule," Kelsey said.

"Mule?" Jacob asked as he struggled to focus on keeping his feet moving.

"Yep," Kelsey replied. "I'd like to say it's a nod to my endowment, but it ain't. They call me mule cause I'm a crossbreed too. My father, if you wanna call him that, was a Demon in human form. He took my momma by force, and here I am."

They walked on in silence.

"What happened to your father?" Jacob asked to break the silence.

"I hope he died a slow and agonizing death for what he did to my momma and me," Kelsey replied.

"What do you mean?" Jacob asked, even though he already had an idea of the answer.

"He ruined my momma's life, obviously," Kelsey said. "And mine for that matter. It's a bitch trying to get by in a human World where you're half animal."

"You're no more animal than me," Jacob responded.

Kelsey laughed. "Nice of you to say," Kelsey said. "But I ain't human and people can sense it. I walk into a saloon and I guarantee you I won't leave without getting into a fight. I can't even tell you how many times villagers have tried to round me up with pitchforks and spades and hoes and lynch me. Or burn me at the stake. That's always an awesome time, let me tell you."

Jacob realized with a start that Kelsey could be foretelling his own future. But at the moment the Beast was curiously absent from his mind.

"We have more in common than you think," Jacob said. "My name is Jacob."

Kelsey nodded. "Stick with me and you'll be alright."

"Where are we going?" Jacob asked.

"To the mine at the base of the Tower," Kelsey replied.

"Shut up," Limm shouted.

"What for?" Jacob persisted.

"To work. We mine iron ore for Skinner," Kelsey answered. "The work ain't bad and they feed us regular. Skinner mines a shitload of iron ore to make weapons."

"Weapons for orcs and Beastsoldiers," Jacob said. "Doesn't it bother you to know you're helping them overrun the World?"

"It's not my World," Kelsey replied. "I don't give a shit what happens to it."

"You live in it," Jacob pointed out.

Kelsey grinned. "Maybe. Best shut up now, unless you wanna get a club upside your head."

Limm raised his club threateningly. Jacob ducked his head and concentrated on putting one foot in front of the other. His head felt as if it were splitting open, and the memory of Kelsey's vacant stare wouldn't leave him.

"The prisoner they were talking about earlier? Bein' one short and all?" Kelsey whispered hoarsely. "They killed him and ate him."

They reached the mine at dusk. Jacob was thrown in a cell with Kelsey. Two other prisoners already occupied the cell. One was a quiet, slim man with a mop of unkempt black hair and tattoos covering his arms and upper body. The other was a blond dwarf with a long, braided beard. He greeted Kelsey warmly.

"Kels," the dwarf said as he clasped the big man's hand. "I wasn't sure I'd ever see you again."

"Here I am," Kesley said. "This is Jacob," he indicated the young Warrior. "He tried to free us. He got ambushed by a snitch."

"Figures," the dwarf said. "I'm Ned. The quiet guy is Nik. He got snagged after they moved you. He's a sailor."

"Really?" Kelsey asked. "All the way from the sea?"

"Aye," Nik replied. "Really."

Jacob leaned against the stone wall and slid down it. His vision was blurred and his head ached fiercely. But what bothered him the most was the absence of the Beast.

"He got hit pretty hard," Kelsey explained. "Right on top of the head."

"Better let me check it out," Ned suggested. Jacob nodded. Ned stood next to him and gently felt the bones of his skull. "You are very lucky. The bones aren't broken. I've seen those animals cave in a man's head with one blow."

Jacob only nodded. The ache in his head was already subsiding. He suspected he wouldn't even remember the pain by morning.

"Rest up," Kelsey advised. "Hurt or not, they'll put you to work tomorrow."

Jacob laid down on the rough stone and was almost immediately asleep. He slipped into a deep slumber that was undisturbed for hours. Shortly before dawn he was visited once again by the spirit of Talin.

"Your luck ran out," Talin said gleefully. "You refused to accept the Beast. See what happens when he deserted you in your time of need?"

"Leave me be," Jacob pleaded. "Tell Slagg I have made my choice."

"It's not that simple," Talin argued. "You can never be free of the Beast. It is part of you. You were captured because you deny him."

Jacob thrashed about in his sleep. Was it true? Was he really that helpless without the Beast? He awoke to a rattling of a tin pan on the bars of the cell. Several guards approached, accompanied by three prisoners pushing a wooden cart loaded with steaming wooden bowls. They stopped at each cell and handed bowls through the bars.

"Breakfast," one prisoner said as they reached Jacob's cell. "Hey Kelsey," he called, "They brought you back?"

Kelsey began to reply when the head guard cuffed the prisoner who had spoken. The prisoner reeled then caught himself and gave the four in the cell a wry grin and shook his head.

"Got up on the wrong side of the cage, eh, Limm?" he asked, then dodged to the side as the guard swung at him again. He pushed the cart to the next cell as Limm growled deep in his barrel chest.

Kelsey shook his head. "Logan's gonna get himself killed one of these days."

Breakfast consisted of a thick stew with chunks of potatoes, vegetables, and some unidentifiable meat floating in a paste like gravy. A thick slab of coarse grain bread had been dumped on top. All of the prisoners ate without hesitation, so Jacob followed suit. The flavor was unusual, but once he started Jacob ate ravenously.

"Don't worry," Kelsey said around a mouthful of bread. "They ain't gonna poison us. They want us to work hard, so they feed us good. Just don't ask what the meat is."

Jacob stopped eating. "What is the meat?"

"I said don't ask," Kelsey laughed.

"Probably rat," Ned said. "Maybe dog. Maybe Beastsoldier. Who knows? It ain't poison, so eat it."

Jacob gagged and forced himself to swallow. He continued to eat, but with much less enthusiasm. As he ate, he felt strength return to his muscles. Then they were released from their cells and herded down into the mines. Jacob paid close attention to the layout of the mine, memorizing every tunnel and shaft he saw. He and Kelsey were assigned to push an ore cart. Jacob paid close attention as they worked, and he was secretly pleased to discover that, despite Kelsey's boasting, he was much stronger than the Mule. That evening they were returned to their cells and were served the same meal they had eaten at breakfast.

"Where do you come from, Jacob?" Ned asked.

"I come from the North," Jacob answered. "Where tall fir trees cover the mountainsides, and the mountains themselves reach to the sky."

"I have no use for mountains," Nik, the sailor, interjected.

"And I have no use for the sea," replied Ned.

"If you fall overboard, the sea will catch you," Nik said. "If you fall off a mountain that reaches the sky you will fall forever."

Ned snorted. "Fall off a mountain! Who ever heard such a thing?"

"Enough," Kelsey said. "Why were you in the desert, Jacob?"

Jacob shrugged. "I'm looking for my father. He was last seen leading an army against the Darklord."

"You think he's here?" Ned asked.

"I don't know," Jacob replied. "But when I saw the prisoners, I thought I could free them and cause him some grief. Any trouble I can cause that man is time well spent."

"Man?" Ned said incredulously. "He is no man. A devil, a fiend, a master of dark Magic, but not a man."

"Bullshit," Kelsey said flatly. "He is a man, trained in Wizardry and committed to Dark Magic, but still a man. Devils and fiends do not eat beefsteak and bread, and they couple with wraiths and shadows, not terrified slave girls."

"Aye," Nik concurred. "And a devil would not try to raise an army of Beastsoldiers and orcs. He would have legions of Demons at his bidding."

"And they would not need steel weapons," Kelsey added.

"He is a man," Jacob said, tiring of the argument. "I know his birth name."

Total silence followed that remark. Kelsey finally said, "And what would that be?"

"I think I better not say it here," Jacob said. "It might draw attention to us."

The talk died down immediately and the prisoners readied themselves for sleep. Jacob drifted off into a sound sleep but was plagued once again by dreams. And his dreams were dominated by Talin.

"Listen to me now," Talin hissed. "You cannot defeat Timon Blackhelm. Not by yourself. But the Sky Rider and I can defeat him easily."

Then, before his eyes, Jacob watched as Talin changed. His face became elongated and his body grew huge. Wings sprouted out of his back. He actually became Slagg, the Mighty, All Powerful Engine of Destruction once again. Slagg took to the sky and he took Jacob with him. The World slid sideways as the incredible beast wheeled in the sky. He dove in on an army, and Jacob realized it was an army of ogres and trolls, Beastsoldiers and orcs. And it was led by Timon. Slagg stooped towards Timon and Jacob clearly saw the fear in the Darklord's eyes. The vision disappeared and Jacob once again lay in his cell. Talin watched him intently.

"See, Dragonspawn?" he said. "We can be invincible. And," he paused dramatically, "I can tell you where to find your father."

"Tell me," Jacob demanded.

Talin grinned. "As you wish."

Jacob felt himself spinning, then he was looking into the cave where he had trained with Mathias and Luke. The *magii'ri* Warrior was busy stirring a pot nestled in the coals as he tended some kind of concoction for dinner. He and Mathias talked easily. Then Luke suddenly straightened with a stricken expression on his face. The barbed head of an arrow protrude from his chest, and as Jacob watched in horror the Warrior was struck by several more. He growled a battle cry and drew his sword, using the last ounce of his strength to defy those who took his life. Then he fell into the fire, his lifeless eyes staring at the ceiling.

"Nooo!" Jacob screamed. He lunged to his feet, and the Beast was ready at his side. Jacob welcomed the Beast. He embraced it. He wanted nothing more than to find Luke's murderers and tear them to pieces. Talin's grin became Slagg's toothy snout.

"Yesss," he hissed before he disappeared.

Jacob realized he was awake and standing in the corner of the cell. His breath came in ragged gasps and his brow was slick with sweat. His cellmates were gathered at the opposite end of the cell, staring at him fearfully.

"Umm," Kelsey began. "You alright, Jacob?"

Jacob struggled to speak. "I'm fine."

"He don't look fine," Ned said.

"I said, I'm fine," Jacob insisted as he walked back to his sleeping pallet.

All three stared suspiciously as he lay down.

"Do you usually talk to Dragonspirits in your sleep, Jake?" Kelsey asked casually.

"Lately?" Jacob said. "More often than not."

"Kels", Ned whispered. "Did you see anything strange about him?"

"Like what?" Kelsey asked.

"His eyes," Ned replied. "Look at his eyes."

Kelsey glanced again at Jacob. He grunted an incredulous curse. Jacob's eyes, which had been a gentle brown when he entered the Tower, had changed to the nearly colorless hue of sea ice. He propped himself up on one elbow.

"Did you actually see who I was talking to?" he asked.

His three cellmates looked at each other and shrugged simultaneously.

"Yeah," Kelsey answered. "We saw him. And if this sort of thing happens around you a lot, then I'm gonna ask to be transferred to another cell."

Despite the situation, they all chuckled.

"What about my eyes?" Jacob asked.

"Well, they're different than when you came in," Kelsey replied. "They were really dark, now they're an almost colorless blue."

Jacob shrugged. He didn't really care what color his eyes were. Something was happening to him though, he was sure of that much. He realized with a start that he had embraced the Beast, and he suddenly felt stronger and more alive than ever before. He heard crickets singing down the passageway and the murmur of voices from other cells. If he strained just a little he could focus on each individual voice and hear them clearly. His muscles burned and swelled as they became engorged with blood and he was filled with nervous energy. The various scents of unwashed prisoners and the acrid stink of the Beastsoldiers filled his nostrils. The confines of the cell seemed to be closing in on him. He rolled to his feet and began to pace. Abruptly, he leaped to the barred window twelve feet above the floor and clung to the bars while he scented the fresh air that flowed down the mountainside.

"Umm, Jacob?" Kelsey said uncertainly. "Is there something else you need to tell us?"

Jacob dropped lightly to the floor. "Only that the Sky Rider told me his blood runs in my veins. I am the Dragonspawn."

Incredulous silence followed that announcement.

"I need to move to a new cell," Kelsey said adamantly.

"That's quite a statement," Ned said. "So, you've talked to a Dragon?"

"Uh,huh," Jacob replied in a disinterested tone.

"What else did he say?" Ned persisted.

Jacob shrugged. "He wants me to join him. Then we can conquer the World. Me, him and his three hatchlings."

"Slagg is nesting?" Ned asked.

"He has three eggs at the root of a mountain," Jacob answered.

Ned released a gusty sigh. "Oh, boy."

"What?" Nik cried. "What does that mean?"

"It means," Ned replied. "That Slagg is going to hatch three eggs. If he succeeds, there will be four Dragons united against all the races of men. Four Dragons serving their own black hearts. It means the end of the World."

"Well," Kelsey ventured his opinion, "the World pretty much sucks anyway."

"It's better than the Abyss," Ned reminded him.

"Maybe," Kelsey agreed. "Maybe not."

Jacob was having trouble paying attention to the conversation. His mind was filled with one thought. Escape. Tear the bars from the stone and run them through the Beastsoldier guards. Leave the foul air of the Tower behind.

"There is another option," Ned said. "It's an old prophecy. Supposedly, if a Dragon bonds with and is reared by a servant of the Light, it too will serve the Light. How long until Slagg's eggs hatch, Jacob?"

Jacob tried to focus on the dwarf's words. Why should he care when the eggs hatched? Oh…the eggs. He needed to defend the eggs.

"Maybe a couple weeks," he said. "I'm not sure."

"A couple weeks is enough time," Ned said.

"Time for what?" Kelsey asked, even though he already knew the answer.

"Time to escape, find the eggs and save at least one," Ned said. "Think of it! Our own Dragon, that serves only us. Maybe even all three Dragon pups. If we're there when they hatch, they'll bond with us. We could defeat any army ever raised."

"You forgot one thing," Kelsey pointed out. "We are prisoners."

"Kels," Ned answered. "You and I know you could overpower any ten guards in the Tower. We can do this."

Kelsey shrugged. "Alright. But we better eat regular while we do it."

"I'll help," Nik added. "Anything to get out of this damn dust and back to the sea."

"No," Jacob interrupted. "I don't want your help."

"Why not?" Kelsey asked. "We all owe the Darklord some grief. If we help you, maybe we get a little revenge."

"Or you end up dead," Jacob said harshly. "That's happened before. Let me handle this. Alone."

It was obvious Jacob was immune to argument. The conversation died and eventually the prisoners drifted off to their sleeping pallets. After a fitful night they awoke to the same meal for breakfast as every other day. Jacob wolfed his meal down and waited impatiently to be let out. He needed the physical labor to drain some of the nervous energy he felt. Once again he and Kelsey were assigned to push an ore cart.

Limm, the Beastsoldier who had taken Jacob prisoner, was overseeing the pushers. He carried a wooden club, his sword, and a silver tipped whip. Jacob and Kelsey passed him numerous times and Jacob studiously avoided eye contact. On the sixth trip, some perverse urge made Jacob glance up and meet Limm's hard stare as they passed the guard. Limm immediately slammed the club down on Jacob's back. Jacob winced from the blow, then he stood up straight and grinned. Limm raised the club for another blow, but Jacob leaped upon him and seized the club with one hand. He backhanded the guard across the face, knocking Limm into the wall and splitting his cheek open. The guard went down while Kelsey watched in shock. Jacob gave the guard a chance to get to his feet.

"I want you to know just how lucky you were on the trail," Jacob said.

Limm started to draw his sword, but Jacob grabbed him by the wrist and forced the blade deeper into its scabbard. He drove short, wicked blows into the guard's face and body. He felt the Beastsoldier's ribs cave in and his face dissolved into a bloody pulp. The Beast inside Jacob was fully in control. He let go of the Beastsoldier's wrist, clamped one hand on his chin and circled the back of his head with the other. Then he broke the guard's neck. Kelsey watched in awe.

"She-it," he drawled. "Get ready. They'll send a squad up here now."

Another Beastsoldier appeared in the passage. Jacob leaped on him. He swung Limm's club in a short arc into the second guards face with such power it broke in half. Then he shoved the splintered end of the club into the guard's mouth, cutting his scream of pain short. The shuffling of many feet sounded in the passage. Kelsey beat him to the attack. All traces of fear were gone from the big Mule's face. Jacob knew he had met his equal in savagery and bloodlust.

A group of guards burst around the corner with a huge orc in the lead. Kelsey charged headlong into the pack, bowling the orc over with his momentum. They rolled down the passage. The orc snarled and growled as he tried to draw his knife. The guards seemed to be immobilized by the sudden show of ferocity from Kelsey, and Jacob was able to wrestle a sword from the nearest one. He slashed at the belly of another. The orc fell to the floor frantically trying to hold his entrails inside his abdomen. Jacob thrilled to the feel of a sword in his hands and his blood sang in his ears as he attacked the remaining guards and cut them down. He turned back to help Kelsey, but the big man needed no help. He stood and spit upon the body of the orc leader. The orc had been a giant among his kind, but he was no match for the incredible strength of Kelsey. Then Jacob saw something that made his heart beat even faster. The orc had a steel hook in place of his right hand, and it now protruded from his own eye socket, effectively locking his wrist to his face. It was Chagg, who had been Jacob's captor after he left Mathias and Luke.

"Well done," Jacob said with a tight smile. "Are you ready for more?"

"Bring them on," Kelsey replied.

Jacob handed the sword to Kelsey and ripped a key from Chagg's belt. "Set all the prisoners free," he ordered.

"What about you?" Kelsey asked. "We need to get out of here."

"Never mind me," Jacob said with a grin. "I told you that last night."

The two charged down the passage. A Beastsoldier attempted to stop Kelsey once, by thrusting his sword out from a recessed doorway. Kelsey cut both of his arms off at the elbow. Jacob snatched the falling sword in midair and charged down the passage to the cells. The prisoners who hadn't yet been released for work were banging their bowls on the bars and shouting. Jacob and Kelsey encountered more guards but none even slowed them down. Jacob saw a passage that led upwards and turned into it.

"The way out is down!" Kelsey yelled.

Jacob paused only long enough to shout back. "Release the prisoners. I'll be back."

Jacob leaped up the stairs going upward two at a time. He climbed until his lungs felt like they were roasting in a blacksmith's forge and his breath came in gasps. The muscles of his thighs and calves were engorged with blood, pumped to the limit. On and on he climbed, forcing his body to respond.

The floor of the passage suddenly leveled out and Jacob burst into a guard room manned by two sentries. The guards were caught completely by surprise and Jacob slashed both of them across the abdomen before they even raised their weapons. An iron barred door dominated one wall of the guard room. Jacob kicked the door completely off its hinges. Several prisoners hung from chains bolted into the rock walls. Only one man even raised his head at the commotion. He had been a formidable warrior at one time, but now he was half starved and covered only in rags. His beard and hair were matted with filth and scars clearly showed where the rags didn't cover his body. A crown of rusted steel was clamped on his head. But there was still life in his eyes.

"Joseph?" Jacob ventured.

"Who calls my name?" the prisoner responded.

"You are Joseph, the Warrior King of Ead?" Jacob persisted.

"I once was," Joseph replied. "Now I am nothing."

Jacob grabbed a torch from the entry and rushed in. Rats scurried away from the torchlight. He hurried over to Joseph. The heavy chains that bound him were held in place by oversized locks.

"The keys," Joseph said as hope flared up inside him. "The guards at the door have the keys."

As Jacob turned back towards the doorway a commotion sounded in the passage. He gripped his captured sword and stepped forward as Kelsey burst into the room with a crazed look on his face. He was followed closely by Ned and Nik. Kelsey carried a beautiful sword that dripped streamers of liquid fire with every movement.

"What are you doing here?" Jacob exclaimed. "You were free!"

"Got nothing better to do," Kelsey offered.

"We thought you needed help," Ned interrupted.

"That, too," Kelsey added.

The passage behind them was filled with the sound of hundreds of shuffling feet, accompanied by growling and snarling and the snapping of inhuman jaws.

"Get ready to fight," Kelsey advised. Ned and Nik raised their weapons in assent.

"No," Jacob said urgently. "There's too many, and we are trapped. If we surrender, we might have a chance."

"Surrender?" Kelsey exclaimed. "Shit."

"It's our only chance," Ned agreed.

"Where did you get that blade?" Jacob demanded.

Kelsey shrugged. "Found it."

"It's Aarden steel," Jacob said excitedly. "Hide it under those rags." He threw his own sword into the passage. "Get rid of your weapons."

Ned and Nik did so reluctantly, as the pursuing Beastsoldiers poured into the room.

"We are unarmed!" Jacob cried. "We surrender!"

The Beastsoldiers halted in confusion and milled about, snapping at each other. One or two lunged at the prisoners, but Kelsey sent them back into the pack with threatening lunges of his own. A new commotion arose from the rear of the pack.

"Back! Back, damn you!" a new voice commanded. Snarls sounded, accompanied by grunts of pain. A tall, slender man pushed his way through the ranks, clubbing any Beastsoldier who moved too slowly. He inspected the situation with a curt glance. A Beastsoldier jostled him, and he retaliated by clubbing it over one eye and shoving it aside. His lip curled in disgust and he wiped his hands carefully on his trousers. Then he stared hard at Jacob.

"So," he began. "You have surrendered?"

Several Beastsoldiers surged forward again. The slender man knocked one unconscious with his short iron club and waded into them, swinging the club indiscriminately.

"Get back!" he shouted. "Back, you filthy bastards! All of you, get out. But not you," he said to the slowest one. "You stay." He fixed his gaze on Jacob once again. "Are you the leader of this little revolt?"

"No." Kelsey stated.

"Yes," Jacob said. "I am."

The tall man looked amused. "You inspire such loyalty. The Mule was just trying to spare you some pain. But I already knew who the leader was of this little insurrection. Chain all of them. But," he gestured to Jacob, "chain this one facing the wall. And send for Skinner. Can you do that?" he demanded of the Beastsoldier who took his orders.

The Beastsoldier nodded sullenly and followed his comrades. The slender man shook his head in disgust.

"I'll never understand why my father insists on creating more of those beasts. A total waste of time. And by the gods, they are so stupid. Ah, but back to your problems instead of mine. I won't kill you. Not yet. But I will make you regret ever being born. Oh, here is the blacksmith," he said as a short, squat, powerful man with a bald head and a thick mat of hair over his shoulders entered the room. The muscles of his arms and shoulders bulged grotesquely.

"Chain them so they can receive their punishment," he told the blacksmith. He tuned to leave. "Oh, by the way. Which of you killed Chagg?"

"Me," Kelsey grunted.

"That was a nice piece of work. Such a beautiful piece of poetic justice. You, sir, are an artist. I congratulate you," he said. "Well, it appears this bit of excitement is over, and look! Here is Skinner. I will leave you in his capable hands." The tall man exited the chamber.

Jacob and the others were shoved against the wall while the blacksmith placed irons on them.

"It should have been me," Kelsey said.

"What are you talking about?" Jacob asked.

He had no time to hear the reply as a powerfully built man dressed all in black strode up to him and jerked his head back.

"He says to give you fifty," Skinner growled. "I don't think you'll last twenty." He shook out the coils of a silver tipped whip in front of Jacob's face.

"We'll see," Jacob replied.

Skinner laughed as the Beastsoldier who remained stripped off his shirt. Jacob closed his eyes and gritted his teeth. The whip whistled through the air and bit deep into the flesh of his back. His body jerked involuntarily. He willed himself to stay upright and kept his mouth clamped firmly shut. More Beastsoldiers crowded into the room. By the tenth lash he sagged in the chains and the Beastsoldiers stomped their feet and howled their approval. They began shoving each other to get closer, snarling and snapping their jaws. The bloodlust was driving them into a frenzy. One ventured too close, and Jacob's eyes flew open. Kelsey caught a bare glimpse of insane light flickering in their depths, then Jacob wrapped his chains around the Beastsoldier's neck and lifted him clear off the floor. The half man hung there, his feet pawing the air, until Jacob gave the chains a jerk and snapped his neck. He dropped him in a limp pile to the floor.

The remaining Beastsoldiers surged forward. Skinner turned his whip on them, his own lips curled back in a snarl. He whipped them unmercifully. Each strike cut deep gashes in their leathery hides. Skinner showed no pity. He whipped them about the shoulders and heads, putting out several eyes in the process, until the room emptied. Skinner walked back to Jacob and pulled his head back. Jacob's eyes flew open again and he spit in Skinner's face. He whirled in the chains, crossing them over his head and lunged at Skinner, his hands extended like claws. The bolts holding the chains to the wall creaked in protest from the strain. One popped out and dust puffed out from the others. Skinner jumped back and wiped the spittle from his face. He smiled, but it was far from pleasant.

"You have spirit," he said. He turned to leave, and called out to one of the Beastsoldiers. "Send for the medicine man to tend to him.

He has too much spirit to die from a whipping. And the rest of you get the Hell out of here!" The whip cracked and snapped and more howls of pain echoed down the passage.

"Gawddamn animals..." Skinner's voice faded as he herded the Beastsoldiers down the passage.

"Who are you?" Joseph asked when the tumult died away.

Jacob uncrossed his arms and turned back to face the wall. He leaned heavily against it. He could feel blood running freely down his back. But it wasn't the pain of the whipping he was fighting. The Beast in his mind was howling, saliva dripping from its jaws, as it wrestled with Jacob for complete control. *It would be so easy,* he thought. *Just let go. Let the Beast rule you. Make all of them pay for every wrong.*

Another voice sounded in his head, cool and confident. "No. Never give in," Luke's voice said.

Jacob struggled to force the Beast back into a dark corner of his mind. Each time it came forward it became stronger. Soon he would have no choice but to give in. But this time he was able to drive it back. His mind became clearer.

"I am your son," he replied to Joseph.

Kelsey and Ned looked at each other in disbelief. Joseph studied Jacob closely. A sad smile tugged at his lips.

"I'd be proud to call you my son," Joseph said. "But I am not your father," he sighed.

"Mathias said..." Jacob began.

"Mathias!" Joseph cut him off. "The Wizard. Of course, he would tell you that. Manipulative bastard." He locked eyes with Jacob. "My son died when he was a baby. I'm sorry. I don't know who your father is."

Jacob sagged against the wall. "Why? Why would he tell me I am the son of Joseph of Ead?"

"Think," Joseph replied. "What, exactly did he tell you?"

Jacob tried to remember the exact conversation. Mathias told him he was a leader of men, the son of a great Warrior King. And he would also be a powerful Warrior King one day. Mathias needed a leader for his army. Who better to lead than the Dragonspawn, fooled into thinking he was on a quest to save his beloved father?

"Damn him," Jacob muttered.

"One day that Wizard will manipulate the wrong person," Joseph said in understanding.

The medicine man chose that moment to shuffle into the cell followed by a half man servant carrying a heavy pack. The half man dropped the pack and the sound of breaking glass caused the medicine man to whirl around.

"Idiot!" he shouted. He lashed out with is foot, connecting solidly with the side of the half man's knee. His knee collapsed and the half man howled in pain, then snarled at the medicine man through bared fangs. The medicine man shrank back, then regained his confidence and shouted at the beast, who cowered and slunk out of the Tower.

"Gawddamn filthy beasts," the medicine man said. "You always have to keep them on their toes. Never let 'em know you're scared of 'em!" he murmured to himself.

He opened the pack and examined the contents. He was a smallish man with a fringe of white hair and pale skin. Blue veins showed clearly through the translucent skin of his bare arms and his beardless face. He approached Jacob and pulled his head back. Jacob involuntarily looked at him and jerked his head to the side. The old man's eyes were absolutely colorless, pink rimmed pools of pure snow melt. He cackled and busied himself with several items from his bag. He pulled out a broken beaker and tossed it aside.

"I needed that," he said. "Oh well." He pulled another vial from the bag and dumped the contents into a flask. Then he removed a covered bowl from the bag, dipped his hands into it and rubbed the contents on Jacob's lacerated back. Jacob winced and grunted in pain from the rough touch of the medicine man.

"Hurts, don't it?" the old man asked rhetorically. "But I gotta get it in deep so's you don't get a fever. Everything is so dirty with those gawddamn, stinkin' animals around. They shit wherever they please, then turn around and lay right in it. Makes me want to puke."

He went back to his pack and pulled out the flask. He held it to Jacob's lips and tried to make him drink.

"Take a couple snorts, it's good for pain," he said.

Jacob refused. The medicine man shrugged and upended the flask in his own mouth. He swallowed noisily, then coughed and gagged.

"It's good for pain," he gasped.

He held it back out to Jacob, who cautiously took a couple sips. The liquid from the flask burned like Dragon fire in his throat and landed like a hot coal in his belly. His eyes watered. The old man cackled with laughter, tipped the flask back to his own mouth and swallowed three times.

"Good for pain," he said again in a hoarse whisper.

Jacob's vision blurred as he strained to make out the face of the old man. He shook his head to clear it and stared at the medicine man. The old man's colorless eyes disappeared and were replace by the burning eyes of Slagg. Then Slagg vanished and Talin stood before him.

"Foolish boy!" Talin hissed, sounding very much like Slagg. "I told you to save my eggs. If you had escaped when you had the chance you would never have been whipped and my eggs would be safe. Now you must hurry before it's too late."

"I don't understand," Jacob said. "Slagg will save his eggs."

"No!" Talin roared. "That Worm is worthless. You must return and save the eggs." *My beautiful little eggs,* he thought.

"You're not really here," Jacob said petulantly.

Talin stepped forward and slapped him. Jacob grabbed him by the shirtfront and shook him. The medicine man squeaked and Jacob realized it was he who had spoken to him. He dropped the old man, who scurried away.

"That's it," he said as he gathered up his pack. "I'm done." He dragged the pack to the reinstalled door and pounded on it. "Let me out!" he shouted, still pounding on the door. "Let me out before one of these lunatics kills me."

Long moments of silence followed the medicine man's exit.

"You gonna be alright, Jacob?" Kelsey finally asked.

Jacob could actually feel the gashes on his back closing as new skin grew. "I'll be fine," he replied.

"What about us?" Ned asked.

Joseph snorted. "We're all in the same pickle now."

CHAPTER THREE

Luke stood up and tossed a pebble into the tracks he had been studying. He had picked up Jacob's trail in the foothills and judging by the condition of these tracks, they were no closer now than they had been three weeks ago. He had led them to Jacob's meeting with Slagg and seen the despair that discovery caused in Mathias. They had followed the same tracks to the bloody battle with the Dragoness and seen the damage Jacob's group had suffered there. To Luke, the story left by Jacob's trail was as clear as a picture book. Jacob had obviously struck a deal with the Sky Rider to protect the girl, whoever she was. To Luke it was just that simple. But Mathias took that news as a sign of treason. The Warrior spat in the dust and went to join the Wizard and the dwarf.

"Same thing," he announced. "He's still heading West with the girl."

"Then we'll follow," Mathias said simply.

"I ain't questioning you," Luke replied. "But we've been on his trail for weeks and I haven't cut any other sign. And I mean none. I haven't seen sign of Jeb or Lynch since that funny lookin' gate and Colin's been missing since we separated. What the Hell is going on, Mathias?"

"I'm not sure," Mathias said.

Luke angrily bit off another chew and rolled it to his cheek. "I get the feeling somebody's playing with us, and I don't like it."

"How many cartridges do you have left?" Mathias asked suddenly.

"Twenty-eight," Luke answered. "Same as the last time you asked. Why?"

"Just checking," Mathias said.

"You know I haven't fired a shot since that ambush and we haven't come across any other gunslingers. The count is twenty-eight," Luke replied as he stalked away from their tiny camp.

Mathias nodded then turned his attention back to the small box of Dragonsand he cradled in his hands. He scowled and pursed his lips.

"You might want to load full," he said, referencing the gunhand's habit of leaving an empty chamber under the hammer to prevent accidental discharges.

Luke groaned. "What do you see?"

Mathias consulted the Sands again. "Looks like disgraced Warriors, probably brought back from the Abyss and headed our way."

Luke drew each revolver in turn and slipped a live cartridge in the empty chambers. "How many?"

"Too many," Mathias replied. "Four…make that five. And a Rider. A bounty hunter also spat out from the Abyss under the direction of Haan."

"How far?"

"It doesn't tell me that," Mathias answered. He looked around. "But they don't catch up to us here. It's in a box canyon."

Luke started throwing things in Lynch's pack. "Let's go," he ordered. "We have to beat 'em there."

Dorro scooped up his camp gear and his axe. He looked around wearily. "Does this mean we have to run again?"

Luke and Mathias grinned. The dwarf was at a severe disadvantage with his short legs, but he did manage to keep up. Luke didn't bother to answer. He took one last look at the campsite and started out at a trot. It was at times like these that Luke felt most at ease. There was an enemy approaching, Hell bent on taking their lives, and their survival depended on his decisions.

He ran on and on, letting his mind ramble from one thing to another, but always aware of his surroundings. The heavy, panting breath of Dorro was a constant sound coming from about twenty feet behind him. It didn't lag or change much, even though the dwarf kept up a staccato stream of cursing. Mathias ran smoothly to his right, sweat streaming down his forehead but with an almost serene expression on his face. Luke felt his muscles loosen up as he ran and he increased the speed to a lope. They had to beat the disgraced Warriors to the canyon.

Some thirty minutes later, the canyon opened up like a wound on the mesa. The small group came to an abrupt halt. Dorro leaned heavily against a boulder, still cursing long legged Warriors and hard as stone Wizards. Luke glanced quickly up and down the canyon. He saw no sign of movement and no dust hung in the air. A camp robber flitted from one cedar tree to another and a squirrel darted out from behind a pile of loose sandstone.

"We did it," he announced. "We beat them here. Which way did they come from, Mathias?"

"They came from down canyon," Mathias replied.

"Five and a Rider?" Luke confirmed.

"Yes," Mathias concurred.

"We'll set up our own ambush," Luke decided. "Dorro, you hide behind the rocks down where that squirrel was. Mathias, you're the bait, so you go up canyon a bit. Let 'em see you."

Mathias nodded. Normally, he would have serious doubts about being used as bait, but Luke knew what he was doing.

"I'll sneak down canyon and come in behind 'em," he finished. "Dorro, let me engage. Then you sink a couple arrows in 'em." He fished around in Lynch's pack, then handed the dwarf a quiver of arrows and a bow that was nearly as tall as he was. "Mathias, you hit 'em with whatever you got. Don't stop until they're all down. Got it?"

"Got it," Dorro replied. Mathias nodded.

Luke grinned. "See ya on the Other Side." Then he trotted off.

"He enjoys this way too much," Mathias murmured. Dorro merely rolled his eyes and climbed down the canyon wall.

Once he was away from the others, Luke slowed to a stealthy walk. It wouldn't do to run headlong into five undead Warriors and a Rider. The Wilding had released all manner of beings, many of which the Warrior hadn't even known existed. The Riders gave Luke the creeps, he had to admit. The disgraced Warriors who had violated the Code and been committed to the Abyss were enough challenge, but an undead bounty hunter mounted on an equally undead horse? That was stretching his abilities. He let the jitters come, like they always did, and when they passed he was calm and deadly. He climbed down the canyon and selected a hiding spot, then settled in to wait.

They came in as quiet as a whisper. Even the horse's hoofbeats were muffled. Luke shrank back into the rock at his back and let them pass. The undead gunslingers filed by, barely stirring the dust, vacant eyes staring straight ahead. They were followed by the Rider. Luke chanced a quick glance at the grinning death's head of the Rider, then quickly looked away. He had seen enough. The Rider was armed with two pistols and a rifle hung in a saddle scabbard. Luke knew he would have at least one knife, possibly a sword and maybe even a tomahawk as well. The Rider's head swiveled in his direction and Luke froze, not even daring to draw a breath. Then the Rider looked away and Luke breathed a silent sigh of relief.

He let them get about a hundred yards up the canyon before he left his cover and began to pursue them. Luke moved quickly but used all of his skill as a Warrior to remain silent. His timing was perfect.

Mathias stepped away from the canyon wall as if he were unaware of any danger for hundreds of miles, and the gunslingers took the bait. They drew and fired almost simultaneously, and Luke thought for a split second that Mathias had waited too long. The Wizard dropped out of sight.

"Hey," Luke called out.

As the undead gunslingers whirled to face the new threat, he drew and began firing. He dropped two with his first two shots, both squarely between the eyes of the gunslingers. They dropped without a sound as Dorro released an arrow that penetrated the Rider's chest from side to side and blew out the far ribs with a gout of black blood. Luke shot a third gunslinger in the side of the head as Dorro released another arrow, this time targeting a gunslinger. His aim was true and that one fell with an arrow in the head. The Rider's horse reared, but he fought it back under control with a savage pull on the reins. He triggered a shot, and Dorro fell back into the rocks. Mathias reappeared among the gunslingers. He thrust his staff at the remaining fighter and his head burst open like a rotten melon.

The Rider spurred his mount forward to face this new threat. He leveled a pistol at Mathias just as Luke triggered another shot. The horse stepped in a hole and stumbled, and Luke's bullet broke the Rider's arm. He wheeled the horse again and drummed his heels into its flanks, driving it straight up the canyon wall. Luke took careful aim and was squeezing the trigger when he heard a report and felt the whiff of a bullet a fraction of an inch from his face. He jerked the trigger and knew he had missed as he dropped to one knee and punched the empties out of his right hand gun.

Four more undead gunslingers were marching up the canyon. Luke grimaced. He dropped his right hand gun in the holster, fully reloaded, as he drew his left hand gun and reloaded it as well. He lunged to his feet and charged his attackers. Flames and smoke erupted from their pistols as they opened fire, disconcerted by the sudden attack. They had expected a retreat or a dive for cover. But the Warrior attacked relentlessly. He drew and fired as he ran straight for their ranks. A bullet opened a gash on his cheekbone, but he dropped that shooter with a bullet to the face. Unmindful of the danger, he ran into their midst. He fired a shot at point blank range into one gunslinger's chest and he dropped. Then he was face to face with the final enemy still standing. They stared each other down over the sights of their pistols. The undead gunslinger's eyes showed no emotion, no spark of life. They both squeezed the trigger at the same time. The gunslinger's hammer dropped with an audible click on an empty chamber, but Luke's did not. The gun bucked with a satisfying report and the gunslinger's face dissolved into a spray of black. Luke wheeled. The fallen gunslinger he had shot in the chest was trying to bring his gun around to bear on the Warrior. Luke shot him in the head and fell backwards. The final enemy gunhand fired a shot that spit rock chips in Luke's face, then the *magii'ri* Warrior triggered another shot and dropped him. Luke jumped to his feet and stood over the fallen disgraced gunhand. Without any trace of emotion Luke shot him in the head.

The *magii'ri* Warrior stood among his fallen enemies, panting from the sudden run. But his hands were steady as he automatically reloaded. He scanned the hillside for sign of the Rider, but he was gone. The fallen gunslingers' bodies began to smoke and they slowly dissolved. Luke continued to watch for more enemies as he trotted back up the canyon to where Dorro had fallen. When he looked around the rocks, Mathias was helping the dwarf to his feet. His side was stained with blood, but he was alive.

Luke stopped and bent over, resting his hands upon his knees. He caught his breath and waited for the inevitable reaction. He kept his hands firmly on his knees so his companions wouldn't see them shaking. With a visible effort, he fought down the urge to puke. When that passed, he shot a hard stare at Mathias.

"You better learn to count," he accused.

Mathias looked stricken. "I only saw five, Luke. I swear, that's what the Sands showed me."

"Then that's the last gawddamned time we trust the Sands," Luke stated. "How's the dwarf?"

"The dwarf will live," Dorro replied. "And how is the Warrior? You've added a little character to your face since I saw you last."

Luke swiped at his cheek. His hand came away bloody, and he realized how bad the gash really was.

"Make a fire," Mathias said. "I need to tend to your wounds."

"What about the Rider?" Dorro asked as he eased out from the rocks, wincing in pain.

"Gone," Luke replied. "You drilled him through the ribs, but I think that just pissed him off."

He began to gather scattered dead wood for a fire while Mathias rummaged around in his pack. It took no time to strike the fire. Mathias wandered off, muttering to himself. When he came back the fire was blazing nicely and Luke had their small pot on to boil. Mathias dropped the herbs he had collected in the water, and when it boiled he dipped a cloth in it and cleaned Dorro's wound.

"In and out," he proclaimed. "You got lucky."

"Doesn't feel lucky," Dorro responded.

"It's a bleeder, though," Mathias said, shaking his head. He laid his knife in the coals. Dorro watched with wide eyes.

"That's not what I think it's for, is it?"

"Yep," Mathias said, matter of factly. "I have to cauterize it."

"I don't think it's necessary," Dorro protested.

"Quit whining," Luke said.

"Bite down on this," Mathias handed Dorro a strip of leather. Luke stepped forward and pinned the smaller man's arms against his sides. Mathias quickly cauterized the wounds on both sides of the dwarf's abdomen. Luke wrinkled his nose in disgust while Dorro cursed.

"Gawddamn, that stinks," Luke complained.

"Yer next," Dorro responded.

"I don't need singed," Luke countered.

"No," Mathias said. "But I do need to sew that up. Your cheek is sagging a half inch on that side."

Luke gingerly explored the wound with his fingers. He shrugged. "Have at it," he said.

As Mathias sewed the flaps of Luke's cheek back together, Dorro laid down by the fire. In minutes he was snoring.

"Does his color look a little off?" Luke asked worriedly.

Mathias looked away from his sewing job for a moment. "It does," he observed. "But it's too soon for infection to show itself."

He finished stitching while Luke winced in pain. As he began putting his tools away, Luke spoke.

"You could have gotten us killed," he observed. "Six in one group is a hell of a lot different than ten men split into two forces."

"I only saw what the Sands revealed," Mathias began.

"That's the problem," Luke interrupted. "Yer relying on a Dragonspirit that you know nothing about. You need to stop." Luke stood. "Thanks fer sewin' me up." He stalked from the camp.

Darkness fell. Mathias tended to Dorro, who seemed to be falling into a deeper slumber. He was sweating freely, despite lying on top of his blanket, and his color had deepened to a fiery red. Mathias muttered a curse and walked out from the camp. When he was well out of the firelight, he pulled the box of Dragonsand from his tunic. He spoke the words of the correct spell and flipped open the lid. The first vision he saw was of Jacob, stripped to his waist and chained to a wall, being whipped unmercifully. He winced as if he felt every lash of the whip. He desperately searched for a clue to Jacob's location but saw nothing he could identify. The second vision came so swiftly he thought it was more of a hallucination. It showed Lynch, his eyes darting suspiciously to and fro as he hid a flat, rectangular object among the stones of a fireplace. Then the images came so fast he had no time to decipher them. Luke rose up silently beside him.

"How's the dwarf?" he asked.

Mathias jumped visibly. "Not so good," he replied as he slammed the lid shut. His mind reeled from the instantly severed connection with the Dragonspirit. "There's magic at work."

Luke spied the object in Mathias' hands. "I warned you, Mathias." So suddenly Mathias had no time to react, Luke grabbed the box from his hands, opened the lid, and scattered the Sands in the wind.

"Nooo!" Mathias actually screamed. He lunged after the grains of sand. Instead of falling to the ground, the individual grains of sand whirled and danced in the moonlight. They formed the shape of a Dragon. An inhuman shriek assailed Mathias and Luke's hearing. Both fell to the ground, covering their ears. The Dragon shape solidified, spread its wings and flew down the canyon seeking a host. The eerie shrieking faded away to silence.

"That's not how I saw that working," Luke commented.

Mathias looked stricken. "I have no idea what will happen now. No one has ever set a Dragonspirit free."

Luke bit off a chew. He chewed silently for a minute. Finally, he spat on a flat rock. "I guess we're gonna find out."

Dorro cried out. Luke and Mathias exchanged glances and ran back to the fire. Dorro's body jerked spasmodically as he bent double, then straightened with such force his spine popped. Luke knelt next to the dwarf, grabbed him by the shoulders and upper body and cradled him to his chest to keep him from bashing his head against the ground.

"Do something," he ordered Mathias between gritted teeth.

Mathias uttered the words of a spell and tapped Dorro's body three times with his staff. The dwarf relaxed in Luke's arms.

"It's poison, ain't it?" Luke asked.

"I reckon," Mathias agreed.

"So what's the antidote?" Luke demanded.

"Only one thing comes to mind," Mathias replied. "The blood of a Rider is the antidote. I can keep him quiet, but without that Rider's enchanted blood, he'll die."

Luke lowered Dorro back to his sleeping pallet. Without another word, he rose and started packing. He took a water skin and some dried meat but left his own sleeping pallet. He also left his sword, but made sure his tomahawk and foot long knife were in his belt. Finally, he spun the cylinders on each Colt. Five rounds in each. He checked the fat brass cartridges on his belt. Only three remained. He took one quick look around the campsite.

"I'll be back," he promised Mathias.

The Rider's trail was as clear as a wagon road to Luke. The hooves of the undead bounty hunter's horse chewed up the mountainside and spat out clumps of sod as big as his fist. Luke didn't try to follow the trail exactly. He zig-zagged up the hill, first at one angle, then back the other way. When the tracks reached the ridge, the Rider turned uphill and Luke followed at a trot. He let his mind wander while his physical senses remained completely attuned to his surroundings. It was an old *magii'ri* Warrior trick. Using it, Luke could run all night and the next day. Once the Rider reached the ridge, he had slowed his horse. Luke kept a wary eye out for a blood trail, but apparently the Rider had plugged his holes with something, for not a drop touched the ground.

"Yeah, you know he's dyin', don't you, you son of a bitch?" Luke cursed. "I'll put a hole in you that you can't plug. Just don't bleed dry before I catch up."

Luke ran on and on through the night, pausing to drink a few sparing mouthfuls of water and chew on a strip of dried meat. As they climbed, the terrain changed. The scrubby trees and brush of the high desert gave way to groves of aspen. Luke noticed a spot where the Rider had paused to let the horse rest, and he grinned.

"You don't tire out, but yer horse does," he muttered with a smile.

The places where the Rider stopped became more and more frequent. Luke slowed his pace. An hour later he was in the middle of a thick stand of ancient aspen trees. He could smell the richness of the torn up earth and the scent of fir trees from farther up the mountain. He slowed to a walk. Suddenly, he caught a glimpse of horizontal movement in a vertical world of tree trunks. He ducked behind an aspen as a bullet shredded a chunk of bark inches from his face. He chanced another quick glance. The horse was riderless, wandering among the aspens. Acting on a sudden hunch, he dodged a quarter of the way around the tree just as another bullet thunked into it right where he had been sitting.

"That's about right," Luke yelled. "You dry gulching, back shooting coward. No wonder all you bounty hunters ended up in the Abyss!"

Silence followed. Luke lunged from behind that tree and rolled to another. Bullets gouged the earth behind him as he rolled. He continued rolling until he could leap to his feet and run to another tree. Shots rang out in quick succession. One struck the heel of his boot and sent him flying headlong into the thick carpet of rotting leaves. He flopped over into a kneeling position.

"Where are you, you son of a bitch?" he whispered hoarsely.

He caught just a flicker of movement and triggered a shot. He was rewarded with a muffled grunt of pain and the crashing of undergrowth.

"How does it feel?" he yelled.

Five more shots rang out, forcing Luke to abandon his hiding place. He dropped behind a slab of rock just high enough to conceal him.

"We can do this all day," Luke shouted. "Or you can show yerself and we can do this the honorable way. If you got any honor left," he added. He sucked in his abdomen and held his breath, expecting another fusillade of shots. None came.

"Let's do this face to face," Luke yelled.

A dry branch cracked with a report like a small caliber pistol *below* him. Luke jumped, then sat up. The Rider entered a clearing below and fifty feet to his right. *"Gawddamn,"* Luke thought. *"This bastard's fast."*

The Rider walked into the clearing with his duster tucked back in his belt. He held both hands out from his sides. His pistols were jammed home in their holsters. Luke stood up, half expecting a hail of bullets, and brushed off the leaves and twigs that clung to his clothes. The Rider nodded. Luke swept back his duster and waited. He focused all of his attention on the Rider's gloved hands. The voice caught him completely by surprise.

"It wasn't by choice, you know," the Rider said. His voice was as dry as the wind rustling through dead cattails.

Despite himself, Luke was intrigued. "What wasn't by choice?"

"Coming back this way," the Rider said. "I followed the Code, but Aard abandoned me."

Luke said nothing.

"You don't believe me," the Rider continued. "Yes, I hunted down outlaws for money. But I didn't break the Code. Aard abandoned me and cast me into the Abyss. And even there my kind are outsiders. The Wilding opened a door back into this World, and we took it. But now we serve Haan, against our own will. I couldn't stop any of this."

Luke nodded. "I understand."

The Rider nodded back. "Whenever you're ready then."

Luke gave the barest nod. His eyes narrowed as he watched the Rider's hands. The Rider's right hand twitched and Luke drew both pistols. He focused his entire being on his target and triggered a shot from each gun. He felt the displaced wind as a bullet sliced through the air a fraction of an inch from his left ear. The Rider's head all but disintegrated as both of Luke's bullets struck home, one in each eye socket. Luke rushed forward. The Rider had an empty waterskin hanging from a cord around his shoulder. Luke ripped it free and held the mouth under the Rider's ruined skull. Thick, black blood dripped from the wounds and into the skin. Luke only hoped it would be enough. Seconds later, the Rider's body began to smoke then it dissolved into a pile of ash.

A sound alerted Luke and he whirled around, dropping into a crouch as he did, and drew both pistols again. The Rider's horse entered the clearing, stripping leaves from the brush as it walked. Fatigue and released stress hit Luke like a hammer. His legs began to shake and he sat down next to the remains of the Rider. *Would he end up the same way?* he wondered. *Would Aard abandon the Warriors who did his bidding their entire lives, even if they followed the Code to the letter?*

Luke had lived his life in the belief that he was doing the right thing, even when it was unpleasant. Even when it meant taking lives, or choosing which life to save and which to abandon. He had placed all of his faith in the Code and taught others to do the same. What if the Code itself was wrong? The thought rattled him. He had never questioned the Code. But the bounty hunter said he had followed the Code and still had been cast into the Abyss. And in the end, what was the difference between himself and the Rider? They both took money to do a job that others were unwilling to do. Luke felt a headache beginning at the base of his skull.

Luke removed his hat and pushed back his sweat slick hair. He took a long drink from his waterskin and bit off a sizable chew of tobacco. The Rider's grazing horse wandered closer. Scalps swung from the leather straps crossing his muscular chest. When Luke stood, the horse cast a quick glance his way then went back to feeding. Luke edged closer and closer until he could reach out very slowly and grasp the trailing reins. The horse tossed its head but didn't rear or try to bolt. Luke sliced the leather thongs binding the scalps to the rigging and left them where they dropped. He slipped one foot barely into the stirrup and cautiously swung up into the saddle. At least he didn't have to walk back.

CHAPTER FOUR

"We have to do something," Kelsey said. "If we stay here, we're gonna die.'

"What about that sword you hid?" Jacob interrupted. "Did they find it?"

"Nope," Nik replied. "It's over in the corner. I have this one" he slid a short sword out of his pants leg.

"That's orc steel," Jacob said. "Not much better than a club. If we had the other blade, we'd have a chance. The Aarden steel blade would cut through these chains like butter. I know me and Kels could rip that door right off its hinges if we could reach it."

"Me and Ned are only chained by one hand," Nik revealed. "If I could get that Aarden steel blade I could cut you guys free. Then you could bust down the door."

"You can't reach it," Ned said.

"Nope, not yet" Nik agreed. "But I will."

Without another word, Nik raised the orc blade high and brought it down with all his strength on his own right wrist. The blade cut through and bit into the stone, Sparks and blood flew. Nik choked off a scream while his cellmates watched in horror. He dropped to the floor, cradling his mutilated arm while his detached hand swung freely from the wall. Nik's body jackknifed in pain as he pulled a lace from his boot and wound it around the spurting stump. He pulled it tight with his teeth until the blood no longer squirted from the wound. He crawled to the Aarden steel sword as his companions looked on in horror. Gritting his teeth, he turned back to Ned.

"Don't move," he warned. Ned stretched his arm out as far as he could and closed his eyes as Nik crossed the cell, his arm dripping crimson on the polished stone of the floor. He raised the sword. He swayed like a tree in a high wind, then slammed the Aarden steel blade down. The orc steel chains parted as if they weren't even there. Ned gasped in relief and caught Nik as he slumped to the floor. He freed Kelsey, then handed him the sword while he turned to tend to his friend. In moments Kelsey freed Jacob. Ned tightened the tourniquet around Nik's arm and fashioned a bandage from torn cloth. Kelsey examined the Aarden steel sword. Not even a nick marred its edge.

"Why?" Jacob asked.

Nik gave him a weak, sickly grin. "I just can't stand the dust here anymore."

Jacob shook his head.

"He's from the sea," Kelsey offered. "Not used to the dust."

"He knows, Kels," Ned interrupted with a shake of his own head.

"What about me?" Joseph said. "You're gonna set me free, right?"

Kelsey looked at Jacob, who shrugged his shoulders. "He's a Warrior king. Or used to be. Set him free."

A wild wind blew through the bars of the window. Joseph turned his face into the wind, a slight smile creasing his lips.

"That's the first breeze I've felt in fifteen years," he said.

Jacob and the other prisoners had no time to wonder at that remark. The wind increased until it howled through the bars, blowing bits of sand so with so much force it bit into their skin. In seconds the cell was filled with a cloud of dust. It began to solidify and take the shape of a Dragon. The Dragon shape hung in the air for only a fraction of a second, then it dove towards Jacob. He held up his hands to ward it off, but it flowed between his fingers and entered his open mouth. It disappeared inside him. The cell was silent.

"Spit it out!" Kelsey shouted.

Everyone in the cell nearly jumped out of their skin at the sudden sound of Kelsey's voice.

"It's gone," Jacob replied. He realized he felt good. Better than good. Better than he'd ever felt, as a matter of fact. But he also felt *different*. Suddenly, his fate and the fate of these men no longer mattered. The was only one thought in Jacob's mind. *Save the eggs.*

Jacob reached the door in three steps, leaving his companions standing flat footed. He wrapped his hands around the thick steel bars and wrenched the door completely off the hinges. The Beastsoldier guards who stood on either side of it spun around in surprise. Jacob had no use for finesse. He simply punched one in the face and felt the beast's bones break. He grabbed the other by the throat and threw him into the stone wall. He never stopped moving. As he ran out the door, he scooped up an orc blade and continued into the passage down. Kelsey, Ned and Joseph exchanged glances.

"Go!" Ned ordered. "I'll help Nik."

Kelsey grinned. "You ready for this, old timer?" he asked Joseph.

"Just give me a blade," the Warrior King replied.

The sounds of combat echoed up the passage as Kelsey and Joseph ran through the guard room. Joseph picked up a sword from one of the dead guards and followed Kelsey down the passage. The evidence of Jacob's transformation littered the passage. Beastsoldiers and orcs lay strewn about. Some were missing limbs or their heads. Others were simply ripped open. But even the Dragonspawn, possessed by a Dragonspirit, couldn't defeat the swarm of Beastsoldiers and orcs that emerged like ants from the tunnels. The main staging area of the mine was clotted with enemies. Jacob's attack had stalled at the mouth of the passage from the Tower. Kelsey saw that, but he didn't even slow down. He barreled past Jacob and plowed into the crowd of enemy soldiers. He blasted a path clear through to the center of the room, knocking everyone he hit to the floor, where he was soon swallowed up by Beastsoldiers. But his attack had created a weakness in the front line. Jacob and Joseph exploited that weakness, forcing their way into the room, slashing and stabbing almost blindly. Their enemies were so great in number there was no danger of wounding each other. They fought like animals, striking at any who were near. But there were just too many Beastsoldiers.

A commotion arose from the rear of the room, then from one side, then the other. The prisoners had returned. The orcs and Beastsoldiers realized they were surrounded and their howls of victory and bloodlust turned to panic. They began to mill about, then one broke for a tunnel to escape. In seconds it became a stampede out of the mine.

Above the din of battle and retreat, a voice rang out. "Hold! Hold, damn you!" the voice cried.

But the Beastsoldiers ignored it and what could have been a defeat for Jacob and his companions turned into a rout. Even Kelsey emerged from a pile of orc bodies, bitten and stabbed and cut, but alive. He spied the son of Timon and attacked. Timon's son, the tall, slender man from the Tower, swung his iron club in a vicious arc. Kelsey took the blow on his shoulder and sealed the slender man's wrist in his vice like grip. He head butted his enemy, disarmed him, and shoved the club down the slender man's throat. Kelsey threw his head back and howled a victory cry. As the cry rang in Jacob's ears the Beast inside him rose to its full height and scented the air, seeking another enemy to attack. Jacob tried to fight it down but realized he was about to lose all control when the Dragonspirit that now inhabited him quelled the Beast and sent it slinking back into a corner of his mind. The prisoners had won the battle of the mine.

Jacob now had a purpose, a reason for being. *Save the eggs,* the Dragonspirit had implored him. Kelsey rejoined Jacob and Joseph.

"I have a mission," Jacob informed them. "But it's for me to do, not you. If you want to be a part of this, that is up to you."

Kelsey shrugged as he inspected a fang hole in his forearm. "I haven't had this much fun in years," he said. "I'll go along."

Joseph appeared distressed. "I want to offer my services," he began, "but I fear fifteen years as a prisoner has dulled my abilities. I'm weak, Jacob. I doubt I could even keep up."

"If you want to help," Jacob replied, "I ask you to strike out for the East. Take these men," he gestured at the escaped prisoners, "to the Wizard Mathias and my teacher, Luke Graywullf. Join them and tell them what happened here."

Ned and Nik walked slowly down the passage, staring in wonder at the destruction of the Beast army. Nik's face was pale with the effort.

"Ned," Jacob called. "I have a mission for you as well, if you're willing."

"What can I do?" Ned responded.

"Take Nik back to the sea," Jacob suggested. "And if you encounter any dwarves by chance or design, ask them to assemble all their might and join the race of men for one last, great battle for Norland."

"And who will I tell them leads the forces of men?" Ned asked.

Jacob hesitated. "Tell them…the *magii'ri* will lead the attack."

Ned nodded. "Consider it done."

Jacob and Kelsey armed themselves. Kelsey picked up a huge double bladed battleaxe. He hefted it and nodded.

"This suits me better," he proclaimed. "Here," he handed the Aarden steel sword to Jacob.

"Now," Kelsey asked. "Where are we going?"

Jacob smiled. "To save some Dragons."

"Yer kidding, right?" Kelsey asked.

"Nope," Jacob replied.

CHAPTER FIVE

Sweat dripped from Luke's eyebrows and cut muddy trails through the dust that coated his weather beaten face. He held perfectly still as one final, annoying drop rolled down his nose and fell with a tiny *plip* onto the sand he lay upon. He thought it was probably the last drop of moisture in him, as he realized he hadn't even needed to make water for the last day and a half and he no longer even had enough saliva left to swallow. He decided he knew what a strip of meat felt like being hung out on a drying rack. Yet he lay unmoving, watching a natural catchment in the sandstone that he knew from the smell contained enough water to save them all. He, Mathias and Dorro had to have that water, but they needed food also. Luke intended to get both at the same time.

A slight movement caught his attention right at the edge of his peripheral vision. A desert ewe, all alone, cautiously picked her way through the scattered rocks to the watering hole. She scented the air, then lowered her head to drink. Luke raised up with agonizing slowness, forcing his cramped muscles to respond. He drew his bow back, lined the fletching up with the ewe's shoulder area and released the arrow. He watched the arrow's flight until it buried itself in the sheep, then watched as it hurtled back up the trail from where it had come. Luke watched it go, then plodded slowly to the water hole, He drank sparingly at first, allowing his parched tissues time to soak up the life giving moisture, even though he craved to bury his face in it and suck up huge draughts until his thirst was appeased. The slight sips he took were like nectar, filling his body with coolness and making his head swim slightly.

The Warrior sat at the water's edge while the strength slowly returned to his body, sipping the warm water and waiting for his sheep to bleed out. He had made a good shot on the ewe. She would not go far. He filled up the waterskins he had carried for miles and followed the blood trail to the sheep's carcass, piled up where she had run into a pile of stone. He field dressed the animal, boned the meat and wrapped it in the hide. Then he started the long trek back to camp. Mathias saw him when he was still a quarter mile away. He had a fire going when Luke reached him.

"You had some luck," Mathias observed.

"Some," Luke agreed. He dropped the meat filled hide. "Here," he handed Mathias and Dorro their waterskins. "There's a seep about two miles ahead."

Dorro gulped greedily at the lukewarm liquid, spilling some in the process. He glanced guiltily at Luke, then drank some more.

"Go ahead," Luke urged. "Drink it all. Next time you go out."

Mathias gave Luke a stern glance.

"Did you get some meat?" the dwarf asked.

"Why?" Luke replied. "You gonna try to finish that off, too?"

"Luke," Mathias admonished.

"What?" Luke said innocently. "I've been foraging for all of us. I just think it's about someone else's turn."

Mathias sighed. Dorro and Luke had been like schoolchildren ever since they left the mines.

"It's only for a few more days," Mathias announced. "Then we'll be at the coast."

"Curse this blasted land!" Dorro exclaimed. "Why would anyone want it bad enough to fight a war over it?"

"What's wrong with this land?" Luke asked.

"Look at it," Dorro responded. "Hardly even a bush in sight, let alone a real tree. Everything that grows here has thorns that tear and claw at your skin if you so much as brush against them. And the heat! I fell that I am melting away to nothing."

"Do you good to melt a little," Luke muttered.

"What did you say, Mr. Longlegs?"

"I said, it would do you good to melt a little," Luke replied, staring pointedly at the dwarf's midsection.

"That does it," Dorro said as she shook his head. "Just because I'm not seven feet tall and made of windburned rawhide like you does not give you the right to criticize me."

"Ain't criticizing," Luke drawled. "Just stating a fact."

"That's enough," Mathias interrupted.

"I'm used to the cool, blue mountains we left behind. Not this parched, sandy Hell you two are fighting for. I just want to sit under the shade of a tree," Dorro said plaintively.

"We are not fighting for this desert. Not specifically, I mean," Luke said. "But it treats you well enough, if you know how to live with it and not fight it. Of course, nobody out here has servants to bring them food and water. I mean, almost nobody." He stared pointedly at Dorro again.

"I said, that's enough," Mathias interjected quietly.

"Well then, maybe you don't need the services of the dwarves," Dorro challenged.

"Maybe not," Luke agreed readily. "They seem like a bunch of greedy whiners anyway."

"I said, by the gods, that's enough!" Mathias shouted. He jumped to his feet. The oaken staff he carried glowed a fiery red. He seemed to grow taller as they watched, and the glow from his staff was reflected as a crazy light in his eyes.

"Gawddamn, Mathias," Luke drawled. "Calm down. We was just funnin'."

"Yeah," Dorro agreed. "You need to relax."

Mathias stared from one to the other. He tried to speak but no words came out. When the mutton was cooked through they ate in silence. Afterwards, Mathias and Dorro stoked their pipes with scavenged tobacco while Luke took a bite from his plug. He worked it in his jaws, spat in the fire and pinned Mathias with a glance.

"Where the Hell is everybody?" he asked, not really expecting an answer. Mathias sat in silence, obviously deep in thought, for several minutes. Finally, he spoke.

"Jeb is with Lynch. We can be fairly certain of that, so I assume he is being watched out for."

"Yeah," Luke said sarcastically. "By Lynch. That ain't much. He's the guy who wanted to leave Mariel behind in the desert because she was slowing us down."

Mathias nodded. "I know. But he has…mellowed since then."

"He's still crazy," Luke insisted.

Mathias merely nodded again.

"Well," Luke said, beginning to lose patience. "It may not bother you, but it sure as Hell bothers me. People have been disappearing while we traipse from one end of Norland to another."

"It does bother me," Mathias replied. "I'm working on a plan. You just have to trust me."

Luke spat his well chewed cud of tobacco into the fire, wrapped up in a tattered blanket and rolled over. Dorro followed suit, but Mathias sat up far into the night. Three days of hard marching later, they stood on a bluff overlooking a seaport town.

"We could have made it here a lot sooner if you hadn't let the horse go," Dorro complained.

"I told you, he wouldn't have survived the desert," Luke replied.

"Don't even start," Mathias ordered.

"Why are we here?" Luke asked. He had followed Mathias' orders and suggestions without fail, but now he was pretty sure the Wizard had lost his mind. "I don't think Jacob would have come this way," he continued. "The attacks have all been in the Borderlands. No one for the last hundred miles has ever even seen a Dragon. And there's been no sign of Timon since we got back to Norland. Or anyone else, for that matter," he added pointedly, reiterating his thoughts.

"You're right," Mathias agreed. "We trailed Jacob and Slagg for far too long. It's obvious we can't catch up. The Sky Rider can outdistance us without even trying. And I don't think Timon is even near Norland at this time. It's time for us to change tactics. Don't you recognize this town?" he asked.

Luke studied the small village and his brow furrowed in thought. "It looks like the village Lynch described from his childhood."

"Exactly," Mathias agreed. "And where would Lynch hide something that meant more to him than his own skin?"

Luke shrugged. "Maybe where he spent his childhood?"

"Now your thinking," Mathias said. "I need the Book of Runes. Lynch had it. I only hope I'm right about where he hid it."

"Then let's go find it," Luke said, ready for the talking to be over and the action to begin. It did occur to him that he should ask Mathias why he needed such a dangerous book. But if the Wizard said it would help them to save Jacob and finally defeat Timon, then he would personally find it and hand it over. No matter who, or what, might be guarding it.

The village streets were deserted at the late hour they chose to explore it. There were no sentries posted and no lights shone through the windows. *It looks like a ghost town,* Luke thought. That idea set him on edge and he readied his weapons for whatever may come. Dorro did the same and gave Luke a quick nod when he noticed. *He feels it too*, Luke thought. Mathias cast a questioning glance at both of them and quickly led them through to the far outskirts of town.

"Where is it, where is it?" he murmured as he quickened the pace. He could feel the Book calling to him, leading him to it. It wanted to be found. Indeed, it needed to be found, to share the knowledge contained within its' pages. They came to the ruins of a small stone house. The walls had long ago crumbled under the weight of the charred roof timbers, but the fireplace remained intact. Mathias clambered over the ruins and made a beeline for the fireplace. He reached for a large slab of flagstone that made up the hearth when he was swatted backwards as if by a giant hand. Luke and Dorro leaped forward and helped him to his feet, brandishing their weapons.

Mathias gave them a sickly grin as he regained his breath. "It's alright. It's protected by magic, as I knew it should be. My eagerness to reach it addled my brain."

He held his staff horizontally at chest level and spoke a string of words neither Luke nor the dwarf understood. Then he thrust the staff forward and an orb of light shot from it. The light was absorbed by the cracks in the stone of the fireplace, then there was the sound of a muted explosion. The flagstone disintegrated. Mathias stepped forward again, narrowly evading Luke's restraining grip. He knelt and reached into the blackness under the flagstone, but immediately withdrew his empty hand with a howl of pain. Luke and Dorro both lunged forward but stopped short when they saw Mathias' face split by a huge grin.

"Sorry," he apologized. "I couldn't resist."

He reached in again as Luke and Dorro fumed, and withdrew a large, leather bound book. He actually breathed a sigh of pleasure when he blew the dust off the cover and saw the insignia.

"You are an asshole," Luke cursed. "You scared ten years off my life."

"Is that it?" Dorro asked. "That's what we walked for a month to find?"

"It is," Mathias replied. "The Book of Runes."

He called upon his staff to emit light and lovingly opened the cover.

"Careful," Luke warned. "Remember what Lynch said. Once you start reading, all bets are off."

Mathias nodded. "I remember. I'll be careful. But there is magic in this Book that we must have."

He sat on the remnants of the fireplace and began to read while Luke and Dorro kept watch. As he read he occasionally made small sounds of surprise and more than once made a harrumphing sound of total disbelief. He read long enough that Luke began to fear for his safety.

Mathias finally said, "Aha! I knew there was a way."

He looked about almost in confusion. "Why are we still sitting in here?"

Only then were any of them aware that the sun was rising. Mathias had been reading from the Book for hours, but none of them felt fatigue.

"Come," he said as he headed for the opening that had been a doorway. "We have to find a forge. Do you know how to forge steel, Luke?"

Luke was taken aback. "I can pound a sickle into a sword, but I have no experience as a blacksmith."

He and Mathias both stopped and looked at Dorro.

"What?" the dwarf asked indignantly. "I'm a dwarf, therefore you assume I know how to forge steel. Isn't that jumping to the wrong conclusion? That's like me thinking you're a gunslinger just because of your appearance."

"Well?" Mathias asked. "Do you know how to forge steel?"

Dorro shrugged and released a heavy sigh. "Of course I can forge steel. I am a dwarf, after all. What do you need me to make?"

"Thought so," Luke said.

"Handcuffs," Mathias replied. He lifted the Book of Runes. "Magical handcuffs."

There was a forge and anvil behind the wreckage of a barn, along with a pile of coal. Behind the anvil the ground was bare and desolate and black with ashes from the forge. It was obvious the forge had been in continuous use for many generations. A few rusty tools were strewn about, but the handles were strong and smooth.

"Doesn't this seem a little odd to you?" Luke asked.

"What?" Mathias asked absently as he searched for items to melt down.

"Lynch has lived hundreds of years. That means this forge is hundreds of years old, but everything looks like it could have been used yesterday," Luke responded.

Mathias shrugged. "It may have been."

Luke groaned. "Magic."

"Yes," Mathias agreed. "Now help us look for pieces of iron."

Luke stood resolutely still. "Do you know what blacksmiths call the crap that comes off when you forge steel? It's called slag," he said. "And what is the name of the Dragon that used to be Lynch's brother? Slagg. Who did this forge belong to? Lynch's family."

"What are you getting at?" Mathias asked irritably.

"I don't know," Luke admitted. "But this all seems like one hell of a coincidence."

He started to help look for iron, but stopped near the forge and sniffed the air. It smelled like coal smoke. Then he lightly touched the forge. It was still very warm. He sighed heavily. "More magic," he complained to himself.

"What was that?" Dorro asked as he dropped several lengths of iron rod near the forge.

"Nothing," Luke dismissed.

Mathias had also found some lengths of iron. He dropped his near the forge and spoke a quick word, then tapped the forge with his staff. The fire leaped to life. It seemed to Luke that it glowed with a peculiar intensity. Mathias worked the bellows while Dorro instructed Luke in cutting the iron rods to the perfect length. Then he heated them one by one in the forge and formed them into interlocking rings. He welded the seams shut, then spent hours hammering and heating and shaping the clasps and locks. When he was finally satisfied, he heated them until they glowed red while Mathias read a spell from the Book. They quenched the glowing handcuffs in a barrel of cold water and Mathias nodded in satisfaction.

"So now we have magical handcuffs," Luke said dubiously. "Who do we slap them on?"

"Timon," Mathias answered. "These handcuffs serve one purpose. They will bind any magical being and prevent them from performing magic. We will lock Timon in these and force him to reverse the Wilding. Perhaps even free Lynch's brother from the imprisoning hulk of the Sky Rider."

"You forgot one detail," Luke reminded. "We can't find him."

"That's because he's not here," Mathias revealed. "The Book has taught me a great deal. I read it as a true servant of the Light and the Book told me many secrets it hid from Lynch as well as many others who tried to use it to serve the Dark. Timon has been using portals to travel to other Worlds and other Times. That is why we can't find him. We must use one of the last active portals to travel to whatever World he is living in now."

"Sounds like a job for a Wizard," Dorro said.

Luke nodded vigorously. "Uh, huh," he agreed. "That's Wizard work for sure. I wouldn't send a Warrior on that job."

"Perhaps," Mathias said. "The plan is to go through the portal, find Timon and get these handcuffs on him. We'll do anything short of killing him to accomplish that. Once these are on, he will be helpless. We'll bring him back here where I will subdue him with Magic, but not cripple him. If this all works out, we can undo the spell on Lynch's brother and free him from the body of Slagg and reverse the Wilding."

"And save Norland," Luke added. He shook his head. "Your plan has a lot of holes in it."

"So, we'll do what your father and Smilin' Jake always said," Mathias replied. "Improvise."

"Lynch said something about always coming through naked," Luke reminded Mathias.

"Again," Mathias said patiently. "The Book is very clear that it is possible to open the portals to accept living flesh and machines. We can go through with our weapons and bring him back in irons. This plan will work, Luke. Do you trust me? Would you be willing to go through a portal with me?"

"As long as we don't end up naked," Luke said. "I'd do it."

"No one is going to be naked," Mathias assured him.

"Then we better get started," Luke said. "I don't want Jacob bein' under the influence of Slagg any longer than he has to be."

"None of us do," Mathias agreed as he placed the magical handcuffs inside Lynch's pack. '*If it's not too late already,*' he thought.

Without warning the fire in the forge flared back to life. In moments the forge was glowing cherry red. Showers of sparks emitted from it. Black coal smoke rose in billowing clouds that shifted instantly into the shapes of Dragons. The smoke Dragons flew in increasingly large circles above the three, and as they rose they grew in size. Mathias appeared mesmerized.

"Magic," Luke spat. He grabbed Mathias and whirled him away from the smoke Dragons. "Run!" he commanded.

Despite his dazed state, Mathias did as he was told. Dorro had already turned to flee and was well on his way to the tree line. Luke herded the Wizard in that general direction then thundered past him just as the smoke Dragons descended upon Dorro. Kicking and writhing, the dwarf was lifted off his feet and into the sky. Luke drew his sword on the run and leaped high enough to slice one smoke Dragon in half. The rest lost altitude from the weight of the dwarf, and Luke slashed at another when his feet touched the earth, severing both front legs. It shrieked in agony and sparks flew from its mouth, but Luke would not relent. He continued slashing and stabbing until only one smoke Dragon remained. Dorro drew his knife and plunged it over and over into the Dragon's side until it burst into flames and disappeared.

"Thank the gods for your long legs," Dorro panted. "Another moment and they'd have had me!"

"You can repay the favor someday," Luke said with a tight grin. The truth was, he had become fond of the tough little dwarf since his wounding at the hands of the Hunter. "Right now we need to get far away from this fell place."

"That we do," Mathias agreed as he came back to his senses. "Our situation is desperate. Desperate times call for desperate measures. Forgive me."

Luke and Dorro both stared at Mathias in confusion. Mathias spoke the words, and both felt energy pouring into their limbs like liquid fire accompanied by a sick and hollow feeling inside.

"Dark magic," Luke managed to accuse. Then they ran.

The spell Mathias cast was powerful, even more powerful than he had intended. All three became unfeeling machines, their legs like pistons pumping tirelessly up and down. They covered hill and dale, desert and scrub brush. And all the while their own minds watched in clinical detachment. Only when their physical bodies had been driven to the point of utter destruction did the spell of Dark Magic relent. All three fell immediately to the ground in a near comatose state and lay there unmoving for a day and a night. As the sun rose on the second day, Luke rolled over to his side and saw Mathias watching him, still unable to move.

"Don't you ever do that again," he warned in a hoarse whisper.

Mathias nodded mutely, his eyes fixed upon something behind Luke. The Warrior rolled over to look. The crater he had tried to cross with Jeb all those years ago lay to the west. The same twisted rails were still tied in knots and fused by a power of such magnitude it was beyond his comprehension. And in the middle of the crater stood a glimmering archway.

CHAPTER SIX

Jacob and Kelsey ran on and on, pausing only long enough to kill and feed on whatever hapless forest creature they chanced upon. Jacob reveled in the physical power he felt, and he marveled at Kelsey's ability to keep up. The big Mule was always at his side, a frightening grin plastered on his face. They came to Slagg's mountain. Jacob thought at first he had lost his mind and led them astray. Slagg was obviously absent. His mountain was lush and green with new growth, not the burned out pile of rubble Jacob had crossed months ago.

Jacob slowed to a walk. The scent of sheep floated to his nostrils. Not the scent of wild sheep, but the heavy, oily smell of domestic sheep. A bell clanged in the distance. *A shepherd pasturing his flock on Slagg's mountain?* Jacob wondered. The scent hung in the air, so strong to Jacob it began to give him a headache.

"Sheep," Kelsey whispered. He raised his axe and tested the edge. "Let's eat."

They crept forward always keeping under cover. In time they came to a clearing. The shepherd had started a small fire and was toasting cheese and making biscuits for his dinner. Jacob's mouth watered. He stared at the shepherd. There was something familiar about him. He tested the air again, and among the scent of sheep he caught a familiar smell. This smell brought back old memories. Memories of a ship's hold, close packed bodies. And a village out on the plains. He laid a restraining hand on Kelsey's shoulder. The shepherd turned to glance out into the darkness. His boyish face betrayed no fear. Jacob knew him.

"He's a friend," he whispered to Kelsey.

"Maybe he'll share his cheese and biscuits," Kelsey said hopefully.

Jacob grinned. His friend seemed to think more with his stomach than his brain. They circled around to come in from the direction the boy faced. Jacob stepped out into the firelight. The boy spotted him immediately and fitted a stone in his sling.

"Easy," Jacob said, holding his hands out at chest height.

The boy recognized him immediately. His face lit up with a huge grin. He leaped the fire and ran to shake Jacob's hand. He pumped it up and down enthusiastically, bobbing his head in time with the handshake. He approached Kelsey with more caution, but accepted him quickly. He gestured at the fire. Jacob nodded. The boy ran ahead and took out a pan of biscuits and dug more cheese from his pack. He took a bite and motioned for the newcomers to do the same.

"Why ain't he talking?" Kelsey asked surreptitiously.

"He can't talk or hear," Jacob said.

"No shit?" Kelsey asked. "Who'd send a kid out into these woods that can't hear danger comin' up on him?"

Jacob shrugged.

"That's just dangerous," Kelsey said.

Jacob chuckled. "Do you care?"

Kelsey was taken aback. "Of course I care. Shit, Jake. I ain't no animal."

"Sorry," Jacob replied. "I know that."

They ate their meager but tasty meal in silence. Kelsey wandered off into the night, muttering about making sure there were no dangerous animals marauding near the camp. Jacob was astute enough to know he had struck a nerve with the Mule, so he stayed in camp. Allie happily prepared his sleeping pallet after he made sure his sheep were bedded down. Jacob sat up, staring into the fire. He was feeling unsettled, like something was stirring within him. The Beast was uncharacteristically dormant and Jacob couldn't identify the sensations he felt. He glanced at the sleeping boy. Without warning, he leaped upon Allie. He tried to pull back, to roll away and leave the boy alone, but he felt compelled to continue. Allie's eyes flew open, but he made no effort to fight. He looked deep into Jacob's frozen gaze and nodded.

Jacob lowered his face towards Allie's. He fought the impulse, but Allie reached around Jacob's neck and pulled his face down until his mouth was only inches from Allie's own. He opened his mouth. Jacob felt like his throat was being ripped out. The Dragonspirit clawed his way out of Jacob and entered the boy. Allie released Jacob's neck as Kelsey came back into the firelight. Jacob flung himself to one side and lay unmoving, but Allie leaped to his feet.

"Uh," Kelsey stammered. "Maybe I should go…"

"No," the voice came from Allie. "It's alright."

Jacob couldn't believe what he was hearing.

"Allie?" he said. "You can talk!"

"I can talk," Allie repeated. "I can talk. I can hear! Jacob, I can hear!"

"How can this be?" Jacob asked.

"It's a miracle," Kelsey whispered.

"No," Allie said. "It's the Dragonspirit. He used you, Jacob, as a vessel to get to me. A Dragonspirit can't be without form for long. He needed you to travel to me. So long ago I've forgotten when, I cast a spell seeking a Dragonspirit. Krone found me."

"Allie, how can you talk so good?" Jacob asked.

"I'm not only Allie," Allie replied. "I am also Nish, the Seventh Scribe. And," he continued, I am now Krone, a Dragon of the First Order. Krone healed the boy."

"Alright," Kelsey said. He walked backwards away from the fire. "Jake, I like you and we make a good team. But strange shit follows you. I'm just gonna go now."

"Wait," Allie ordered. Kelsey stopped. Allie rubbed his forehead. "I… have so much information to process. Krone is a treasure trove of knowledge. Let me sort through this for a moment." Allie's eyes went blank.

"Can we go?" Kelsey pleaded.

"No," Allie said. His eyes lit up again. "You are one third of the Prophecy of Six. This prophecy says that the war to end all wars will be decided by an alliance of the races of men and half-men, giants and dwarves, Beast and half-beast. You two must maintain this alliance."

"So, you have a Dragon inside you?" Kelsey asked.

"No, it's a Dragonspirit. One of the first and most powerful Dragonspirits," Allie replied.

"I don't understand the prophecy," Jacob interrupted. "Beast and half-beast? What is that?"

Allie sighed. "The Beast is a Dragon. You are the half-beast."

"Jake is half Beast?" Kelsey asked. "What does that make me?"

"Yes, Jacob is half-Beast. You are half-man," Allie answered. "Now please, stop asking me questions. As a Scribe I am duty bound to answer any query asked of me."

"Alright," Kelsey agreed. "But Jacob said something about saving some Dragons. Are we still gonna do that?"

Allie groaned. "You are too late. The Dragon's eggs have already hatched."

"Are you sure?" Jacob asked before he could stop himself.

"Yes!" Allie shouted. "I am sure."

"Sorry," Jacob muttered.

"It's alright," Allie replied. "I'm just not used to talking anymore."

"Can I ask another question?" Jacob asked.

"By the gods!" Allie said. "Yes, ask what you will."

"What is the Beast inside me?"

"The Beast is your Dragon side. You must learn to control it, Jacob. Control it and it will serve you."

"Did you hear that, Kels?" Jacob asked. "You're the Half-Man. I'm the Beast."

"Half-Beast," Allie corrected.

"What about me?" Kelsey asked. "Why am I here? Why do I even exist?"

Allie laughed. "That is a very deep question. You are here to fulfill the Prophecy. You exist because your mother was raped by a Demon." He looked into Kelsey's eyes. "I'm sorry, I am programmed to speak only the truth."

Kelsey shrugged, his face an unreadable mask.

"You've taken the first steps in fulfilling the Prophecy," Allie informed them. "Create an alliance between the entities I have named. Send word far and wide that the fate of the World hangs in the balance. Gather the armies of the Light."

"What are you gonna do?" Kelsey asked.

"I am going to try to tame some Dragons," Allie replied.

Jacob digested that remark. He still felt responsible for the eggs, which were Dragons now.

"Maybe I can help?" he suggested.

"Yes," Allie agreed. "But it is dangerous. Dragons grow very fast. They will be taller than a man by now and capable of ripping you apart."

"Umm," Kelsey mumbled as he fidgeted uncomfortably. "Is it gonna be dark in there?"

"We'll take torches," Jacob offered. "It won't be too bad."

Kelsey looked at the mountain looming behind Allie. "It's just that I don't really like it when it's completely dark. And closed in places bother me some too."

"You don't have to go," Jacob said.

"Are you goin'?" Kelsey asked.

"I reckon so," Jacob said. "I think it's what I'm supposed to do. But you can go on, Kels, and find my teacher, Luke Graywullf. Tell him about this prophecy. Maybe Joseph will be there too."

"I...don't do so well around full blood men, and I might have crossed the *magii'ri* a time or two." Kelsey scuffed his toe in the dirt. "Okay, you twisted my arm. There's a bounty on my head. I guess I'll stick with you."

Jacob smiled. "Take your axe. That'll make you feel better." He turned to Allie. "Let's go."

"Sleep, now," Allie suggested. "Dawn will be soon enough."

They arose in the quiet light of a new day. The sheep were beginning to scatter a little, looking for forage, but Allie knew there was enough feed close by. They wouldn't go far. By midday they found a shaft that drilled right into the side of the mountain. The tailings pile below it made it look like a raw wound.

"Be very, very quiet," Allie warned. "We don't know how they will react to us."

Jacob nodded. Kelsey examined the edge of his axe for the hundredth time. They entered the gloom of the Dragon's lair. The dwarf tunnel was straight as an arrow with a level, sandy floor. But as the circle of daylight grew smaller behind them, Kelsey became more agitated until Jacob struck a light in a pine knot torch he had found outside. Then the big Mule breathed an audible sigh of relief. They continued on, walking straight into the heart of the mountain.

The slight sounds of their passing were strangely muffled, but the mountain groaned and creaked like a living thing. The air had a damp, musty quality, but eventually they came to an air vent that tunneled straight up. A tiny window of light was visible at the top, but it was several hundred feet away. Kelsey stood under that shaft as long as he dared, staring longingly at daylight and freedom. Then he hurried to catch up to Jacob and the meager light of the torch.

Allie forged ahead, sometimes outdistancing Kelsey and Jacob by a hundred feet or more. He was relying on Krone's senses now, not his own vision, so he needed no light. He stopped at the junction with a larger tunnel and was standing there when Jacob approached. Kelsey nearly bumped into them in his haste to stay close.

"Do you hear that?" Jacob breathed.

Allie nodded. Kelsey strained to listen, but all he heard was dripping water and the groaning of the mountain.

"What is it?" he whispered.

Jacob held his hand to his lips. Faintly, Kelsey heard what sounded like the call of a loon. It seemed to be coming from straight ahead. It was answered immediately by a similar call to their right. The calls continued back and forth, then faded away. Allie turned to his companions, his face a white mask of fear.

"I can't ask you to go any farther," he whispered. "The Dragons are hunting something. Maybe us."

"Yeah, I've seen enough," Kelsey whispered back.

"Take the torch and go back," Jacob said. "Wait for us. If we're not back in three days, get out of here as fast as you can."

Kelsey looked longingly back down the tunnel. "No, I'll stick with you for awhile."

Jacob gave Kelsey the torch. One tunnel went straight, one left and one right.

"Three choices," Allie whispered. "We should split up."

"No way," Kelsey argued. "I don't care which way you go, Dragon boy, but I'm stickin' with Jacob."

"I'll go straight then," Allie said. "You two go left."

Jacob nodded. Allie slipped silently down the tunnel and disappeared. Jacob took the lead to the left. That passage almost immediately began to enlarge. Soon they came to a wide hall which was lined on both sides by smaller rooms. Kelsey cautiously peered inside one of the rooms. It held a rough wooden table and a couple of overturned chairs. Dust covered garments hung from hooks imbedded in the rock. They had reached the living quarters for the dwarves who carved the maze of tunnels from the mountain.

Jacob once again led the way through the hall. The interior of the mine was as clear as midday to him, but he knew Kelsey was limited by the ten foot ring of torchlight. They passed through another hall. Kelsey heard water running behind a partition and took the time to look behind it. There was a long pool with water running in one end and out the other. A bench ran the full length of the pool. He hurried to catch up to Jacob. The next room contained a huge kitchen. One entire wall was lined with cookstoves with pots and cookware still sitting on them. The next room was filled with heavy wooden tables. Crockery and utensils were laid out at each place setting. If it hadn't been for the thick layer of dust covering everything it would have seemed the place was still inhabited.

"What happened to everyone?" Kelsey whispered.

They didn't have to wait long to find out. The next room was filled with coats and miner's tools. They passed through it quickly. Then they entered a great passage with ruts worn in the floor from the heavy ore carts that rolled through it for centuries. The carts at the far end were still occupied. Jacob grimaced. The ore cart drivers had been burned alive, frozen by fire in the posture of their death. Some had their hands raised as if to ward off their own demise. Others still clutched weapons that were only half drawn. But all had been burned by Dragonfire. And in the dust next to the last ore cart was a perfectly defined, three toed track.

"They're here," Jacob breathed. "Alive."

"They did this?" Kelsey asked.

"No," Jacob replied. "This was Slagg. Come on."

Kelsey hesitated. He turned a slow semicircle, studying the destruction wrought by one mature Dragon. When he turned around, Jacob was gone.

"Jake?" he whispered.

There was no answer. He felt the darkness closing in.

"Jacob?" he called, louder this time. He heard a sound in the passages behind him. *Chirrup, chirrup.* It sounded like a bird, but bigger. Much bigger. Then a drawn- out hiss. Kelsey ran blindly deeper into the mountain.

CHAPTER SEVEN

The tracks La'Nay was following were fresh, no more than a couple of hours old. She had been trailing Jacob for so long she knew without a doubt that she was following the Dragonspawn, and there was no need to go slowly. She had been catching up, slowly but surely, for weeks. It had taken some time to sort through the chaos in the mine at the Tower, but in the end she was certain that Jacob had escaped. And now he had a companion, a man who could match him stride for stride. She ran on, intent upon making up even more time, when a sudden plume of smoke rose into the startling blue sky.

"Dammit," she cursed under her breath. The smoke could only mean she was too late to save yet another village, or outlying farm, or the manor of some lord with designs on running the World. The Sky Rider struck without prejudice, destroying men and Beasts alike.

Suddenly, she caught a ghost of movement to her left, and a moment later, another to her right. She had been so intent on making up time she had grown careless. She slowed to a trot and scanned her surroundings more carefully. Three more figures became visible, and the Dragonwitch knew she was in trouble. Without warning, she muttered the words of a spell, veered off the trail and doubled her speed. She headed for the thickest growth in the forest. Her magic lent speed and agility to her feet, and she leaped upon a huge, toppled tree. Light as a feather she raced down the trunk, then leaped to another. Soon she was racing from tree to tree, sometimes as high as fifteen feet above the forest floor. Three more pursuers joined from the rear. *Eight to one*, she thought. *Too many*. Thorns and brambles snagged her clothing and soon her dress hung in tatters.

Her only chance was to hope her magic was strong enough to outrun them. In desperation, she sent a silent plea into space. *Slagg, I am here!* La'Nay knew her rescue by the Sky Rider would depend upon a whim as chancy as the direction of the wind, but it was a chance nonetheless. She felt the tree trunk under her feet tremble slightly as one of her pursuers landed on it and the others appeared directly below her. Without another thought, she leaped right in the middle of them, drawing her sword as she fell. She landed squarely on top of a Beastsoldier, crushing him to the ground and breaking her fall.

Her first strike entered the base of one attacker's neck and nearly decapitated him. As he fell sideways, she struck again and opened a gash across another's belly. Yet another sealed her forearm in an unbreakable grip, as another wrapped one long arm around her waist. She drew her knife and stabbed the arm that held her wrist. Her blade went clear through his arm and was wrenched from her grasp. In desperation she flung her head backwards and smashed it into the face of the man who held her. She was rewarded with a grunt of pain and heard the Beastsoldier's nose break. But he didn't release her. He simply let his weight bear her to the ground. In moments her hands and feet were solidly bound.

"Who are you?" La'Nay hissed.

Her attackers didn't speak. One simply threw her over his shoulder and they set off at a trot. The strength and stamina of her captors dumbfounded La'Nay.

"Who sent you?" she demanded.

None answered. She may as well have been speaking to a tree. La'Nay gritted her teeth and focused on the ropes that bound her, but they seemed to be enchanted. Then all she could focus on was surviving that nightmarish run through the forest. On and on her captors ran. They seemed to be more beast than man, but La'Nay had yet to get a good look at any of them. They ran through that day and the night that followed. La'Nay blacked out before the sun rose on the second day. She was only semiconscious when she was lowered to the ground. Then there was silence.

An hour or more passed as La'Nay slowly became aware of her surroundings and the fact that she was actually free of her bonds. As that thought registered, she realized she could hear a trickle of water and she was incredibly thirsty. Her vision was blurred and she was dizzy but she could crawl. She followed the sound of water until her searching hands found a tiny stream. She smelled the water first, then dipped a finger in it and touched her tongue. It seemed pure. She cupped one hand and took a sip from it. The water was icy cold and as she swallowed it sent a sensation of pure relief through her body. She took another small sip and lay on her back, trying to regain her strength. Finally, she was able to sit up. She felt no ill effects from the water, so she drank her fill. Then she looked about as her vision slowly cleared.

She was in a well lit cave with a sandy floor. There was an opening high up on one wall, but it appeared to be covered in iron bars. She was a prisoner, then. Struck by the hopelessness of her situation, she sank back against one wall. She had no idea who her captors were, where she was, or what they intended to do with her. She felt for her weapons, but of course they were gone. She did, however, discover a wafer of trailbread tucked in the remains of her shirt pocket. Since she had no intention of dying on a completely empty stomach, La'Nay nibbled on it until it was gone. Amazed at how much better she felt after such a simple act, she carefully examined her surroundings.

A rustling sound accompanied by a fleeting shadow caused her to spin around. She saw nothing. An identical sound came from behind her and she turned quickly enough to catch a glimpse of something as it disappeared behind a rock formation. She wasn't able to identify it, but the fine hairs at the base of her neck stiffened. Without a word or another pause, La'Nay ran across the cave and into the darkest shadow she could see. It was an opening, and she ran inside.

A passageway opened up before her. It was dimly lit, almost too dark to see, but she charged headlong down the passage. Back in the cave she could hear growling and snapping sounds accompanied by inhuman, high pitched shrieks. Terrified, La'Nay ran deeper into the mountain. The passage became smaller and smaller until she was forced to slow down. In places she actually had to crouch and turn sideways to proceed. Behind her, she heard more growling and scratching sounds as the beasts who chased her tried to pass through the smaller passage with no success.

The passage abruptly opened up again. La'Nay ran into that chamber, but her foot became entangled in something and she tripped. She stifled a scream as she fell. Nearly sobbing in terror, she whirled around and felt her stomach roll when she saw what her feet had become entangled in. It was the lower half of a human body. She recoiled and scurried backwards. *What kind of place was this?*

La'Nay's mind reeled as she searched the new chamber. Her eyes were drawn back to the mutilated body on the floor. There was a metallic glint around what had been the waist. Intrigued, she crept closer. It was a gunbelt with loaded cartridges still in the loops. Gagging, she unbuckled it and pulled it out from under the detached legs. A pistol was still nestled in the holster. La'Nay looked in wide eyed wonder at the fine craftmanship of the belt and holster as she slid the pistol free and examined it. The hammer slipped back with a solid click as the cylinder rotated smoothly and locked in position. The Dragonwitch touched the fingers of her right hand reverently to her brow.

"Thank you for your gift, gunslinger," she said as she buckled the belt around her hips.

Another belt was visible, now that she had removed the gunbelt. La'Nay unbuckled it and slid it out from under the corpse as well. Four throwing knives hung from it in individual sheaths as well as a small bag of cartridges. La'Nay drew the pistol, opened the loading gate and rotated the cylinder again. Four of the cartridges in it had been fired. Four shots fired, and still this Warrior had fallen? What manner of monster lurked beneath the mountain?

La"Nay punched out the empty cartridges and replaced them with loaded ones. She hesitated, then slipped the boots off the detached legs and tried them on. They were a little big, but better than trying to run in bare feet. Then she forced herself to look closely around the cave. On the far side she found what remained of the rest of the gunslinger. He had been torn in half. Not cut cleanly or hacked, but torn as if two giant dogs had been playing tug of war. Resolutely, La'Nay rolled the body over and looked into its lifeless eyes. Despite herself a slight sigh of relief escaped her lips. It was no one she knew. She retrieved the Warrior's hat and settled it firmly on her head. Then she looked for a way out.

There were two passages to choose from. One reeked of snake and water dripped from the ceiling, but the air moved with a tiny stirring. The other was dry and held no smell at all. La'Nay desperately wanted to take the drier passage, but at the last moment she changed her mind and entered the other tunnel.

The snake smell grew stronger as she walked. Then, without warning, La'Nay burst from the tunnel and walked two steps right into Slagg's den. She stopped and stared in shock at the vast treasure the bull Dragon had amassed. She realized immediately where she was and that she had placed herself in grave danger. But the memory of the monsters that pursued her left her no choice. She picked her way across the Sky Rider's den and breathed in the unmistakable scent of fresh air coming from the main tunnel. La'Nay hurried down the main tunnel until she could clearly see light at the opening. She was sure she was going to escape. No more than fifty yards remained to fresh air and freedom when three distinct figures emerged from the gloom.

La'Nay recognized her captors immediately, and without another thought she drew and began firing. The first wild shot took one Beastoldier squarely between the eyes and blew a four inch hole out the back of his skull. As his blood and brain matter spattered his companions, La'Nay shot the nearest survivor in the chest, then triggered two more shots into the belly of the third. He slithered down to his knees, staring stupidly at his own intestines in his hands. La'Nay dropped into a crouch and searched for more targets. None came. She looked down in disdain at the Beastsoldiers who had been her captors and just beyond them, saw another body lying half buried in the dirt. It was bigger than a Beastsoldier, much bigger than a man, and the head was in a shape that was definitely not human. La'Nay crept closer. The outline of the body became more distinct and she realized it wasn't really buried. It was perfectly camouflaged to match the desert sand. It was the body of a juvenile Dragon, and even in death she could see it had been emaciated. The hindquarters of the fallen Dragon, thin as it was, had been gnawed clean of flesh. Slagg's eggs had hatched, then, and now his offspring were starving. That was the terror inside the cave. Juvenile Dragons that had grown from birth with no guidance, no help to tap into their instincts. Now they were no more than mindless eating machines, intent on survival. La'Nay ran out into the bright sunlight, to stand on the ledge Slagg liked to perch on to survey his domain.

Her breath came in gasps, more from terror than from exertion and her hands began to shake. She willed them to stop as she once again opened the loading gate on her liberated pistol, punched out the fired shells and slid loaded ones into place. She began to feel that she had a chance to survive the ordeal when she made the mistake of looking below the ledge.

The entire hillside was covered with the remnants of human skeletons. Crows hopped about, pecking scraps of flesh from the bones. Here and there a piece of clothing rustled in the slight breeze.

La'Nay gagged and retched, but held down the contents of her stomach with a long, low moan. Here was the evidence of Slagg's true nature. No matter what being was held captive by the immense hulk of the Dragonform, the Sky Rider truly was a bloodthirsty monster. The ancient race she, as a Dragonwitch, had pledged loyalty to was no more than a myth.

La'Nay ripped a sleeve from her torn blouse and wrapped it around her nose and mouth. She steeled herself against this new terror and began to pick her way down the hillside. Despite her misgivings, she kept a sharp eye out for anything useful. She pulled an intact leather vest off a very fresh corpse with the head missing. One skeleton yielded a bow, another a quiver of arrows. She emerged from the bonepile fully outfitted and completely disillusioned with Dragons.

CHAPTER EIGHT

Kelsey was lost. The pine knot was burning out and he knew he would be engulfed in darkness within scant minutes. His unnatural fear of the dark had a firm hold on him and he was almost sobbing. In desperation he broke into a run, made clumsy by the six foot field of vision afforded by his torch. But he had a firm grasp on the handle of his battleaxe. The tunnel he was in suddenly widened into a great hall. Piles of gold coins littered the floor and on the far side of the cavern, Kelsey saw a pinprick of light. Hope flared within him. The torch sputtered and died. He moaned in terror as fear temporarily paralyzed him.

He stood rooted to that spot, afraid to move or make a sound. Just as he had vowed to make a break for the light, a loud, drawn out *huff* came at his back. Kelsey felt his hair flutter as the sound was repeated. *Huff, huff.* Droplets of moisture struck the back of his neck. Tears flowed down the big man's cheeks as he turned ever so slowly to face the terror behind him. He came face to face with a juvenile Dragon.

The Dragon stared at him with unblinking, reptilian eyes as it sized up its prey. Kelsey's left eye began to twitch. The Dragon opened its jaws and hissed. It extended its neck and thrust its face inches from Kelsey's. Corrosive saliva dripped from its fangs. One drop struck Kelsey's hand where it sizzled and smoked.

"Gawd *damn* you!" Kelsey snarled. He jerked his battleaxe upwards. The Dragon blocked his thrust with its forepaws and struck with open jaws towards Kelsey's face. Kelsey fell backwards, rolled once and leaped to his feet. He was still in the air when he swung the axe. The Dragon had also attacked and Kelsey felt the blade bite deep into its side thwarting the beast's attack, but only momentarily. Its momentum carried it past Kelsey, but it wheeled and slashed at Kelsey with a hind foot. If it had been a mature Dragon with foot long talons, the fight would have been finished. Even so, the juvenile's hind claw was long enough to open a wicked gash in Kelsey's side, just missing his intestines.

Kelsey roared in pain, matching the growls of the juvenile. Warmth cascaded down his side and wet his breeches. He swung his axe again. The juvenile had rushed back in, emboldened by its earlier strike and driven by starvation. It reached for Kelsey with one foreleg and his vicious swing severed that leg. The Dragon hissed in pain and leaped upon Kelsey, driving him backwards. His legs gave out and he fell to the floor, taking the brunt of the impact on his shoulders and upper back. The Dragon's hind feet flailed as it tried to disembowel him with its talons. Simultaneously, it reached forward and bit at his face. Kelsey jammed the handle of his axe in the beast's jaws and fought back with all his strength. Each slash of the Dragon's talons opened wounds on his legs. In desperation, he held the beast back with one hand, drew his knife, and plunged it into the Dragon's belly. It paid no heed. But then Kelsey heard another growl and something struck the Dragon with a massive thud and suddenly its great weight was lifted from him.

He rolled to his hands and knees and started to crawl towards the distant light. Then he was struck again. He was flipped on his back and found himself staring into Jacob's face. His friend was almost unrecognizable. His eyes blazed with an insane light and his face was screwed into a mask of animalistic rage. Jacob drove his fist into Kelsey's face again and again.

"Jake!" Kelsey cried. "Stop, Jake! Stop! It's me, Kelsey!"

The attack stopped. Reason returned to Jacob's eyes. He scooped up Kelsey's battleaxe and whirled to face the Dragon. It attacked. Jacob darted to one side and chopped one hind leg off at the knee. The juvenile roared in pain and propelled itself in a long leap back towards Kelsey. Jacob dove upon its back, raised the axe high and split the beast's skull. Its snout plowed a furrow into the cavern floor inches from Kelsey's face. He looked into its eye as the light within it died. Jacob dropped from its back, light as a fly, and knelt for a moment beside it. He touched three fingers of his right hand to his forehead in deference, then turned to his fallen friend.

"I'm sorry, Kels!" he cried. "I'm so sorry!"

Kelsey groaned an unintelligible reply as Jacob scooped him up in his arms and carried him to the exit. For perhaps the first time in his young life, Jacob felt real fear and concern for the safety of another. He had felt responsible for Anja and Michael, and in time he may have felt much more for Anja. But the thought of this strange young man he knew as a friend dying because of him filled him with dread.

"Don't die," he pleaded. "Please, don't die!"

"I held my own, didn't I?" Kelsey whispered.

"You sure did," Jacob agreed. "Hold on. I'm getting us out of here. Just hold on."

CHAPTER NINE

A foreign sound caused La'Nay to stop. She strained to make out what it was. Then she heard it again. Voices. Human voices. She hurried back through the grisly remains of Slagg's voracious appetite and climbed the slope to peer over its edge just in time to see Jacob emerge carrying another man. Crimson stains bloomed on the carried man's clothing. Jacob pleaded with him not to die. Jacob dropped to his knees and gently lowered the other man to the ground. Unmindful of her own safety, La'Nay rose into full view. Jacob's entire body stiffened and he went into a defensive posture over the fallen man, brandishing an axe.

"Jacob," La'Nay said as calmly as she could muster. "Jacob, you know me. I am La'Nay. I'm your friend and I'm here to help."

Jacob studied her. Her voice felt good inside his head, cooling the flames of rage. His nostrils flared as he tested her scent. Her scent was cool and calming as well, like the deep, black timber after an afternoon rain. And it was familiar.

"I know you," he said.

La'Nay breathed a huge sigh of relief. "Let me help your friend. He's losing a lot of blood."

"Yes," Jacob quickly agreed. "Help him."

La'Nay knelt beside the fallen man and examined his wounds. She began to draw her knife but a warning growl from Jacob stopped her.

"I'm only going to remove his clothes so I can see his wounds, Jacob," she assured him. She moved very slowly while Jacob watched closely. La'Nay grimaced. "I need cloth to bind these wounds." She thought quickly. "Jacob, find the cleanest clothing you can from over the hill. Hurry."

Jacob leaped over the hill. It was a terrible risk, La'Nay knew. But she had to stop the bleeding. She would deal with the risk of infection later. Jacob flew back over the crest of the hill with an armload of salvaged clothing. La'Nay ripped the cleanest into strips, made compresses, and bound Kelsey's wounds. She looked about. There was almost no vegetation anywhere near the ledge, and nothing but scrub brush immediately below.

"Can you carry him?" La'Nay asked. "We have to get him near water, and I need to find herbs to make medicine."

"I can carry him," Jacob assured her. He scooped up the two hundred eighty pound Kelsey as if he were a child.

La'Nay watched in amazement. She led the way down the slope and through Slagg's bone pile. Jacob never stumbled or jarred his wounded friend.

"Will he live?" Jacob asked.

"I think I have stopped the bleeding," La'Nay replied. "If he doesn't get an infection, he has a good chance. The rest depends on his will to live."

Jacob nodded. "He'll live. Because of you," he said pointedly to La'Nay.

"Is he a friend of yours?" La'Nay asked.

"He's my only friend," Jacob replied. He stopped and tested the air. "There's water this way."

La'Nay followed him to a small spring. Jacob lowered Kelsey to the ground. He dipped a finger in the water and sniffed it, then he tasted it.

"It's clean. What can I do to help?" he asked.

"I need a fire," La'Nay said.

"It's risky," Jacob said.

"I know," La'Nay agreed. "But he needs it. What is his name?"

"His name is Kelsey," Jacob said. "I'll get wood and start the fire."

La'Nay searched around the small seep and found some herbs she could use. She soaked rags in water and hung them over the fire until they steamed. Then she pounded the herbs into a poultice and packed it inside the makeshift bandages. When Jacob wasn't watching, she directed a quick spell of healing into the poultices. Then she very carefully removed Kelsey's compresses one by one and replaced them with poultices. The bleeding had stopped. She cleaned up the gashes left by Jacob's fists and applied a layer of smashed herbs to those as well. She placed her cheek close to Kelsey's nose and mouth. His breath came slow but steady. She cast another quick spell of general good health. Satisfied she had done her best, she leaned back against a boulder and studied Jacob.

"What happened?" she asked.

Jacob shrugged.

"I can see you've changed," La'Nay said.

"Why didn't you tell me?" Jacob said suddenly. "Why didn't you tell me I'm a monster?"

"You're not a monster," La'Nay insisted.

"Look at him," Jacob said. "I saw him fighting with that Dragon inside the cavern. I saw him, my friend, being killed by a Dragon. And what did I do? I attacked him!"

"Tell me exactly what happened," La'Nay suggested.

"I just did," Jacob insisted. "There's something inside me. A monster, a Beast. Sometimes it comes forward and takes over. It makes me do bad things. I can't control it. I saw Kelsey fighting with the Dragon and the Beast told me to stop him."

"Jacob," La'Nay said. "You did control it. You stopped attacking Kelsey when you realized he was your friend. Then you protected him. You controlled the Beast and protected your friend."

Jacob shrugged uncertainly.

"It's true, Jacob," La'Nay said. "You can control the Beast. You can control your own life."

"I've never been in control," Jacob said. "Someone, or something, has always told me what to do. First it was Mathias, always badgering me to be faster, stronger, more of a leader. Then Luke. And Slagg."

"Do you resent Luke?" La'Nay asked.

"No," Jacob was quick to answer. "Luke taught me things. He let me be me. He just taught me right from wrong."

"And that's all you need," La'Nay said with a smile. "And Mathias?"

Jacob's expression darkened. "Mathias made me into a monster."

"You are not a monster," La'Nay said again. "I can teach you to control the Beast at all times. You can use the Beast to honor the Code."

Jacob nodded. "I want that."

"Good," La'Nay said. "I'll teach you all you need to know. I need to know one more thing, Jacob. It's about Slagg. Actually, it's about all Dragons. Do you still feel a kinship with the race of Dragons?"

Jacob considered that. He suddenly realized the bond he'd felt with Slagg was gone. He consciously thought about Slagg's eggs and felt...*nothing*. He forced himself to remember the fight with the juvenile Dragon inside the cavern and all he felt was animosity. With a start, he realized he felt *whole*. The Beast was still there, crouched and ready. But the divisiveness fostered by Slagg was gone.

"I feel nothing for Slagg," Jacob said truthfully. "Nothing at all."

La'Nay grinned. Suddenly, Kelsey groaned and tried to sit up. La'Nay and Jacob rushed to his side. Kelsey saw Jacob, and fear registered on his face for a moment. Then he had a chance to look into Jacob's eyes and the fear melted away. He shyly studied La'Nay.

"I thought you were a dream," he said.

"Kels," Jacob said, relief evident in his voice. "Are you alright?"

Kelsey tried to pull off a weak smile and barely made it. "I'd be better if you hadn't pounded on my face."

"I'm sorry," Jacob replied sincerely. "I was out of my head. It won't happen again."

"Good," Kelsey said weakly. "I won't be going inside any more dark places either."

Jacob grinned as La'Nay looked from one to the other questioningly.

"Tell her," Kelsey said.

"Kelsey's afraid of the dark," Jacob said.

"And small, tight spaces, too," Kelsey admitted. "And you can add Dragons to that list now." He suddenly sobered. "What about that kid?"

Jacob suddenly looked distressed. "I lost him. I thought I was good in the dark, but he left me behind. Then I heard you fighting the other Dragon. I don't know what happened to him."

"Should we go back in and look for him?" La'Nay asked.

"No," Kelsey said forcefully. "I won't go back in there and I won't let you either," he said to La'Nay.

"I have to agree," Jacob said. "Allie is probably safer by himself."

La'Nay nodded in agreement. "Fine. Jacob, we have years of work to catch up on. Kelsey," she smiled. "You need to rest."

La'Nay left the glowing embers of the fire after she was sure Jacob and Kelsey slept. She crept quietly away from the campsite and sat down on a log in the moonlight. Only then did she relax. It was a good thing she was sitting, she thought, because her shaking legs probably would have given out. The Beast inside Jacob had grown strong, almost too strong for her magic to have any effect. It had been a massive gamble, casting a spell on the Dragonspawn, but it was the only way she knew to calm him enough to be rational. The raw energy and lust for destruction she had witnessed left her doubting her own ability. The question that remained was, how long would her spell keep the Beast inside Jacob at bay?

"Damn you, Mathias," she muttered under her breath.

If she had only been allowed to continue nurturing the boy when he was a child, the whole process would have been so much easier. Now she could only hope that Luke had been able to imprint strongly enough on Jacob to ingrain the Code of the *magii'ri* in his brain. Teaching would never be enough. The Code had to be an integral part of Jacob, or the Beast inside him was sure to take over. She returned to her blankets and fell into a fitful sleep.

She arose early the following morning, but Jacob was already awake. He had a small fire going and was heating water for tea. Two rabbits sizzled on a spit. Her mouth watered. Kelsey stirred and sat up very slowly.

"I'd rather have beef," Jacob said without turning around, "but rabbit was all I could find. Slagg is devouring everything else."

"Rabbit will be wonderful," La'Nay replied.

"Anything will be fine," Kelsey added. "Remember the biscuits and toasted cheese we had with Allie? That was good. Not as good as biscuits and gravy and eggs, but then everything's better with gravy." He glanced at Jacob and La'Nay who regarded him with irritation.

"Sorry," he said. "Rabbit will be good."

They ate. La'Nay took Jacob aside and began his teaching. She started with the earliest times, when men and Dragons coexisted as equals. She stressed that neither race was superior, and both races were stronger because of it. Dragonmagic was taught and used freely, until Haan intervened. The Guardian of the Abyss twisted Dragons to serve his own ends and the long peace with men ended. But Dragonmagic survived. La'Nay presented Jacob with the arm band she had taken from a Warrior in Slagg's bone pile.

"This arm band was worn by the Dragonlords," she said. "I have cast powerful spells of Dragonmagic on it to enhance the magic it was instilled with when it was forged. Wear it, and it will only allow you to use the power you have to honor the Code of the *magii'ri*. This is a powerful talisman, Jacob. It will always protect and guide you."

Jacob eagerly took the arm band and encircled his right wrist with it.

"Feel the magic," La'Nay encouraged. "Feel the inner peace it bestows upon you. You are your own master, Jacob. I know you will do what is right."

Suddenly confident, Jacob looked within himself. The Beast was still there, but it now stood at his side, ready to do his bidding. They moved and thought as one. He felt calm and more at peace than he had in years. He suddenly realized he hadn't felt that good since his time as Luke's 'prentice.

"Thank you," he said simply.

La'Nay smiled. "You are most welcome, Jacob." She drew a deep breath. "Now we must discuss Slagg."

Jacob nodded. "He must be stopped. I had the Black Arrow, but lost it when the Rider shot me."

"Without it, or a weapon of equal power, it would be suicide to attack the Sky Rider directly," La'Nay said. She took a chance. "Can you reunite with Slagg and trick him into doing our bidding?"

Jacob shook his head uncertainly. "I can influence him, but he is beyond control. I believe he's going insane."

La'Nay frowned. Dragons were unpredictable at best, even when they were in a rational state of mind. But an insane Dragon? The World would be destroyed. Unless his anger could be deflected away from the meager defenders of the Light.

"I can't ask you to do this, Jacob," La'Nay said. "It's too dangerous."

"I'll do it," Jacob volunteered. "After all, what choice do we have?"

"None, I fear," La'Nay conceded. "But Jacob, you must be so very careful. One misstep, one moment of carelessness when Slagg is near and he will turn on you without warning."

Jacob gave her a weak smile and nodded. He knew all too well what Slagg was capable of. He would have to be constantly on his guard or the Sky Rider would see his true intentions.

"What about me?" Kelsey asked. "What can I do?"

"Heal first," La'Nay instructed. "Then you and I will search for a Black Arrow. And if we encounter some Beastsoldiers along the way, we can make their lives miserable."

Kelsey grinned. "I like the sound of that."

CHAPTER TEN

Joseph of Ead skirted wide around yet another burning village. He shook his head in sorrow. For the hundredth time he wished he could turn back the clock and listen to Mathias' advice to delay his attack on Timon Blackhelm. He had been so sure, so confident of himself and his men. Now his confidence was shattered. The battle had been hard fought. That much was true. But in the end, Timon had been victorious. And he wasn't content to merely defeat the army of Ead. He had executed all the survivors his Beasts could run down, and forced Joseph to watch. His proud Warriors died well. But Joseph broke. He begged Timon for mercy, not for himself, but for his men. And Timon had refused. He, Joseph of Ead, was responsible for the death of his entire kingdom. He now had two choices. Run from the truth, or make Timon pay for what he had done.

Joseph knew he couldn't defeat Timon. He knew he would never again be the Warrior King who led thousands into the face of danger. His own physical strength was on the wane. A brutally honest assessment of himself revealed that he just wasn't strong enough. He could still die with honor on the battlefield. But he intended his death to mean something. Somehow, he would navigate the war torn country of Norland, evade Slagg, and deliver a message to the armies of men. The Dragonspawn lived!

Joseph kept to the roughest country he could find, since that was where he found the most cover. He worked his way East. Eventually he dropped into the same canyon where Jacob had encountered the Rider. The Warrior King surveyed the battle site. He studied each set of remains dispassionately, poking through the bones. He had no idea what he was looking for, only that he needed to understand the enemies the forces of the Light faced. Joseph followed the all but invisible tracks Jacob left farther up the creek to the site of Jacob's battle with the Rider. The leather wrapped bundle on the edge of the pool seemed innocuous at first, but the longer he studied it, the more he realized it was very familiar. His heart racing and his hands shaking, Joseph carefully unwrapped it.

"The Black Arrow," he whispered reverently.

The Black Arrow. The same arrow Joseph had used to kill the Dragon who's head hung in his hall. The one weapon he knew of with the inherent power to slay any Dragon. His aim had been off a fraction of an inch, or Slagg would now be nothing but a gigantic skeleton. It was a turning point in the battle. With the Black Arrow lost, Slagg had been free to turn his destructive attention fully on Joseph's army. Joseph closed his eyes. The memory of the battle would not leave him. He could still hear the screams of his men as

Slagg dove upon them, fully under Timon's control. The Darklord controlled the Sky Rider and enjoyed watching the imprisoned Talin writhe in agony with each Warrior killed.

Joseph wrenched his attention back to the present. His first thought was to find Jacob and present him with the Black Arrow. But why? The Arrow was his. It belonged to him and the glory he could gain by driving it through Slagg's black heart would cement his name as one of the greatest Warriors of all time. Now he had another purpose. He would have vengeance, and the Black Arrow was the vehicle to achieve it.

It took a week to work his way to the coast. Ships were few and far between, but he managed to secure passage to Gryllis. From there he intended to cross the Sothron Desert, evade the Sand Wyrms, and approach the King of the Eastern Provinces to raise an army to join the *magii'ri*. Rejuvenated by his new lease on life, Joseph found he was actually looking forward to the journey. He would return with an army. All he needed was one shot and Timon's greatest weapon would fall.

CHAPTER ELEVEN

Jacob made his way easily through the dense growth of the forest, running lightly along a massive fallen log one moment, then leaping to land soundlessly on the constantly damp carpet of aspen leaves that covered the forest floor. He moved so easily, effortlessly and silent, that he seemed almost to be an apparition. His nostrils flared as he unconsciously tested the breeze for scent. His brain instantly categorized each individual smell. Most he dismissed almost immediately, but if any were unfamiliar or classified by his instincts as dangerous, he stopped and scanned the area for threats. And so it was that he was being extra cautious with his senses on high alert as he neared a clearing he had spotted earlier.

His sense of smell was assaulted by a myriad of scents. He detected Beastsoldier, which was rank and sour, and the smell of troll which could just as easily have been a rotting sheep carcass but with a subtle difference. There was at least one giant among them, with the characteristic woody scent peculiar to their kind. Jacob could also smell horses, and wafting through all of that was the unmistakable fragrance of men who had been on the trail for too long. They smelled of sweat and woodsmoke, and the sweat of the horses they rode.

Jacob crept closer. His curiosity was a burning thing. Why would men and Beastsoldiers and trolls and…he sniffed the breeze again. *What was that?* A scent he had no experience with drifted through the trees. He could not identify it, but the smell made Jacob uneasy. The Beast inside him stood tall, muscles quivering, straining forward with its claws extended, ready to spring. Jacob slipped closer until his view into the clearing was unobstructed. What he saw froze his blood in his veins. The banner of King Titus was planted in the center of the clearing. The camps of his men extended behind the banner. But what had Jacob staring in disbelief was the easy camaraderie between the men and Beasts and trolls he had already identified. They shared campfires and food, and all were armed. As Jacob watched, a man dressed in an embroidered cloak, wearing a silk hat adorned with a peacock plume, emerged from a large embroidered tent. He walked purposefully forward across the camp. Another figure emerged from the trees on the far side of the clearing, and Jacob's entire body tensed. This was the creature he had sensed. It stood eight feet tall, and claws adorned the ends of its muscular arms. The face was hideous, with three sets of interlocking pincers that it clicked open and shut like a nervous tick. It glimmered as it moved, fading almost entirely from sight before it reappeared. Then it crouched, and the creature's entire body spasmed. As Jacob stared, the monster's deformed body was replaced with that of a man. His skin was covered in slime. A soldier rushed forward with a cloak, which the monster wrapped around his newly hatched body.

"Traegor," the man said as he extended his hand.

Traegor, the King of Demons, stared in disdain for several long moments at the man's proffered hand, then he reluctantly took it in his own.

"You're a messenger from King Titus," he acknowledged in a deep voice. "Why have you offered this parley?"

"I am King Titus' right hand man," the speaker corrected. "I am Lord Dunmore. I think we could be mutually beneficial to each other."

"You have nothing that interests me," Traegor responded, contempt dripping from his words.

I think I do," Dunmore replied. "I know where Lynch can be found."

Despite himself, Traegor was intrigued. His head swiveled around. "Lynch? Where?"

"Not so fast," Dunmore said, certain he held the upper hand. "We can make a trade."

"A trade?" Traegor asked. "What kind of trade?"

"I'll tell you where to find Lynch," Dunmore said. "And in return I want your help. The petty arguments and squabbling of men must end. The World needs one King, and I intend to be that man. You can help me achieve that, and in return I'll reveal to you the location of the Dark Wizard Lynch."

Traegor's face twitched and his perfect human body convulsed until he fought it under control again. "Is that all you have to offer?"

"No," Dunmore continued. "I want to rule the World, but I have no interest in what happens Under. The underworld kingdom will be yours, and Lynch will be your plaything."

Jacob could not believe what he heard.

"I have control of Titus' military. My armies will join with the Beasts and trolls. I approached the ogres, and I think they will also join me. I have only to sway the Dark Elves and Nightriders and with the support of the Demons my army will be invincible," Dunmore said.

Traegor smiled slightly. "You'll put your race under the bootheels of an army of the Dark?"

"To achieve domination, yes," Dunmore agreed. "At least temporarily."

Traegor shrugged. "Very well. Provide me with the location of Lynch and I will offer my help."

Jacob silently backed away. *Titus was being betrayed by his own men.* How could the power of the Dark be so firmly entrenched in every level of Norland? Despair at the flimsy loyalty of men overwhelmed him. He circled wide around the clearing, now even more cautious than he was before. Part of him longed to launch himself into the center of the gathering army, but even the Dragonspawn had limitations. He was outnumbered three hundred to one. But there was an equalizer somewhere ahead, an equalizer that went by the title of the Sky Rider. All he had to do was convince Slagg not to kill him on sight, then deceive the Dragon into believing he wanted to join him again. And then they would return to find this army and make them pay for their deception.

Jacob searched unceasingly for Slagg. He left the cool comfort of the mountains and ranged throughout the foothills. Most of the villages he passed through were deserted. He never spent any more time in those than he felt absolutely necessary. The empty, dark windows and doors seemed to watch him, and more than once he thought he could feel hostile eyes on his back as he hurried onward. Several times a day, Jacob paused and allowed his mind to roam, but Slagg's presence was always absent. But he knew the Sky Rider had not simply ceased to exist. He was in Norland, watching and waiting, biding his time. A tiny bit of Jacob insisted that it was true. Somehow, they were still connected. He could deny it. He could fight it, and he could try to expel the Dragon from his being. Nothing could change the fact that he shared blood with the Sky Rider. And he could feel the Dragon.

The absence of people confounded Jacob. He understood that most would flee the coming war, but surely some stalwart would stubbornly refuse to bow before the storm. But the countryside he roamed was utterly deserted. Not even a stray cat or an escaped milk cow remained. And there were no bodies. There had been no battle. The village huts stood ready to accept inhabitants.

After weeks of travel, Jacob found himself outside the walls of Titus' kingdom. He had slipped by the sentries easily enough, but now, with a powerful ally just inside the walls, he felt the sudden weakness of doubt. Would Titus believe him? He had to make sure the king's advisors could not interfere. He needed a private audience. Without another moment of hesitation, he waded into the stinking waters of the moat. Black mud sucked at his boots and every step released a putrid stench like rotten eggs. He drew in a deep breath and plunged under the water. He stroked powerfully until his hands brushed the rough stone foundation of the castle. He emerged from the water silently. His searching hands found tiny cracks and ledges and he began to climb. As nimble and light as a fly, Jacob fairly skipped up the stone wall. When he reached the top, he lunged over a ledge and dropped into a crouch. His searching eyes darted back and forth. Sentries appeared in blots of livid red, but they were oblivious to his presence.

He timed their patrol, and in the split second when he was out of sight of all the guards, he darted across the ledge and leaped to cling to the next level. He resumed his silent ascent until he reached the tallest spire. A faint glow came from inside. Jacob peered through a window opening. Titus sat hunched at a desk, poring over sheafs of paper. Occasionally he sipped wine from a jewel encrusted goblet and gnawed on joints of roasted meats. He licked and sucked the grease from his fingers. Saliva spurted in Jacob's mouth. Without even a whisper of sound, he dropped through the window and entered the light. Titus dropped a turkey leg on his papers and knocked over his wine.

"I mean you no harm," Jacob stated.

Titus swallowed noisily. He nodded. His eyes darted to the door, where a sentry stood guard in the hall.

"You have been named as a good and decent man," Jacob said. "A man who may unite the World under one ruler. Who do you serve?"

"I serve Aard," Titus guaranteed.

Jacob nodded. "There is a traitor in your court," he said.

"What?" Titus demanded. "Who are you? Who do you serve?"

"My name is Jacob. I am *magii'ri*."

Titus' eyes narrowed. "The *magii'ri* are outdated relics who have outlived their time. Still, the Warriors have the reputation of upholding the Code at all costs. Why are you here?"

"I told you," Jacob said. "You are being betrayed by a man named Dunmore. He has an army of men and Beasts and creatures of the Dark camped fifteen days march North of here. He means to rule the World."

Titus leaned heavily back in his chair and released a heavy sigh. "Dunmore has been my friend since we were boys. Why would he betray me?"

"Ambition and greed and the lust for power," Jacob replied, drawing on Luke's teaching. "The common sins of men. Has there been a slight or misunderstanding between you two?"

Titus was silent for so long Jacob began to think he had lost this gamble. His forehead was furrowed as he scowled, deep in thought. Finally, he spoke. "A woman."

Jacob nodded. "So there is something that could turn him against you."

"So it would seem," Titus agreed. "But even though you are *magii'ri,* you can't expect me to blindly put my trust in you."

Jacob shrugged. "Is Dunmore here?"

"No," Titus admitted. "I sent him on official business to some of the farther reaches of my realm. His absence is expected."

"And convenient," Jacob said. "If you don't believe me, send a scout to investigate."

"I will," Titus said. "In the meantime, will you enjoy the hospitality of my home?"

"I can wait a bit," Jacob said. "But I have business of my own to tend to. I can't wait thirty days for your man to make the round trip."

Titus nodded. "At least rest a day or two and have some food. You must be hungry."

"I could eat," Jacob admitted.

"Good. It's settled then," Titus replied. He rang a bell, and a moment later a servant girl appeared.

"Send for Fargus," Titus ordered. "I have need for him this very night. And have cook prepare food for a special guest."

The girl bowed her head and disappeared. Titus returned to his chair where he studied his visitor with unabashed curiosity. Jacob squirmed under his scrutiny until he finally began to stalk around the room. Paintings adorned the walls and Jacob studied them closely. Some were done with such skill it seemed the artist had captured his subjects and somehow trapped them inside the frames. The images left him feeling oddly unsettled.

"What is the name of your sire?" Titus finally asked.

Jacob was taken aback at the directness of the question.

"Grimwullf," he replied. "My name is Jacob Grimwullf."

Titus nodded. There was a sudden knock at the door.

"Enter," Titus ordered.

The doorway was filled by a brutish giant of a man with shoulder length hair and a wild, unkempt beard. His skin was permanently darkened by the elements. Jacob recognized him as a very dangerous adversary, but he also sensed that he was even more dangerous than the newcomer. The bearded man crossed the room, his heavy, hobnailed boots clumping loudly on the floor. Another man came in behind him, having been completely obscured by the man Jacob took to be Fargus. He was correct.

"This is Fargus," Titus said, indicating the big man. "He's my chief scout. Fargus," he said, turning to the scout. "Jacob is *magii'ri*. He saw a large force assembling fifteen days march to the North. I need you to investigate without being seen. Report back here in no more than twenty days."

Jacob's brow furrowed. Fargus nodded and left without a word. The man who had accompanied him nodded at Jacob in a friendly fashion.

"Jacob Grimwullf, this is Pembroke, one of my chief advisors," Titus said with a pointed look at Pembroke.

"Jacob Grimwullf," Pembroke said with a slight smile. He cocked his head at Jacob and watched him expectantly.

"Pembroke," Jacob replied, not really interested in the newcomer. "Titus, I don't think Fargus can make it back in twenty days. I moved fast and it took me fifteen just to get here."

"He can do it," Titus dismissed with a wave of his hand. He turned back to Pembroke. "Have you ever heard of this young man?"

"Jacob Grimwullf," Pembroke mused. He muttered under his breath, then looked in Titus direction and shrugged.

"What?" Jacob asked. "What's so interesting about my name?"

Titus seemed confused for only a moment before he regained his composure

"Excuse us for a moment," Titus said. He turned Pembroke towards the door with a hand on his shoulder. As they left the room, Titus said, "Check on the cook. I'd like something extra special for our guest."

Pembroke nodded and hurried down the hallway.

Titus returned to the room and carefully closed the door behind him.

"Have you told anyone else about Dunmore?" he asked.

"No," Jacob responded. "I haven't seen another person in over a month."

"Good," Titus said. His confident smile returned. "We need to keep this quiet until I can deal with Dunmore in person. No need to give it away."

Jacob shrugged. "Whatever."

In his mind he had already done his part in warning Titus about the traitor. Now he only wanted some food and a brief rest so he could leave. He was already thinking about places Slagg might have chosen to hide and lay in wait. A light tap sounded at the door. Titus hurried over and accepted a tray loaded with food and two flagons of beer.

"Here we are," he said. He placed the tray on his desk and slid a chair up to it. Then he sat down on his padded seat. "Dig in," he offered.

The smells from the tray were heavenly. Jacob sat down and devoured everything he was offered and washed it all down with huge swallows of beer. He drained his flagon and Titus pushed his own across the tray with a grin. Jacob drained it as well.

"You had quite an appetite," Titus observed, "More beer?"

Jacob leaned back in his chair. He studied Titus closely. A strange feeling washed over him. His arms and legs tingled and suddenly felt heavy as lead. He shook his head and nearly lost his balance, even though he was seated. That slight motion made his head swim. His eyesight dimmed and turned black, then slowly returned.

"What did you do to me?" he asked thickly.

"Me?" Titus asked innocently. "I did nothing, my young friend. It was your own hunger that betrayed you."

Jacob heard the door open again, but his eyesight deserted him again before he could see who had entered. A heavy hand clamped down on his shoulder. Jacob reacted so quickly he caught the newcomer and Titus completely unprepared. They thought the magic infused in the tainted food would render Jacob helpless. They were wrong. He spun out from under Fargus' hand, grabbing the bigger man's wrist as he did. He twisted it without mercy, allowing the turning motion of his body to lend the movement even more power causing the scout to groan and curse in pain. But he was slower than usual. Fargus backhanded him across the side of the head. His ears rang from the blow and he lost his grip on Fargus' wrist. He dodged a couple more blows that the scout aimed at his head, and the Beast awoke within him. He reacted totally on instinct, ducking his head and charging the bigger man. He wrapped both arms around the scout's midsection and drove him through the doors leading to the balcony. They splintered under the impact. Jacob lifted and drove Fargus backwards. Fargus rained blows down on his back and shoulders. Then they struck the low stone wall around the parapet, but Jacob didn't let up at all. In a fraction of a second they both flew over the wall and into space. Fargus screamed in terror as they fell. The wind whistled in Jacob's ears for what seemed like an eternity, then there was a tremendous impact. Time slowed. Jacob was only dimly aware as Fargus' body struck the ground first and seemed to explode. His own impact was cushioned by the bigger man's body, but the wind was driven from his lungs. His head struck Fargus', and everything went black.

Pembroke was the first to the scene, followed closely by Titus. He stopped and stared in disbelief.

"Gawddammit," Titus cursed. "That crazy bastard knew he was going over the edge with Fargus but he didn't even slow down. Who the Hell does that?"

Pembroke shook his head. "Someone with absolutely no fear of dying." He looked back at Titus. "Who *is* he?"

"I told you. Jacob Grimwullf," Titus replied.

"He is *not* Jacob Grimwullf," Pembroke informed the king. "Name spells are extremely powerful, but mine had no effect on this boy at all. The only explanation is, his birth name is not Jacob Grimwullf."

Titus shrugged. "What difference does it make? He's dead as a post now."

Titus and Pembroke both nearly jumped out of their skins as Jacob suddenly groaned in pain. The groan metamorphosed into a growl.

"*Gawddamn,*" Titus hissed. "He's still alive. Get a spell on him and get him in an enchanted cell!"

Jacob rose to his hands and knees. Then he slowly straightened his body and rose to a kneeling position. He drew his knife and lunged at the king despite the tearing pain in his ribs. He missed Titus by a few inches as the king hastily backpedaled and Jacob fell flat on his face. Once again the growl sounded from deep in his chest, louder and stronger this time.

"Now would be good, Pembroke!" Titus shouted. "Before he gets to his feet and rips both of us apart."

Pembroke hastily began crafting spells. "Get me some help!" he shouted after the rapidly retreating Titus. He looked back at the battered and bloody Jacob. "*What are you?*" he whispered.

Jacob was pinned to the ground by the immeasurable, crushing weight of Pembroke's hastily constructed spells. The frightened court Wizard, ruled by his own awestruck fear, overreacted and hurled such a number of spells at the battered youth they would have killed any other man. As it was, Jacob was paralyzed, but aware. He glared at the Wizard with such malevolence it was clear to Pembroke his own future was forfeit. The Wizard had a sudden premonition of his own demise at the hands of the boy on the ground before him, and he prepared a killing spell. Before he could say the final words, Titus reappeared with a squad of guards and Pembroke's own cluster of apprentices.

"What a beautiful creation," Titus murmured.

The apprentices wrapped Jacob's inert form in enchanted chains and the soldiers bore him away to a magical cell.

"You must kill him," Pembroke suggested.

"Never," Titus argued. "What an incredible creature. Did you feel the life force churning inside him? It was barely contained. He is a geyser of life, Pembroke. I must study him and learn how to harness such power!"

"He will be the doom of us all," Pembroke insisted. "I want to kill him, before he can kill me."

"Nay," Titus said. "I order you, as my court Wizard, to heal that boy. No harm must come to him. If he is harmed, Pembroke, I promise you tenfold will be done to you."

Pembroke shook his head. "As you wish, my king. I am duty bound to follow your orders."

As the guards carried Jacob up flight after flight of stairs, he slowly forced the Beast inside him to subside. He focused on the armband La'Nay had given him and let his body relax. Already he could feel his broken ribs knitting together, and his blurred vision cleared. He didn't struggle. His time would come, and when it did he would rip the traitorous king's arms off and beat his Wizard to death with them while the king bled to death. Comforted by such gory thoughts of revenge, Jacob actually drifted off into a healing sleep before the guards even reached the cell at the top of the tower. They dumped him unceremoniously on the solid wooden slab that served as a cot and hurriedly left the cell. Pembroke grasped the thick, enchanted steel bars the sealed the cell and stared at Jacob's inert form.

What are you? The thought ran through his mind over and over, accompanied by the vision he'd had. In that vision, he was flat on his back, mired in deep, stinking black mud, pinned there by Jacob's incredibly solid weight. Rain poured down, and as he stared into the icy, emotionless eyes of the youth lying on the bed, Jacob grabbed his head and plunged it underwater, over and over. But just as he was sure he was going to drown, Jacob released him. He sat up and an agonizing pain exploded in his chest. He stared stupidly at Jacob and the gory mess he clutched in his fist. Then he realized the pulsating mass in Jacob's hand was his own beating heart. The Wizard stared at it as he died.

Pembroke shook his head violently. *No.* He would not allow that vision to be realized. He crafted the most powerful killing spell he could imagine and hurled it vehemently at Jacob's sleeping form. Then he watched in growing satisfaction as Jacob's breathing slowed and finally stopped. Whatever punishment Titus could render was nothing compared to his fate if Jacob was allowed to live. He nodded to himself. He could pass it off as injuries from that incredible fall. Titus would never know. Pembroke retreated to his own chamber, stopping by Titus private wine cellar on the way. He grabbed a bottle of particularly strong spirits and proceeded to get blindly, roaring, falling down drunk.

He awoke with a magnificent hangover. The castle keep was quiet. Pembroke squinted his eyes and tried to think. Even that hurt, but he persisted. There should be activity, noise, confusion. Servants should be scurrying to hide in the shadows as Titus roared and fumed about the unfortunate death of the prisoner. But all the Wizard heard were the normal sounds of an everyday morning. A rooster crowed and another answered from across the courtyard. Birds sang in the still morning air and bees buzzed around the flowering vines that twined across the rough stone walls outside his chambers. Something was definitely wrong.

Pembroke arose and began the climb to the tower without bothering to change his clothes. The climb winded him and he had to stop more than once to make the world stop spinning. He heard the voices well before he reached the enchanted cell. But there was no cursing and shouting, no voices raising the alarm. These voices were calm, if not rational. He paused at the last landing.

"You are obviously a very special creature," Titus voice floated calmly through the passage. He spoke in such a soothing tone an uninformed observer would have thought he was addressing a favorite pet. "My Fargus was a marvelous animal. I had him since he was a boy. I kept him in the cellar and I was the only human he had any contact with. I fed him. I trained him, and he served me. But he was wholly without human feelings and emotions. He lived to serve me, and I never saw his equal for ferocity or his desire for carnage. Until last night," Titus continued. "When you showed up and you utterly destroyed him."

Pembroke was sure his lord had finally lost his last marble. He knew Titus was insane, but the king could manage to keep up an appearance of being normal. But was he now conversing with a corpse? The Wizard tiptoed around the corner. His amazement was betrayed by a sudden, sharp intake of breath which revealed his presence. Titus swiveled his head to fix the Wizard with a stare. Jacob sat on the wooden slab that served as a bed in the tower fortress, devouring a steak the size of a serving platter and a huge mound of fried potatoes.

"It's not possible," Pembroke stammered.

Titus smiled. "Not only did he survive the fall," he said. "But he is fully healed."

The head jailer's body lay between Titus and the door to the cell. Titus indicated him with a tilt of his head. "Berret got a little too close when he brought breakfast." The lunatic king chuckled. "The boy slammed him into the bars so hard he almost pulled him through. In pieces."

Pembroke grimaced at the misshapen head and body of the jailer. His stomach was in no condition for such a sight this morning. Jacob fixed him with a baleful stare, and slowly, dramatically, winked one eye. Pembroke staggered backwards so suddenly he had to clutch frantically for a handrail to prevent falling head over heels down the steep stairs he had just ascended.

"I…should tend to my duties," the Wizard stammered.

Titus nodded, his attention already firmly back in place on his newest prize possession.

Pembroke began to turn away. Without warning, Jacob leaped from the rough cot and slammed his body into the wrist thick steel bars that contained him. Dust sifted down from the ceiling. Jacob snarled and wrapped his hands around two of the bars. The muscles of his shoulders and upper back bulged and the veins in his neck stood out like ropes as he began to try to spread the bars. Titus fell over backwards in his chair and a wet spot bloomed in his breeches. Impossibly, Jacob began to bend the enchanted steel. The bars cracked and popped from the strain and fractures appeared in the foot thick stones that encased the steel. Pembroke created and cast every spell of containment he could think of, but the bars moved inexorably farther apart. Finally, the Wizard cast a spell of Dark Magic intended to control a Dragon, and Jacob reluctantly released the bars. He sat back down on his cot and resumed his meal.

Pembroke didn't wait for his liege. By the time Titus had regained his feet and bellowed for a fresh pair of breeches, the Wizard had already descended three flights of stairs. He didn't slow down until he had run into the courtyard. The maniacal laughter of King Titus floated from the fortress prison, but the Wizard was not laughing. He ran all the way to his own chamber. After casting a furtive glance around, he removed a loose stone from the floor and felt around inside the opening with his hand until he found what he sought. He retrieved it and blew dust from its surface. It was a small, leather bound book embossed with a foreign seal. Pembroke opened it and began to read.

"The Dragonspawn will arise in a time of turmoil and utter destruction. He will cast his enemies from the land without thought or fear of Death, for he is endowed with the gift of Regeneration. Once a man is marked as an enemy, there is no forgiveness or leniency for those condemned in his mind, and the Beast will not rest until he has exacted his vengeance. The Dragonspawn may be slaughtered by removal of the head or heart. No other injuries will be mortal."

"Could it be possible?" the Wizard said aloud. Did someone actually create the Dragonspawn? *'No, no, no,'* a voice inside his head screamed. He had endured far too much, had given his life in servitude to a maniac in return for a comfortable life of comparative ease, to lose everything at the moment of victory. *Because of an aberration,* the voice in his head insisted. Of course, he agreed. The Dragonspawn wasn't even human. He was a monster, not human, not Beast. To kill him would be an act of mercy. But how? He stayed in his chambers, feigning illness when Titus sent for him, as he debated the best method to engineer Jacob's demise.

Jacob, hopelessly trapped by the tangled web of spells cast by Pembroke in his panic, relaxed upon the slab of wood that served as his bed and let his strength build. He kept his eyes closed as he tried to ignore the incoherent ramblings of the man many considered to be the most qualified to rule Norland. After his outburst when he nearly escaped the cell, he had focused on regaining his strength and healing the injuries from the fall. The food Titus eagerly supplied helped immensely. Jacob knew the lunatic King intended to enslave him and use him as a weapon. The only plan that seemed to have any chance of success was to feign servitude, then tear the King limb from limb. He allowed the Beast a few minutes to revel in that thought, then rolled over and went to sleep. Titus rambled on for hours oblivious to the fact that his audience was deep in slumber.

"People," he finally mused aloud, "are not capable of deciding what is actually best for them. They must be led or herded like sheep, down the right path. That is where people like me come in. I have known my entire life what is best for the people around me. Is it a crime that the decisions I make result in profit and power for me? I think not. That is the one thing Timon and I actually have in common. But, he has lost interest in Norland. There's another World, he says, that is infinitely richer than Norland and the people there have all but forgotten their Fathers. They have no common sense, a relaxed moral Code and no guidance. All of that makes this new World an easy target. So, he has handed the mantle of power to me in our World, and I, my young weapon, intend to take full advantage of it."

At the mention of Timon's name, Jacob had fully awakened. He lay still and listened.

"Timon may be the most powerful Wizard of all time," Titus said. "He claims to have found many doorways to the new World, each leading to a different time, a different pathway. And people call me crazy." The King snorted with derision. "All I know is, Timon is gone from Norland. I care not what World or what path he is on. Soon my combined army will roll over Norland like a cleansing wave from the sea. Then I will systematically destroy the ogres and trolls and Beastsoldiers and I will rule supreme."

Jacob could no longer restrain himself. "When is it enough?" he asked quietly.

Titus laughed quietly. "Never," he stated. "It is never enough."

Jacob closed his eyes and feigned indifference, but inwardly he seethed. Everything Luke had taught him was true. Greed and the lust for power ran rampant, not just in Norland, but everywhere. And as a prisoner in a magical cell, he was powerless to stop it.

"What do you want, Jacob?" King Titus asked.

Jacob shrugged.

"Come now," the King chided. "Surely you have desires. Do you wish for money? Servants to do your every bidding? A life of ease? Or perhaps your tastes are a bit more salacious. Is it sex that rules your mind?"

Jacob pursed his lips as if deep in thought. "I…" he began, then stopped.

"What?" Titus leaned forward. "What is your desire?"

"I… want another steak. Bigger than the last one, and tell cook not to leave it on the fire so long this time," Jacob replied.

Titus cursed under his breath. "Don't toy with me, boy. I will conquer all of Norland, with or without you. If you join me, we will go forward together. If you persist in this nonsense I will either leave you in this cell for all eternity or kill you myself. Your choice."

"I'm sorry," Jacob said with as much sincerity as he could muster. "I wish to be at peace with myself. That is my one great desire. Can you provide me with that?"

Titus shook his head. "No one is truly at peace with themselves. Your one desire is futile."

"I was afraid of that," Jacob said with a wry smile. "Which is why I asked for a steak."

Titus smiled, and Jacob returned it.

"You shall have your steak. You can have the whole beef," Titus said, suddenly magnanimous.

"I appreciate that," Jacob replied. "And, if it's not too much trouble, I do find myself in want of the company of a woman."

Titus grinned. "That's the spirit! Why throw your life away for a set of outdated ideals? Enjoy your life! I can provide you with a parade of women who will make your pulse pound."

Jacob saw his opportunity and seized it. "I do desire a woman, but not just *any* woman. One woman has captured my imagination."

"Only one?" Titus asked. "A young man, virile and rugged as you, and you only desire one specific woman?"

"Yes," Jacob responded. "But such a woman as you have never imagined. Her eyes are as blue as the summer sky, her hair is black as a raven's wing, and her body will torment your dreams. She is brave and extremely independent. She is beautiful, wild and free."

"Who is this incredible woman?" Titus asked. "I might keep her for myself."

Jacob hesitated. Here was the most precarious point in his gamble.

"She is called La'Nay. She is *magii'ri*."

"*Magii'ri*, eh?" the King mused. "The *magii'ri* are dangerous and unpredictable."

"Which makes her all the more attractive to me," Jacob replied. "Since I can't have inner peace, if you bring this woman to me, here, in my cell, I will pledge fealty to you and your cause."

"I will consult with my Wizard," Titus said.

"No," Jacob interrupted, nearly in panic. "Do not mention this to Pembroke." He arose and calmly approached the bars of his cell. Titus watched warily. Jacob leaned forward and whispered in a conspiratorial tone. "Your Wizard tried to kill me."

Titus scowled.

"It's true," Jacob insisted. "Remember his reaction earlier? He wasn't just surprised when I nearly broke out of this cell. He was shocked that I had survived the killing spell he cast upon me last night."

"You expect me to believe that you survived a killing spell? How?" Titus demanded.

Jacob shrugged. "I don't know how. How did I not die in the fall from the turret? A fall that blew up your murderous slave like a rotten tomato."

"Are you a Wizard?" Titus asked.

"No," Jacob stated. "I am not. I don't even like Wizards. I was trained as a Warrior."

"You are *magii'ri?*" the King asked.

"I am," Jacob replied. "I was trained as a Warrior by Luke Graywullf."

"But you carry no gun," Titus mused. "I know guns are not found under every rock, but most Warriors have sniffed out at least one pistol in these trying times."

Jacob shrugged again. "It doesn't matter. I'm telling you the truth. Your Wizard hates me for reasons of his own. I'm not trying to force you to make a choice between us. By all means, keep him around and working for you. Just keep him away from me."

"Are you afraid, Jacob?" Titus asked.

Jacob grinned. He rose and walked slowly forward. Titus back up until his bootheels hit the wall.

"I'm afraid of no man, whether they are a Wizard, a Warrior or a King," he stated flatly.

Titus made up his mind. "I will find you this woman, this *magii'ri* woman named La'Nay," he promised. "And you will be true to your word. I will see to that, or you'll watch this woman die a horrible death knowing that you caused it."

Jacob nodded. "I agree. We have an accord."

Without another word, Titus left the Tower. Jacob sat heavily upon his cruelly hard bed and rubbed his hands over his face. It was a huge gamble, but he was betting that La'Nay could break the magic that bound him. The thought did cross his mind that he may have drawn La'Nay into a situation that could prove to be deadly. But he honestly felt he and La'Nay together could vanquish any enemy. *"And then,"* he promised himself silently, *"Titus will suffer the punishment suitable for a traitor."*

CHAPTER TWELVE

The days of Jacob's imprisonment dragged into weeks and then months. He managed to maintain a façade of calmness and serenity, even when Titus felt the perverse need to harangue him with his peculiar ideals for endless hours. He ate ravenously, instinctively building his strength, and did every manner of exercise possible in such a confined area. The head porter had been replaced after Jacob bashed his head in on the bars of his cell, and the new porter was an agreeable young simpleton name Linus. Jacob befriended him, which was a fact so totally foreign to Linus that he became more loyal to Jacob then he was to his own liege. In reality, Linus was an outcast, a poor boy from a servant family with no political ties. He had been the butt of cruel jokes by his peers his entire life, so when Jacob offered him his sincere friendship, the boy was flabbergasted. He kept their friendship secret, at Jacob's suggestion, but he guarded that secret with the fiercest loyalty. And so Jacob managed to glean news about the happenings in the kingdom.

The lunatic King had indeed been true to his word. Search parties were sent out in all directions, seeking news about a beautiful *magii'ri* woman with jet black hair and diamond blue eyes. But the search had been fruitless. One of the search parties failed to return at all. All of them had suffered losses. Piece by piece, the survivors returned emptyhanded. Jacob began to despair. In such a mindset it was almost impossible to control the Beast within him. He began to spend hours leaning against the stone wall of his cell, knees drawn up against his chest, stroking the steel armband La'nay had given him. Only then would the Beast retreat enough to allow him to rest.

He began to toy with the idea of pledging loyalty to Titus. Perhaps then he would be released from the cell. And then he would have the exquisite pleasure of squeezing Pembroke's neck until his eyeballs exploded from his head. One night, in such a mood, he confessed to Linus that he could not bear to be confined any longer.

"I'm going crazy," Jacob said. "I need to feel the wind on my face. I need to hear the sounds of the night as I run through the woods. I must be free, or die."

Linus was greatly troubled to hear his friend talk of dying, and he resolved to do something about it. That night he did something he could never have dreamed of before meeting Jacob. Linus actually sneaked out of the servant's area and, at exactly three minutes after midnight, found himself standing outside of the door to Pembroke's apartments. His resolve faltered and he stood there in indecision. All of his young life he had been told awful stories about people who had drawn the ire of Titus' Head Wizard. It was rumored the Wizard had cursed a servant who spilled his wine and turned the old man into a hound dog with great drooping jowls and a steady stream of drool dripping from his jaws. Linus did not want to be a hound dog. But he could not bear to watch his one friend suffer any longer. With a shudder and a low moan of fear he twisted the knob, half hoping it would be locked. It yielded easily. He gritted his teeth and stepped inside.

Linus was an observant boy, and he knew Pembroke frequented the whorehouses on most nights. He had seen the Wizard hastily leaving the castle grounds that evening. Most nights the Wizard didn't return until after dawn. But there was still a fraction of a second when he stepped inside the room that he thought he would be struck dead. Nothing happened, and Linus released his breath.

The rooms stank of chemicals and moldy books. Linus gagged before he slipped a kerchief over his face. Workbenches lined two of the walls, filled with beakers and vials. Linus ignored these. He made his way straight to Pembroke's desk. Papers were stacked deep upon it and he hastily rifled through them. He tried the desk drawers, but they were locked. Unreasonable fear caused him to nearly panic and abandon his quest. *If he were a mighty Wizard, where would he hide a key?*

He searched through the pockets of Pembroke's robes hanging from hooks on the wall. It was impossible. There were just too many places the Wizard could have hidden the key. Perhaps he even kept it hanging from a cord around his neck where he could absentmindedly fondle it while he plotted Jacob's death. In his haste, he turned too quickly and slammed a knee into a large stand covered by an embroidered blanket. Pain shot up his leg.

"Gawddammit," he muttered through clenched teeth.

"Gawddammit," a voice mocked from under the blanket. "Gawddammit."

Linus fell over backwards. Visions of hanging from the gallows flashed through his mind.

"Aawk, gawddammit," the voice said again.

Linus screwed up all of his available courage. He crawled to the stand and lifted the blanket. A parrot, perched on a roost, cocked his head and fixed one eye on the servant boy. But Linus had lost interest in the bird. The gold flake coated cage was locked, and jutting from the lock was a key that seemed much too large. *Of course*, he thought, *hide it in plain sight.* Linus retrieved the key and slipped it into his pocket. He hastily straightened the room as best as he could and ran down the hall. A dim light appeared at the far end of the hall. Linus grimaced and ducked into the first door he found. It was the kitchen. Despite his current dire situation, he was still a teenage boy, and the delicious smells that assailed him left him almost lightheaded. The door slowly opened and an older woman with a bonnet and apron peeked inside. Linus grabbed a meat pie and took a quick bite. The woman caught her breath when she saw him, then she slowly smiled.

"Get on with you," she said. "Don't let no one else see ya."

Linus ran all the way back to the servant's quarters. He burst through the door and surprised his old dad, sitting next to the fire nursing a chipped enamel cup of whiskey.

"Yer in a hurry," he observed.

"Sorry, Dad," Linus said. He could think of nothing else, so he offered up the meat pie he still clutched in his left hand. "Me and some other boys stole a few pies from the king's larder."

The old man grinned. "Go on to bed," he said. "But cut that pie in half and leave me a piece first."

Linus ducked his head in agreement and chopped the pie in half. He left half by the stove. His father nodded. *It was good to see the boy finally making friends and getting into mischief,* he thought.

Linus closed the door to the closet that served as his room and lit a candle. With shaking hands he retrieved the key and lay it reverently on the stool next to the candle. He ate the meat pie slowly, relishing each bite, as he tried to imagine Jacob running through the woods. He fell into a deep sleep.

The tumult of horns jarred him awake the next morning. Certain that he had been found out and that the sheriff's men were being summoned to hunt him down, Linus leaped up from his straw pallet. He scooped up the key as he did and jammed it deep into his trouser pocket. He flung open the door and peeked into the street. His father was already gone, off to care for the King's horses which would be charging down the street carrying armed men to slaughter him, he was sure. But the commotion was in the courtyard. Linus gathered his courage and walked in that direction. Other boys went running by. Usually, Linus would have ducked away from them to avoid their insults and pummeling fists, but today he was not himself. He grabbed a running boy by the arm.

"What's up?' he demanded.

"Get yet hands off," the boy said with a curse. "They found her. That *magii'ri* woman for the prisoner."

Everyone in the kingdom had heard the story in one form or another, and now it seemed that every citizen had turned out to see this mystery woman. Linus plunged his hands into the pockets of his threadbare coat and clutched the key as he wound through the gathering crowd. *'What am I going to do?'* he wondered. The Tower would be packed with guards by now. And Pembroke was certain to notice his missing key. He would toss the kingdom upside down until he found it. And then Linus would dance on air hanging from the gallows. He rubbed his neck. He could feel the noose tightening already. It was becoming hard to breathe and black spots danced in his eyes. And then he saw her.

La'Nay was not bound. Her hands and feet were free, but she was surrounded by a solid wall of guards. Linus caught his breath. He had heard Jacob's description of this woman, but it did not do her justice. She was the most beautiful woman Linus had ever seen, but it was the way she moved with a wild and primitive grace that caught his attention. She wore the traditional *magii'ri* gunfighter's garb, even though her holsters were now empty. Her piercing gaze cut through the crowd causing the onlookers to fall silent as she passed. Linus realized he was staring at her, and then her eyes met his. She cocked one eyebrow at him and a tiny smile tugged at the corner of her lips. Linus was in love. He hastily averted his eyes before she could read the emotions within them.

King Titus met the cavalcade at the entrance to the Tower. He bowed low, tossing the tails of his robe to one side in a grand flourish.

"Please forgive me, my lady," he greeted her. "I hope my men were clear that this is an invitation only, a chance to meet a most amazing specimen that has come into my possession."

"Why was I disarmed?" La'Nay replied without preamble. "A Kingdom that is loyal to Norland and the Code has no reason to disarm a soldier for the cause."

"I feared you might misread my intentions," Titus said. "And the *magii'ri* do have the reputation of making snap judgements that result in violence. People could die," he added in a conspiratorial tone.

"So you are loyal to Norland and the Council?" La'Nay asked.

"Of course," Titus replied glibly. "Now, I do have something I think may interest you in the Tower. Would you like to see?"

"Lead the way," La'Nay answered.

Her mind raced as Titus fell in step with her. The boy in the courtyard was most certainly an ally, but who was he? And what could he offer? She felt the spell tickling at the edges of her mind and quickly cast a cloaking spell. Nothing that would seem obvious, just enough magic to conceal her thoughts and make them seem hazy.

She did not want to reveal her power to an enemy. She surreptitiously glanced about. She spotted the Wizard immediately. He was a slightly built man of average height with jet black hair who fell in behind the phalanx of guards. He was closing the distance between them until they reached the entrance to the Tower. Then he stopped in his tracks. La'Nay saw a tiny, fleeting smile cross Titus' features. Then it disappeared.

They climbed on and on. Titus kept up a steady stream of inane conversation which she ignored as she counted steps. After one hundred steps, La'Nay's confidence dropped sharply. At two hundred she knew she had no chance of escape. Four hundred and twenty steps later they reached a landing and La'Nay knew she'd have to sprout wings and fly from such a height. Then she saw Jacob. Her heart sank even as he leaped from his log bench.

"Yes!" he cried. "You have found her!" He turned to La'Nay. "They did not harm you, did they?"

"No," she replied shortly. She turned to face Titus, "What is going on here? This boy has done nothing against the Code. Why is he a prisoner?"

"So you know him?" Titus asked the obvious.

"I know him," La'Nay replied. "He is Jacob Grimwullf, a *magii'ri* 'prentice."

"He is more than that, I assure you," Titus said. "He rode Fargus from the parapet outside my chambers. Fargus is now nothing more than a stain on the cobblestones, but this boy survived and is now stronger than ever. He has powers yet undiscovered. Magic contains him. He has requested your presence and in return, he will swear fealty to me. Isn't that right, Jacob?"

"Leave her here with me," Jacob replied. "And I will swear to do your bidding."

"Wonderful!" Titus said with a clap of his hands. He motioned to his guards. "Place her in the opposite cell."

"Wait!" Jacob shouted. "You said you would bring her here to me!" "And I did," Titus replied. "You will be right across from each other. Talk through the day and into the night, young man. In the morning, you will swear to do my bidding."

Jacob leaped onto the bars of his cell. Pain from the spells cast upon the steel bars tore through him, but he ignored it. An inhuman growl rose from his chest. Veins stood out like ropes in his neck as he strained to tear the bars from the stone. The entire Tower creaked and groaned. Dust fell from the ceiling. The guards exchanged panicked glances. One bolted from the room. Even Titus backed away. Droplets of blood appeared in Jacob's nostrils as Pembroke's magic tore away at him. His pupils became glittering diamonds the color of sea ice as the Beast threatened to take full control.

"Yes," Titus urged. "Show me who you are!"

La'Nay's voice cut through the fog in Jacob's mind even though she did not speak aloud. Her words soothed him, and the Beast retreated. Jacob dropped to floor, shaking and retching.

"You were so close," Titus complained. "Why did you stop? No matter," he continued. "You will become the beast in time." He nodded to the other cell. "This is your home now," he said to La'Nay. "Protected by magic, and we all know *magii'ri* Warriors such as you don't practice magic."

"If I had my guns you'd eat those words," La'Nay promised.

"That's exactly why you have been disarmed," Titus agreed.

"What do you want from me?' Jacob moaned. Pembroke's magic had made him feel as if giant fishhooks were imbedded in his flesh and eyes when he attempted to escape.

Titus turned back to him. "I want you to be true to yourself. I want you to let that beautiful Beast take complete control. Become the Beast that you are, Jacob."

"No," Jacob growled.

"You will," Titus guaranteed him. "Or you will bear witness as we inflict incredible pain upon the one person you seem to care about." He stared pointedly at La'Nay.

Jacob gathered himself to leap upon the bars.

"No," La'Nay said calmly.

Jacob relaxed. La'Nay smiled sweetly at Titus.

"Lay a hand on me," she promised. "And you will endure agony beyond anything you have ever dreamed. After I cut off your privates with a dull knife."

"So beautiful," Titus mused. "And so violent." He turned with a flourish. "See you in the morning."

After the Tower was deserted, La'Nay spoke again. "Jacob, what have we gotten into here? I thought Titus was a staunch ally of the Light."

Jacob drew himself into a sitting position against the stone wall of his cell. "He's a traitor," he spat venomously. "He has allied himself with the worst forces of the Dark. He wants to rule Norland. Can you break the spells on these bars? I can break us out if you get rid of the Magic."

La'Nay focused her mind on the magic in the Tower. "I can't, Jacob," she said. "I need to probe the mind of the Wizard who constructed these spells. Then I have a chance."

Jacob pounded his fist on the stone floor in frustration. "I am so stupid. All I managed to do is make you a prisoner as well."

"You are not stupid," La'Nay reassured him. "If the Wizard comes close enough I will determine the origin of his spells. Then I can break them. And then," she turned her glowing eyes to Jacob, "I want you to promise me that you will kill Titus."

"I'll kill him," Jacob stated. "Even if it kills me to do it."

"Then we might as well sleep," La'Nay said suddenly. "Calm yourself, and rest. We're going to need our strength."

Sleep did not come easily. La'Nay did eventually doze off, but she woke often and every time she did, Jacob was pacing the length of his cell like a wild animal. Voices carried up the winding stairwell, growing louder as they approached. La'Nay hoped to see the Wizard who had crafted such punishing Magic, but it proved to be King Titus and a small squad of guards. He approached Jacob's cell and spoke without preamble.

"I had an absolutely marvelous idea. I took your warnings to heart and I will not harm such a lovely lady. But, I fear I have not been entirely open with you."

Any faint glimmer of hope La'Nay had felt at the beginning of Titus' speech was dashed by the tone of his voice.

"I have a hobby which could prove quite interesting to you. But, rather than try to explain I think I'll just show you," Titus said. "Chain them," he ordered the guards.

Pembroke the Wizard stepped from the rear of the group. He raised his hands and began to chant under his breath. La'Nay listened closely. Her eyes widened. This was not the familiar magic of the *magii'ri*. It was an exotic, foreign type of magic with hints of the Dark arts. The weight of the spell crushed her to the floor. Even Jacob was forced to his knees. A white faced guard rushed in and chained him with enchanted handcuffs. La'Nay received the same treatment and the whole troupe was escorted down the long, winding staircase.

Titus babbled on as they descended, but no one actually listened. The guards seemed unnaturally tense. Beads of sweat formed on their foreheads even though the passage became cooler as they dropped beyond ground level. The air grew stale and dank and their nostrils were assailed by a scent that La'Nay could only identify with what had to be a horde of mice. A chittering, scurrying sound reached their ears as they entered a large chamber lined with steel cages.

"Some of my works in progress," Titus gestured at the cages.

As the torchlight illuminated the cages La'Nay was astounded to see mice the size of large dogs. Their incisors were three full inches long and the grating, grinding sound they made as they were gnashed together made La'Nay shudder. Jacob felt only rage at the abominations of nature created by Titus' fevered mind. He wanted to crush them, to destroy them and erase their existence from the face of the World. Titus grinned. He thrust a two inch thick board inside one cage and laughed like an idiot as the occupant snapped it with one violent snap of its jaws. They passed through that chamber and entered another. The cage in that one was covered with a gaudily colored tapestry. A horrible stench filled the room. Titus stopped in front of the cage and lovingly caressed the tapestry.

"This was where I created Fergus," Titus explained, lost in the memory. "He lived here since he was a small child, until he was ready to serve me. And now he resides here for eternity."

He thrust the tapestry to one side. The corpse of Fergus lay in the cell. One of the guards retched and puked. La'Nay covered her mouth and nose with her hand. Jacob stared impassively.

"He was my greatest creation," Titus lamented. "But you," he grabbed Jacob by the shirtfront, "you are so much more! And today you will show me. I am willing to sacrifice something which I value to see what you can become. That is worth something, is it not?"

"You're insane," La'Nay managed to choke out.

"Takes one to know one," Titus replied.

He led the way from that chamber down a long passage. It was obviously manmade. The walls still bore the scars and toolmarks of excavation. Suddenly, the passage ended and opened into an underground arena surrounded by a mesh of interwoven steel cables as thick as Jacob's index finger. The bottom level was solid rock with two doorways cut into it. A cage at least ten feet tall jutted out from a shaft cut into the floor. Jacob's eyes narrowed when he saw it.

"Jacob," La'Nay said softly.

He turned to her. His eyes were wild and his nostrils flared with the bitter scent of old blood.

"Jacob," she pleaded. "Listen to my voice. Stay calm. Focus on the words I taught you."

Titus grinned in satisfaction.

"He already knows," the lunatic King said. "He knows what's coming and he can't wait!" He clapped his hands together gleefully.

"Don't do this," La'Nay begged. The crazy King ignored her. "I'm asking one last time, don't do this," her voice took on a warning tone.

"Take them below," Titus ordered as people began to file into the seats protected by the steel mesh. Titus took his seat of honor, separated from the crowd, and waited impatiently. The guards took La'Nay and Jacob down more stairs. The clink, clink, clink of chain moving over massive cogs could be heard, and when they reached the next level the cage had been lowered from the arena floor. Jacob cocked his head to one side. From far away he could hear strange grunts and growls, but even beyond that he heard a whisper of sound. It was oddly familiar but totally out of place and he couldn't identify it. Then he and La'Nay were shoved roughly into the cage and it began the inexorable journey back up to the arena.

When they emerged from the arena floor they were greeted by a chorus of catcalls and boos. The cage door popped open and Jacob leaped out. He ran across the arena and leaped ten feet up the wall, but a blast of magic repulsed him and he flew backwards with his arms flailing. As he landed he realized the arena floor was littered with fragments of bone from previous combatants, but there were weapons as well. He scooped up a massive battleaxe with a four foot blade which seemed much too large for him. But the Beast had come forward, and Jacob swung it back and forth easily. La'nay stepped onto the arena floor with trepidation. Jacob's chains unlatched and fell to the floor, but hers remained clasped. The seats were filling rapidly and Titus' people were chanting for blood.

"Jacob," La'Nay pleaded once more. "You don't have to do this, not for me."

Jacob was beyond hearing. Titus leaned forward in his seat, his eyes locked in rapt attention on Jacob. The cage dropped from sight. Jacob crouched in front of La'nay, his eyes fixed on the open shaft. A gurgling, squealing growl sounded from the elevator shaft. Once more the massive chains clanked over the cogs and the cage emerged. Jacob and La'Nay had time to register a huge creature that looked like a cross between a giant and a troll, with an elongated batlike face thrown in for good measure, when the cage door flew open. The crowd erupted in a deafening cheer. They expected Jacob to be cast aside like a piece of cotton on the wind, and the prospect of watching La'Nay being torn to bits excited their bloodlust into a frenzy. Jacob leaped nimbly aside as the creature charged, but he spun in midair and brought the battleaxe crashing down. The creature's body plowed a furrow in the floor as it fell and ground to a stop, but its head continued across the floor and rolled into the wall leaving a crimson trail in its wake. The crowd was silenced. Not a sound was heard. It seemed as if the entire audience had ceased to even breathe. Jacob raised the axe high, threw back his head and screamed a primordial battle cry.

Titus had risen halfway from his seat and was frozen there. A satisfied smile tugged at his lips and his eyes gleamed speculatively. He made a chopping motion with his hand and the cage dropped back through the floor. The crowd burst into cheers again. Not many made it past the first opponent, but when they did Titus always had an entertaining backup on hand. The creature that emerged from the floor filled the entire cage.

It rested on all fours, but it was coiled and tensed to spring as soon as the doors opened. Its body was hairless and covered by a pebbly, leathery skin that clearly showed the musculature beneath it. The head was shaped like a Dragon, but it was attached to the body by a short, powerful neck with a magical collar around it and it had no wings. It stamped one hind foot impatiently and steel hard talons clicked audibly on the cage floor. Saliva dripped from its open jaws and sizzled as it struck the floor. The creature hissed between razor sharp fangs.

Jacob realized his only chance to save La'nay was to distract the creature, keeping its attention focused on him until he could kill it. This one was no dumb brute that could only focus on the kill. Jacob looked into the creature's eye and saw intelligence there, as well as boundless sadistic cruelty.

"Come on then," he taunted. He flung his arms open wide. "You want a piece of this?" He tossed the battleaxe to the side. Titus came clear off his chair. The cage door opened and the creature bounded out. Jacob and the creature charged each other at full speed. Jacob ran directly at the toothy snout of his adversary. The jaws popped open as the creature prepared to snap them down on the puny human's body, but Jacob dropped into a slide and slid right under the belly of the creature. It frantically dipped its head almost between its front legs as it attempted to latch down on Jacob, who reached up just in time to wrap his hands around the monster's magical collar. Jacob reversed his body and planted his feet. The monster's head was pinned and it flipped. Its tail end flew up in the air and its body slammed into the floor with enough impact to shake the arena. Dust fell from the roof. The tail itself crashed to the floor only inches from La'Nay, who dodged nimbly to one side. Jacob moved with unbelievable speed.

He released the collar, grabbed the monster by the front of the lower jaw and brutally jerked it down. The grinding, tearing sound was audible to all as Jacob wrenched the creature's jaw downward and tore it completely free of the joint. Slicing talons swished by him as he leaped again, this time to grab the monster by the snout. One desperate strike caught him by surprise and the razor sharp claws sliced through two of his ribs. An inarticulate cry of rage and pain burst from Jacob's throat as the Beast within him completely took over. He spun around and snapped the creature's neck, which cracked like a dry branch. But he wasn't done. He scooped up a discarded sword and disemboweled the monster with one backhanded strike. Without warning, he turned and threw the sword towards King Titus with all his strength. One of Titus' guards leaped upon the King, knocking him from his seat. Then he howled in pain as the well-aimed sword pierced his leg and pinned him to the rock wall behind him.

Titus stood slowly and dusted himself off. He watched in mingled admiration and fear as Jacob's challenging cries of rage filled the arena. He caught the head guard's eye and gave an exaggerated nod. The head guard shook his head in disbelief, but Titus nodded even more forcefully. A few people in the crowd began to chant Jacob's name.

"Well, that's it then," Linus' father Luther told him with a shake of his head. "No one can stand against the horde."

Linus stood with the few, pumping his fist in the air and shouting Jacob's name.

"He's got to, Dad!" he cried. "Get on your feet!" he shouted.

Luther reluctantly stood. Slowly, a few more people stood, mostly peasants and servants from the castle.

"Is he doing it?" Linus asked. "Did he signal the release of the horde? I can't see!"

"He did," Luther said with a sad shake of his head. Then he resumed chanting and pumping his fist in the air. More and more people stood and in minutes the arena rang with the sound of Jacob's name.

"Jacob!" La'Nay shouted. "Jacob! I'm sorry!" She realized something truly terrible was about to happen and she only knew one way they could survive. She bowed her head and focused all her power on the steel armband which Jacob wore. As she broke her own spell, she crumpled to the floor.

Jacob felt like something exploded inside him. He and the Beast were one. He eagerly sought out another enemy. The cage was slowly coming into view. Jacob scooped up a tomahawk and a battlesword. He clashed the blades together as the occupants of the cage hooted and howled. They resembled apes, but were bigger with incredibly exaggerated muscles. Their faces were longer and their jaws, studded with long, pointy teeth, protruded out from their faces. They climbed the bars of the cage and across the roof. Jacob was startled to hear intelligible speech coming from their mouths in a guttural tone. They repeated one word over and over.

"Kill!"

Jacob paused only long enough to glance once more at the new arrivals. His stomach sank. There were too many. He knew he couldn't possibly protect La'Nay. At least one enemy was certain to get past him while he was fighting the others. The horde hooted and screamed as they swarmed up the wall and across the roof of the cage like a pile of spiders. As the cage door began to open, Jacob hurled himself at the new enemies. He threw the tomahawk as he ran and his aim was perfect. The first Beastsoldier out of the cage ran right into it and the blade cleaved his face in two. Then Jacob was in their midst. He spun around, slashing and stabbing. The sword was torn from his grasp and he went down under a pile of Beastsoldiers. Teeth and claws tore at him. He broke one's arm and punched another until his ribs caved in. He caught a glimpse of an exposed neck and sank his teeth into it until he felt the hot spurt of the Beast's life blood in his mouth.

Jacob's savage transformation was so complete the Beasts actually halted their attack for a split second. Jacob caught sight of La'Nay standing over him with a shortsword. Her face and arms were spattered with the black blood of the Beasts. With a roar of rage, Jacob flung the Beasts off. He leaped to his feet and caught one Beast by the arm. He slammed it to the floor, ground one foot into its ribs and jerked the arm from the shoulder socket. The remaining Beasts circled him, shocked into momentary inaction by such savagery. What manner of enemy did they face?

"Go!" Jacob shouted to La'Nay. "Get in the cage!"

La'nay hesitated.

"Now!" Jacob ordered. "I can't protect you!"

As he spoke, he lunged back into the ranks of the Beastsoldiers. La'Nay knew Jacob had a better chance of survival if he only had to worry about himself. She rushed into the cage and slammed the door shut as several Beastsoldiers slammed into it. One leaped and clung to the side of the cage. La'Nay allowed herself a grim smile as she thrust her sword into his groin with all her strength. He leaped violently away with a squeal of anguish. The momentum of his leap pushed the cage off balance. The next thing La'Nay knew, she was falling. The cage landed with a crash atop three of Titus guards with such force that La'Nay was knocked to her knees. She lunged forward and slammed her shoulder into the cage door but it held fast.

"Aard!" she cried. "Hear me! I am a loyal servant of the Light! Help me!"

She shoved the cage door once again, but it was sealed shut. "Can't one thing go right?" she groaned. "If you won't help me now, Aard, then curse you! I'll serve myself!"

A slender youth appeared from the shadows. La'Nay raised her sword as he approached the cage. He held out his hands with his palms up.

"I'm here to help," he assured her. "I'm Linus. Jacob's friend."

"Get me out of here," La'Nay demanded. "I must help Jacob!"

The din of battle and the cheers of the insane crowd drowned out normal speech. Linus stepped forward and yanked on the cage door but it held fast.

"It's locked!" La'Nay screamed at him.

Locked? Linus thought. Locks. Keys. He had a key. *Why not?* He thought. He withdrew Pembroke's key from his pocket and slipped it into the cage lock. It turned easily and the cage door sprung open. La'Nay rushed out. She kissed Linus full on the lips.

"Thank you!" she cried as Linus' face flushed a deep red.

A massive impact shook the entire castle. Dirt and rocks fell from the ceiling. The crowd upstairs went silent. An unearthly roar rent the air. The castle shook again.

"Slagg," La'Nay breathed.

"My Dad's up there," Linus stammered.

"Then let's get up there and save him," La'Nay said. She absentmindedly reached for her guns, but of course they weren't there. Linus noticed the motion.

"I know where your guns are," he announced.

La'Nay hesitated only a moment. She didn't know this boy, but he had already been a godsend.

"Can you show me?" she asked.

Linus nodded eagerly. He had fallen in love with this lovely Warrior the instant he set eyes on her. He would do anything for her, and as a servant of the castle he had explored every secret passage and hidden trapdoor he could find. He led the way to what looked like a blind corner to an expertly concealed tunnel. The light was almost too dim to see, but he trotted unerringly from one passage to another until they came suddenly into the armory. La'Nay stared in total disbelief. The walls were lined with racks of long rifles and recessed cupboards full of ammunition. Her pistols hung behind a locked steel grate. Linus rushed forward and slid Pembroke's key into the lock. The door popped open.

"You dear, sweet boy," La'Nay said.

She scooped up handfuls of loose pistol ammunition and filled her pockets. She strapped on her guns and realized with a start how much she had missed their comfortable weight. The castle shook again, and now there were human screams of terror and pain mingled with the roar of the Sky Rider.

"Go, find your Dad," La'Nay ordered. "Get as far away from the castle as possible, and take all the servants you can find with you."

Linus nodded as the din of battle grew even louder.

"Is this the end of the World?" he asked.

"It's the end of Titus' World," La'Nay promised. "Now go!"

"No one is going anywhere," a new voice interrupted. It was Pembroke, the Wizard. "You'll dangle from a rope, boy, when this is done!"

La'Nay felt the sting of his spell, but she had been crafting one of her own even as Pembroke had betrayed his presence. Her spell prevented Pembroke's from incapacitating her, as he had planned, and turned much of the energy of his own magic against him. He reeled backwards as his face registered disbelief. He raised his hands and began to craft a new spell. La'Nay grinned, and Pembroke felt terror run up his spine. The Warrior Dragonwitch drew and shot him in the face. The Wizard was flung to floor. His shattered teeth flashed stark white against the crimson gore that had been his face. Linus retched, but his empty stomach had nothing to yield.

"Go!" La'Nay urged.

"But what about you?" the boy managed to ask.

"I'll be fine," La'Nay assured him. "Just get out of here."

Linus disappeared into yet another passage as La'Nay retraced her steps back to the dungeon holding area. Once there, she climbed atop the cage, unmindful of the arms and legs of Titus' men that protruded from under it. Hand over hand she climbed the thick rope to the floor of the arena, which was strangely quiet. She peeked out from the opening just in time to see Jacob as he dropped an unidentifiable Beastsoldier body part to the floor. His shirt had been stripped from his body and his torso was bathed in black Beastsoldier blood. His own blood from a dozen wounds mingled with that of the Beasts and his eyes were wild as he crouched and turned a slow circle, searching for more enemies. La'Nay emerged from the opening. A whisper of sound alerted Jacob and he whirled to face her with a snarl of rage. The gentle boy La'Nay had known was gone. In his place stood a supreme predator, a killing machine, but La'Nay felt no fear.

"Jacob" she said in a soothing voice.

Jacob shook his head. A Dragon's bellow sounded from far above them. Jacob whirled and ran to the steel cables surrounding the arena. He leaped high, and this time there was no magic to repel him. He growled deep in his chest as he grasped two of the cables. The cords in his neck stood out like ropes and the muscles of his arms and upper back bulged with effort as he ripped the cables apart. He slipped through and ran to the top of the stadium and out of the arena.

"Gawdammit," La'Nay cursed.

She forced her tired body to respond. She climbed the steel net, slid through the opening and followed Jacob. The Warrior Dragonwitch climbed several flights of stairs before the hardships of the previous weeks caught up with her. She stopped and leaned against the stone wall.

"Damn you, Titus, and your stupid stairs," she panted.

She climbed more slowly after that, and when she finally reached a level that had window openings she looked out upon what was left of Titus' kingdom. The realm that had been touted as the new center of Light was a smoking ruin. But what astounded her the most was the picture of a young man, bare to the waist, face to snout with a massive bull Dragon. Slagg had grown in stature and power since her encounter with him in the desert and he towered over Jacob. Neither made a sound, but La'Nay was certain they were deep in conversation. What she didn't know was that she was witnessing the ultimate contest of wills as each struggled for dominance over the other. The Sky Rider trembled with rage as he was forced to retreat. The roar that was ripped from his throat betrayed the first defeat the Dragon had ever known. La'Nay sought the first exit she could find and burst into the courtyard, gripped by panic. Slagg and Jacob noticed her immediately. The great bull Dragon covered half the distance to her in one leap, but he froze as if stayed by a gigantic hand.

"I know you," Slagg's voice melted in her mind. "The Dragonwitch."

"Hold," Jacob ordered. "She is not an enemy."

The Sky Rider complied.

"How…" La'Nay stammered.

"How am I here?" Slagg finished for her. "I felt the call of the rise of the Beast. It led me here. I sensed that my son was in danger."

La'Nay groaned as she saw the shocked expression on Jacob's face.

"Or how does anyone rein in anything as magnificent as myself?" Slagg continued. The great beast rolled his eyes. "As much as it pains me to admit, the bond between the Dragonspawn and myself is complete. I find myself unwilling to incur his wrath."

"Destroy this place," Jacob growled. "And all the abominations the King of the lunatics created."

"As you wish," the Sky Rider agreed. His appetite for destruction was fully aroused. He leaped into the air and rose to the clouds before hurtling downwards to crash into the castle walls.

"Wait!" La'nay shouted. "There's weapons in there," she said to Jacob. "Weapons we can use to defeat Timon."

But she was too late. The Sky Rider was beyond reason. He thrashed and clawed and bashed his great bulk into the stone walls with abandon. La'Nay watched in dismay as the cache of guns was buried under tons of rubble.

"Did he speak the truth?" Jacob asked in a tone as still as death.

La'Nay bit her lip. "Partially," she began.

"Partially?" Jacob argued. "Either he did, or he didn't."

"You are a wondrous being," La'Nay said.

"I am a monster," Jacob interrupted. "I am the son of a monster."

"No!" La'Nay denied. "You are the son of a great man, a great Warrior. I am the monster, Jacob. I used my magic as a Dragonwitch to introduce the awesome power of a Dragon to your being, to meld it with your ability as a Warrior to make you invincible."

"You saw me," Jacob argued. "I was no different than the Beasts created by Titus."

"You are different," La'Nay said vehemently. "You use your savagery and power to serve the Light. You are a Trueblood son of Luke Graywullf!"

Jacob froze. "Did you say I am the son of Luke Graywullf?"

"Yes," La'Nay stated. "I should have told you long ago. Luke Graywullf is your real father. The Sky Rider's essence merely gives you greater power."

Jacob's knees buckled. Luke was his father? He realized the truth of the statement as memories of his childhood with Luke came flooding back.

"Why didn't he tell me?" Jacob demanded.

"He didn't know," La'Nay replied, her voice trembling with emotion. "Mathias made me conceal your identity. To protect you and Luke, he said."

"Mathias," Jacob repeated. His hands flexed. The Wizard who held him in contempt, who had always been disappointed in him, had denied him his own family.

"Who is my mother?" he asked.

"A *magii'ri* maiden named Mariel," La'Nay explained. "She was Mathias' sister. She died when you were very small."

"I'll kill him," Jacob stated calmly. "The next time I see him, he's a dead man."

"Jacob, no," La'Nay pleaded. "I know, he did a terrible thing." She hesitated. "We did a terrible thing. We should have never hidden your identity from either you or Luke."

"How is this possible?" Jacob wondered aloud.

"It's magic, Jacob," La'Nay reassured him. "Magic concocted in desperation to save our entire World."

The din of Slagg's destruction reached a crescendo that prevented conversation. The Sky Rider reveled in leveling Titus kingdom, and when he was done the castle was a mound of rubble. But he wasn't satisfied with that. His wrath was so complete he took to the sky and circled the entire castle and enveloped everything in Dragonfire. Every scrap of timber was reduced to ash along with even the smaller stones. Everything else was fused together in a melted heap. The inability to converse during Slagg's destruction gave Jacob time to think. As Slagg rose once more to the clouds, Jacob wheeled around and began to walk away without another word.

"Jacob?" La'Nay called after him.

Jacob reluctantly turned back.

"Where is Kelsey?" he demanded.

"I sent him to gather as many allies as he could. He told me what the boy, Allie, said to you before you went into Slagg's den," La'Nay answered. "He's a Scribe, Jacob. What he told you is a prophecy that we can't ignore. It's time to prepare for the last, desperate battle of our time."

Jacob sighed. "I know."

"Whatever the outcome, our World will never be the same," La'Nay predicted.

Jacob nodded in agreement.

"Can you actually control him?" La'Nay asked. "Slagg, I mean."

Jacob shook his head. "No one controls the Sky Rider. I can influence him. That's all."

"His attention must be diverted away from the forces of the Light," La'Nay reminded him. She indicated the annihilation of Titus' kingdom. "Slagg could destroy our entire army."

"I know," Jacob sighed. "I am true to the Code and the Light. I'll keep Slagg busy, if I can." He gave La'Nay a wry smile. "If I can't keep him busy you'll know, because I'll be dead and he'll be upon you."

La'Nay stepped forward and suddenly embraced Jacob. He shied away, then reluctantly returned her hug.

"I'm so sorry," La'Nay said. "So much has been thrust upon you. I hate to add to it, but Titus must not be allowed to live."

Jacob grinned, and it reminded La'Nay of the wolfish snarl that Lynch called a smile.

"He's not going to escape," Jacob assured her.

A shudder went down La'Nay's spine when she thought of Titus' fate, but he had chosen his own path.

CHAPTER THIRTEEN

Jacob stood impassively as rain fell from the sky in sheets, plastering his long, normally unruly hair to his skull. It ran down his face in rivulets and his clothes had become so saturated they could absorb no more. Dense clouds of smoke, trapped low to the ground, ran here and there like living things. A rain such as that could quench a brush fire, but Dragon fire burned with unrivaled intensity. And so Jacob stood in the rain and the smoke, feeling nothing, as he watched the last stronghold of King Titus burn.

He scanned the areas beyond the moat, near the pickets that could repel armies, and watched for survivors. His eyes were cold and unfeeling as they picked up a heat signature. It was a member of the Palace Guard, who glowed in Jacob's vision even in the pouring rain and smoke. Jacob nocked an arrow on a bow as thick as his forearm, pulled back to full draw and drove the arrow completely through the man as he crouched behind the pickets. Almost immediately his heat signature began to fade to a dull orange. Jacob grimaced and wrinkled his nose as the acrid scent of the man's blood reached his nostrils. It reminded him of the lunatic King. Titus had begged like a wretch at the end. Jacob spat on the wet ground and studied his bloodstained hands. What he had done to Titus had been savage and without even a vestige of human mercy. But it was done and the skinned body of the lunatic King hung from the crossed timbers of the gate to the village. Slagg soared into view on the far side of the compound signaling Jacob that the raid was over.

Jacob nodded. "Let's go," he thought.

Slagg ascended into the swollen clouds and disappeared. Jacob took one last look at the destruction of the man who would have ruled Norland, then turned and trotted to the East. He always preferred to be alone after a raid. Slagg had picked up on that fact after their first attack as a team and now the Sky Rider simply left Jacob to fend for himself. They would meet up again, perhaps in a few days, maybe even a week or two. Jacob never told Slagg he needed the time to calm down his Dragon senses and return to as normal a human state as he could manage.

He ran at a trot well into the night. As the sun sank the rain slowly transitioned into heavy, wet snowflakes. By midnight the ground was covered and Jacob's deep draughts of air were exhaled as puffs of steam. The heat and cold didn't seem to bother him anymore, not since he had surrendered to his Dragon side. Nothing seemed to bother him. He remembered the disgust and fear in Anja's eyes when they had parted, but it felt as if he were looking at a portrait of someone he didn't even know. He could see the hate etched on Link's face and feel the despair of the old Warrior, Michael, but he felt no empathy with either. It seemed to him he was merely a detached observer with no real interest in the experiences of the past or the consequences of his actions in the future.

Suddenly, he caught the musky scent of elk in the soggy air. He skidded to a halt and pulled his bow from his shoulder. As always after surrendering to his Dragon side, he was famished. He tested the air currents until he determined the direction the scent came from and began a slow and stealthy stalk. He found the small band of elk in a clearing no more than thirty yards across. His approach was so perfect they didn't even know he was there. To his hybridized eyesight the elk appeared as livid red blots. Jacob picked out a smaller blot and sent an arrow on its unerring flight. He heard the arrow strike home and seconds later smelled the scent of blood. The yearling animal crashed into the brush on the far side of the clearing and lay still.

Jacob waited a few minutes before giving in to the predator that lived within him. He approached the fallen animal carefully, but once he was sure it no longer breathed he leaped upon it and quickly disemboweled it. He reached inside the abdomen and sliced off one lobe of the liver, then retreated farther into the trees to feast on his prize. It was still hot, and Jacob did not bother with a fire. Indeed, he found he now preferred not to cook his meat. He bit off great chunks and gulped them down until his hunger was satisfied. Only then did he return to the kill and take the choice cuts from the carcass. He wrapped them in the hide and continued farther into the forest.

Jacob had no way to gauge the surrender of his human side. He controlled the Beast within him through the power of La'Nay's knowledge and guidance. Or, he thought, it was more accurate to say he *directed* the Beast. When he allowed the Beast to come forward there was a fine line between giving in completely and using the Beast to his own ends. Added to that was the fact that he walked a razor's edge when dealing with Slagg, which put him well within the range of the Sky Rider's deadly talons and fangs. To say that his life was stressful was an incredible understatement. How he longed for the days of his youth. Even training under Mathias had been easier than pulling a doublecross on the Sky Rider.

Jacob realized the Dragonspawn was gaining a reputation as a cold blooded killer and an ally of Slagg. But he also knew from before that King Titus had been touted as perhaps the one leader who could truly unite all of Norland and perhaps even the World under one government. That would be a great disaster. Every instinct he had screamed that message. There could never be one ruler, a leader with so much power he could control the entire World. The loss of human life and the utter destruction he and Slagg were wreaking on Norland weighed heavily on him, as did the appearance of his apparent loyalty to the Dark. It was widely believed that he was under the guidance of the most soulless creature in the known World.

The moments Jacob actually felt like he was really a part of the human race were fleeting. It was in these quiet moments after the battle, when the Beast had been fed, that Jacob remembered Luke and the teachings of the *magii'ri*. He could recite the Code, which he did with maniacal fervor, willing his human side to fight the Beast. He tried desperately to remember his pleasant childhood memories, mostly involving the time he had spent with Luke. And he missed that. Luke had been gruff and unwilling to show his emotions, but Jacob knew the Warrior had cared for him then. And probably still did. Jacob swore and broke into a faster run. He reveled in the physical effort and let his mind go blank.

He smelled Slagg well before he knew where the Sky Rider actually was. Only then did he realize the Dragon had selected a spot very near to his den as their meeting point. Jacob realized they hadn't been there in weeks. He slowed to a walk and rubbed his temples. Why, of all the creatures in the World, had he been cursed with a connection to a being as totally self-absorbed as Slagg? Most of the time the Sky Rider couldn't even remember hatching the eggs and he certainly had no idea only one survived. Jacob wondered which of them would go insane first, himself or the Sky Rider?

"You took your time," Slagg's voice felt like a blast furnace inside his head.

"I had to feed," Jacob said defensively. "Which reminds me, when did you last feed your young?"

"I sent the servants out to forage," Slagg replied.

"But when did they last feed?" Jacob pressed.

"I don't know!" Slagg's voice roared in his mind. "Why don't you go inside and find out if they're hungry?"

Jacob grinned. "If I go in, it's hard telling what might come out."

Slagg swiveled his massive head to fix Jacob with one great eye.

"Are you threatening my young?" he demanded.

Jacob could feel the barely contained rage inside the bull Dragon. Slagg was fighting his own internal war, very similar to his own. Jacob wondered briefly what would be left of this World if they both lost their humanity completely. It would be a wasteland. He touched his hand to his brow in deference.

"I apologize, Sky Rider," he said in a flat tone.

Slagg growled a response, then pointedly looked away from Jacob. He wondered sometimes why he had accepted the young man's offer of his life for the girl. He should have just eaten that tasty morsel and gone on his solitary way.

"Why don't you forage for them yourself?" Jacob couldn't believe the words had come from his lips. *What the Hell was he doing?* Jacob thought.

Slagg's rage flared to life again. "Because there's nothing left!" he roared. The great bull Dragon hooked Jacob's shirtfront with a curved talon and pulled him so close their cheeks almost touched. Jacob stared into the shining black orb. At first he saw only his reflection. Then that faded and Jacob saw a huge Beast army gathering for a final assault. The forces of the Light resisting them were pitifully small and the landscape between them was a barren desert. The *magii'ri* faced certain defeat, but they stood steadfast to the last man. He felt the connection Slagg had allowed beginning to break, but at the last possible moment he saw something else.

Something he was sure Slagg wasn't even aware of. A massive force of men arriving on ships.

He forced his mind to go blank.

Slagg sighed. Smoke seeped from his fire vent. "Why do you try me, Dragonspawn?" he asked peevishly. "You and I are one, are we not?"

Jacob nodded silently.

"I loved my beautiful, little eggs," Slagg reminisced. "My young were going to be the start of a new age of Dragons. But look at them. Two turned on their brother, killed him and ate his flesh. Dragons don't do that, Jacob. We are noble creatures."

That news chilled Jacob. Of course, he knew only two of the Dragons had survived. But he had assumed the other egg simply hadn't hatched. He was amazed that Slagg had not yet discovered that one of his young had been killed and Jacob was the killer. The truth was, Slagg didn't even venture into his own lair, not even to count his treasure. That fact reinforced the thought that the Sky Rider was losing contact with reality.

Jacob hated not knowing Allie's fate. The memories of that day in the cavern haunted him still, when he allowed himself to think about it. With a sudden start, he realized Slagg was studying him closely. He was very careful not to make eye contact, lest the Sky Rider read his true intentions.

"I had such grand plans," Slagg sighed.

It was at times such as these that Jacob didn't know if he was speaking to Slagg or to Talin.

Indeed, the farther Slagg seemed to dip into insanity the less distinction there was between the two. Without warning, Slagg dove off the ledge and sailed away.

Relief washed over Jacob. He wasn't ready to face the Sky Rider. Not yet. But one day he would face off with the bull Dragon, and only one of them would survive. The kinship he'd felt with the Sky Rider had dissolved. He was beginning to realize there could only be one ultimate being in Norland. The Beast within him leaped to its feet, eager for the challenge, and turned its ravenous attention to defeating Slagg. Jacob didn't know or care if he was giving in to the Beast or if his human side was winning. He only saw Slagg as a rival. There would only be room for one of them in Norland. Jacob intended to be the one.

La'Nay was still the one being left in the World who thought Jacob still had a spark of human decency. The Dragonwitch followed Jacob and Slagg from one chaotic battle site to the next, reading the role of each participant in the fight from the signs left in the blood and mud. The savagery of the Dragonspawn was apparent, but La'Nay was certain he served the Light. She pursued Jacob and Slagg relentlessly, stealing moments alone with Jacob to reinforce the teachings of the Light.

La'Nay reached the elk carcass when it was still warm. She skinned another section of the animal and packed it full of meat, then slung it over her shoulder. The entire operation took only a few minutes. She followed Jacob's tracks to the fringe of trees lining the clearing and saw where he had squatted to enjoy his dinner. The Dragonwitch did not stop. She had sliced off a strip of the animal's liver herself, and she munched on it as she walked. The trail was clear. Even Jacob's scent still hung in the damp air. She was closing the gap. And soon she would look into the eyes of the Dragonspawn once again and convince him to remain true to the Code. If she failed, no one would ever know because she would die trying. But if she succeeded, she just might save the World.

CHAPTER FOURTEEN

Luke and Dorro polished off the last crumbs of trailbread as they squatted next to the ashes of a dying fire. The Dark Magic spell Mathias had cast on them had burned up every reserve of energy they had, and their bodies had demanded to be fed with a ravenous hunger none of them had ever experienced. Some of the inedible contents of their packs still lay strewn about the bare campsite, but anything that had any nutritional value had been consumed. Moments earlier, Luke had watched with detached curiosity as Mathias gathered some of the items and stuffed them in Lynch's pack. Now he stood staring into the glimmering archway which they all assumed was a portal to another World. Luke rose and walked over to stand beside Mathias. The Wizard alternately stared into the portal and at the heavy book that he cradled in his hands. Luke stood in silence for several minutes until he lost patience.

"What do you see?" he finally asked.

Mathias made a startled sound and whipped his head around as if he had no idea Luke had been standing there.

"Not as much as I'd like," the Wizard admitted. "I actually came out here to make water. Did you want to help?"

"Hell, no," Luke replied. He cast a sideways glance at Mathias and saw his amused smile. "So why are you really out here?"

"The Book has shown me the way, but I can't see the final outcome of our quest."

"Not this again," he groaned. "I've told you a dozen times, Mathias, no one can tell the future. Not me, or you or even a cursed

Dragonspirit living in a box of sand. Or a blasted book of magic," he added.

Mathias smiled patiently. "I have learned just enough," he said. "Here," he handed Lynch's pack to Luke and slid the Book back inside it.

Luke shrugged and shouldered the pack. *What the Hell*, he thought, *he'd already carried it from one end of Norland to the other. Might as well carry it a little further.*

"What's the plan?" he asked.

"I have to tell you something," Mathias said, rushing on before he lost his nerve. "But first, the plan is simple. Exactly as I told you before, we have to find Timon in the other World. Somehow, and I mean any way short of killing him, we have to weaken him enough to get those handcuffs on his wrists. Then get him back here to confront Slagg. That will release Lynch's brother and, I hope, dissolve the influence the Sky Rider has over Jacob. Then if Timon is the author of the Wilding, he can reverse it."

"Just like that?" Luke replied. "All our troubles taken care of in one fell swoop?"

"I think it will work," Mathias said. "It may be our last shot."

"Best get on with it then," Luke said.

"One last thing," Mathias said. "Jacob Grimwullf is not who you think he is."

Suspicion flared on Luke's face.

"What do you mean, Mathias?" he asked.

"Forgive me," Mathias pleaded. "His name is Jacob Graywullf. He is your son, and he is the Dragonspawn."

Luke's disbelief was evident in his shocked expression. Mathias spoke a few quick words, and Luke felt like he was mired in quicksand, only it enveloped his entire body. Then Mathias gave him a hard shove towards the portal. Luke lost his footing and fell headlong through the opening. He tucked his shoulder and rolled completely over. Reacting purely from instinct, he drew both pistols as he rolled. He landed in loose soil much like where he had been standing in Norland, but he never stopped moving. The *magii'ri* Warrior leaped to his feet and lunged back towards the hazy opening so quickly he nearly made it back through. The last thing he saw before the portal closed completely was the stark white of Mathias' face, and that picture was framed by the sight of his pistol.

Dorro stared at the Wizard, cup still in his hand, slack jawed and round eyed with disbelief. The cup fell from his suddenly nerveless fingers and clattered on the rocks. The sound jarred him from his stupor.

"You…cut that pretty close," he said uncertainly. "Another half second and he'd have shot you."

Mathias turned to face the dwarf. His own shock was evident in the pasty white color of his face. "By the gods," he whispered. "I think you're right."

"I'm not questioning you," Dorro continued. "But do you think that was the best decision you could have made, sending a gunslinger to retrieve Timon?"

"That part was the absolute best decision," Mathias retorted. "Now that Luke knows Jacob is his son, he'll move heaven and earth to return to Norland with Timon."

"Well," Dorro said. "From what I can see, that part has it's drawbacks as well. Cause when Luke gets back you're gonna have one very pissed off Warrior looking for you."

CHAPTER FIFTEEN

Luke dropped to his knees then toppled over on his side as a wave of dizziness rolled over him. Black spots danced in his eyes and threatened to blot out his vision entirely. He drew in several deep breaths and forced himself to concentrate. His nostrils were filled with the scent of crushed sage and a sudden miniature dust devil kicked up sand in his face. He rolled to his back and looked up into the hazy blue sky, then shut his eyelids tightly until the dizziness stopped. The Warrior holstered his pistols and patted down his chest and legs to confirm that he was, indeed, still fully clothed. At least he wasn't naked. Then he sat up and took a long, slow look around. As far as he could see there was no movement. He paused to think.

His fury startled even him. Would he have actually shot Mathias? He wondered briefly. He guessed he would never know, but there was no doubt Mathias was lucky he closed the portal when he did. So…he had a son. That reality staggered him. How could Mathias, his own blood brother, hide such a thing from him? And Jacob was the Dragonspawn? He allowed himself a tiny smile. He knew there was something special about that boy all along. But that damn Wizard had kept them separated and prevented them from actually being a family. And now, after revealing the truth, Mathias had separated them again, now with time and space that completely boggled Luke's mind. Why? He asked himself that question over and over. Why would Mathias hurl him through the fabric of time and space immediately after telling him he had a son?

The answer was obvious. Mathias knew he would sacrifice anything to find Timon and return to Norland, even if only to have the chance to punch a certain Wizard in the mouth. With a heavy sigh, Luke stood and surveyed his surroundings. The surrounding country was harsh, with rock strewn hillsides bisected by water worn canyons. In the distance he could see the green of a broad valley. Sunlight glinted off objects in the valley which Luke assumed were buildings. Buildings meant people, and people could offer much needed information. He had to find out where he was and track down Timon, then find a portal and return to Norland. The enormity of the task was too much for one Warrior. He needed help. Magical help. And since he seriously doubted Timon would assist in his return to Norland, that left the only other Wizard which Luke thought might inhabit this World. And that was Lynch. It seemed that his only chance hinged upon the presence of a Dark Wizard and a *magii'ri* 'prentice in this new World. But, if Timon really was here, it seemed logical the others who had disappeared from Norland might also be there.

"Mathias," he said aloud, "you manipulative son of a bitch."

At least the Wizard had gotten the magic right. He was fully clothed and his weapons were intact. Lynch's magical pack rode upon his shoulders, as light as a feather. So, he reasoned, if he could round up Lynch and Jeb they might just have a chance to return to Norland.

The *magii'ri* Warrior turned downhill and began walking. As he walked, one whisper of thought kept gnawing away at his conscious. Mathias obviously had more than one reason to send him through the portal instead of going himself. Luke dredged up every memory he could that concerned the Dragonspawn, until the truth made him stop dead in his tracks. Mathias did not want Luke in Norland. He knew they were getting closer to confronting Jacob and Slagg and he did not want Luke to be there when they did. Luke cursed aloud. If Jacob was indeed under Slagg's influence and Mathias could not convince him to support the Light, then the Wizard meant to end his creation. Mathias intended to kill Jacob.

Luke felt that truth as a hard, cold knot of fear in his belly. Even as the thought struck him he knew it was true. Mathias had pushed Jacob to realize his potential as a servant of the Light for his entire life, and when the boy had been nothing more than a normal boy, he had given up on him. Once again the Wizard had not seen only the Light or the Dark, he had seen the shadows that were neither and felt he had lost control. But Luke knew Jacob had the potential and the training to honor the Code. He only needed the chance to choose. The certainty he felt lent urgency to his steps and he descended into the valley.

By midnight the *magii'ri* Warrior stood concealed in some bushy spruce trees ringing an immaculate expanse of neatly trimmed grass. The night air was refreshingly cool and the scent of the trees was heady after the heat of the day. Luke stood as motionless as the trees and waited with the infinite patience of a born predator, studying the perfect yard and the neat stone house which sat in the center of it. He was rewarded after more than a half hour by a whisper of movement on the porch. A match flared briefly, followed by the winking glow of a cigarette. Moments later Luke smelled the burning tobacco.

"Well," a deep, pleasant voice said from the porch, "You ain't a mountain lion or a bear. If you was, my stock would be going crazy right now."

Luke said nothing. The cigarette glowed again.

"You ain't a meth head or an opie either," the voice continued. "They don't have the woods sense to sneak up on anyone or the patience to stand still for more than half a minute. But I know you're there. Might as well show yourself."

Luke considered that as the speaker took another drag from his cigarette.

"Just so you know," he continued, "I got a twelve gauge shotgun loaded with five rounds of double aught buck and I can hit you in the dark as good as the light."

Luke grinned. "Comin' out," he said. He slipped across the yard as silent as a shadow and stood at the base of the steps.

"Yer good," the speaker said. "Quiet and fast, so not a government man either. But you are trespassing. What are you doing on my ranch?"

"I don't have any idea where I am," Luke said truthfully. "I'm just trying to find my friends."

The man on the porch chuckled. "Then you're in a pickle, cause I can guarantee you your friends are not on my ranch." He struck another match and a lantern flared to life, illuminating both of them. He studied Luke suspiciously. He cocked his head to one side to get a better look at the sword hilt protruding from the sheath on Luke's back. His eyes widened when he noticed Luke's duster was tucked behind the smooth, worn grips of his revolvers. The handle of Luke's oversized knife jutted ahead of the holster on his left side. As casually as he could manage, he reached down and retrieved his shotgun. Luke merely stood at the ready, his hands hovering over his pistols.

"You didn't draw," the man on the porch observed.

"No need," Luke replied. "You're not going to shoot me."

"I might," came the reply.

Luke shrugged. Then, without seeming to move at all, he drew his right hand gun. He stood empty handed one moment, and a millisecond later the big bore revolver was pointed at the other man's belly. His eyes bugged out and his jaw dropped.

"Jesus," he whispered.

Luke holstered the pistol. "I didn't come here looking for a fight," he said. "I just need to know where I am. Tell me that, point me in the right direction, and I'll be long gone."

The other man studied him for several long moments. "Ok." He lowered the muzzle of his shotgun. "I'm Zeke." He held out his right hand.

Luke didn't hesitate. He stepped forward and clasped Zeke's hand in his own while he studied him. Zeke was a little taller than average with a solid build and graying hair. His hand was calloused and hard as a rock.

"I'm Luke."

"You're not from around here," Zeke observed.

Luke laughed. "I sure as Hell ain't," he agreed. "Like I said, I'm lost."

"Maybe," Zeke agreed. "And maybe you're right where you are supposed to be." He indicated the sword on Luke's back. "That's a Hell of a pig sticker. What else are you packin'?"

Luke slowly opened his duster. "Colt .45's," he replied. He pulled the knife from its sheath. Zeke gave a low whistle at the ten inch blade. Then Luke reached to the small of his back and withdrew Lynch's tomahawk.

"Damn," Zeke exclaimed. "Are you lookin' to start a war?"

"Just came from one," Luke answered.

Zeke laughed quietly, but his laughter was cut short by the expression on Luke's face and the hardness in his eyes.

"Well," he said, "if you get caught with all that hardware they'll lock you up or hang you."

Luke grinned. "What about you?" He indicated the shotgun still in Zeke's hands.

Zeke grinned widely. "What they don't know won't hurt 'em. Come inside," he invited. "I'd like to know more."

Luke followed Zeke inside. The older man indicated a chair at the kitchen table. "Have a seat."

Luke sat and lowered Lynch's pack to the floor beside him.

"You hungry?" Zeke asked.

"I could eat," Luke replied

"Got some leftover chicken fried steak and mashed taters," Zeke said. "Real beef, too. None of that gawddamn garbage grown in a test tube."

"What are you talkin' about?" Luke asked "Beef is beef, ain't it?"

"Now I know you ain't from around here," Zeke said. "Everybody knows the only meat the government allows is tank meat."

Luke shook his head. "I don't know what you're talkin' about. Like I told you, I'm not from around here." He nodded at the empty seat across from him. "Better sit down." Zeke sat and regarded Luke suspiciously. "I'm from a land called Norland," Luke began. "I'm a *magii'ri* Warrior. In Norland, Warriors are entrusted to uphold the Code, a set of laws handed down by the gods. I was sent here by a Wizard to find the man responsible for initiating a spell called the Wilding, which will destroy Norland if we don't stop it."

Zeke stared at Luke in silence. He began to speak several times, only to lapse back into thoughtful silence each time. Finally, he said, "Where exactly is Norland?"

Luke smiled without humor. "From what I've been told, Norland exists on another plane of reality, separate from this World."

A smile stole across Zeke's face, then expanded into a huge, gap toothed grin. "Gawddamn, you had me goin' for a minute," he exclaimed. Then he burst into a long fit of laughter. Luke sat impassively.

"This is one of those prank shows, isn't it?" Zeke asked. "You do have an amazing costume." He got up and peered out the windows, then scanned the counters and cupboards. "Where's the camera?" he asked.

Luke nodded. "Go ahead and laugh. I would too, if we traded places."

Zeke's laughter died. "You're not joking?"

"Nope," Luke replied. He had a sudden idea. He retrieved Lynch's pack and upended it on the table. The Book of Runes slid out. Lying on the table it appeared to be much too large to fit inside the pack. Luke shook it again, and the magical handcuffs fell on the table with a metallic clink. Then he reached in and withdrew Lynch's crossbow and a packet of bolts, a bottle of whiskey with barely a sip left in it, a woman's corset and Jeb's leather ball.

"How...?" Zeke asked.

"Magic," Luke answered. "This pack belongs to a Dark Wizard named Lynch, and it is absolutely saturated with magic."

Zeke sat before his legs gave out. "Let me see that," he suggested.

"Sure," Luke replied as he pushed the pack across the table.

Zeke cautiously reached inside and drew out the first item he touched, an ornately carved pipe. He reached in again and drew out a glass eye, a full sized buffalo robe, a fiddle and bow, and a Dragon's talon. Zeke held the talon up. It jutted more than a foot from his fist. Just for fun he slammed it down on the edge of the table. It sliced through the one inch maple like it was butter.

"Jesus," he whispered.

He shook his head in disbelief and reached deeper. That time he pulled out a human upper leg bone and a withered, dried up scalp, which he hastily dropped. Luke scooped the items up and stuffed them all back inside the pack, except for Jeb's leather ball. The pack expanded, then settled back into its original shape. He leaned against the counter behind him and worked the ball in his hands.

"Pick it up," he suggested to Zeke.

Zeke did as he was asked. The pack felt almost empty.

"How can that be?" he exclaimed.

"I told you," Luke said. "This pack belongs to a Dark Wizard. It's magic, and Lynch is…unique. But what I'm telling you is real. Magic and Dragons and other monsters exist in Norland. I need to find my friends, if they are here, and get back to Norland before it's too late. I can't waste any more time trying to convince you."

Zeke looked at Lynch's pack, then back into the eyes of this hard faced, young stranger. The young man in his kitchen, who had appeared out of nowhere in the middle of the night, looked like he belonged in a spaghetti Western. Zeke reached his decision.

"I believe you," he said quietly, half surprised at the words that came from his own mouth. "What can I do to help?"

"I'm beholden to you," Luke replied. "What can you tell me about this World?"

Zeke laughed humorlessly. "That is gonna take some time."

He rose and began to putter about the kitchen. He put a pot of coffee on to boil and reheated a heaping plate of leftovers, which he placed on the table in front of Luke. When the coffee was ready, he joined Luke with the pot and two mugs. Luke didn't hesitate. The food smelled heavenly. While he ate, Zeke began to talk.

"To sum it up," he said. "Our World has gone to shit. No one can say they really know when it all started, but it's been a downhill slide for a lot of years. People got soft. Their values changed. No one wanted to actually work for a living anymore. When I was a kid, growing up on a ranch, I didn't even know what a restaurant was. We raised our own beef, had chickens and a few pigs and a vegetable garden. I didn't know you could go into town and buy a hamburger until I was fifteen years old."

Zeke paused, lost in memories.

"Technology was responsible for a lot of it, I guess. But that was only possible because of mankind's inherent laziness. Men made machines to do the majority of the hard work and that evolved until people didn't want to work anymore. They had a lot of free time, so they invented ways to fill that time. Idle hands, you know. Then they got bored so they legalized drugs and passed their days lost in a haze. People lost their ability to cope with adversity, and the government said it was ok, we'll put you on a program that gives you food and pays for a home with heat and water and electricity and you can just stay high all the time.. And it built upon itself. In time, the majority of the population had no idea where their food came from or how to change a flat tire. They couldn't pluck a chicken or tell a potato plant from nightshade. They just wanted to escape. That started a whole new drug crisis. People abused opioid painkillers because they make you feel nothing. So, the government spent billions of dollars trying to help these drug addicts. In some cities they overloaded the health care systems. My opinion, and people call me every name in the book because of it, is that you should just let the addicts die when they overdose. Problem solved."

Zeke rose and paced about the kitchen. "I shouldn't get so worked up over this. Anyway, technology reared its head again. Some brilliant scientist came up with a way to grow meat in a test tube in a laboratory. The extreme Greenies got hold of that idea and pushed it forward until the citizens of this World decided it was evil to grow a cow for beef, or a pig for pork, or even a chicken. After flip-flopping on the issue for fifty years, scientists decided eggs were like a time bomb in your guts and they were declared illegal. You could buy legal marijuana on any street corner but not eggs. So, now it is illegal to raise cows or pigs or chickens. All meat is grown in giant tanks in factories. We call it tank meat, regardless of what it's supposed to be."

He laughed at the expression on Luke's face.

"No, that wasn't tank meat," Zeke said. "I'll be damned if the government is gonna tell me I can't raise a cow on a ranch that's been in my family for generations. And I'll starve before I eat tank meat."

Luke nodded vigorously. "Me, too. I have to admit I didn't understand everything you said, but I think I got enough of it. What else can you tell me?"

"Eventually the extreme Greenies basically took over the government. They outlawed cars and trucks, basically every type of carbon based energy. They set off an EMP, that's a device that destroys most technology, including cell phones. Then they issued new cell phones free of charge to everyone, whether you wanted it or not. I tossed mine out in the desert fifteen minutes after it was issued. They can track every thing you do with those cell phones. The Greenies ran the country for a decade. They decided we had a little too much freedom, so they set up cameras everywhere in the major cities and they outlawed guns."

Luke perked up at that piece of news. Zeke noticed.

"Yep, you know what I'm talkin' about there, don't you?" he said. "Anyway, we had an election. People had had enough, and we voted in a new President. But the career politicians and big business hated him. He had a touch of common sense and they couldn't stand that. So all they did was fight. The old faction didn't even show any interest in running the country, all they could think about was how to get rid of the president."

Luke scooped up the last bit of gravy with his fork. "That was good. Thanks, Zeke."

"No problem," Zeke said. "So now what are you gonna do?"

"I have to find my friends," Luke said. "Then I have to find the man I was sent for and return to Norland."

"Well, maybe I can help," Zeke suggested. "What are your friends names?"

"Colin and Lynch," Luke answered.

"What about last names?" Zeke said. "I need both names."

"I don't know their last names," Luke admitted. He thought for a long moment. It was a long shot, but he had to try. "How about Jebediah Steel?"

Zeke's expression brightened. "That's a start." He disappeared into another room and returned with a laptop computer. "I worked as a deputy sheriff for twenty-five years," he told Luke. "When I retired, I liberated this from the department. I can still access the database." He sat down and opened up the computer. Luke watched in confused silence.

"I use my neighbor's wifi to connect to the internet," he explained. "If they trace the ISP, it'll lead the Watchers right to him."

"Whatever that means." Luke said. "What happens then?"

"They'll haul his ass off to the work camps, I guess," Zeke said. "It don't matter. He's a shithead anyway."

Luke looked over Zeke's shoulder. His eyes widened in amazement. "Is that magic?"

"Hell no," Zeke replied. "Downfall of society, that's what that is." He typed, then leaned back. "Bingo. Jebediah Steel, age seventeen. Arrested for conspiracy to riot. Released from the work camps seven months ago."

"Seven months," Luke repeated. "How long was he in there?"

Zeke scrolled down the screen. "Two years."

"How can that be?" Luke wondered. He shook his head. "He's been gone eleven years. He should be more like twenty one or two. Does your magic box tell you anything else?"

"It ain't magic," Zeke growled. "Let me see. He was picked up in Tucson."

"Too-sonn," Luke repeated. "Where is that, from here?"

Zeke rose and produced a map from a desk in his living room. He spread it out on the table. He studied it briefly, then stabbed a spot with his finger. Luke looked, then looked again.

"Tuxin," he said. He looked closer at the map. In a wrinkle in the map he saw another familiar name. He pointed to it. "Felix," he said.

Zeke looked. "Phoenix," he corrected. "Phoenix and Tucson."

"And where are we?" Luke asked.

Zeke pointed again. "Flagstaff," he stated.

"How do I get to Tuxin?" Luke asked.

"Tucson," Zeke corrected. "Normally, you'd take the rocket train."

"The what?" Luke said.

"The rocket train," Zeke repeated. "Jesus, you really are lost here. The rocket train connects every city of more than ten thousand people. But it don't go to Tucson anymore. The government came in and shut that track down. Said it was too dangerous. On the order of the President," he added with an obvious sneer.

Suddenly restless, Luke rose and wandered around the room. A few pictures hung on the faded walls, most showing a much younger Zeke with a very pretty woman. Then there was a succession of photos of a young boy as he grew through boyhood to a young teenager. Then there was one photo of the boy in a military uniform, but no more. Luke glanced down at a pile of newspapers stacked by a threadbare recliner. He paused, then returned to sit by Zeke.

"So," Zeke said casually. "Does this feller you came for have a name?"

"He does," Luke replied. "But you already know him."

Zeke licked his suddenly dry lips. He could do it. Drop to the floor and roll once, grab the shotgun as he rolled by it and come up with it pointed at this odd stranger.

"Who is it?" he choked out.

"There's a likeness of him in those papers by your chair," Luke answered. "I didn't see his name."

Zeke's brow knitted in confusion. He tried to remember the photos from the paper. No one he knew, he was sure of that.

"Go look," Luke urged.

Zeke walked across the living room floor, his skin crawling with tension. He glanced down and froze in disbelief.

"You have got to be kidding me," he said as he picked up the paper. "You came here for the President?"

"If that's the President, then I reckon so," Luke responded.

Zeke thought for a moment. "He ain't really the President, you know. The President I was tellin' you about? He got ran out of office by the career politicians. Then this Blackhelm feller comes in. He goes to the White House and tells them damn fools that they need to make him president. Those idiots couldn't kiss his ass fast enough. He was sworn in and moved the United States capital to Phoenix." Realization blossomed on his face. "You two are from the same place."

"I reckon," Luke said. A mountain of tension was lifted from his shoulders. Jeb was here. Timon was here. And he'd bet money Lynch was close by. If that Dark Wizard didn't want to be found, he would not be found.

Luke considered what he discovered. Timon was in this World. He had left Mathias and Luke and all the *magii'ri* fighting a war and he wasn't even there. Was Timon even behind the Wilding? The enormity of such a possibility was too much to consider. If Timon wasn't behind the Wilding, they would be back at square one with time running out. He focused on the information Zeke had provided.

"You said something about a bodyguard?" he asked.

"Yep. Head of security for the president. Huge man named Colin. Timon Blackhelm snaps his fingers and men disappear. Colin Laborteaux is the guy who makes that happen," Zeke offered.

Luke felt a cold weight drop in his stomach. It couldn't be. His own mentor had thrown in with Timon. Shock gave way to rage and a burning need for vengeance. Treason was punishable by death under the Code. Colin knew that. Luke drew each revolver and slowly rotated the cylinders, even though he knew exactly what they contained. Five shots in each. He grimaced and cursed under his breath. He would never be able to shoot his way through Timon's guards with ten shots. He forced himself to think. Lynch had told him he had to be smarter than Timon.

He lifted Lynch's pack and sat it back on the table and rummaged through it until he felt the cold metal of Mathias' magical handcuffs. He pulled them out again and stared at them thoughtfully. Mathias believed they would contain Timon's magic, so he assumed it was true. But then again, Mathias had deceived him for years. Could the Wizard be trusted? Luke knew the answer. Mathias had dedicated his entire life to the restoration of the kingdom of Norland. If he said the handcuffs would render Timon helpless, then they would do just that. Sitting there, he realized he still held Jeb's leather ball in his hands. It was a huge relief to know the boy was still alive. He made up his mind. One way or another, they were all going back to Norland.

"I need to get to Tuxin," he said.

Zeke frowned, then he said, "Oh, you mean Tucson."

"Yes," Luke agreed. "Too-sonn. I need to find Jeb Steel. I'd bet he knows where Lynch is."

"Then you go after President Blackhelm?" Zeke asked.

"I reckon so," Luke agreed. "I hope the plan comes together after I find those guys."

"What about the bodyguard?"

"He broke the Code," Luke replied. "There's only one way that can end up."

Zeke tried to match Luke's gaze, but he averted his eyes after a few seconds. There was something wild and primitive in the younger man's eyes that left him feeling unsettled. He felt like his soul had been laid bare and his sins tallied. What had this figure who looked like he belonged in the old West seen with those glacial, blue eyes?

"By the way," Luke suddenly said, "you wouldn't have made it."

"What?" Zeke said.

"The scattergun," Luke answered. "You thought about makin' a try for it earlier. You wouldn't have made it."

Zeke studied the young Warrior. He saw no gloating, no bragging. Just a simple statement of truth. He had seen his share of dangerous men during his career in law enforcement, but none of them would have stood a chance against this stranger.

"I reckon you're right," he agreed. "I can get you to Tucson, but you'll have to walk the last few miles. We can't openly drive down the highway. Gawddamn Greenies got cars outlawed even before they outlawed growin' cows for red meat. But there's still a few of us that got the balls to live free. The rest of 'em are like a bunch of sheep."

Luke nodded. The last part was all he really understood. Too often he had seen people blindly following the one in front of them, even if they were led straight to slaughter.

"It won't be light for hours," Zeke suggested. "We can get started tonight, if you feel up to it."

Luke eagerly agreed. Now that he had at least an idea of what to do, he was ready to get on with it. Then he could get back to Norland and straighten things out with Mathias. His stomach felt hollow at the thought of his blood brother deceiving him for so long.

"Eat some more, if you want," Zeke said. "I'll bring the Jeep around."

Luke nodded and filled his plate again as Zeke took the shotgun and disappeared outside. As he ate a feeling of bone deep weariness descended upon Luke. He ate and stalked about the living room, looking at all the photos until he sank down in Zeke's easy chair. The harsh conditions in Norland caught up to him and he closed his eyes. He had only been asleep a short time when the clapping of the screen door jolted him from a dream. He leaped to his feet and drew both pistols before he was fully awake. Zeke dropped the armload of firewood he had carried in and stared in open mouthed astonishment.

"Don't shoot!" he managed to shout. "It's me! Zeke! Don't shoot!"

Luke blinked the sleep from his eyes. Only his training as a *magii'ri* Warrior had stopped him from squeezing the triggers. Even half asleep he had paused to identify his target.

"Sorry," he mumbled as he slid his pistols home.

"Ok," Zeke said, still in shock. "I should have known better. My son was the same way when he got home from the war." Zeke looked around. "Guess we can go anytime you're ready."

"Might as well," Luke replied.

Zeke followed him out the door and walked around to stand by the driver's side of a battered International Scout. The fenders were rusted through but the oversized, deep lugged tires looked brand new. He waited and watched expectantly.

"We're going in that?" Luke asked.

Zeke smiled. "I know she ain't much to look at, but after the Greenies set off that EMP in 2025 it kept right on running. All those more modern cars with electronic ignitions were dead as rocks, which is exactly what the Greenies wanted."

Luke shrugged. "I don't understand most of what you say, but if this carriage will get us to Tuxin then I don't really care."

"It'll get us there," Zeke laughed.

He climbed in the driver's seat and waited until it became clear that Luke had no idea how to open the door. He reached across the driver's seat and opened the passenger door. Luke tossed his pack and sword in the back seat and slid in. He stared apprehensively as Zeke turned the key and the big V-8 engine roared to life. Zeke grinned proudly and they were off. He drove slowly and carefully, but Luke still kept a firm grip on the arm rest. They drove in silence for forty five minutes, then Zeke spoke.

"All the liberals and yuppies and Greenies used to laugh at us preppers," he said with a chuckle. "Now look at us. Everything we were worried about came true. Nobody's laughing now."

"What's a prepper?" Luke asked.

"That's what people call someone who believes in being prepared for any type of disaster," Zeke replied.

"Oh," Luke mused. "We could have used a few more of those in Norland. Didn't anyone stand up to the Greenies when they took power?"

"Sure," Zeke said. "Some people are still resisting. That's why your friend Jeb Steel got arrested and tossed in the work camps. 'Inciting to riot' they call it. That just means he was at a demonstration supporting Ray Benson when it got raided."

"Wait a minute," Luke said as he swiveled in his seat to stare at Zeke. "Did you say Ray Benson?"

"Yep," Zeke replied. "He's organizing a rally in Tucson. Chatter among the preppers says if you attend you better come well armed. Do you know Ray Benson?"

"We've met," Luke said. "But not here."

Could it be possible, he wondered? Did Mathias' magic actually transport him here to correct the reality Timon had disrupted?

"When is this gathering?" Luke asked.

"You know a lot more than you're letting on," Zeke responded. "I interrogated enough suspects to know when somebody is holdin' back." He waited but Luke merely stared out the windshield. "Ok," Zeke finally said. "Have it your way. The meeting is one week from today."

One week. Seven days to alter the reality of two Worlds. His head began to ache. *Gawddamn you Mathias,* he thought irritably, *I need you here. I can't do this alone.*

"I met Ray Benson in Norland," Luke confessed. "We have to stop this rally at all costs. Timon Blackhelm is not just a powerful man, he's a Dark Wizard. He's going to send Ray Benson and his followers to Norland. Then there will be no one left to oppose him in this World. And Norland will turn upon itself and tear my World to bits. Timon must be stopped."

Luke drew in a deep breath and released a gusty sigh. Then he told Zeke everything about Norland, including the information about Wizards and Dragons and the *magii'ri*. Zeke continued driving while Luke talked, following an almost invisible track deep into the desert. Finally, as the sun rose he pulled the Scout over into a patch of brush and killed the engine. For some time, he simply stared straight ahead in silence. At length, he spoke.

"So you're a lawman?" he said.

"I am," Luke replied. "I am a *magii'ri* Warrior. I am sworn to uphold the Code with these," he indicated his pistols. "And by any other means necessary. But guns are useless against magic and Dragons."

Zeke nodded. "I was a lawman, too. That is, until the powers that be decided I was too old. I know what it means to honor a code." He tapped his fingers on the steering wheel. "Let's just say I believe you. It sounds crazy, but no one would have believed meat was gonna be growed in tanks twenty-five years ago either, and look at us now."

"So you'll help?" Luke asked. "I mean, besides giving me a ride out here?"

Instead of answering, Zeke said, "You can find Jeb Steel at 1430 Prickly Pear Drive in Tucson, Arizona. Do you know how to do that?"

Luke shook his head irritably.

"That's what I thought," Zeke said. "Truth is, you're just about helpless without me. I feel obligated to come along just to save yer ass."

Luke grinned. "Glad to have you."

They covered the Scout with a camouflage tarp. Zeke patted the hood as they left.

"I'll be back," he said. He slung his shotgun under his shoulder and put on a tan duster very similar to Luke's gray one.

They walked for hours until they could see the sunlight glinting off the steel and glass high rise buildings of Tucson. A few minutes later they crested a dune and looked down into a broad valley. Train tracks bisected it and in the middle was an arched opening leading undergound. Luke realized with a sudden feeling of growing dread that he was looking into the valley where he and Jeb had encountered the Sand Wyrms in Norland. But the tracks were intact, not twisted and welded into huge knots of steel. Zeke noticed the look of apprehension on the younger Warrior's face.

"That's the end of the line for the rocket train," he explained.

"I've been here before,' Luke said. "But the whole valley looked like it had been turned inside out."

"Really?" Zeke exclaimed. "That's interesting. Timon Blackhelm has been preaching that this whole area is unsafe. He wants to bomb it. That's why Ray Benson chose Tucson for the rally."

Luke remembered how the valley had been totally destroyed. "Is there enough bombs in this World to destroy this whole valley?" he asked.

Zeke laughed humorlessly. "Humans could destroy this entire World and have bombs left over," he replied.

The feeling of dread returned. "Why would anyone want to possess such power?" he asked.

Zeke shrugged. "With some people, it's never enough."

"What's the fastest way to Too-sonn and out of here?" Luke asked.

"We'll take the tunnel," Zeke answered. "Like I said, the rocket train don't come through here anymore. The tunnel is abandoned."

The feeling of dread wouldn't leave Luke, but he smothered it and slid down the dune into the valley. As he neared the arched entrance, he noticed elaborate drawings and insignias in brilliant colors on the concrete barriers that surrounded the opening. Zeke noticed his attention.

"Those are gang signs," he explained. "They fight over turf all the time, even way out here. The gang that could claim control of this area, with the reputation that it's getting, would gain a huge amount of prestige."

Luke studied each sign as they passed. Most made no sense to him, but as they neared the final one he stopped and stared. It was a Dragon with wings flared and streams of smoking flame jetting from it's fire vent. It was almost perfect, he realized. The artist had to be very familiar with Dragons to achieve such perfection. Who in this World, he wondered, could have even seen a real Dragon? Timon certainly had, but gang wars were far beneath his aspirations of power. Who then? Who would adopt the Sky Rider as the sigil of their gang?

As they entered the tunnel and left the daylight behind, lights recessed in the roof leaped to life. Luke watched in awe as they lit up exactly one hundred feet ahead, then dimmed the same distance behind them. He didn't feel even a trace of magic in this World, but there were definitely some wondrous discoveries.

"What made you become a lawman?" he asked Zeke to break the tension.

"Ideals, I guess," Zeke replied "I grew up watching old Westerns on TV with my Dad. I wanted to be just like those old time cowboys." He paused. "They were a lot like you, as a matter of fact."

"Would it bother you if I told you I don't understand most of what you say?" Luke asked.

"Not a bit," Zeke answered with a chuckle.

"Were you good at it?" Luke asked. "Were you true to your Code?"

"I was," Zeke said. "Then the powers that be took even that away from me. Said I was too old. They had a new breed of lawman, they said, younger, faster, stronger. Truth is, they're nothin' but brainwashed soldiers taught to act like robots."

They walked in silence after that until Luke had lost track of time. Finally, they emerged on the outskirts of Tucson. The sun was setting and a brownish haze hung over the city. The air had a foul taste to it. Luke's expression belied his disgust.

"That's Too-sonn?" he asked.

"It is," Zeke said. "It ain't exactly magical, is it?"

"That's a fact," Luke agreed. "It looks like Hell and smells like ass."

"There's a lotta people piled up in there," Zeke said. "You should smell it right after a rain. Smells ripe enough to turn my stomach. But, it ain't no better or no worse than any other big city."

Luke stopped and offered his right hand to the older man. Zeke stared first at Luke's hand, then into the glacial blue eyes of the younger Warrior.

"I came this far," Zeke said. "I don't intend to quit right at the finish line. Besides, in my World, you're still wet behind the ears."

Luke smiled. "I reckon so. I gotta tell you though, I think we're walkin' right into a war and neither side knows who we are."

Zeke shrugged. "I can handle myself," He opened his duster to show Luke his shotgun dangling from a strap. A bandoleer of shotgun shells crossed his chest.

"Looks that way," Luke agreed.

They continued walking. The streets were nearly deserted. The few pedestrians they encountered avoided them from a long distance.

"Can I ask you something?" Luke said.

"Fire away," Zeke replied. "Fire away and stand back." The older man couldn't explain it, but he felt better than he had in years. It was good to actually be doing something, not just sitting around waiting for the end of the world.

"Back at your house, kind of hidden in the hall, there were very old pictures of men hanging on the wall. Who were they?"

"You don't miss much," Zeke said. "Those men were my ancestors."

"Your fathers," Luke clarified

"Yes," Zeke agreed. "My father, grandfather, and great grandfather."

"Back to the first of your blood?"

"Not all the way, but yeah, pretty far back," Zeke said. "All the way back to old Jericho Sipowicz."

Luke felt as if he'd been punched in the guts. "Did you say Sipowicz?"

"Yep. My great great grandfather was Jericho Sipowicz. Him and his twin brother Jake were some of the first cowboys to ever ride the hills around my ranch."

"So, you are related to Jake Sipowicz?" Luke asked.

"Well, yeah," Zeke answered. "He was my great, great uncle. But he disappeared when he was still in his early twenties. The old stories say him and Jericho were kinda wild, but in a good natured, hell for leather kinda way. Fun loving, a little crazy, happy go lucky types. They were rounding up cows together. Jericho said Jake went after a stray and rode his horse right into a shaft of bright light and just disappeared. Jericho searched for days but never found any sign of him, his horse or the beef they was chasin'. He never actually stopped lookin' for his brother, right up until the day he died. He swore Jake was out there some where."

Luke drew a deep breath. "Jericho was right. I didn't know your great, great grandfather, but I did know the son of his son. He was called Smilin' Jake Sipowicz. He was a *magii'ri* Warrior and my friend." He looked again at Zeke and shook his head. How had he missed the similarities?

Zeke rolled his eyes. "Is this some kind of joke?" he asked. "Cause if it is, it ain't funny."

"It's not a joke," Luke assured him. "I see a lot of Smilin' Jake in you. You became a lawman because it's in your blood. You are a *magii'ri* Warrior."

Zeke laughed. "I'm a retired sheriff's deputy who wants to set things straight so I can get back to living the quiet life on my ranch."

Luke was not laughing. Perhaps he had been wrong in his earlier assessment. There just might be a tiny bit of magic left in this tired World, he thought.

"All the same," he said, "I'm glad you got my back. We'd best get on with it."

CHAPTER SIXTEEN

Lynch hurried back and forth between the corroded work benches in the basement of the dilapidated ranch style rental he and Jeb lived in. He had chosen the falling down old rat trap with peeling paint and curling shingles for one simple reason. No one else wanted to live there. And Lynch didn't need anyone poking about in his business.

The Dark Wizard had fumed and cursed after bringing Jack and Diane back to their own World, especially when he discovered the incredible scarcity of magical energy he needed to recharge his own magicometer. The fact was there wasn't enough magical energy left to go around, and Timon snatched up anyone who showed even an inkling of interest in the dark arts. He stashed those people away in prisons and work camps and siphoned off their magical energy anytime his own tank needed topping off.

Then Lynch had gone through his period of despair. During that time he tried to drink himself to death and nearly succeeded, but there was still enough of the old Lynch left that he had survived. He tried mind altering drugs and fasting, starving himself, really, and overindulging in the whores in the seedier districts. He had tried to screw himself to death, he admitted. And that's where Jeb found him. Leave it to that skinny kid to shame him out of his self pity. Together they had come up with a plan, and only recently a new development had appeared which Lynch believed virtually guaranteed their success.

The Dark Wizard began to hum as he worked. He was in rare good spirits, especially for the trying times. Then he began to sing.

Mushrat, mushrat, dynamite.
Building me a bomb
And building it right
This time Saturday evenin'
Timon's gonna be screamin'.
And he whirled and he twirled and exploded
And scattered his guts to the heavens above.
How's that for some half brother love?

The sudden slamming of the screen door above and the sound of heavy footsteps on the floor over his head jolted him out of his reverie. A puff of smoke erupted from one of the glass tubes Lynch had arranged in pockets sewn into a Kevlar vest and he winced in preparation for the detonation, but it didn't come.

He cleared his throat. "Who is it?" he called out as innocently as he could manage.

"Jeb," came the squeaky reply. "And I brought Colin, like you asked."

"Be right up," Lynch said in a sing song voice.

He looked around, stuffed a cork in the open glass tube and threw a tattered blanket over the whole contraption. He went up the stairs two at a time. Jeb perched on a barstool while Colin draped his massive form over most of the couch. Lynch stifled a chuckle and hid his smile behind his hand. He and Jeb reserved the couch for company, mostly because they hadn't been able to identify most of the stains on it. The big man didn't seem to mind.

"Well?" Lynch asked.

"Good to see you, too, Lynch," Colin said.

"Forget the formalities," Lynch replied. "Me and the kid have been watching you long enough to know you've thrown in with Ray Benson. I personally never thought you were enough of a yellow bellied skunk to join that asshole Timon. So, let's put everything on the table. What's your game?"

"Same old Lynch," Colin said. "Whatever. Timon has something of mine that I value more than my own life. That's all you need to know. I worked for him to save that. Now I can see he's gonna destroy two Worlds unless someone stops him. When the kid showed up, I knew it was my only chance. What's your plan and how can I help?"

Lynch grinned his trademark, feral grin. "I need to get within fifty feet at the rally. Then I'll blow him, me and you and probably a whole bunch of other people into crowbait."

Colin sighed. "That's your wonderful plan? Blow everyone at the rally to bits?"

"Why not?" Lynch answered. "They're all Blackhelm supporters. The rest of us are just collateral damage."

"Yer crazy," Colin replied. "Just crazy enough to actually do it."

"Oh, I'll do it alright," Lynch said. "I have nothing to lose. By the way, are you still carrying Graywullf's guns?"

Colin grimaced. "Yep. Blackhelm requires it."

"Wonderful," Lynch replied. "I don't want to carry a trigger, my concoction is..ummm…somewhat unstable. So, I'll need you to shoot me at the rally. It would not do to blow myself and an entire city block up by tripping over a stray dog on my way down the street."

Colin shook his head in dismay. "You really are crazy as a bedbug."

Lynch nodded in agreement. Jeb rolled his eyes and nodded in the background.

"Alright," Colin said. "I guess it's come to this. I'll make sure you're on the security detail backstage."

Lynch grinned. "It'll work. Wait and see."

"It better," Colin said. "I'm not sure what he's planning, only that he's gonna open up a huge portal. Something really big is either comin' in or goin' out."

He stood and looked down at Lynch. "You better come through. Remember, I'm gonna shoot you one way or another, and I still have that magic bullet."

Lynch laughed. "I wouldn't expect any less."

"I have to go," Colin said. "He keeps me on a short leash these days. There's been some kind of disturbance at the doorway. He wants to check it out in person."

"Stay in touch," Lynch suggested. "We have one week."

Colin raised one hand in a casual salute as he walked through the door. Lynch watched him thoughtfully.

"What do you think?" he asked Jeb.

"He seems sincere," Jeb replied.

"Follow him," Lynch said. "But stay out of sight."

Jeb nodded. He didn't need to be told to stay out of sight, and Lynch knew it. He hurried out the door and across the street to a row of abandoned houses. Two other youths joined him at the rear of one. All three pulled off their baggy shirts. They all wore identical under shirts. The sleeveless design was the perfect accent to draw attention to their matching Dragon tattoos. Without a word they slipped off into the darkness.

CHAPTER SEVENTEEN

"How much farther to Prickly Pear Drive?" Luke asked.

"We're on it," Zeke replied. "The damn thing's five miles long. Couple more hours, probably."

They walked steadily through the mostly deserted streets. The few other people they met either ducked their heads and hurried by or slipped silently into yawning black alleys.

"Where are all the people?" Luke asked.

"Mostly home," Zeke said. "There's a permanent curfew in place. Has been for years. Shuttles run workers to and from the food factories. Those things run day and night."

The buildings they passed were nearly all dark. Occasionally Luke caught a glimmer of light around a blackout blind. But about every three blocks there was a glaring exception. Those buildings were adorned with a flashing neon green sign adorned with one word. They all said "GRASS" in big, bold, capital letters. After the third identical sign Luke couldn't control his curiosity.

"What are those?" he asked, pointing at the sign.

Zeke's expression showed his disgust. "That," he replied, "is the only state sanctioned restaurant chain in the whole country. There isn't one speck of meat on the menu. Everything served there is plant based. They don't even sell tank meat."

"I don't understand," Luke commented. "Why did the government turn against ranchers and farmers?"

Zeke shrugged. "If you can believe it, it all started with cow farts."

Luke laughed. "Cow farts?"

"Yep," Zeke replied. "Some brilliant scientist decided that cow farts were polluting the environment. That gave the Greenies a foothold and they ran with it. See, most of the population of this World lives in cities. They got no freakin' idea where food actually comes from, and well, most of 'em left their common sense on the farm when they migrated to the cities. So, they all agreed that cow farts were gonna ruin the World. Never mind that it was their cars and factories that were ruining the environment. Anyway, the Greenies used cow farts to start their whole radical movement."

Luke shook his head in incredulous wonder.

"The whole Greenie philosophy exploded and became more radical until the economy basically collapsed," Zeke said.

Another pedestrian appeared from around a corner. He spotted Luke and Zeke and hesitated a moment, then resumed walking towards them. He wore a hoodie that concealed his face, which was focused on a light emitting device he cradled in his hands. As they drew nearer, it illuminated his features for just a moment when he glanced up. Then he dropped his gaze back upon the rectangular device he held.

"Dumbass," Zeke growled as they passed.

"What was that?" Luke asked.

"Cell phone," Zeke answered. "We gotta get off the street. That damn fool is calling the Watchers right down on top of us."

"What are you talking about?" Luke asked.

"Never mind," Zeke responded. "I'll explain later."

They came to an abandoned two story warehouse. The windows on the ground floor were all broken and the door hung askew on one hinge.

"In here," Zeke ordered.

He carefully opened the door and closed it behind them exactly as he found it.

"The Watchers will be here in two minutes," Zeke explained as they explored the warehouse. "They enforce the laws now. That dumb kid is breaking curfew and they'll trace his phone's location within fifty feet. He'll be in a work camp by dawn. And so will anybody else they find on the street."

They went upstairs and stood by a window on the far end of the building. The kid had stopped directly below them. He still stared as if mesmerized at the illuminated screen in his hands.

"Great," Zeke growled. "When they get here, don't move. Don't make a sound."

Luke nodded. Everything in this strange World was foreign to him, but he was beginning to get the picture. And it was a bleak picture indeed. This World was not only devoid of magic, it was also nearly out of hope. Free will was crushed under the bootheel of a government that demanded compliance. Every citizen was controlled by their dependence on technology and the ruthless enforcement of the agenda espoused by a radical faction. That faction had originally been empowered by their pursuit of a once noble cause which had long ago been lost in chaos and confusion. All that remained was the demand for total compliance to the laws of those currently in power, no matter how ridiculous those laws might be. The only good thing he could see was the apparent dearth of magic in this World. He was shaken from his ponderings by the approaching roar and squealing tires of several large vehicles.

The kid tried to run, but it was a weak and pathetic attempt. Each vehicle regurgitated four men all wearing body armor. The boy was tackled in seconds and his cries of pain when he hit the pavement were plainly audible. Luke and Zeke watched impassively. But then another vehicle arrived. It was long and low slung and purred to a smooth stop. A giant emerged from the driver's seat.

Luke's breath caught and his hands went instinctively to the grips of his pistols. He clenched his jaw in anger. He wanted to draw and send several ounces of lead crashing through the big man's head. It was Colin. He had expected Timon and hoped to find Lynch and Jeb. But Colin? His anger blossomed into total disbelief when his former mentor opened the rear door and Timon Blackhelm climbed out. Timon grabbed the kid by the hair and jerked his head back. He shook his head and threw the kid back into the arms of the Watchers.

"Take him to the meat factory," he ordered. "And be alert. There was a disturbance at the Gate earlier. Somebody, or something, got through."

The enforcers sped away. Colin held the door for Timon while he climbed back in the car, then they followed the Watchers. Luke realized his heart was pounding and his palms were slick with sweat. He wanted to move, to give chase, to do *something*. But he felt like his feet were nailed to the floor.

"Gawddammit," he whispered hoarsely. After all this time he still felt fear at the sight of Timon Blackhelm.

"You two have history," Zeke observed.

"He beat me," Luke explained. "I challenged him, one on one. He disarmed me and beat the shit outta me. Left me for dead."

Zeke stared at him. "He beat you in a stand up, face to face, fair fight?"

Luke shook his head. "It ain't ever a fair fight with a Wizard. He magicked me. I could take him without magic. The thing is, he'll see me comin' and magic me again. How can I get close enough to slap these enchanted irons on him?"

"Knock him down from a distance," Zeke suggested. "You said you want him alive? Gut shoot him, slap the irons on him and...do what you want with him."

Luke thought about that for a moment. A slow smile stole across his lips.

"Now I know you're a *magii'ri* Warrior," he said. "I'm gonna need a rifle."

Zeke expelled a gusty sigh. "That ain't gonna be easy. Guns have been outlawed for decades. But," he admitted, "I may know a guy."

Luke nodded. "Good. Do you think the Watchers are gone now?"

Zeke shook his head. "They probably got eyes in the sky on this whole neighborhood until tomorrow. We'd best hole up here. We could both use some rest."

Luke agreed. He was suddenly keenly aware of just how exhausted he was. They rounded up some old tarpaulins and machinery covers to make sleeping pallets. Within minutes they were both sound asleep.

Luke awoke before dawn. He lay silently in his sleeping pallet trying to pinpoint exactly what had disturbed him. Zeke's slow, steady breathing indicated that he was still asleep. Luke rose and padded quietly to the window overlooking the street. Something was off. He felt something, some foreign presence that didn't belong in this World any more than he did. The street was deserted as far as he could see. The hair on the back of his neck stiffened.

Suddenly, by a dumpster across the street there was a blurred shape where nothing had been only a moment before. Luke stared as the shape solidified into a man and was joined by another, then three more. They all wore long, gray dusters and broad brimmed hats. But he couldn't see their faces. Luke's palms itched. His breathing quickened and the blood sang in his ears. Then it was gone, leaving him cold and dangerous. He heard Zeke as the older man rose and joined him.

"Who are they?" he asked.

Luke grunted an unintelligible reply.

Zeke studied him for a moment. "They look like you."

"They look like *magii'ri*," Luke replied. "But they can't be. This is more of Timon's magic, I reckon. They're disgraced Warriors, returned from the Abyss."

"What's the plan?" Zeke asked as he checked his shotgun.

"You stay here, out of sight," Luke advised in a hoarse whisper. "They'll be fast, faster than you could ever believe. They're here for me, you can bet on that. If they get me, you go on back to your ranch, live out your days as your gods intended."

Then he was gone. He descended to the ground floor and exited a back door into an alley. He noted the position of everything in the alley, took a deep breath, and stepped around the corner of the building. As he had hoped, all five of the men across the street noticed him and started his way. He knew they would be fast, but even he was surprised at how quickly they reached him. He barely had time to dive behind the dumpster before they flanked both sides of the alley. When they advanced, he leaped out of hiding to attack, drawing as he moved. Time seemed to slow to a crawl. Luke had enough time to see the surprise in their faces at his decision to attack instead of retreat, then he shot the first two in the face.

Instead of running, he planted his feet and waited a fraction of a second. As another attacker swung his gun around the corner of the building, Luke fired again. His bullet struck the fully loaded cylinder of the gunfighter's revolver. The live ammunition in it exploded, blowing the gun and his attacker's hand to pieces.

Luke dove for the doorway as another gunhand appeared. He actually saw the fire from the muzzle blast and knew he could not avoid the bullet. It sliced through the thick muscle at the base of his neck as he rolled. The impact felt like he'd been kicked in the head. He slid through the doorway across the concrete floor, lunged to his feet and lurched behind a massive drill press.

The remaining two gunhands did not hesitate. They burst through the door and paused a fraction of a second as their eyes adjusted to the gloom. Luke hurled Lynch's tomahawk. His throw was perfect. It lodged deep in the skull of the nearest attacker. As he fell, Luke swung his gun to cover the last man. Their eyes locked for a moment, and Luke saw the despair in his eyes, but he would not give up. He started to swing his pistol up when Zeke stepped into the doorway and shot him with his shotgun. The impact of the blast sent the gunhand flying over his fallen comrade, where he lay twitching on the floor.

"I don't like being left behind," Zeke explained.

His eyes widened and his jaw dropped wide open as Luke swung his pistol. He thought it was pointed straight at his face. Luke pulled the trigger before Zeke could react. He actually felt the displaced air from the passage of the bullet and heard it thump solidly into something behind him. He turned in time to see the last gunhand fall, cradling his mutilated hand to his chest and his other pistol in his remaining hand.

"I guess you had it under control," Zeke managed to say.

Luke nodded as he came out from behind the drill press where he had taken cover. "Better take anything of use," he said as he knelt and began to strip the cartridge belts from the fallen men.

"You're bleeding," Zeke said. "How bad is it?"

"Burns like Hell," Luke replied. "But I'll live, I reckon."

They hurriedly gathered the gunhand's weapons and exited into the alley. Luke stopped in his tracks. The alley was blocked by a rider on a horse. But this rider was no man. He wore the same gray duster and broad brimmed hat, and his legs were encased in dusty jeans. Worn out boots were jammed into the stirrups. But this was not a man, at least not anymore. His face was a grinning death's head. His eyes sockets were vacant and black. Human scalps hung from the horse's rigging. He drummed his heels into the horse's flanks. It leaped out of sight around the corner of the building and its hooves beat a staccato rhythm on the concrete sidewalk. Luke charged after the fleeing figure and triggered two shots down the street. Both hit their mark, he was certain of it, but the Rider did not fall. Then he was gone.

He turned back to Zeke, who's mouth worked for several seconds before any sound came out.

"What the Hell was that?" he finally managed to say.

"Something else from Norland," Luke replied. "A Rider, I believe. A bounty hunter for Haan, the Guardian of the Abyss."

Zeke nodded. "Ok. I don't think I want to go to Norland."

Luke laughed. "Neither of us is going anywhere if we don't get outta here first."

They grabbed their belongings and ran. After they had gone a couple blocks, Zeke pulled up. His breathing came in gasps.

"I can't keep up," he wheezed. "And we gotta get off the street. We gotta hide until things cool down."

"Where?" Luke demanded as he looked around.

A siren sounded. It blew a long, piercing blast followed by two short ones. Zeke scowled.

"That's the signal to shelter in place," he said. "What the Hell is going on?"

"Shelter in place?" Luke asked. "What does that mean, and what does it mean to us?"

"It means stay wherever you are, whether you're at work, or on the train or in the hospital. Whatever. You just ain't supposed to be out on the street."

"Shit," Luke summed it up with one word. He looked up and down the street. "I see a steeple up ahead. You have churches in this fucked up world?"

"Yes," Zeke said with new hope. "Let's check it out."

They ran in the direction of the church steeple. There were others on the street, but they ignored everyone around them, desperately scurrying about like ants to get out of the open. The lone subway entrance for blocks in any direction was covered up with a clot of people, all yelling and screaming at each other. Fistfights broke out. As they ran by, a man with filthy, matted hair, dressed in castoff clothing, fixed them with a threatening gaze. His eyes followed them until they rounded a corner and were cut off from view. That sight added to the sense of urgency Luke felt.

They reached the front doors of the church, but they were covered with sheets of plywood. Luke skirted around the corner of the building with Zeke right on his heels. A set of concrete stairs led down to a basement doorway also sealed with plywood. Luke descended the stairs two at a time, planted his left foot and drove his right bootheel into the door. The rotten doorjamb splintered and the door swung inward with a crash. Stale, musty air rushed out. Luke slammed his shoulder into the door and plunged inside.

He stopped for a moment just inside the room. Dim light filtered in through the grimy windows. The basement must have been used for Sunday school at one time. Child sized desks and chairs were strewn about. Luke stepped aside and motioned for Zeke to enter, then he pushed the door firmly shut. The silence that ensued was only broken by Zeke's labored breathing. Luke waited for several minutes.

"Wanna tell me what's that all about?" he finally asked.

"Presidential decree," Zeke answered. "When the sirens go off, everyone's supposed to go to a government shelter, national guard armory, hospital, some designated site. Wait there until they get the all clear signal on their phone. Anyone caught outside is supposed to be shot on sight."

"What!?" Luke exclaimed.

"Yeah," Zeke replied. "He's herding everyone together."

A terrible premonition flashed through Luke's mind. Something was horribly wrong.

"How long does it last?" Luke asked.

Zeke shrugged. "It's never been done before."

Luke sighed. He unslung Lynch's pack, placed it on a desk and rummaged inside. He pulled out the nearly empty whiskey bottle and a semi-clean rag. He didn't want to think about Lynch's purpose for having such a rag in his pack. He gingerly shucked his duster and pulled the neck of his shirt aside. Zeke's eyes widened when he saw blood pulse from the bullet hole in the thick muscle at the base of Luke's neck.

"That was close," he commented. "Let me help."

Luke reluctantly handed the rag and whiskey to the older man.

"Clean it good," he instructed. "Don't worry about stopping the bleeding yet. And," he added, "don't worry about hurting me."

"This is gonna burn," Zeke observed.

"Do it," Luke ordered.

Zeke held one corner of the rag under the wound and poured whiskey into the hole, then he worked it deeper into the wound. Luke gritted his teeth and stared straight ahead. Zeke repeated the process with the exit wound.

"Sumbitch," he muttered. He took a few deep breaths.

Zeke looked inside Lynch's pack.

"Huh," he exclaimed in disbelief. He reached inside and withdrew a roll of camouflage duct tape and a roll of gauze. He held it up for Luke to see. Luke shrugged, then winced in pain.

"Magic pack," he commented. "Sometimes it knows what you need."

Zeke bandaged the wound and bound it in place with tape.

"Thanks," Luke said. "I'm beholden to you." He paused as he looked around, deep in thought. "Something's wrong. This is Tuxin, right?"

"Too-sonn," Zeke corrected.

"Whatever," Luke replied. "And you mentioned Ray Benson."

"Yep, he's supposed to be organizing a rally here," Zeke answered.

"Timon said there was a disturbance at the gate and he wanted Colin to check it out. I'll be gawddamned. I think Timon's getting ready to send Tuxin through the gate with Ray Benson and his followers. And anybody else caught in it. Like us," he said pointedly to Zeke. "I don't care what the opposition is, we have got to get out of here."

"We have to wait," Zeke argued. "The streets will be crawling with Blackhelm men."

Luke paced in the narrow confines of the cluttered basement. "Two hours," he said. "We can wait two hours and no more. Then we go."

He sat on the floor and leaned back against an upended desk. Inwardly, he fumed. It sure looked like Mathias had sent him to the wrong *when*, if not completely the wrong World. Zeke found an adult sized chair and sat down, watching the younger gunslinger. Luke unloaded and inspected each of his guns carefully. He wiped them down with an oily rag and cleaned the bore and each individual chamber in the cylinder. Then he retrieved the gunbelts he had stripped from the fallen disgraced *magii'ri* Warriors. He shucked the cartridges from each. After he had filled the empty loops in his own belt, he had fifteen bullets left. He slipped five loaded rounds in each gun and reholstered them, then he dropped the extra shells in his duster pocket.

"How many rounds do you have for the scattergun?" he asked Zeke.

"Forty-nine," Zeke replied. "The bandolier holds fifty. I fired one."

Luke gave a satisfied nod. "Can I see your weapon?"

Zeke shrugged and slipped the shotgun off his improvised shoulder strap. Luke made sure the chamber was empty, then he looked it over. He shouldered it and sighted down the sixteen inch barrel.

"This might be just what we need," he commented. "It's not much good for longer range, but against a crowd, up close, it will be devastating." He racked the slide and chambered a round. "That sound right there is the most intimidating sound there is in a close-up fight." He cleared the chamber, inserted the shell in the magazine and handed it back to Zeke.

"I know you're experienced," Zeke said. "But how many men have you killed?"

Luke looked away uncomfortably. "I haven't kept track. It's not the *magii'ri* way."

"I only ask," Zeke continued, "because you never even blinked during or after that fight at the warehouse."

"I had several good teachers," Luke replied. "The *magii'ri* Warriors are taught to follow the Code, and the Code says that some offenses are punishable only by death. Also, if a Warrior's life is threatened or if the life of an innocent is threatened, deadly force is not only justified, but encouraged."

"I'm not saying there's anything wrong with that," Zeke said. "I understand. But, well, that guy back at the warehouse was my first. I was a deputy for thirty years and never had to fire my weapon in the line of duty."

"And it's weighing on you,' Luke finished.

"Well, yeah," Zeke admitted.

Luke shrugged. "My first kill wasn't even human, so I guess you could say I was broke in slowly."

"Not human?" Zeke said in disbelief.

"Nope," Luke replied. "He was a Beastsoldier, more animal than man, bred by the Darklord Timon to fill the ranks of his army. I shot him with a rifle from a tower called the Citadel."

"So you shot the one Beastsoldier and that was it?" Zeke asked.

"Nope," Luke replied. "I shot dozens of 'em that day, but it was payback for what they done to Smilin' Jake."

"My ancestor?" Zeke said.

"I reckon," Luke said.

"What did they do to him, or do I want to know?"

Luke let the memories of that day wash over him. He felt the rage and despair and sorrow all over again. But the dominant emotion was admiration. Smilin' Jake had died a hero's death, true to the Warrior's Code to the very end. Luke told Zeke how Smilin' Jake had slain the Dragon and then gave his own life to vanquish an army.

When he was done, tears flowed freely down his cheeks. He roughly brushed them away, embarrassed at the unfamiliar revealing of his emotions. But Zeke's own bristly cheeks were wet with tears as well.

"I believe you," he said, his voice choked with emotions too complex to define. "You loved him, didn't you? Not in a weird way, but as a brother."

"I did," Luke admitted. "He was my teacher, my substitute father and my Warrior brother all in one."

"I wish I could have met him," Zeke said.

"Someday, when your time has come, you will be invited to the Feast," Luke assured him. "That is where all the *magii'ri* gather on the Other Side, and he will recognize you as a Warrior."

"I hope so," Zeke said. He cocked his head to one side and listened intently. "It's really quiet out there."

"We should go," Luke suggested. "We need to keep moving."

"Let's do it," Zeke agreed.

"I'll go first until we get out to the main street," Luke said. He loosened his revolvers in their holsters. "Then we move together, smooth but quick."

Zeke gave a short nod. Luke focused his thoughts, pulled the door open and ascended the stairs with Zeke close behind. The back street was empty. The sirens had stopped and an eerie silence filled the city. They made their way back to the main street. A gunshot sounded in the distance. The pair traversed half the distance to the corner subway entrance when a man stepped out of an alley with a semiautomatic handgun. He raised it to aim at the pair. Luke drew his right hand gun and shot him between the eyes. Almost immediately more Blackhelm men emerged from around corners and out of alleys. They began firing at the pair. Luke plunged ahead, drawing his other pistol as he did and returned fire. Car windows erupted in showers of shattered glass, but Luke's uncanny Warrior's sense allowed him to beat each Balckhelm man to the shot by a fraction of a second. His right hand gun clicked on an empty chamber. He dropped his left hand gun into the holster and shucked the empties from the right hand gun. A bullet plucked at his sleeve and a sudden grunt of pain announced that Zeke had been hit. His hands performed the trick of reloading without benefit of his vision, which he kept trained on his enemies. Suddenly, all conscious thought was drowned out by the bellowing roar of Zeke's shotgun. The sudden looks of panic on his enemies' faces would have been amusing in any other scenario. They broke ranks as Zeke fired his seventh shot. By then Luke had reloaded. He coldly shot several of the retreating soldiers and as they fell, he and Zeke took shelter in the stairwell of the subway entrance.

"How bad you hit?" Luke asked as he reloaded his left hand gun.

"Clipped my shoulder. Didn't hit a bone," Zeke replied. "Burns like Hell."

Bullets whizzed by and ricocheted off the concrete walls. Luke and Zeke were forced deeper into the subway tunnel.

"Too many of 'em," Luke said. "Let's go."

They plunged downward and climbed over the turnstiles to enter the platform area. As one they skidded to a stop. The platform was covered with bodies.

"What the Hell?" Luke cursed, but his earlier premonition had proven true.

They ran over the bodies and dropped onto the empty track. Luke trusted his instincts and ran north. Dim emergency lighting illuminated the tunnels.

"Does this train go to the station where we came in?" Luke shouted over his shoulder.

"It goes to a substation," Zeke said. "Slow down."

Luke slowed to a fast walk.

"The rocket train was the only one that goes where we came in," Zeke said. "We follow this track to the substation, then take the rocket train track back out. Why are we going back out?"

"This has gone bad," Luke said.

He didn't know it was about to get worse. They rounded a slight bend in the tunnel. The track was blocked by the subway train. Luke groaned. They forced open an emergency exit and entered the last car. It was filled with dead passengers. Nearly all of them cradled their still glowing phones in their hands, staring at them with dead, sightless eyes.

"My god,' Zeke moaned. "He did it. He really did it." His eyes showed too much white as he looked at Luke. "He poisoned everyone. They're all dead."

"Everyone?" Luke asked.

Zeke nodded. Luke gritted his teeth and plunged ahead. They navigated the entire train and emerged on the other side. They walked in silence as the overhead lights came on in silence ahead of them and blinked into blackness behind them. They walked for hours until they reached the substation. Zeke pointed to the track for the rocket train and, without a word, they entered it.

Every train they encountered and every platform they passed was filled with corpses. Men, women and children, Young and old, all frozen with bewildered expressions still on their faces as they stared at their phones waiting for the signal to emerge from shelter that never came.

Luke pushed Zeke as hard as he dared. The urgent need to escape this strange World filled him and he was consumed by a growing sense of dread. The events of the past few hours were beyond his understanding, but he was certain they had implications for Norland as well as the World he was in now. Finally, the hazy, arched outside entrance to the rocket train came into view. Beyond it, Luke could see the twin rails clawing through the sun baked landscape.

"We have to get out," he announced.

"So, let's get out," Zeke said with a shrug. He immediately regretted the movement as pain flashed through his wounded shoulder. He impatiently walked ahead, but as he neared the entrance his footsteps slowed as if he were mired knee deep in mud until he was forced to stop while he was still inside the tunnel.

"No," Luke breathed in disbelief. He tried to walk past the older man but was also stopped short.

"It's a portal," he announced in despair. Realization blossomed inside him. This was the portal outside Tuxin, but the rails still ran straight and true, not twisted and welded together by an unimaginable force. And Tuxin, the Tucson of this World, still stood behind them. "Son of a bitch," he muttered.

"What is it now?" Zeke asked in an exasperated tone.

"We can't get out without activating the portal," Luke said. "And if I'm right, when Timon activates this portal the entire city is going to be sucked through. Then, he's going to use that power you assured me exists in this World and he's going to blow the whole thing all to Hell."

"Can you open it?" Zeke asked.

"I'm a Warrior, not a Wizard," Luke answered.

Zeke thought for a moment. "What about that book? Is there something in there we can use to open it?"

Luke shrugged. *'Gawddamn you Mathias,'* he thought. *'It's your fault I'm stuck here. You and your Magic.'* Even as he thought it, another thought sneaked into his mind. Even though he had never had any magical power in his entire life, he had always listened when Mathias talked about Magic. And the thing he remembered the most was, magical power needed only one thing to succeed, and that was people who believed in it. He hated magic, that point was beyond contention. But there was no disputing the fact that he believed in it heart and soul. He retreated from the portal and opened Lynch's pack. Zeke joined him. The Book of Runes slid out and plopped open. Luke and Zeke exchanged glances. Suddenly, from far down the tunnel, lights began to spring to life. Their pursuers were close.

Luke and Zeke scanned the pages the Book had chosen to reveal.

"That's it,' Zeke said. "I don't believe it, but the Book knew what we needed."

"I can't believe I'm doing this," Luke said in disgust. He stood before the portal and began to read in a halting voice. He finished the rune and stepped forward. Once again, he was stopped short.

"You read it wrong," Zeke accused.

Luke cast a murderous glance his way. "I don't read that much," he said defensively.

The lights behind them clicked on steadily closer.

"Try again," Zeke said. "Smoother this time."

Luke read the rune silently several times. "I've got it now," he said. Once again, he read the rune aloud, but nothing changed. "Son of a bitch," he cursed. He read the rune a third time, and before he finished the haze began to shift. As he said the last word, he and Zeke lunged forward as one and fell into the sand. Luke knew immediately he was back in Norland. He could *feel* it. He looked down at his hands and body and nodded in satisfaction. Not only did he open the portal, but by the gods, they had also come through fully clothed. He glanced around quickly as he climbed to his feet and dusted himself off. Zeke also looked around.

"It looks like the desert outside Tucson to me," he said.

"Trust me, it's not," Luke assured him.

"I don't see anything different," Zeke argued.

"Well," Luke drawled. "Take a look over by the Eastern horizon. But be quick, cause I think we better find cover real soon."

Zeke looked where Luke indicated. At first he thought he was looking at a plane, but this flying object glided among the mountaintops, dipping and climbing like a swallow. As he watched, it veered into a straight flight towards them. He was amazed at the speed with which it ate up the distance.

"Come on," Luke urged. He ran towards the dubious shelter of a pile of boulders, hampered by the ankle deep sand that sucked at his boots. Zeke labored to keep up, and Luke grabbed him by one arm and half-dragged him through the sand. They crawled in among the boulders, panting and sweating, just as the first of their pursuers emerged through the portal. The man shielded his eyes from the sudden glare of the sun. Zeke swore and struggled to shoulder his shotgun, but Luke slapped a hand around the forearm and forced the gun back down.

"No," he whispered hoarsely. "No shooting. No talking. No sound at all and *do not move*." The last words were delivered with such urgency Zeke could not have ignored them if he had tried.

More of their pursuers fell through the portal. Most of them clambered to their feet and looked around in a dazed manner. The sudden roar and whistling of wind over outstretched wings drowned out whatever sound they may have made. Then Slagg was upon them. Several fell to his razor sharp talons, sliced to ribbons. Then his powerful neck dipped and bobbed. Each graceful movement was designed to inflict the maximum amount of damage on the interlopers. Several of the men were able to bring their weapons to bear and fired off a fusillade of shots, but the Sky Rider's scales were impervious to bullets. In moments the arch was spattered with blood and gore and all of Timon's men were dead. Zeke's mouth dropped open. Luke very slowly and almost imperceptibly shook his head.

"No sound," he mouthed.

Slagg's snout was covered with blood. His head moved with agonizing slowness until he fixed the pile of boulders with one obsidian eye. The Sky Rider stared at their hiding place until Luke was certain they had been found out. But then Slagg suddenly whipped his head around. Smoke spurted from his fire vent, followed by jets of flame that shot fifty feet inside the entrance to the rocket train. Then he scooped up three of the men in his jaws and leaped into the sky. In moments he was gone. Once again, Zeke's mouth worked, but no coherent sounds came out.

"Welcome to Norland," Luke said in a soft voice.

"This is Norland?" Zeke asked in disbelief.

"It is," Luke drawled as he scanned the desert out to the horizon in all directions, "and then again, it ain't."

The whites of Zeke's eyes showed plainly. He appeared to be going into shock. In a matter of minutes he had seen a lunatic unleash a terrible weapon that apparently killed most of humanity and then been sucked through a doorway into a World where flying monsters ripped people limb from limb with impunity. Now his guide, this young, weather beaten gunhand who hadn't been fazed by anything seemed to think they had landed in the wrong World.

"What do you mean?" Zeke managed to ask. He seriously hoped Luke was going to say something about Dragons not actually existing in Norland.

"Somethin's not quite right," the Warrior answered. "I can't put my finger on it, but I get the feeling we should already be moving."

"Then by all means, let's move out," Zeke replied. In truth, he couldn't wait to leave the blood soaked sand in front of the archway far behind. And right now this hard bitten gunslinger was the only thing he felt he could actually trust to be real.

They set off across the desert. Luke chose a path that followed the ridgelines where the sand wasn't as deep and they moved at a good pace. The elevation also gave him a fairly good field of view. Even after walking for over an hour the urge to get away from the entrance to the rocket train drove him onward. They walked steadily and by midafternoon he judged they had covered five or six miles. Zeke kept up without complaint, and Luke started to breathe a little easier. He thought it was about time to stop for a rest and began to turn to tell Zeke when a massive concussion rocked the entire World. He and Zeke were tossed about like children's playtoys and thrown to the ground which undulated beneath them. They flopped about like fish on a riverbank, unable to get back on their feet. Luke landed face up when the earth finally stopped shaking. He spat out a mouthful of sand and opened his eyes. He blinked. He was staring at a tear in the sky. Utter blackness showed through even though the sun still burned in the distance.

"Jesus," Zeke exclaimed. He was on his hands and knees, spitting sand. "Was that an earthquake?"

"I don't think so," he said. He jerked his head skyward. Zeke looked up.

"Holy shit!" he cursed. "What the Hell is going on here?"

Luke shrugged and sat up. Once again he blinked in amazement. The answer appeared in the desert. The skyline of Tucson had emerged from the sand amid a cloud of dust. He pointed towards it.

"I'll be gawddammed," Zeke swore. "That's Tucson."

"Nope. Not here it ain't," Luke corrected. "That's Tuxin. And I'll bet a hunnerd dollars them tracks we followed are twisted and tied in knots like a pig's tail. Somebody set off them bombs you was talking about and just about blew a hole in the sky." Luke shook his head. "I've been here before. But not in this *when*."

They both sat in the sand and stared.

"What do you mean by that?" Zeke finally asked.

"I'm not sure yet," Luke responded.

"Do you mean you were here in a different time?" Zeke persisted.

"Not just a different time," Luke answered. "A different *everything*."

Far to the West a small plume of dust caught his eye. He watched it intently. It wasn't a dust devil. It moved in a straight line, like it had a purpose. Luke watched it intently for at least fifteen minutes. Finally, he delved into Lynch's pack and found the Dark Wizard's scratched and tarnished brass spyglass. He laid down, steadied the spyglass on the pack and peered through it.

"Huh," he grunted, not quite believing what he saw.

"What is it now?" Zeke asked.

"It looks like a kid with three dogs running through the desert," Luke replied.

Zeke's skeptical laugh was cut short by the humorless expression on Luke's face. It was obvious the gunslinger was not joking.

"What next?" He wondered aloud.

"It gets even better," Luke replied. "I think I know that kid, but he ain't supposed to be here." He stowed the spyglass, stood and shouldered the pack.

"Let me guess," Zeke said. "We're going back, ain't we?"

"I reckon so," Luke answered. "If that's the kid I think it is, I have to head him off. He's about to get into a world of trouble." Luke studied the older man. "You doing alright?" he indicated Zeke's wounded shoulder.

Zeke nodded. "It quit bleeding a while ago."

"We'll clean it good when we make camp," Luke assured him. "There'll be water and bandages, maybe even medicine and food, back there in Tuxin."

"You already know what we're gonna find, don't you?" Zeke accused.

Luke nodded. "I reckon so."

"So you've been here before?" Zeke demanded.

"Yep," Luke answered. "But it was in a different time. Like I said before, a different *when*. The kid was older than he looked today, and we came in from the other direction. He went inside the buildings, which were half buried in drifted sand, and found some stale old foods." His face was bleak. "The homes were full of dead people, all dried up. Mummified by the heat, I guess. We passed through, and the sand Wyrms almost got us." He started to walk, but Zeke stood stock still.

"Sand Wyrms?" he repeated.

Luke looked back. "Yep. Giant worms. Big enough to eat a horse in one bite. They tunnel under the surface, then explode out and snag their dinner."

"And they were at the underground entrance to the rocket train?"

"Yep," Luke answered.

"But they weren't there when we came through," Zeke corrected. "They didn't show up until…well, until the explosion and Tuxin appeared, right?"

"I reckon," Luke agreed. "What are you getting at?"

Zeke rubbed his temples. "Let me see if I can make sense of this." He thought as they walked. "I got it. The doorways don't lead to different Worlds. It's all the same World, but different times. No… you had it when you said it wasn't just different times. It's a different *when*. The gateways lead to alternate realities on the same World."

"I don't even pretend to understand what you just said," Luke replied.

Zeke persisted. "That has to be it. You might even exist here, in this World, in a different *when*. You must be younger, and in a different place, because you know you weren't here when the kid came through."

Luke laughed incredulously. "I can't imagine the gods having the humor to create more than one of me."

"That's the point," Zeke said. "There is only one of you. I watched enough time traveling movies to know that you can't exist in the same time and space as your alternate." He stopped.

"Gawddamn. You can't go down there and interact with that kid. As a matter of fact, we need to find a way out of here right now. Anything we change here could change our Worlds in ways we can't even imagine."

"Well," Luke drawled. "I'm going down there and stop that kid from making a huge mistake and the Hell with the consequences."

"You can't" Zeke pleaded. "Let the kid make a mistake and learn from it. What could be so bad about that?"

"Because in this case," Luke stated flatly, "this mistake gets him killed." He looked sideways at Zeke. "I'm going down there to save his life."

"Oh," Zeke mumbled. In his mind he could hear an authoritative voice saying something about a butterfly flapping its wings and rain forests, but he couldn't remember the exact quote. He caught up to Luke. "Ok, so we save the kid and then we get out. Right?"

"Right as rain," Luke said.

CHAPTER EIGHTEEN

Jeb slowed down as he entered the first street lined with incredibly tall glass and steel buildings. Dried tears had cut trails through the grime and dust on his cheeks, but the tears had stopped hours ago. He had seen more than his share of violence and bloodshed in his twelve years, but his entire world had been turned inside out in the last day and it had rattled him more than he cared to admit. The dogs romped and played and more than once he looked at them with a hungry, thoughtful expression in his eyes. All he could think about was fried chicken. When he had lived under Dez's house, he always looked forward to Sunday. That was the day Mary Alice, Dez's on again-off again wife, would fry up a whole mess of chickens. Dez always slipped a couple pieces through the gaps in the floorboards for him. He looked at Milo, the hound dog closest to him, and he saw a huge, walking fried chicken leg. Milo approached and licked his hand.

"Nasty old dog," he murmured as he stroked the dog's velvety muzzle. "Shit. I couldn't eat you. But I am mighty gawddamn hungry."

The dogs ran in and out of open doorways, licking their chops. Jeb screwed up his courage and followed them. The interior was even stranger to him than the outside had been. Glass cases and metal shelves held objects that he could not identify. Still, Dez had told him food could be found there. It wouldn't be what he was used to, but it would keep him alive. He recognized a foil packet that Dez had brought home previously. He's told him it was dried taters. He ripped it open. The super thin, dried potatoes inside were crusted with salt, but he stuffed them in his mouth with abandon. He found a shelf stacked high with short, cylindrical cans and scooped at least a dozen into a discarded cloth bag along with an armload of water bottles. Then he looked behind the counter. He backpedaled so suddenly his buttocks crashed into a shelf and he fell over backwards. He leaped to his feet and ran back into the street, but kept a wary eye on the vacant eyes of the dead bodies sitting calmly behind the counter. *'At least they're fresh,'* he thought, *'they don't even stink yet.'*

He was surprised at how low the sun had sunk. There was no way he could get out of the city before dark. He reluctantly chose a small corner park as a campsite for the night. After he gathered several steel mesh trash cans together to use the contents as fuel, he struck a fire with flint and steel. The dogs had run off, but he wasn't worried about them. He knew they'd come back after exploring and foraging. The dried taters had done nothing to satisfy his hunger, so he took out one of his cans and examined it. He spied the ring on the lid and, more out of curiosity than anything, he pulled on it. The lid popped off and Jeb sniffed the contents. *'Not too bad,'* he thought. *'Better than Mary Alice's squirrel stew.'* He scooped up a glob on his knife blade and scraped it off with his teeth. *'Way better than Mary Alice's stew,'* he thought. He glanced at the label on the can, shrugged, and took another bite. He emptied that can and ate another. He drained a water bottle and had started on his third can when the gunslinger stepped into his meager firelight. Jeb sat as if frozen, mesmerized by the silent appearance of such a foreboding character. He had seen plenty of desperadoes at the way station, but this was no two bit outlaw. This was a character straight out of the fairy tales the whores used to tell him before bedtime.

"Yer a *magii'ri* Warrior," he stammered.

"I am," Luke replied. "And your name is Jeb."

"Gawddamn," Jeb breathed. "You know who I am."

"Yep," Luke said. "My name is Luke. Do you remember me?"

Jeb shook his head. "I never met a real Warrior before."

Luke nodded as Zeke stepped into the light. "This here's my partner, Zeke." Luke said. "Mind if we sit?"

Jeb scrambled to his feet. "Sure, sit wherever ya like. Want some grub? I got some potted cat meat that ain't half bad." He held out the can so they could see. "Plenty more where that came from too. Them dead people don't need it anyhow."

Luke took the cans Jeb handed him. Zeke did the same, and burst into laughter.

"That ain't potted cat meat," he exclaimed. "It's cat food. Food made for cats to eat."

Jeb shrugged. "I saw the drawing of a cat on the can. Figgered it was cat meat. It ain't bad."

Luke popped open a can and dug in. Zeke gagged and looked away. When Luke finished his cans, Zeke tossed his at Luke's feet. Luke shrugged and tucked them into the pockets of his duster.

"Thanks for the grub," Luke said. "So, what's a young feller like you doin' out in the desert all alone?"

Jeb hesitated, but this was a *magii'ri* Warrior. An almost mythical being endowed with superhuman speed, strength and endurance. He stared at the smooth butts of Luke's pistols protruding from the holsters. Luke noticed his gaze.

"Wanna see one?" he asked.

Jeb nodded. Luke casually glanced away, then half turned and drew his right hand gun. Jeb's eyes went as big as saucers at the speed of the Warrior's draw. Luke dumped the cartridges into his left palm and spun the cylinder to make sure it was empty. He handed the revolver to Jeb, who took it wonderingly. He hefted it.

"So heavy," he commented.

"You get used to it," Luke replied. "So, why are you out here all alone?"

Despite his earlier bravado, Jeb's eyes teared up at the thought of events that had led him here.

"My Pa got bit by a window spider," he explained. "It killed him, but not before he killed that bitch Mary Alice. He sent me to fetch my Uncle Philbert before he died, but I never trusted Phil anyway. So I lit out. And here I am."

"Headed to Old Town?" Luke asked.

"Yep," Jeb answered. "The whores will take me in. I know some of 'em."

Zeke watched the exchange in silence. His eyebrows rose a good half inch at Jeb's mention of the whores, but he still kept his mouth shut.

"That'd be fine," Luke said. "I reckon the whores would treat you nice enough. You got any friends in Old Town, besides the whores, I mean?"

Jeb shook his head.

"Well," Luke said, "I reckon it'd be a whole lotta trouble and you'd probably slow us down some, but you could trail along with us."

Zeke hid a smile behind one hand.

"Do ya mean it?" Jeb gushed.

"I have to ask my partner," Luke interrupted.

Jeb cast a plaintive glance towards Zeke.

"I reckon we could use another hand," Zeke said.

"It's settled then," Luke stated. "You can trail along with us, and I'll teach you how to be a *magii'ri* Warrior."

"Gawddamn," Jeb exclaimed. "This day started out bad and went to shit, and now look! It couldn't get much better."

Later, after Jeb finally settled down enough to sleep, Zeke and Luke sat on the hard park benches and watched the fire die. The dogs had wandered back in before Jeb laid down to sleep, and now Luke sat and absentmindedly scratched Milo's ears. The old hound dog was in heaven and sat with his chin resting on Luke's thigh.

"So, you think doing this will save the kid's life?" Zeke's question broke the silence.

"Yep," Luke said. "If he had gone on to Old Town, them mean kids down there would have beat him to death."

"Do you wonder what else might have changed because of what you did?" Zeke asked.

Luke shrugged. "I saw a chance to save the kid. That's all that matters." He pushed the dog off his leg. "Better turn in. We got a lot of walkin' ahead of us."

Luke stretched out on his bench and began to snore softly almost immediately. Zeke shook his head and followed suit. In minutes he was asleep.

Zeke didn't know what woke him. Every sense he had screamed danger, but he forced himself to lie still. He opened his eyes to slits. The dogs had piled around Jeb and were obviously still asleep. Luke's bench was empty, but from the silhouette in the moonlight near the sleeping boy, Zeke assumed the gunfighter was checking on the boy. But something was very wrong. He swung his legs off the bench. The silhouette near the boy rose and turned towards Zeke and he realized it was not Luke. He began to swing his shotgun around but the lean figure by the boy drew and covered him with a pistol nearly identical to Luke's.

"That ain't a good idea," the gunman said.

Zeke raised his hands to shoulder height. "Who are you?" he asked.

"They call me Ding," the gunman said. "Short for Dingus McCray. And you?"

"Zeke," came the reply.

"Who's the kid?" Dingus asked.

"Just a kid," Zeke responded.

"But yer guardin' him," Ding observed. "Is he a Wizard?"

"I don't think so," Zeke answered.

"Good," Dingus holstered his pistol. As he did, Luke stepped away from his spot of concealment near a dumpster. Dingus' hand flashed towards his gun, but Luke beat him to the draw easily.

"Stand down," Luke ordered.

It was the newcomer's turn to raise his hands.

"Unbuckle and let 'er drop," Luke ordered. The newcomer did as he was told. "Now back away," Luke continued. He holstered his own weapon and scooped up McCray's rigging. "Why did you sneak into my camp?"

Dingus shook his head and shrugged. "I didn't mean to start somethin'. But with the war on Magic you just can't take anything for granted. I was hopin' to bag me a Wizard."

"War on Magic?" Luke repeated. "When did that start?"

Dingus chuckled. "Where you been? I know damn good and well yer a Warrior and yer gawddamn fast so you have to be involved in the war."

"I've been away a long time," Luke said impatiently. "Tell me about this war. Start at the beginning and be quick about it."

The interloper eyed Luke with open suspicion. "Ok. It wasn't too long after the Revolution. Everybody realized the Wizards had become way too powerful. Then we figgered out that pretty much every disaster that ever happened in Norland started with magic. The Council got together and abolished all forms of magic. Well, that didn't set too well with the Wizards and they started fightin' back. We been fightin' back and forth for years now. There's a standing kill order on all Wizards. Shoot on sight."

Luke felt physically sick. Sure, in a fit of anger he had drawn on Mathias, but he wasn't going to actually shoot him. Or was he? Would he have pulled the trigger if he'd had another second or two? The fact that he didn't really have the answer confused him even more.

"Who issued the order?" Luke asked.

"Lorn Graywullf," Dingus stated. "Who else?"

Luke's mind reeled. "Did you say Lorn Graywullf?"

"Yeah. General Lorn Graywullf, the leader of the Warriors," Dingus said. "Him and Lynch have been tryin' to kill each other for years."

It was not possible. His father was alive. Lynch was here. And they were mortal enemies. Luke shook Jeb.

"What is it?" Jeb asked crossly.

Luke motioned Zeke over and handed his shotgun to Jeb, "Cover him," he pointed to Dingus. "If he moves, just pull the trigger." He turned back to Dingus McCray. "He's barely even a 'prentice and he's half asleep. If you move he'll probably cut you in two."

Luke led Zeke away from the makeshift camp while Dingus stood like a statue.

"Something wrong?" Zeke asked.

"Everything," Luke replied. "We're lost. I have no idea where we are."

"Do you mean this isn't Norland?" Zeke demanded.

"Oh, it's Norland," Luke replied. "But it's nothing like the Norland I know. Remember what you said earlier about alternate Worlds? Well, I think you're right. We landed in a different reality. I went to your World looking for a Dark Wizard named Lynch. He's here. And so is my father."

"That's wonderful news!" Zeke said. "Isn't it?" he asked as he saw the expression on Luke's face.

"No," Luke said. "It's not. My father died when I was a boy. He and Lynch were closer than brothers but here, in this reality, they are sworn enemies trying to kill each other."

Zeke chewed his lip while he digested that information. Luke fished around in his duster pocket and slowly unwrapped a plug of tobacco. He bit a corner off and situated it in his cheek.

"Do you suppose we caused this?" he finally asked Zeke.

"I don't think so," Zeke replied. "In all the TV shows I ever watched, anything that changed occurred after someone meddled in time. I'm sorry, but that's all I have to go on. We just got here and everything is different."

"I need to learn a lot more about your World," Luke mused. "But I agree." He walked back to face McCray. "I want to see General Graywullf. Can you arrange that?"

"That's not a good idea," Zeke interrupted. "We should get out of here as quickly as we can, before we change something else."

"I can take you right to him," MaCray said. "Just give me back my guns." He jerked his head towards Zeke. "He might wanna come along. Smilin' Jake's there too, and by the look of him they could be twins."

"Smilin' Jake Sipowicz is there?" Zeke asked.

"Hell yes, he's there. Him, Ox and Bill McCurry," McCray replied.

Luke tried to swallow the lump that formed suddenly in his throat. His father and all the men who raised him like he was their own son were alive in this World. The men who made him what he was. Nostalgic memories hit him like a chest high, cold wave causing him to suck in his breath.

"We're going," Luke announced. "I'm keeping your guns," he told Ding. "Try something," he said. "And I'll blow your head off."

"You are one untrusting son of a bitch," McCray said. "We're *magii'ri* Warriors, and *magii'ri* Warriors stick together." He gestured to the East. "I got a string of horses behind that dune. I was bringin' in replacements for the Warriors when I smelled the smoke from your fire."

"Sounds good to me," Zeke grumbled. "Walkin' in this sand wears me out."

"We'll go at first light," Luke decided. "Jeb," he called, "get some sleep."

Jeb gratefully handed the shotgun back to Zeke and curled up in Luke's duster.

"I was supposed to have that remuda back to the General by dawn," Ding said.

"I guess yer gonna be late," Luke replied. "Cause I ain't gonna take a walk in the moonlight on your say so. After all," he drawled, "There just might be an ambush waitin' for us."

Ding shrugged. "Yer the boss." He stretched out and started snoring almost immediately.

Zeke waited for a few minutes as he studied Luke's face. The meager light from the fire cast shadows on the hard planes of the gunslinger's face. The scar from the cursed Warrior's bullet showed up as a stark white line on Luke's cheek.

"What are you thinking?" Zeke asked.

Luke shook his head. "Everything feels off," Luke said. "We got to be ready for anything."

He shook Jeb awake when the sun showed a faint glow on the eastern horizon. The boy grumbled and blinked his bleary eyes, but he packed up and was ready quickly. He scooped the contents of another tin can into his mouth as he plodded tiredly behind Luke. He drained a plastic water bottle he had scavenged and dropped it in the sand. Luke heard the small sound it made and stopped with a thoughtful expression on his face. He wheeled around and dropped to one knee and scooped up the bottle. He slipped an empty cartridge inside it and firmly screwed the cap back on while Zeke and Jeb watched curiously. Then he carelessly dropped it and resumed the march. No one spoke as they left the street and slogged through the loose sand. Luke kept a close eye on Ding, watching for even a hint of betrayal. The younger gunslinger's expression was serene. He showed no trace of anxiety as they topped the dune. In the hollow below there was a temporary rope corral holding ten horses. He turned back to Luke and shrugged.

"See?" he said. "Just like I said."

Luke nodded. "So far. Let's go."

After they were mounted, Luke guided his horse next to Zeke's.

"Watch for signs of an ambush," he said in a low tone. "Sun glaring off anything, dust, anything out of place."

Zeke nodded and looked around like his head was on a swivel, but the ride was uneventful. They reached the outskirts of a large encampment in two hours. A sentry challenged them, but Ding was expected and they were allowed to pass. They approached a large tent in the center of the camp. A man emerged and Luke sucked in his breath. He waited for Lorn Graywullf to acknowledge him. He felt the rake of the older man's gaze, but when he spoke it was to Ding.

"Who are they?" he asked. "And where are your guns?"

"He's *magii'ri*," Ding replied. He flushed red. "He's got my guns."

"So you bring him right into camp?" Lorn Graywullf's tone was caustic. "Who are you?" he demanded of Luke.

Luke's heart sank. A cold weight settled in his belly. The man he faced was Lorn Graywullf, but he was older than Luke remembered. His face was etched with deep lines and his eyes were sharp with bitterness. Luke also thought he detected a hint of cruelty which he had never seen on his father's face.

"He said his name was Graywullf," Ding offered.

Luke laughed, but it was forced. "I said Graywold," he corrected Ding. "You misheard me."

"Who did you 'prentice under?" Lorn asked.

Luke took a desperate chance. This man was Lorn Graywullf, but he was not his father. "Colin Laborteaux." He responded.

Lorn nodded as three men came out of the tent. Lorn didn't even look behind him. "A Trueblood *magii'ri* Warrior will know these three men. From left to right, what are their names?"

Luke didn't hesitate. "Smilin' Jake Sipowicz, Ox Duvay and Bill McCurry."

Zeke sat upon his horse staring in openmouthed astonishment.

"Yer partner better shut his mouth before he starts catchin' flies," Smilin' Jake said with a chuckle.

Luke casually rested his right hand on his thigh. Something was very wrong.

"Give Ding his guns," Lorn ordered. "Real slow."

"Sure," Luke agreed. "But I'm keepin' mine."

"Keep it holstered," Lorn suggested. He made up his mind. "Put the horses up and get some grub. The mess tent has bacon, and bacon, and biscuits. Help yourself. But don't wander off. I'm gonna have a chat with Colin before I decide if I can trust you."

Luke nodded. He breathed a sigh of relief as he turned his mount and rode towards a corral, following Ding.

"One more thing," Lorn said. Luke's skin crawled between his shoulders. "Who's the boy?"

"Just a boy," Luke replied. "Picked him up on the trail."

Lorn dismissed them by turning his back. "Watch the kid," he ordered Ding.

They rode to the corral and handed the horses over to the wranglers.

"She-it," Ding said with a laugh as they dismounted. "I thought the General was gonna smoke you."

Luke shook his head. "So did I. Does he do that often?"

"Don't cross him, that's all I can say," Ding replied. "Cross him once and there won't be another time. I was actually glad you disarmed me. Prob'ly the only thing that kept him from drawin' on me."

They followed the scent of frying bacon to a huge tent crowded with men sporting all manner of weapons. Luke felt saliva spurt into his mouth. He hadn't eaten since Zeke's kitchen in the other World. They joined the line and Luke watched in amusement as Jeb loaded his plate with bacon and biscuits and gravy. Then he shrugged as he and Zeke followed suit. They sat and washed the food down with huge tin cups of black coffee. Four horses thundered by. Ding grinned happily.

"There goes the General," he crowed. "Goin' to have a chat with Colin. He's camped about six miles away." He stared at Luke. "When he gets back there'll be Hell to pay if you were lyin'."

Luke shrugged nonchalantly as he chewed and swallowed. He took a big gulp of coffee before he replied.

"Where can we bunk?" he asked Ding. "I've been goin' short on shut eye for too long."

Ding led them to a tent and plopped down on a wooden stool outside the entry and began to whistle a mindless tune. Luke made sure he wasn't watching and held his finger to his lips in an exaggerated motion for silence.

"We can't stay here," he whispered to Zeke. "At best we have two hours, and I'd rather have an hour head start on the General. So we got one hour to get the Hell out of here." He knelt close to Jeb who regarded him with mixed curiosity and trepidation. "How sneaky can you be?" he asked.

Jeb's eyes lit up. "I lived under Dez's house for months and Mary Alice never even knew I was there. I could even sneak past the dogs," he bragged.

Luke grinned. "You can leave the dogs with us. I want you to sneak out that back tent flap and find a real good place to hide. When the commotion gets going, you meet us on the East side of camp and come a runnin'. Got it?"

"Sure, but what do I have to do?" Jeb asked.

"Don't get caught, and don't get found," Luke replied. "That's all."

Jeb nodded.

"Go," Luke ordered.

He watched as Jeb wiggled under the back wall of the tent. He gave the boy ten minutes.

"Act like your belly's hurtin'" he told Zeke. "I want Ding to come in and sound the alarm."

Zeke smiled. He laid down on a cot and rumpled the blankets. Then he started to moan loudly. The whistling stopped. Zeke moaned again.

"Gawddamn," he cursed in a choked voice.

"What's goin' on in there?" Ding said in a loud voice.

Zeke moaned and made a retching sound.

"You better not be goin' at each other," Ding warned as he flung back the tent flap.

Luke waited while Ding scanned the entire tent, then looked again.

"Where's the kid?" he demanded.

Luke looked surprised. He turned and searched the tent with his eyes.

"Well, I'll be," he declared.

Ding's face went white. "He can't be gone." His eyes went crazy. "The General will skin me for sure."

"Well," Luke drawled slowly. "He ain't here."

"Oh, Hell," Ding moaned.

Zeke matched his moan with an even louder one. He rolled to his side, gagged and spit on the floor. Ding looked disgusted.

"You two stay here," he decided. "Gawddammit. Why do I get the shit details?" He rushed from the tent and stormed back through the camp yelling orders left and right.

"Let's go," Luke ordered. "We gotta move fast. Come on, dogs." He ran from the tent towards the horse corral with Zeke on his heels. The entire camp seemed to be in an uproar. Even the horse wranglers were gone. Luke grabbed three horses that wore halters and muscled them to one side and handed the lead ropes to Zeke.

"Hold 'em," he said. "No matter what."

Zeke nodded and leaned back with his heels planted.

"Sick 'em, dogs!" Luke cried. "Hiii-yaw!" He shouted as he rushed the remaining horses. Milo, the half hound of Jeb's, rushed in growling and barking and snapped at one horse's heels. It bolted and took the rest of the herd with it, right through the rope fence. The horses stampeded away from the camp into the desert. Lorn grabbed two lead ropes from Zeke. He leaped astride one as Zeke mounted his. They raced to the east side of the camp. Luke wheeled his mount one way, then back the other.

"Jeb!" he bawled. "Where are you, boy?"

Jeb emerged from hiding almost under the horse. Luke leaned down low to that side and lowered his arm. Jeb grabbed it and Luke swung him astride the remaining horse. Luke drummed his heels into his mount's flanks and they raced out of camp. Jeb wrapped one hand in his horse's mane and hung on like a tick. Zeke threw back his head and laughed uproariously.

"Ha-ha-ha, by God! We showed them," he cried.

Luke shook his head as he focused on avoiding prairie dog holes and other obstacles as they galloped away from the pseudo *magii'ri* camp. It seemed Zeke's similarities with Smilin' Jake were more than skin deep. *They're both crazy*, Luke thought. His first instinct was to lead them away as fast as possible, and once they had put a few miles behind them he slowed the pace and began to formulate his next step.

They needed help. The entire World was different from the Norland he knew. It seemed he didn't even exist in this one. That thought made him pause and an ironic smile twisted his lips. Maybe he wasn't even necessary. In fact, maybe the World was a better place than the Norland he called home. He slowed the horses to a walk.

"I do believe we need a Wizard," he announced.

Jeb made a rude sound. "Huh. Them Wizards are nothin' but trouble. Outlawin' magic was the best thing the *magii'ri* ever did."

"Magic has been outlawed?" Luke asked in disbelief.

"I'm startin' to think you ain't *magii'ri*," Jeb replied. "Of course it's outlawed. That's what started this war in the first place."

"I'm *magii'ri*," Luke said roughly. "More than them wannabe's back in that camp."

"Arguing won't get us anywhere," Zeke interrupted. "I just want to know one thing. Can we get back to my World?"

Luke shrugged. "That's why we need a Wizard. And I know where Wizards go when they don't want to be found."

CHAPTER NINETEEN

Mathias poked a stick into the coals of the cooking fire and added a little kindling. He looked longingly at the staff leaning on a boulder nearby, then leaned down and blew on the coals until the flame caught. In the old days, he'd have simply struck a spell and had a fire instantly. *And then the Warriors sensors would go off and they'd have your location. Your last secure location,* he thought. He shook his head and sighed. Lynch came out of the cave and stretched. His back popped in three places. He took a step and winced at the tightness and pain in his hip.

"This is ridiculous," he observed. "We live like animals when we should be kings."

"We've gone over this before," Mathias argued.

"I know, I know," Lynch agreed. "Are you sure this is the right *when*?"

Mathias nodded. "Absolutely. They'll be here. This time, try not to provoke him. I'd rather not go through all this again, and we don't know how many tries we have left."

"It wasn't my fault," Lynch insisted. "He was madder than a wet cat when he got here, just looking for a fight."

"And you opened your big mouth and we both got shot," Mathias finished. "I remember."

A new voice rang out from the dense fir trees surrounding the campsite. "Don't move," it ordered calmly. "Don't touch the staff, and don't try to magic me."

It was Luke. He emerged like an apparition from the trees. He held both pistols at the ready.

"Behave yourself," Mathias admonished the Dark Wizard.

Lynch managed to appear hurt by the comment.

"I need one really good reason not to dust both of you," Luke announced. "And I never thought I'd say this," he said while pointedly staring at Mathias. "But you'd be my first target."

Mathias held out his hands in a placating manner. "I understand that you're upset," he began.

"Upset?" Luke shouted. "I am far beyond upset, Wizard. You denied me my only chance for a real family."

"You're not doing well," Lynch whispered to Mathias. "Want me to give it a try?"

"No," Mathias refused. He locked eyes with Luke. "I'm truly sorry. I was wrong."

Luke thumbed back the hammer of his right hand gun. "I'm not sure that's enough."

Mathias winced, expecting the roar of detonating powder and the sledgehammer thud of the bullet crashing through his body. It didn't come. Luke lowered the hammer and holstered both pistols.

"We're in a pickle," he explained as Zeke and Jeb came out of the trees.

"Oh shit, Warrior," Mathias cursed. "What did you do this time?"

"What do you mean?" Luke pressed.

"You have someone from yet another *when* and you have the boy with you," Mathias groaned. "Why?"

"I've had enough of this," Luke announced as he drew and cocked both pistols.

"Here it comes," Lynch said through gritted teeth.

"This boy is worth saving," Luke argued. "And Zeke too. I am. So are you," he said to Mathias. "And even *you,*" he said to Lynch. "We all are. So somebody better clear this shit up for me so we can get on with saving this World."

"Ok. Sit down and listen. I hope it sticks this time," Mathias said. "I can't explain it so I won't even try. But somehow, someone has meddled with the universe. That takes really, really big magic. Apparently there are many Worlds out there, all existing at different times with different situations. But the Worlds have become intertwined and inhabitants from other Worlds have, ummm… infected Worlds where they are not supposed to be. We, meaning Lynch, you, and I, have been here in this exact moment before. Every time, we send you back to try a different approach to fix things. None of them have worked."

"Wait," Luke said. "Do you mean I've been *here* before?"

"Many times," Lynch butted in.

"How many?" Luke demanded.

"Forty- seven," Mathias answered.

"This will be forty-eight," Lynch corrected.

"Whatever," Mathias replied. "The outcome is always the same."

"And what is that?" Luke asked.

"We use magic to send you back. That rings the little alarm bell for the Warriors, who storm our position and shoot us to death," Mathias replied.

"Gawddamn," Luke cursed in awe. "Forty-seven times, huh?"

"Yes," Lynch said. "And it hurts."

Mathias shook his head. "Please get it right this time. I can't put up with him any longer."

"You're gonna do it again?" Luke asked incredulously.

"What choice do we have?" Mathias answered.

"Use our magic to fight back," Lynch suggested.

Mathias sighed. "I can't do it even one more time," he pleaded with Luke. "You have to remember what we tell you this time. You have to do exactly what we tell you. Apparently, going through the gates scrambles your brains a little, and you've been forgetting the plan."

"And that is?" Luke asked.

"First," Mathias began. "Everyone must be in their own World, in their own *when*," he said. "That means Jeb can't go with you. He must stay here. This is his *when*."

"What will happen to him?" Luke asked.

"I can't say for certain," Mathias answered. "But I think he'll be alright."

"You think?" Luke asked. "What about Zeke? What happens to him?"

"I have no idea," Mathias replied.

Luke glanced at Lynch who merely shrugged. "We have every reason to believe you can change the course of all the Worlds. If you are successful, Zeke and Jack and Diane will at least have a chance."

Luke removed his hat and ran his hand through his hair.

"Take your time, Warrior," Lynch said sarcastically. "The *magii'ri* will be here soon enough. Then you can try to shoot your way out of this, just like you Warriors always do."

"I hate leavin' that kid,' Luke replied.

"I'll be alright," Jeb insisted.

"I'd really rather not die here," Zeke interrupted. "So maybe we can hurry this up a bit?"

"Alright, I'll do it," Luke decided. "Tell me what to do."

Lynch stepped forward. He held out a shiny, rounded piece of polished granite.

"Keep this talisman with you," he told Luke. "We have enchanted it with magic to help you remember what to do."

Luke reluctantly held it up and inspected it dubiously.

"It would be best if you swallowed it," Mathias suggested. He held out a flask of water. Luke hesitated. "Forty-seven times, gunslinger," Mathias reminded him.

"Forty-eight comin' up," Lynch said.

Luke took the flask, popped the talisman in his mouth and washed it down with tepid water. He gagged a little and swallowed noisily. He actually felt it when the talisman landed in his belly. Images of events in the past and present flooded his mind, along with many he couldn't place. But there was one moment in time that stood out, and suddenly he knew what to do.

"I'm ready," he announced. "Where's the gate?"

"You're standing in it," Lynch laughed. "We were gonna send you back whether you agreed or not."

He and Mathias chanted a spell. Zeke glanced about fearfully and edged a little closer to Luke. An arch appeared. Luke realized he had seen in in Zeke's World. The his vision went dark and the whole world began to spin. It stopped suddenly. He opened his eyes and looked around.

"Well," he announced to Zeke, "we're not in Norland anymore."

"What are you talkin' about?" Zeke demanded. "I'm telling you, we have to get off the street and lay low. That stupid kid is callin' the Watchers right to us."

Luke shook his head as if the clear it. The stupid kid. The one with the glowing thing in his hands. He was back on the streets of Tuxin. *Of course!* He ran back to the kid, who shrank away in far of the towering, lean gunslinger in his face. Luke stripped the kids' phone away from his hands, slammed it on the concrete sidewalk and ground his bootheel down on it.

"Hey man, that was my phone!" the kid accused. "You can't do that!"

Luke whirled back to face him as he pulled his duster back. The kid's eyes went round at the sight of Luke's well worn pistols jutting from their holsters.

"Holy shit!" he said. "I don't want no trouble, man." He backed away with his hands at shoulder height.

Luke scooped up the mangled phone and dropped it into a nearby storm drain. He nodded in satisfaction when he heard it splash in the putrid water below.

"That won't do any good," Zeke commented. "Them things are waterproof and damn near indestructible."

Luke ignored him. He cocked his head to one side and listened. "Ya hear that" he asked. "That water's moving. That thing will be in the nearest river before they find it. All we have to do is go in the opposite direction."

Zeke nodded in approval. "It just might work."

CHAPTER TWENTY

"Are you sure this is the right house?" Luke demanded.

He and Zeke stood in the deepest shadows looking at the run down house. The windows were open and Quiet Riot's "Bang Your Head" issued forth at such a volume they could actually feel the bass. The front yard was strewn with trash, mostly pizza boxes, fast food containers and empty beer cartons. A mixed breed hound dog slept in the desultory light that came through the open front door. Zeke checked the numbers he had written on a scrap of paper and stuffed in his shirt pocket.

He shrugged. "Yep. This is it."

Luke shook his head. The dog presented a possible problem, but the music was so loud he doubted anyone inside would even know if the dog barked. Then he recognized the dog. It was Milo. He reached his decision.

"Come on," he said.

They walked straight up the uneven sidewalk. The dog raised its head and thumped his tail on the porch. Luke led the way inside and followed the source of the music downstairs. He stopped at the bottom of the stairs and watched Lynch feverishly mixing up some kind of concoction for a full minute. The dog stood patiently behind Zeke. Finally, Luke walked right up behind Lynch. Zeke yanked the power cord for the radio out of the wall socket and Lynch whirled around to look right down the muzzle of Luke's pistol.

"Hello, Lynch," he said.

"Hello, Luke," Lynch replied without missing a beat. "This isn't the first time I've looked down the barrel of a gun held by a

Graywullf." He gave the dog a scathing look. "Some watchdog you are. So," he said as if they hadn't been separated by time and space for years, "I'm guessing you were the disturbance at the gate that has Timon up in arms."

He continued mixing ingredients until one glass beaker erupted in flames. He grimaced and hastily doused it with water, which only spread the flames. Then he threw a ratty old blanket over it, wrapped it up and tossed it on the floor well away from the other glass beakers on the bench. He stomped it until the flames went out.

"We should go upstairs," he said. "I'm not sure what those fumes will do to us."

They retreated upstairs, but not before Lynch plugged the radio back in and turned the volume down. The hound dog was already back out on the porch. Lynch grabbed a six pack of beer from a filthy refrigerator and led them out to join the dog. He handed each of them a bottle and poured a generous amount in a battered pie plate for the dog.

Luke sighed. He introduced Zeke and Lynch. "Zeke Sipowicz, meet the Dark Wizard Lynch."

"Sipowicz, eh?" Lynch said "I see Smilin' Jake in you. So, Graywullf, what brings you to this World?"

Luke chuckled. "Does anything surprise you, Lynch?" He didn't wait for an answer. "Mathias thinks he has found a way to end all this," he gestured widely.

"I've got that covered," Lynch replied. "I'm building a bomb. I'm gonna blow myself and Timon to bits. Yessir, gonna go out just like Smilin' Jake did, in a blaze of glory."

"What about the Sky Rider, and your brother, and our entire World?" Luke said in disbelief. "If you kill Timon here it won't change anything there."

"There's no quit in you, is there?" Lynch said in response. "Just like your father, always following the Code and doing the honorable thing." He took a long drink and belched loudly. "I've tried to get back a hundred times. I simply can't power up my magicometer enough to open the portal, nab Timon, and get through with the weapons we need. It can't be done."

"Mathias says it can," Luke said as he pulled the Book of Runes from Lynch's pack.

"I read that from cover to cover," Lynch said dismissively.

Luke lost patience. "Listen to me. I have to get back to Norland. Jacob Grimwullf is actually my son, and he is the Dragonspawn." He paused to judge the effect of that news upon the Dark Wizard. He saw amazement.

Lynch sank down on a filthy lawn chair. "Well, I'll be damned." He chuckled. He shook his head and erupted in gales of laughter. He laughed until tears were streaming down his cheeks and he gasped for breath. Finally, he calmed himself enough to speak. "Oh, this is rich! The good Wizard who dedicated his life to serve the Light has pulled off a scheme that makes me look like a rank amateur." He studied Luke. "You really didn't know, did you? Oh, by the gods, you didn't! Doesn't that make you feel stupid?"

"Not helping, Lynch," Luke advised.

"Oh, of course," Lynch agreed. "That was uncalled for." He shook his head again. "I just can't believe Mathias Bulwyn actually pulled this off."

"Well, Lynch," Luke drawled. "I reckon if he's smart enough to pull that off, then he could probably figger out a way to beat Timon and the Wilding, too."

Lynch's expression became cunning. "I'll be gawddamned. You're right." He took a deep breath. "Tell me what the good Wizard has planned."

Luke summarized everything Mathias had told him, at least what he could remember, emphasizing that the Book had to be read with a pure heart. Lynch held up a hand at that news.

"You know I can't do that," he protested. "I'm a little too far gone down the Dark path to be turning back now. But maybe the kid can read it for me."

"Where is Jeb?" Luke said. "I should have asked earlier, but you almost blew up the house and all."

"I did no such thing," Lynch replied indignantly. "Jeb is close by. Actually, he should be here very soon."

"How's he doing?" Luke asked. "Is he alright?"

"He's fine," Lynch said. "He got in with a group of boys about his age, some kind of Dragon gang or clan or something."

"Lynch!" Luke said in a threatening manner. "You're supposed to be taking care of him."

"Don't blame me," Lynch protested. "I'm no father figure. I didn't ask to be a role model. The kid is fine, it's just a phase. Besides, there are no Dragons in this World."

Luke couldn't even respond. Zeke looked from one to the other and simply shook his head. Now he knew how Luke felt stepping into a new World. He had no idea what was going on. Lynch fidgeted uncomfortably until a quail called from the darkness. He brightened up immediately.

"Come on up," he called loudly.

Jeb walked into the ring of light thrown by the bare bulb on the porch followed by Colin. Luke leaped to his feet and drew both pistols before anyone else could even move. He trained both of them on Colin's chest.

"Give me one reason not to blow your treasonous guts out," he hissed.

Jeb stepped to one side. Colin held his hands at chest height, palms out.

Lynch grinned. "He's workin' with us, Graywullf."

Luke didn't waver. "Since when? We saw him with Timon Blackhelm last night."

"Not long," Lynch admitted. "But he's working a doublecross on ol' Timon. Put the guns down, Graywullf. He's in our camp now."

"It's true," Colin interjected. He met Luke's gaze. "I have a family in Norland," he said simply. "Timon is holding them, using them for leverage. He's been blackmailing me for years. But now I see that we are all doomed unless we stop Timon Blackhelm once and for all."

Relief coursed through Luke. He slowly lowered his pistols and holstered them. Zeke very casually tucked his shotgun back out of sight under his duster.

"Well," Lynch said brightly. "The gang's all here. Let's make plans."

Luke descended the steps and wrapped Jeb in a bear hug.

"It's good to see you, boy," he said.

Jeb awkwardly returned the hug and hastily stepped back.

"I never thought I'd see you again," Jeb said.

"Same here," Luke admitted. "It's been years." He turned to Colin. "I'm mighty glad I didn't have to shoot you, Colin."

"So am I," Colin replied with a sincere smile. "You might be even faster than I remember."

"Has Lynch been takin' care of you?" Luke asked Jeb.

Jeb shrugged. "We eat regular. That's about it."

Luke shot Lynch a warning glance.

"Well," Lynch said hastily. "We have a lot to do. Best get to it."

The group went back inside. Luke introduced Zeke to Jeb and Colin. Then he outlined Mathias' plan once again. When he was done, dubious silence filled the room. Luke looked from one face to another, hoping to get some reassurance that Mathias' plan wasn't simply fantasy.

"It could work," Colin finally said. "I can get you within about six hundred yards. Any closer and he would sense you. Can you pull that shot off?"

"I can," Luke guaranteed.

Lynch rubbed a palm over his bristly cheeks. He started to speak, stopped, and said, "Colin, will a bullet drop him?"

Colin shrugged. "A normal bullet probably won't do it. But," he added, "we have this one." He slipped his enchanted cartridge from his belt and held it out in his palm. "Timon insists I pack your guns from Norland, Luke. I'd give 'em back to you but he'd know right away."

Lynch nodded excitedly. "That would do it! But we have to pull the bullet and reload it in a rifle cartridge. And we need a rifle."

"Umm," Zeke said. "Like I told Luke, I know a guy who can probably get us a rifle. What caliber?"

".45-90," Colin said quickly. "The bullet is .45 caliber, and we need a pretty good dose of powder behind it."

"Even if we get the rifle," Zeke said, "we have to find someone who can reload it for us."

"Lynch knows somebody," Jeb interrupted.

Lynch shook his head. "No, I don't."

Jeb stared at him. "Yes, you do. And you know where we have to go to recharge your magicometer to open the portal. You just have to swallow your pride and ask for help."

Lynch cast a murderous glance Jeb's way while everyone watched expectantly.

"It's Jack and Diane," Jeb explained. "She chose Jack over Lynch and he never forgot it. They live near Roswell. There's gonna be a shitload of people who believe in magic coming to Roswell real soon. They're gonna gather at the site of the spaceship crash and make plans on storming Area 51."

"That would do it," Zeke said. "This Jack, is he a former sheriff from New Mexico?"

"One and the same," Lynch replied.

"Well, then we're all on the same page," Zeke said. "I worked with Jack when I was a deputy. I know for a fact he's got several old breechloader rifles and reloading equipment. He's a prepper, too," he added happily.

"We still have to get to Roswell, get the rifle and ammo, sight it in and get back here before Saturday," Lynch said. "And we have to get to the believers to harvest a truckload of magic and open the portal after Luke pulls off a six hundred yard shot."

"I can get a car," Colin suggested. "I'm supposed to go to Roswell and check things out. Timon's heard that rumor about Area 51, but nothing is showing up on his sensors."

Luke nodded. "It's coming together."

CHAPTER TWENTY-ONE

Mathias and Dorro sat on opposite sides of a tiny campfire. Both slowly sipped the last of their coffee after a meager supper of trailbread, dried meat and a small, moldy block of cheese. The Wilding continued unabated, gaining momentum with each passing day. Beastsoldiers roamed about during the brightness of day, no longer confined to the hours of darkness. Ogres and trolls and Nightriders congregated without fear. Most of the villages they had come to were deserted and Mathias had the distinct feeling they were being herded together like cattle to slaughter. He knew his companion would fight to his last breath, as would he, but the end felt inevitable. They were going to lose. Dorro shook the last crumbs of tobacco from his pouch and tamped them into his pipe. Mathias gave him a stern glance. Dorro stared back defiantly and lit his pipe.

"You know our enemies will smell that from miles away," Mathias said.

"Our enemies know exactly where we are," Dorro replied. "And you know that. They are driving us wherever they desire, and if I'm gonna die tomorrow I'm gonna enjoy one last pipe before I do."

Mathias had no argument for that. Pushing Luke through the portal had been a huge gamble and it looked like it was not going to pay off.

"I'm curious," Dorro said. "If we caught up to Jacob tomorrow, what would you do?"

"He has left me no choice," Mathias replied. "I have to put him down."

Dorro chuckled. "Is that even possible?"

Mathias shrugged. "I don't know. But he chose his side."

A stone rolled outside the ring of firelight. Dorro simply dove to one side, pipe firmly clenched in his teeth, and grabbed his axe. He lunged to his feet and whirled around. Mathias sat as if frozen. For a split second Dorro thought Luke may have returned, but the person who held a knife to Mathias' throat was too short and slender to be the Warrior. Then Dorro realized the figure dressed in a duster, jeans and a broad brimmed hat was a woman.

"You will not kill Jacob," La'Nay hissed.

"La'Nay?" Mathias gasped.

The Dragonwitch released Mathias and took a seat by the fire. Mathias and Dorro both openly stared at her. A pistol jutted out from her hip and stubby brass cartridges gleamed in the firelight. Her belt bristled with knives. She had tied her hair back and her face was leaner and more angular.

"Is there more coffee?" La'Nay asked.

Dorro gave her the last cup from the pot. La'Nay took a slow sip and sighed. It was weak, but it was hot and it was coffee. Dorro hastened to hand her a wafer of trailbread and a slice of cheese. She nodded her thanks and bit off a corner.

"We thought you were dead," Mathias said. "What are you doing here?"

"I'm not dead yet, as you can see," La'Nay replied. "And I'm here to save you from making yet another mistake, Mathias."

"What are you talking about?" Mathias demanded.

"I heard you talking about killing Jacob," La'Nay said. "You owe it to him, as do I, to fight for him until your last breath. You will not give up and try to take the easy way out, Mathias. I begged you to let me nurture him, to show him the way of the *magii'ri*, but you knew best. As always," she added venomously. "Now look where we are."

Mathias looked miserable.

"But," La'Nay continued. "As I have done before, I pulled your ass out of the fire. I did what I should have done so long ago. I told Jacob he is the Dragonspawn, and I am teaching him to control the Beast inside him."

"Then why have he and Slagg joined forces to destroy Norland?" Mathias demanded.

"Things are not always as they appear," La'Nay replied. "I have faith in Jacob. If he persuades Slagg to attack an enemy, there is a legitimate reason."

Mathias stared in disbelief. "Are you trying to tell me Jacob is using Slagg?"

"That's exactly what I'm telling you," La'Nay responded. "It was his idea. I tried to talk him out of it. But he thought using Slagg to eliminate some of the true enemies of Norland might buy us enough time to stop the Wilding."

"That is an incredibly dangerous and foolhardy plan," Mathias argued. "If the Sky Rider suspects Jacob at any time, he'll kill him. No questions asked."

"You were planning that very action yourself not ten minutes ago," La'Nay retorted.

"When I thought Jacob had gone to the Dark side, yes," Mathias admitted. "What of the Dragon?" he asked. "Once you felt a kinship to Slagg. You served him."

"I served the ancient race of Dragons," La'Nay corrected. "Slagg has become nothing more than a perverted shell of the true Sky Rider. He must be destroyed."

Dorro watched them both as if they were mad. "You both speak as if we have a chance to accomplish either task," he said. "We have no chance against the Sky Rider or the Dragonspawn."

La'Nay agreed. "You're right. We can't fight both of them. But I believe Jacob is true to the Code and the Light. He is the son of two Trueblood *magii'ri* and he will honor the Code. He can defeat Slagg." She turned back to Mathias. "He found the Black Arrow, but then it was lost. He was made a prisoner and a slave, even if for a very short time. He's been through much, Mathias. He found Joseph of Ead by chance, and rescued him. He knows Joseph is not his father."

Mathias was silent as he digested that information. Finally, he spoke. "Can he beat Slagg without the Black Arrow?"

"Not without our help. If we can find the Arrow, he could use it to slay the Sky Rider. He will be true to his father." She gave Mathias a hard glance. "Speaking of Luke, where is he?"

"I saw one last chance to stop this madness and I took it," Mathias replied. "I sent him to the other World to bring Timon back."

"And did you tell him he has a son?" La'Nay asked.

"I did," Mathias replied.

"Well," La'Nay said after a pause. "At least you did that, albeit fifteen years too late."

"Everything I have done, I did for Norland," Mathias said in his defense.

"I know," La'Nay replied in a softer tone. "Even at the expense of your friendships. But who am I to criticize? I devoted my life to the creation of the very being you have set out to destroy."

"We have both made mistakes," Mathias agreed. "If I am still alive when he returns, Luke may make me pay for mine with my life. If that is so, I won't fight him."

"Will he return?" La'Nay asked.

"You know him," Mathias answered. "I told him Jacob is his son. Nothing will stop him from finding his way back."

La'Nay considered that. She nodded. "I only hope he's not too late." She cast a sly glance at Mathias. "You see, I told Jacob he's Luke's son. He a little pissed off at you, Mathias."

CHAPTER TWENTY-TWO

Colin pulled up at dusk in a Cadillac. They stowed Luke's sword and Zeke's shotgun in the trunk, followed by several dusters and assorted gunbelts, and finally their distinctive hats. Luke sat in the front with Colin while Jeb, Zeke and Lynch piled in the back. Milo, the half hound, half pit bull mongrel, lounged on the porch in a shaft of sunlight.

"I can drive," Lynch said as he was squeezing into the back seat.

"Oh, hell no," Colin replied. "I saw the reports on all your wrecks, right before I shredded 'em."

"Alright," Lynch agreed. "But you have to make one stop on our way. I know a guy that's got something we need."

Colin shrugged. "Tell me which way to go, but hurry it up. We're on a tight schedule."

Lynch led them down a myriad of nearly identical streets until Luke was totally lost. Finally, after thirty minutes of twisting and turning, he directed Colin to park on a side street.

"You all wait in the car," he ordered. "I'll be back in a few."

"This better be important," Colin demanded.

Lynch exited the car and slammed the door carelessly. "It is," he said. Then he disappeared down an alley.

"What's he after?" Luke asked Jeb.

"Beats me," Jeb replied with a shrug.

Colin left the car idling and turned on the air conditioning. Passerby stared curiously at the luxury car purring at the curb, but none had the courage to approach. The four passengers fidgeted and squirmed in their seats until Lynch finally appeared carrying a brown paper bag and a twelve pack of Busch Lite beer.

He slid back in the rear seat and a maddeningly delicious aroma filled the car. The paper bag rustled as Lynch dug around in it, then he removed something and more paper rustled as he opened it. Then there was a loud crunch as the other four passengers stared at Lynch with open animosity.

"What?" Lynch mumbled around a mouthful of food. "I wanted tacos."

"Gawddammit, Lynch," Colin threatened. "If you make us too late…"

"I brought enough for everyone," Lynch offered. "That's what took so long. Hell, I got twenty of 'em."

"Hand 'em over," Colin demanded. He slipped the car in drive and accelerated smoothly up to fifty miles per hour.

"Is that tank meat?" Zeke asked.

The other three stopped eating immediately.

"Nope," Lynch assured him. "I do not eat tank meat. This is real Grade A beef. Like I said, I know a guy. Same guy runs a black market fast food chain through the whole Southwest. That's where me and the kid got our burgers and pizza, too."

Colin navigated his way to the interstate and the car was filled with the sound of crunching taco shells and popping bottle caps until the food and beer was consumed.

"I was wondering," Lynch started to say.

"Driver gets to choose the music," Colin interrupted. He turned the radio on and cranked up the volume. Def Leppard's "Pour Some Sugar on Me" rattled the windows. Colin had the entire "Pyromania" album on compact disc and he played it continuously through the desert. After the second continuous play of the entire album, Jeb reached over the font seat and hit the power button. They drove on in silence for several hours until Lynch tapped Colin on the shoulder.

"I gotta take a piss," he announced.

"I'm not surprised," Colin replied. "You hogged most of the beer."

But he did pull over and everyone piled out. Empty beer bottles rolled out of the floorboards as they lined the shoulder of the road. Lynch yawned and stretched with both arms over his head. Everyone scattered.

"Good grief, Lynch," Colin complained. "Yer peeing all over the place."

"Oh," Lynch exclaimed with a laugh. "Sorry. I wasn't paying attention."

Before they climbed back in the car, Zeke stopped Luke. "This bunch is gonna save the World?" he asked quietly.

"It's the best I could do in a hurry," Luke said.

They all piled back in the car. After a few minutes of desultory conversation most of the passengers either slept or feigned sleep. Finally, as they neared Roswell, Jeb tapped Colin on the shoulder and pointed to an exit. Colin nodded and took the exit, tires squealing. He skidded to a stop in a convenience store parking lot and killed the engine. Silence ensued.

"I'm driving back," Lynch announced.

"Fine," Colin replied. "Where's this Jack feller?"

Lynch shrugged and looked out his window. Jeb shook his head.

"We're close," he said. "Better walk. If he sees a car he'll run for sure."

They grabbed their weapons and gear from the trunk. Luke offered Lynch his pack, but Lynch just shrugged.

"You keep it," he said with a careless wave of his hand.

"What about these?" Jeb asked, as he held up the captured pistols from the fallen gunslingers.

"You take one," Luke directed. He held the other out to Lynch. "You want this?"

Again, Lynch shrugged. "I never had much use for one," he admitted. But he took it and strapped it on out of sight beneath his duster.

"What about the tomahawk?" Luke asked.

"You keep that," Lynch advised. "I've seen you use that. It's in good hands."

Jeb led the way down back alleys and side streets to a neatly painted, little pink house with a white picket fence. A detached garage sat about fifty feet behind the house. As they stood in the shadows of a perfectly manicured hedge, Jack left the house and entered the garage. Lynch showed little interest.

"Good grief, Lynch," Luke said. "Pull your head outta your ass and do something. It's time to put up or die trying. Otherwise," he flipped his duster back from his pistols, "I'll smoke you right here."

Lynch reacted as if he'd been slapped in the face. There was no mercy in the younger Warrior's eyes. "You're right," he said. "It's time to deal the final hand."

He drew a deep breath and led the way down to the garage. He slipped the door open and all five men entered silently. Jack Parsons turned away from his workbench. His mouth worked like a fish out of water.

"Oh, shit," he finally managed to drawl.

After he recovered from his original shock, he shook hands all around. Zeke introduced himself. Jack sank back on a stool and looked at the group in front of him.

"I knew this day would come," he said. "I always told Diane that our past would catch up to us."

"We need your help," Luke said. "We have a plan to take Timon Blackhelm out of power once and for all. Can we count on you?"

Jack looked from face to face once again. He saw nothing but steely eyed determination. It was obvious this was the final hand. These men would not stop until they'd won or died trying.

"What do you need?" he asked.

After listening carefully to their needs, Jack opened a ramshackle cabinet to reveal a steel gun safe. He dialed the combination and pulled out two breech loading rifles. Luke gratefully took one and shouldered it. Then he lowered it and admired the craftsmanship. The thirty two inch barrel gleamed in the light cast from a bare one hundred watt bulb that hung overhead. The stock was oil rubbed walnut, and it came with an adjustable elevation rear sight, which Jack was quick to point out.

"Elevation adjustments out to eight hundred yards," he said proudly. "Otherwise you could just use Kentucky windage, I guess."

That statement was met with blank stares by everyone except Zeke.

"That means you just guess how high to hold it," he explained.

"This'll do," Luke announced.

"So," Lynch said as casually as he could muster, "Where is Diane?"

"Working," Jack replied without hesitation. "At the cannery, where she swore she'd never work again. Remember?"

Lynch nodded. "We're gonna set things right."

Several hours later, Jack proudly showed them a batch of fifty dull brass cartridges topped with identical hard cast lead bullets.

"I weighed that special bullet you have," he explained. "These are all within a few tenths of a grain of that same weight. They'll shoot the same, I guarantee it. Now you got enough to practice a bit." He held up one single cartridge loaded in a shell casing that was colored black. "This is your magic bullet," he said with just a trace of a smile.

"We're beholden to you, Jack," Luke said as he stowed the special bullet in an inside pocket in his duster.

"If what you have planned sets things right, then I can't do enough to help you," Jack replied. "This ol' World is so screwed up, something has to change. I'm glad to do my part."

"Are you set?" Colin asked.

"All set," Luke replied.

"Good," Colin said. "So, me, Lynch and Jeb will head back to Tucson. Hopefully, if Timon has been watching them, that'll throw him off your trail. And you and Zeke will stay here, so you can sight in the rifle. I'll be back in three days. Right?"

"That's the plan," Luke agreed.

Luke shook hands with Jeb. "Take care of yourself," he said as they left.

Jeb grinned. "I always do."

"Come on," Colin urged. "We're gonna have to drive all night to get back."

The three walked down the street. Lynch was already arguing that he should get to drive back. Luke simply shook his head.

CHAPTER TWENTY-THREE

The day of the rally for Timon arrived. As Lynch had predicted, the town square filled up quickly with Blackhelm supporters. Colin had driven back into town the night before with Lynch and Jeb. He smuggled Luke and Lynch into the bell tower of the local church, which had been deserted for years. As the sun rose, Luke sighted down the long barrel at a trash can, then the podium Timon was to speak behind, and finally at a uniformed security guard. Satisfied with his estimate of the range, he settled down to wait.

"I make it out to be a shade over six hundred yards," Lynch said.

"Ya think?" Luke asked. "I'm not sure. Looks like a shade under to me."

"Nope," Lynch said assuredly. "It's six-fifty. Hold on his chin."

"If you say so," Luke agreed.

"There's Colin," Lynch said excitedly. "It's time. Kill him, Graywullf. Kill him for all of us."

"Uh-huh," Luke agreed. He rolled his tobacco in his jaws and spat. He shouldered the long rifle and sighted at the podium. The rifle felt like a part of him. They were one weapon of destruction with one purpose. Kill Timon Blackhelm. *'Wait,'* A tiny thought gnawed at the edge of his brain. Colin looked around nervously.

"Calm down," Lynch said as if the big man could hear him. "Don't give us away." He stared through the spyglass in his hands. "There's a breeze, left to right."

"Not enough to worry about," Luke assured him.

"Remember, hold on his chin," Lynch reminded him.

Luke gave a tiny nod. The crowd cheered loudly. Timon entered the stage from the rear. As he did, Jeb stepped into the clear in the front of the crowd. Luke perched Timon's chin on top of the front post sight and began to apply pressure. Timon froze for a split second. At that moment, Luke knew he had been there before. He paused for a second, adjusted his sight picture, then squeezed the trigger. The heavy rifle bucked in his hands as two hundred and twenty grains of lead were sent downrange at almost three thousand feet per second. He lost his sight picture from the recoil, but Luke was certain the shot went true.

"He's down!" Lynch said excitedly. "Did you hold on his chin?"

Luke grunted an unintelligible reply. He reloaded the big rifle. A security guard ran towards Timon's fallen form and Luke shot him through the body. As he reloaded again, Luke saw Colin draw and fire into a group of three more Blackhelm men. Jeb ran to Timon and began to fasten the handcuffs on his wrists. Zeke stood guard, shotgun at the ready. The crowd panicked. Chaos ensued.

"Come on, Jeb," Luke implored.

"Behind the trash can," Lynch said.

Luke grinned. He sighted and fired. The heavy, hard cast lead bullet penetrated the trash can completely and hit the Blackhelm man behind it. Timon's men were scattering. Jeb stood and waved both hands in the air.

"Time to go," Lynch announced.

They ran down the stairs two at a time and crossed the distance to the stage in a few minutes. Colin and Jeb stood over Timon. Zeke still stood guard. Luke and Lynch approached Timon.

"Gawddamnit, Graywullf," Lynch cursed. "You missed. I told you to hold on his chin."

"I hit right where I aimed," Luke stated. "It was six hundred yards."

Timon groaned and the entire group held their breath. His eyes fluttered open.

"Lynchie," he sneered through his gritted, blood stained teeth. "You'll pay for this." He muttered the words of a spell. Lynch actually held his hands up to ward off the spell.

"I told you to kill him," Lynch growled.

Luke, Lynch and Colin looked from one to another. Luke shrugged.

"I don't feel a damn thing," Luke said.

"Me neither," Colin agreed. A huge smile lit up his face. "So far, so good."

"Can I kill him? Please?" Lynch begged.

"That's not the plan," Luke asserted.

"Then let's get on with it," Lynch said. "We don't have all day."

Colin threw Timon across his shoulders as if he were a child. Timon moaned in agony.

"Hurts, don't it?" Lynch asked. "If Graywullf had held where I told him your head would be gone."

Colin looked questioningly at Luke, who simply shrugged and nodded.

"Get the car, Jeb," Luke said. Jeb ran off and returned a minute later driving the Cadillac. Milo, the half breed hound dog, sat happily on the seat beside him. The car squealed to a stop and Jeb popped open the trunk. Colin unceremoniously dumped Timon's prostrate form in the trunk and slammed the lid.

"Slide over," Lynch ordered.

Jeb gave Lynch an irritated look but slid to the center of the front seat, pushing the dog over as he did. Luke jumped in the passenger side while Zeke and Colin climbed in the back.

"Hang on," Lynch suggested.

They made the thirteen hour drive to Hiko in eleven hours, stopping only once. There was no sign of pursuit. As they coasted into town on fumes, Lynch pulled the car over and rubbed his eyes. He waited until Luke and Colin got out and stood at the rear of the car before he popped the trunk open. Luke and Colin both stepped back involuntarily, expecting an attack of some sort, but none came. They both leaned in.

"Well?" Lynch asked as he exited the driver's seat. "Is he alive or not?"

"He's alive," Luke replied. "Barely," he added.

"Barely alive is enough," Lynch said. "As long as he lasts until we get back to Norland."

"He'd be dead as a post if I'd held where you told me," Luke reminded the Dark Wizard.

"Yep," Lynch agreed. "And this farce would be over. But since he's alive I guess we'd better play it out."

"Where's your driver?" Luke asked.

A huge military truck rounded a corner up the block, tires squealing. Black smoke rolled from the exhaust pipes as the driver accelerated straight for them. Luke flipped his duster back behind the butts of his pistols. Zeke glanced at him and readied his shotgun.

"Right on time," Colin said. "Here's our ride."

The truck rocked to a stop and Ray Benson jumped out.

"What's up, Ray?" Colin asked. "You weren't supposed to be driving."

"Change of plans," Ray replied. He looked at Timon. "Is he alive?"

"Barely," Luke and Lynch said in unison.

They loaded Timon in the back with their weapons and gear and strapped him down. Colin climbed in the driver seat while the rest of the group climbed in the back. Milo jumped in and immediately turned back to leap up and place his front paws on the tailgate, tongue lolling from his happily grinning jaws. Colin directed Ray to the passenger side.

"It won't do for the future president to be seen driving a vehicle used in a kidnapping," he explained. "Strap in," he yelled to the passengers in the back. "Ray said the perimeter fence is guarded. It might get rough."

Colin accelerated smoothly through the gears, revving the big diesel up high enough to make the turbocharger whine.

"Here we go," Lynch said happily.

Colin pushed the big truck hard. They fairly flew down the road. In minutes they came to a series of military installation warning signs. Colin pressed harder on the accelerator, squeezing every drop of speed he could out of the truck. In the distance he saw a gate across the road. Armed men flanked it.

"Get down!" he yelled. "We're gonna take fire!"

Bullets whined off the pavement and ricocheted off the sheet metal of the truck. Divots appeared as if by magic in the windshield. The guards pulled a sedan across the road. Colin made no effort to slow down. He plowed through the gate as guards dove to the sides and struck the car dead on. He pushed it down the road for a hundred feet before it slid to one side. He drove another half mile and the road suddenly dipped downward. A quarter mile ahead and some fifty feet deeper in the desert sand stood a huge set of steel doors. Berms of sand held in place by reinforced concrete lined the roadway.

"What now?" Colin asked Ray.

"Go, go!" Ray shouted. "Head for the doors!"

"They better open," Colin said through gritted teeth.

Just as it seemed they would smash into the doors they swung inward allowing them to pass. As soon as they were inside, the doors swung shut. Colin slammed on the brakes and skidded to a stop. He killed the engine. Silence ensued for a long minute, followed by the sound of one pair of hands clapping. Another joined in, then another and another as a crowd erupted in applause. Colin climbed down and looked around.

"Who are all these people?" he demanded.

Ray grinned. "We needed a safe place to hide. Couldn't have a bunch of believers discovered by Timon at the last second, could we?"

Inside the truck bed, Luke and Jeb picked themselves up off the floor. Zeke grinned as he unbuckled his seat belt, which was the only thing that kept him from joining them on the floor. Lynch leaned back, his eyes close, as he basked in an atmosphere absolutely soaked in magic. He sucked it in, absorbing all the magical power he could hold.

"Oh…yeah," he whispered. His magicometer was pegged on the high side.

Luke leaned in close to Timon. The Dark Wizard's eyes opened. He could sense the potential magical power floating about as well as Lynch could.

"Better hope these handcuffs hold, boy," Timon warned. "If I get loose, you're history. All of you."

Luke smiled and clubbed Timon across the face with his rifle butt. Lynch laughed as eager helpers climbed into the truck to unload the now unconscious Timon. Lynch's laughter was abruptly cut short by Diane's appearance. They locked gazes for a moment before Lynch spoke.

"Jack said you were working at the chile plant," he said. "What are you doing here?"

Diane shrugged. "What else could I do, Lynch? I told Jack to lie to you and to anyone else who came looking for me. I've been part of the resistance since its inception."

Lynch stared at the crowd of people gathered around the truck. "This is the resistance? A bunch of people waiting for aliens to swoop down out of the sky and take them away?"

"Don't put us down, Lynch," Diane warned. "How's your little magicometer doing right now?"

Lynch laughed. "My magicometer is anything but little, and it's running full, thank you."

"You're charged up because of us," Diane reminded him. "Hop down from there and let me give you the dime tour."

Colin appeared at the rear of the truck. "I'll take Timon in. I've been here. Place gives me the creeps." He waved to Luke, Jeb and Zeke. "You guys might want to see this too."

"Hello, Diane," Luke said.

"Oh my god," Diane said. "Luke! There was chatter about a gunslinger but I didn't know it was you. And Jeb!" She enveloped Jeb in a hug. He backed away as soon as he could, blushing furiously.

Luke introduced Zeke, who shook Diane's hand and smiled.

Diane led the way down a huge passage.

"How did you get in here?" Luke asked as they walked.

"We stormed the facility," Diane replied casually. She laughed at the look of disbelief on Luke's face. She laid a hand on his arm. "It wasn't that hard. Security is primitive since the EMP of 2025. The guards let us walk right in. Most of them have joined us since then. And this place was designed to keep secrets, so we've been here undetected for years now."

Lynch worked his way between Luke and Diane. "Why is this place so important to the Believers?"

"I'm about to show you," Diane said as they came to another set of doors. "What you're about to see has been kept secret for generations."

She held her hand palm up on a scanner. The door buzzed and opened. She led the way to a huge, glass enclosed case.

"Exhibit A," Diane said.

The case held another smaller case filled with liquid. And inside floated a creature that was all too familiar to Luke, Lynch and Jeb.

"We call him Raptor," Diane said. "It's the closest creature to him we could think of. He's eight feet tall, twelve feet from snout to tail. The research indicates his saliva was corrosive as well as flammable. He has eight inch talons on each hind foot and his teeth are about four inches long. He was found in the desert near Roswell, New Mexico. He killed one hundred and twenty five men before he was subdued." She turned to Lynch and sweetly said, "You told me aliens don't exist."

Lynch smiled just as sweetly. "I hold firm to my statement. You see, that's not an alien. That is a juvenile Dragon. And you're lucky he didn't kill many more."

Diane paused, but only for a moment. "I thought you might say that. Come along, we have much more to see."

The next case held a bipod creature with a hugely exaggerated cranium. His musculature was underdeveloped to the point that his neck didn't seem strong enough to support his head.

"This one also came from Roswell," Diane said. "He was armed with those weapons," she pointed to another case holding two lance shaped items. "And," she said with a flourish as they rounded a corner, "he arrived in that ship."

She noted with satisfaction the apparent awe with which the group regarded the ship resting on concrete supports in a massive hangar.

"What do you have to say now, Lynch?" Diane asked. "I was right."

Lynch nodded. "Yes, you were right. And so was I. I told you if aliens did exist, you would not want them to visit your planet because they would only want to eat you. I would say they haven't been back because it's just not dinner time yet. You must admit, those creatures did not look friendly."

"Maybe," Diane said. "But we don't have time to debate the matter. The item you're looking for is in the next hangar."

Luke, Jeb and Zeke paused to stare at the massive ship.

"Did you know about this?" Luke asked Zeke.

"Nope," Zeke admitted. "The government kept this a secret. Probably one of the few things they did right."

They hurried to catch up to the group in the next hangar, where they were gathered around a huge archway leading nowhere. Colin stood over Timon's inert form, fidgeting nervously, with Ray Benson by his side.

"I think this is what you came for," Diane said.

"Looks like it," Lynch said. He motioned to Jeb and Luke. They joined him and Jeb slipped the Book of Runes from Lynch's pack.

"Open it, Jeb," Lynch suggested. "Just open it wherever the Book wants you to open it."

Jeb flipped the Book open.

"What do you see?" Lynch asked.

Jeb shrugged. "It's a spell to open locked items."

"Read it," Lynch ordered.

Jeb read the spell aloud as Lynch repeated it. He finished and closed the Book. Nothing happened. Lynch shot an accusing stare in Luke's direction. Timon began to stir.

"Try again," Lynch suggested.

Jeb opened the Book once again. "This one's a spell to counter a concealment spell."

He read it aloud and once again Lynch repeated it, with the same result.

"Give me that shotgun," Lynch said to Zeke. "I'm gonna blow Timon's head off and be done with it."

"No," Luke said in a tone that would not be denied. "Let me think for a minute."

"Oh, that's rich," Lynch sneered. "The Warrior is going to think our way out of this. You can't shoot the arch, Graywullf."

Luke drew both pistols and trained them on Lynch's head. "I can shoot you. That'll shut your mouth up once and for all."

"Stop," Diane ordered. "Give me that Book."

Jeb handed her the Book. She opened it to a random page. "Here it is. Activating a portal. Plain as day."

Jeb looked over her shoulder. "It says that's a transformation spell."

Luke also looked. "It's a blank page."

"No, it isn't," Diane argued. She began to read the lengthy spell. By the fourth line the arch began to hum. She continued reading. The arch glowed. Without warning, the space within it cleared, revealing a sandy hollow.

"Guess we didn't need you," Luke told Lynch. "What the Hell did you do to Jeb, teach him Dark Magic?"

"Is that Norland?" Zeke asked, before Lynch could reply. "The real one, I mean?"

No one answered.

"One way to find out," Lynch said. He stepped through as Diane reached out to try to stop him. The Dark Wizard was clearly visible. He turned back and said something but his words couldn't be heard. He shook his head irritably and stepped back through.

"It's Norland," he announced. "But damn close to the fortress where I originally imprisoned Slagg and hid the Book. We better hustle." He locked eyes with Diane. "Come with me."

Indecision clouded Diane's expression, but she finally shook her head. "This is my World, Lynch."

"Fine," the Dark Wizard said. He stared at the group. "What are you waiting for?"

Colin grimaced as he leaned down to grab Timon by his collar. He unceremoniously dragged Timon through the portal. Ray stepped aside to let Jeb pass.

"You comin'?" Luke asked Zeke.

"I have to agree with the lady," Zeke replied. "As screwed up as it is, this is my World. I'll stay."

Luke extended his hand, which Zeke took in a firm grip. "I'm beholden to you," Luke said. "I got a feeling we've been here before. I hope we got it right." He stepped through the portal, leaving Lynch behind. Luke watched his blurred outline through the haziness of the portal. The Dark Wizard approached Zeke and embraced him, then turned and hugged Diane. Without another word, he stepped back through the portal. Zeke, Ray Benson and Diane watched him go.

"Now what?" Ray asked of no one in particular.

"Now we wait," Diane replied.

Zeke glanced at his wrist. He stopped so suddenly he almost skidded on the smooth, concrete floor. "I'll be damned. He stole my watch."

CHAPTER TWENTY-FOUR

"It's almost over," Slagg hissed. His voice was almost unbearable, even to Jacob. It scalded and smoked in his mind.

It was true, Jacob realized. He and Slagg had been an unbeatable tandem, destroying villages and kingdoms alike. The problem that arose, in Jacob's mind, was it no longer seemed any of the humans he encountered were actually true servants of the Light. The *magii'ri* were decimated. The few who survived were so totally handicapped psychologically by the horrors they had witnessed they were incapable of meting out justice. He and Slagg tried to weed out the humans who served the Dark, albeit without the Sky Rider's express knowledge of that pursuit, but that only resulted in the near extermination of humankind. They were simply running out of targets and soon there would be nothing left but the monsters. But they had not been able to find Dunmore and Traegor's army.

Jacob felt the animosity growing between himself and the Sky Rider. They both recognized in each other the most powerful beings left in Norland. The day would come when they would face off and only one supreme being would remain.

"Yes," Jacob agreed. He had one last gamble to try. "Slagg, how long has it been since you checked on your eggs?"

"The eggs hatched long ago," Slagg dismissed.

"Did they?" Jacob feigned confusion. "Are you sure? Why haven't we seen your young?"

Slagg ignored him.

Jacob shrugged his shoulders and pretended indifference. "It's ok," he said. "I'm sure the eggs are fine. The Dragoness wouldn't hurt them anyway."

Slagg jerked his head around and Jacob knew the hook had been set. It had become obvious to him long ago that the great bull Dragon was insane. Slagg didn't know if he had hatched the eggs or eaten them himself. His left eye twitched. He stared down into the valley.

"Can you sense them?" Jacob asked innocently.

"I cannot!" he roared.

Jacob recoiled involuntarily from the lava flow Slagg's roar released in his head. He took his last shot.

"We could go check on them," he suggested. "It would only take a few hours."

"Yesss," Slagg agreed. "Yesss. We should check on the eggs."

He dipped his neck and allowed Jacob to climb on his back. As always, Jacob reveled in the feeling of freedom he felt during the few times the Sky Rider lowered himself to be ridden. The flight to Slagg's mountain took less than a quarter hour. After the Sky Rider alighted, he barely gave Jacob time to leap from his back before he entered the passage into the mountain. In his haste and his current unstable frame of mind, he didn't notice the newly repaired iron doors that hung at the entrance. Jacob waited only a few seconds before he gritted his teeth and swung the mighty doors shut. As he struggled with the massive beam to bar the doors La'Nay dropped from her hiding place and began crafting spells to seal them. Kelsey climbed up from below and helped Jacob drop the thousand pound, solid iron beam in place.

A terrifying roar shook the mountain. In his earlier years, Slagg may have been able to squeeze through one of the side passages. But, after having eaten so many villagers and their livestock, he could only exit through the main tunnel. The mountain shook again, this time from the impact as Slagg slammed into the doors. They bulged outward as La'Nay frantically crafted more spells to hold them. The Sky Rider mindlessly butted the doors with his head, over and over. Each blow dislodged bits of rock from the mountain above.

"Will it hold?" Jacob asked as they backed away.

"It'll hold," La'Nay assured him. "It has to. At least, long enough."

CHAPTER TWENTY-FIVE

"It's good to be back," Timon said. "It's fitting, is it not, Lynch? That the end of all things should come here, where your journey into the Darkness began."

"Shut up," Lynch growled. He adjusted his duster and checked the pockets. "At least the spell worked. Now what?"

"Mathias didn't have the rest planned out," Luke replied. "I guess he figured he'd wait and see if we made it back first."

"I say we take Timon to Slagg's lair and blow his brains out," Colin offered.

Jeb nodded silently.

"That would end the Wilding," Lynch agreed. "And save Norland."

Timon looked from one to another. "How?" he asked. "How could such a bunch of idiots have bested me?"

Colin slapped him across the back of the head, knocking him on his face in the sand.

"But it wouldn't save your brother, Lynch," Luke said. "And brothers always have each other's back. Always."

Lynch was silent, a faraway look in his eyes. It didn't seem possible that he was so close to realizing his lifelong pursuit. To bring Timon to justice and free Talin from the imprisoning hulk of the Sky Rider. Nostalgia washed over him, so strong he felt he was drowning in it. Had he wasted his life? Did he ever even have a choice? He knew he didn't. He owed that much to his brother.

"How bad is he wounded?" Lynch asked Colin.

Colin gave Timon a quick once over. "Luke did his job. He centered the guy. But if it hadn't been an enchanted bullet this son of a bitch would have walked away. He'll live until we blow his brains out."

"Then we take him to the top of Slagg's mountain and hold him there," Lynch said, taking charge. "Colin, you keep watch. If things go bad, you kill him and you make damn sure he's dead. Me, Luke and the boy will search for Mathias. If we can't find Mathias," he told Luke, "then we find Slagg and lead him here. One way or another, we're gonna end this."

Luke took a deep breath. "One way or another," he promised.

"Wait," Jeb said suddenly. "Did you feel that?"

"Feel what?" Luke asked.

"I felt the ground shake," Jeb replied.

They all heard a muffled roar and dust flew from the various air vents on the side of Slagg's mountain. The earth shook again.

"What the Hell?" Luke asked.

"Slagg's home," Lynch replied. He had heard the same roars of frustration and rage so many years ago, when he had been the one to imprison the Sky Rider.

"Your time is almost up," Timon sneered. He laughed as he nodded at the mountainside and valley below them. "Behold my army."

As far as they could see, the valley below was filled with camps of Beastsoldiers.

"You're too late," Timon said. "My Beasts will wipe out the rest of your paltry resistance. They'll free me from these blasted handcuffs and I will make all of you pay. I should thank you for bringing me back to Norland."

"What do we do now?" Jeb asked.

"We fight," Luke said.

"Can I kill him now?" Lynch begged.

"Not yet," Luke said. "How about it, Lynch? We're up against impossible odds. Thousands of Beastsoldiers are about to overrun Norland. When that happens, no one will even remember the Dark

Wizard Lynch. You'll be forgotten. But fight with me now and your name will be sung as a hero."

Lynch grinned. "No one will ever forget the Dark Wizard Lynch." He unbuckled his gunbelt and handed it to Jeb. "You better have this," he suggested.

"You don't have a weapon," Jeb protested.

"I *am* a weapon," Lynch replied. "This is it, Graywullf. The last, great battle of our time."

Luke nodded as he drew each pistol and rotated the cylinders. He carefully counted the bullets in each gunbelt, including the one he had liberated from the undead gunslingers. He freed his knife in its sheath and made sure the tomahawk was in place in his belt. He unslung his sword and handed it to Lynch.

"I know you're a weapon and all," he drawled, "but it won't hurt to have a blade."

Lynch grinned his feral grin.

"What the Hell am I supposed to do?" Colin demanded. "Stay here and babysit?"

"Guard the Portal," Lynch said. "Don't let anything in or out. You have that big rifle, don't you?"

Colin raised the rifle so they could see it.

"If they get close," Lynch suggested. "You can persuade them to turn back with that. But save one bullet for Timon. Make it count. Ready?" He asked Luke and Jeb.

"Ready as I'll ever be," Luke replied. Jeb nodded, tight lipped with worry.

They began to walk down the mountain to meet the Beast army.

"It'll be close work after the pistols run dry," Luke told Jeb. "Then it's all about luck more than training. Keep moving, all the time, never stop. If they pin you down, it's all over."

"Ok," Jeb said.

"One more thing," Luke said without taking his eyes off the advance scouts that were coming into range. "I'm proud of you."

Jeb smiled.

"Remember what I taught you, too," Lynch said, not to be outdone.

Luke chuckled but it was cut short as a Rider and three disgraced gunslingers arose from the rocks. He estimated the range. Too far for a pistol.

"Get ready," he warned.

They heard the bullet passing over their heads before they heard the report. The Rider slapped one hand to his face and was swatted from the saddle. He had barely hit the ground when the big rifle boomed again and a gunslinger took two more steps without a head. Luke charged the remaining two. He drew on the run and the instant he was in range he fired both guns simultaneously. The last two gunslingers went down with the muzzles of their guns spurting fire. Luke and Jeb unbuckled their belts and jerked them from around their bodies as they began to smoke. They were both full of shiny, loaded cartridges. The undead gunfighters dissolved into ash. Jeb's face went white.

"You'll do fine," Luke assured him.

He turned and led the charge into the mass of Beastsoldiers.

CHAPTER TWENTY-SIX

U p on the stony ledge, Jacob whirled back to look at La'Nay. "Did you hear that?" he asked. "Gunfire. That must be *magii'ri.*"

"Or one of those nasty Riders who shot you before," Kelsey reminded him.

Jacob stared until even his keen eyes watered. "No," he finally said excitedly, "it's *magii'ri*. I think one of them is Luke!"

"We have to get down there," La'Nay ordered. "Now. You two go ahead," she almost laughed at the look of indignation on Kelsey's face. "It's alright. You two are much faster without me. I'll catch up. Now, go!"

Jacob and Kelsey charged down the mountainside, leaping boulders and deadfalls at the risk of life and limb. La'Nay followed as fast as she dared. Jacob and Kelsey plowed into the flank of the Beast army. Kelsey wielded his axe like a farmer cutting hay, sweeping it back and forth with mighty strokes that severed heads and limbs. Jacob slashed and ducked, stabbed and parried, all with unbelievable speed. Enemies fell before him by the score.

At the head of the Beast army, Luke and Jeb scooped up swords from fallen Beastsoldiers. Luke whipped out his tomahawk. Strength from the many spells Lynch had cast upon it flowed up his arm. He moved with deadly grace from one enemy to another, leaving them dead or dying in his wake. Jeb's face was a pasty white, but he fought with dogged determination, always trying to keep Luke in sight and protect his back. Lynch held back for only a moment, muttering under his breath. Luke and Jeb both felt the spell of Dark Magic he cast, but Jeb had no idea what it was. Luke felt it as a glowing coal in his core that radiated strength and endurance, and he recognized it immediately.

"Damn you, Lynch!" he shouted. "No more magic!"

Lynch was beyond hearing. The spell he cast upon himself was much more powerful. He let the Dark Magic take control, then he waded into the Beasts. His sword flashed in the sun, spraying droplets of black blood in a fine mist. The Beasts he encountered inevitably panicked when they saw him. Many turned and ran, crashing headlong into their companions.

Jacob outpaced Kelsey. He drove into the center of the Beast army, and then he let his own Beast take control. He felt enemies before they could even strike, and his counterattacks were performed with uncanny speed. He armed himself with a battleaxe and a massive sword, and he turned and whirled in a graceful ballet of blood and death.

A commotion arose from the far side of the Beast army, near the head. Explosions sounded. Beastsoldiers and parts of Beastsoldiers were flung fifty feet in the air. Flashes of light followed, like lightning during a summer thunderstorm, and the acrid stench of burned hair and Beast hide followed.

"Mathias," Luke whispered.

The tide of Beastsoldiers turned towards the new threat. Panic churned in Luke's gut.

"No," he grunted as he fought off another attack and stabbed a Beast in the stomach. "No!" he repeated with more urgency as he heard Mathias' cries of rage and pain. He charged through the ranks of the Beasts, leaving Jeb behind as the 'prentice worked away doggedly at the wall of soldiers who blocked his way. He was surrounded, and drew his pistol. Six shots cleared an escape route and he ran through.

Luke drew both pistols and ran headlong into the clot of Beasts who blocked his way, firing as he ran. His pistols ran dry and he jammed them home in the holsters. Suddenly, he broke through. Mathias was trapped in a depression surrounded by boulders. As Luke leaped to the top of one he saw Mathias go down. A primal scream of rage ripped from his throat as he jumped into the middle of the Beasts. He hacked and stabbed and slashed at the Beasts until he stood over his fallen friend. He glanced down. Mathias blinked and opened his eyes. A gash on his head pumped blood down one side of his face, but he saw Luke and recognized him. Luke stood over Mathias. He automatically drew and reloaded his revolvers without looking.

"Thank you, Warrior," Mathias groaned.

"Brothers do that," Luke replied. "I'll punch you in the mouth later."

"Deal," Mathias said. "Are we winning?"

"Hard to say," Luke grunted as he fought off another Beast. The truth was, they were destined to lose. There were too many Beasts. But Luke vowed they would not harm the Wizard while he lived.

Midway down the Beast ranks, La'Nay joined the fight. She drew her pistol and stood like a duelist. Each shot dropped a Beast. When that cylinder ran dry, she flipped a loaded one from a pouch at her belt, slipped the empty out and replaced it and resumed firing. A Beast reared up close to her, swinging his sword high. La'Nay grabbed wildly for her own blade to parry it when the Beast's head dissolved in a fine spray that speckled her face. A moment later she heard the boom of Colin's heavy rifle. She gave him a quick salute and resumed her own attack.

A horn sounded. The Beasts paused, fear registering on their faces. Another horn blew from the rear of the army. Chanting rose above the din of battle. The chanting of hundreds and hundreds of dwarves, feet stomping and weapons banging on shields. The dwarves attacked and the side of the Beast army collapsed.

"Warriors!" a deep voice shouted from the rear. "Attack! Attack! Slay them all!"

Luke strained to catch a glimpse of this new force. He saw the standard of the Eastern Provinces, flying high. In the forefront of the Eastern Warriors, a tall, lean Warrior led the charge. A battle cry rose from the throat of Joseph of Ead as he plunged into battle. Hope blossomed inside Luke.

Kelsey and La'Nay reached Jacob, and the three fought their way down the center of the army. Jacob was covered in blood and gore. Kelsey gasped for air, but Jacob showed no fatigue. The growls of the Beastsoldiers were turning into cries of fear. The new arrivals were fierce and showed no pity. Suddenly, shouts of panic rose from the Easterners in a palpable wave. They pointed to the sky. Luke followed their gestures. A Dragon swept down the mountain, flying so low and so fast the fir trees were bent over in his wake. The Beasts cheered, until the Dragon dove on them and flames erupted from his fire vent. A man clung to his neck. The Dragon scorched the army of Beastsoldiers from one end to the other, turned, and swooped in again. This time it flew so low to the ground it's wingtips actually brushed the larger boulders. It dipped and weaved, slashing its talons through all it encountered. The Beasts broke rank and began to scatter. They ignored the combined armies in their haste to escape, and they were cut down by the score. Jacob couldn't contain his disbelief. The young man riding the Dragon was Allie. He leaped in the air and cheered as he pumped his fist at the sky. Allie directed the Dragon through the Beast army several more times, then they rose to the clouds and disappeared.

Luke was dumbstruck by the sudden fortunate turn of events. He bent over, hands on his knees and tried to regain his breath. He was bleeding from a dozen cuts and was battered and bruised, but he was alive. He turned his attention back to Mathias. The Wizard was struggling to his feet. Luke helped him to stand.

"We won," he whispered. "I don't know how, but we won." He met Luke's eyes. "Did you bring Timon back?"

"I did," Luke replied. "With some help. Can you make it up the mountain?"

"Somehow, I will," Mathias assured him. "This is not over yet."

Mathias had a large gash on his head and various cuts and bruises. He also had four puncture wounds in his calf where he had been bitten. When he bent to examine that wound, he discovered two of the fingers on his left hand were missing. He held up his hand and stared at it blankly. Luke grimaced. He tore off the tail of his shirt and bound Mathias' wounded hand and began to help the hobbling Wizard up the hill.

"I'm sorry, Luke," he apologized. "I handled everything quite badly."

"I won't argue that," Luke said. "But I won't hold it against you either. It's the kid you need to be worried about."

"Just get me up the hill," Mathias promised, "And I'll set it all right."

The Easterners, led by Lance L'orinel, and the dwarves advanced up the battlefield finishing off the wounded Beasts. Occasionally, the big rifle in Colin's hands boomed as he spied an enemy with fight left in them. Joseph of Ead also worked his way towards Jacob, La'Nay and Kelsey. Two more shots rang out from the mountainside.

"He's out," Luke announced. The *magii'ri* Warrior's practice of counting expended bullets had him frowning in consternation. "He was supposed to hold one back for Timon in case things went bad."

Shouts from the battlefield made him turn around. What he saw made his blood run cold. A pack of trolls burst from hiding near a huge boulder and charged Jacob and his group. Luke dropped Mathias and ran headlong down the mountain, but he knew he would never make it in time. La'Nay drew her pistol and triggered three shots into the nearest troll. He dropped to one knee and fell forward on his face, but there were still three more. Jacob attacked. He ran forward and slid between the legs of the nearest troll and struck upward with his sword. It went in to the hilt and was wrenched from his grip, leaving him unarmed. Kelsey also attacked. His recent wounds and fatigue left him slower and weaker than usual, and the troll drove him back with repeated blows from a club the size of a sapling tree. La'Nay refused to leave him. She dropped her empty revolver back in the holster and drew a short sword. As the troll went by her in pursuit of the backpedaling Kelsey, she hacked at its hamstring. The troll's leg collapsed, but he swung his club with a backhand swing and knocked her flying. Jacob jumped at the wounded troll who wrapped him in a bear hug and squeezed. It roared and lowered its gaping jaws down to engulf Jacob's entire head. Luke screamed a wordless cry of rage. Jacob freed one arm and jammed it under the beast's jaw, then slipped the other arm out. He slammed the heel of his hand into the troll's upper jaw and straightened his arms. He tore the troll's lower jaw loose. It shrieked in agony and threw Jacob thirty feet to the side. One of the remaining trolls lumbered towards La'Nay's fallen form. As he reached for her, Joseph leaped from a nearby boulder and landed on its back. He stabbed the monster between the shoulder blades repeatedly. It squealed in pain and frantically tried to reach the human on its back. Joseph could have jumped to safety, but he made no effort to flee. The troll finally caught him in one massive hand and began to fling the annoying human from his back. Joseph wrapped both hands around the hilt of his knife and plunged it through the beast's skull. The troll's eyes crossed, but it continued its throwing motion and hammered Joseph into the ground. He lay in a crumpled heap.

Luke was finally within range. The last troll was crawling towards an exhausted Kelsey. Jacob was struggling to regain his feet. Luke drew on the run and shot the monster in the eye. It grunted, then let out a groaning squeal and pitched forward on its face. The entire attack was over in less than a minute.

Luke and Jacob both ran to La'Nay, who was struggling to sit up.

"I'll be alright," La'Nay assured them. "Check on Joseph."

Jacob ran back to the fallen Warrior King and gently rolled him over. Joseph gasped in pain. His eyes fluttered open and he recognized Jacob.

"I failed again," he moaned. "One last chance for glory and I blew it."

"No," Jacob insisted. "You save La'Nay's life. You enlisted the army from the Eastern Provinces and you came back to fight with us. You have been true to the Code, and you will be welcomed at the Feast."

Joseph smiled. He coughed and blood welled up in his throat. He choked on it, spat it out and whispered, "The Black Arrow rides upon my back. I wanted another shot at Slagg. Looks like you're gonna have to take it for me." His body went limp.

Jacob felt Luke's comforting hand upon his shoulder and turned to look up into his familiar face. "He died with honor," Luke said.

"Our Fathers will be waiting for him. But we still have business to tend to."

Jacob rose. Luke reached for him awkwardly. He grabbed Jacob's hand and wrapped one arm around his shoulders.

"For crying out loud," La'Nay exclaimed. "Jacob, meet your Father. You both know it."

Luke and Jacob were both suddenly shy.

"By the gods, men are so stupid," La'Nay remarked. "Give your son a proper hug, Luke."

Luke shrugged and turned red. Jacob reached around Luke and enveloped him in a powerful hug and lifted him off the ground.

"Easy, now," Luke protested.

The mountainside shook. Dust flew from the massive iron doors covering Slagg's den. His roar of rage echoed down the valley. Jacob dropped Luke, ran to Joseph and took the Black Arrow from its leather case. He scanned the battlefield.

"Here," Kelsey called. He climbed to his feet holding a bow as tall as he was and as thick as his wrist. Jacob ran to his friend and took the bow.

"You gonna make it?" Jacob asked.

"Wouldn't miss it," Kelsey replied with a grin.

"Let's get up the hill to Mathias," Luke ordered.

Jacob scooped La'Nay up in his arms despite her protests that she could walk. Luke helped Kelsey and they hurried up the hill. Slagg's cries of rage were growing more intense. Each time he roared, Jacob cringed in actual pain. Colin met them part way up.

"You're supposed to be guarding Timon and the gate," Luke gasped, fighting for air as they struggled up the hill.

"Got it covered," Colin replied. He slung Kelsey over his shoulder and lumbered back up the hill.

They reached the gate. Timon knelt at the entrance. Lynch stood slightly to one side and behind him. Mathias sat thirty feet behind Lynch with Jeb at his side.

"They made it," Luke breathed a sigh of relief.

Jacob's body stiffened at the sight of Mathias. He stopped and gently lowered La'nay to her feet. His body went cold. Mathias, the

Wizard who made him a monster, was at his mercy. The Wizard who was never satisfied and who denied him his own family, was helpless before him. He nocked the Black Arrow and pulled the bow back to full draw and aimed it at Mathias' heart.

"No," La'Nay's voice cut through the red haze in his mind.

Luke turned to look. "No, Jacob." He said. "Stand down."

"He made me a monster," Jacob said through clenched teeth. "I'm not even human."

"This is your chance, Jacob," Luke said. "This is where you make your choice."

The iron doors on Slagg's den parted and were flung out and down the mountain. The Sky Rider emerged and took to the air with one beat of his wings. Lynch began reciting spells under his breath. Slagg was upon them in seconds. He stooped, flames already jetting from his fire vent, and swept downwards.

"Kill him," Slagg's voice boiled in Jacob's brain. "Shoot him, cut him, slay him!" the Dragon's voice cried.

Slagg was all but upon Mathias and Lynch when Jacob released the Arrow. At the last possible moment, he changed his point of aim. Lynch grinned, reached inside his duster and jerked out Zeke's shotgun. He jammed the barrel against the back of Timon's head and pulled the trigger. The shotgun boomed, and at the same moment the Black Arrow struck home in Slagg. But not in his heart. Jacob had waited a fraction of a second too long. The Arrow entered the Sky Rider's flank and erupted from the far side in a gout of black blood. The Dragon writhed and bit at his side. The impetus of his flight carried him into the gate. A sound wave radiated outward from the gate and knocked everyone sprawling in the sandy soil. Even the soldiers in the valley were knocked down by its force.

Jacob was the first to his feet. "He's gone," he said in disbelief. "Son of a bitch. He's gone."

Everyone turned to look at the gate. The Sky Rider had vanished. Lynch looked from the gate to Timon's headless body, then back to the gate. There was a shadow there, where nothing had been before. Lynch crawled towards it.

"Can it be?" he asked. He struggled to his feet and limped to the entrance of the gate. "Talin," he whispered. "My brother." He dropped to his knees and cradled Talin in his arms.

Talin's eyes opened and he tried to smile. "Lynch." He gazed up into the cloudless sky. "I'm finally free."

"I'm sorry," Lynch cried. "I tried, I really did."

"I know," Talin replied. "I know." He encircled Lynch's neck with his hands and pulled the Dark Wizard close. Sobs wracked Lynch's body as Talin's life expired.

"I'm leaving now," Kelsey's voice cut through the sudden silence. La'Nay shot him a murderous look. "I know," he said as he held his hands out at chest height and backed away. "I've seen some weird shit, but nothing like what I've seen since I joined you people."

Luke approached the Dark Wizard and laid a hand on his shoulder. Lynch looked up. Luke offered him his other hand and helped Lynch to his feet.

"You did what you could," Luke assured him. "He died as a man, not a prisoner inside the Sky Rider."

"But where did Slagg go?" Jacob asked.

"Oh, crap," Lynch said. "He went through the gate."

"Hey!" Kelsey shouted. Everyone jumped and turned to look. He pointed down the valley. "What's happening?"

The hazy quality of the air was gone. The sky was a brilliant blue and the mountains were clearly visible. As they watched, the valley below turned green again. The hordes of Beastsoldiers who had fallen in battle dissolved. Grass and shrubs sprouted where they had lain. The peak of Slagg's mountain was capped with snow. A spring bubbled to life in the valley below. Fir trees appeared surrounding the gate, and birds and squirrels flitted among their branches. As one they all drew a deep breath of the amazingly refreshing air.

"The Wilding is broken," Mathias proclaimed. He slumped back against a boulder, covered his face with his hands and wept with relief. They all stared in wonder at the transformation that was taking place.

"Norland will heal," La'Nay said. "It's all over. I can't believe it."

"We should celebrate," Kelsey said as he tromped back up the slope to join them. "Has anybody got any biscuits?" The others just shook their heads. "Does anybody have what it takes to make biscuits?" Kelsey persisted. "No? Does anybody even know *how* to make biscuits?"

"I don't know about you, Kels," Jacob said.

"I just want some biscuits," Kelsey replied.

A breeze swept through the valley below, gaining intensity as it climbed the slope. The trees bent before it as it blew ever harder towards the portal. The survivors watched with trepidation as the litter of dust and leaves was sucked through the gate and disappeared.

"Grab something!" Luke yelled. He latched onto a sapling tree with one hand and snagged Jeb as the teen actually began skidding across the ground. The wind snatched all further words from their mouths and whipped them down the mountainside. He could see La'Nay crouching over Mathias as he hugged the ground, her mouth working in a silent shout. Lynch clung to the edge of the portal opening with one hand and both booted feet like a giant spider while he furiously worked on something with his free hand. The wind shrieked in Luke's ears. Suddenly he was struck a numbing blow as the sapling Jacob clung to was uprooted and he flew right into Luke. He caught a glimpse of Jacob's face inches from his own, then they were flying through the air into the mouth of the portal. Lynch grinned like a maniac as they went by. Then he launched himself into the air and was sucked through the portal behind them. Once inside the portal he dropped with a thud. A sudden, sharp intake of breath in the deafening silence revealed he had landed on a vulnerable companion.

"Gawddammit, Lynch," Luke growled. "Get your knee outta my balls."

Lynch extricated himself from the pile. He lunged at the portal and was repelled by a force so powerful he was forced to his knees. The others joined him, but the gate was shut. They could clearly see Mathias, La'Nay and Kelsey, but no sound penetrated the portal.

"Get away!" Lynch shouted. He pounded on the invisible barrier between them. "We need to go," he said to his companions.

He cast another glance into Norland. La'Nay was crawling away in a shallow depression, keeping as low to the ground as possible. Kelsey threw Mathias over his shoulder and leaned nearly perpendicular to the ground as he carried him down the mountain. Lynch nodded in satisfaction.

"They'll make it," he said to himself. "We really need to go," he insisted.

"We need to get back through," Jacob argued.

"Ain't gonna happen," Lynch said as he hastily walked away.

Realization blossomed on Luke's face.

"What did you do?" he demanded as he caught up to the Dark Wizard.

Lynch didn't answer. Instead he broke into a run and cast a fearful glance back at the portal. His panic was contagious. All the others ran after him. Their pounding footsteps were muffled by the dust that lay thick upon everything they could see. Even in the dim light and running hellbent for leather Luke realized the place was familiar. It was the cavern in Area 51, but it was empty now. It didn't seem possible, but Lynch actually picked up the pace. Luke began to doubt the Dark Wizard's sanity when he suddenly realized Lynch was counting aloud. The Wizard had reached fifty-three when they came to a massive steel door.

"Here it is," Lynch gasped to himself.

He shoved the door open just enough to enter and frantically motioned the others to follow him. He continued counting as they did. With Jacob's help he slammed the door shut.

"Fifty-nine, sixty," Lynch gasped. He held his breath. Nothing happened.

"What's goin' on?" Luke demanded.

Lynch put a finger to his lips. A moment later a huge explosion rocked the mountain. Emergency lights glowed to life as rocks and dust and chunks of concrete fell from the ceiling.

"Good grief, Lynch," Luke groaned. "What did you do now?"

"Closed the door," Lynch replied with a satisfied smile.

"Why?" Jacob demanded.

"Yeah, why?" Jeb added. "What happened to everyone being in the World they belong in?"

"What makes you think you don't belong here?" Lynch said to all of them. "Being sucked through the doorway was a pretty clear sign."

Emergency ventilation fans groaned to life and quickly cleared the air.

"It was a sign," Lynch assured them. "Whatever this World is, we belong here and the doorway needs to be closed. Forever."

"So you planted a bomb in the doorway?" Luke asked incredulously. "Where did you get it?"

Lynch grinned. "I wore it. That was the explosive vest I was working on."

Luke stared in disbelief. "That's why you said you were a weapon."

Lynch shrugged. "Not completely. After all, I am the Dark Wizard Lynch."

"Yer an idiot," Luke replied. "You could have brought the whole mountain down on top of us."

Jacob grunted a crude affirmation. Lynch shrugged indifferently.

"Do you think this is the World Slagg went to?" Jeb suddenly asked. "He went through the door right before we did."

"What do you think, 'prentice?" Lynch responded.

Jeb fidgeted uncomfortably. "I don't know."

"Sure you do," Lynch insisted.

Luke and Jacob watched the exchange with mounting interest.

"Why are you hackin' on him?" Luke demanded of Lynch.

"He knows," Lynch replied. "Slagg was invited here."

"What? How?" Luke asked.

"Totems and sigils, maybe some amateur Dark magic. Perhaps even the initiation of a Dragoncult," Lynch answered.

Images of the Dragon gang sigil at the rocket train entrance flashed through Luke's mind.

"Jeb?" he asked. He turned to Lynch. With a sudden curse, he grabbed Lynch by the shirtfront. He knotted his gnarled hands in the fabric and slammed Lynch into the stone wall at his back. "Gawddamn you, Lynch," he growled. "What did you do?"

"I did it," Jeb interrupted. He tried to step between Lynch and free the Dark Wizard from Luke's cruel grip. Lynch's face turned purple. "Let him go," Jeb pleaded.

With a muffled curse, Luke released the Dark Wizard.

"You don't know what it's like here," Jeb said. "I asked Lynch to teach me a few things. He taught me some minor magic and how to fight his way."

"His way?" Luke repeated.

"Dirty," Jeb admitted.

"Fight to win, at all costs," Lynch corrected.

"Jeb…" Luke began.

"I remember everything," Jeb said. His eyes were haunted. "I remember Dez and Mary Alice and how his arm blew up when Phil tried to chop it off with the hatchet after the window spider bit him. I remember them boys stomping me to death and the taste of blood and shit and puke in my mouth. I remember Daisy, and you and the guys rescuing us from the Abyss. But there's nothing in Norland that can prepare you for the cruelty in this World. Too many people want what other's have busted their asses for, and they'll stop at nothin' to get it. The leaders of this World are corrupt and allow themselves to be ruled by greed." His expression turned savage. "They deserve to have Slagg turned loose on them."

Luke had no answer. He turned back to Lynch and Jacob with a shrug. How could he argue?

"Bravo," Lynch said, his voice hoarse. "Bravo!" he said louder. "In all my centuries I have never created the mayhem you have released upon this World in one fell swoop. They'll never know what hit them. Slagg will be merciless. None will escape."

Jeb nodded enthusiastically, but Luke and Jacob both shook their heads.

"Slagg won't be choosy," Jacob pointed out. "He'll kill the innocent along with the wicked."

"That'll be like six people," Jeb argued.

"Six people are worth saving," Luke stated. "What about Jack and Diane?" he asked. "And your friends?"

"We could warn them," Jeb said.

"And then what?" Luke asked. "They'd survive the first attack and have to live like fugitives for the rest of their lives."

"I don't care," Jeb said.

His mind was made up. He drew his pistol. Lynch groaned. He expected Luke to draw his own weapon. He waited expectantly for the thunder of guns, but it didn't come. Luke merely watched with a small sad smile. Jacob started forward, but Luke stayed him with an upraised hand. Jeb waved the pistol threateningly.

"Open the door," he ordered Jacob.

Jacob chuckled in disbelief, but then he shrugged and pulled the door open. Jeb slipped out. They could hear his muffled footsteps as he ran towards the entrance.

"I can stop him," Jacob said. "There's still time."

Luke shook his head. "Every *magii'ri* Warrior must face the time when he has to make the decision that shapes the rest of his life. This is Jeb's time."

"So, what are we going to do?" Jacob asked.

"Follow the Code," Luke said. "We have to try to hunt Slagg down and kill him."

"We might get killed trying," Jacob asserted.

Lynch nodded. "The good guys don't always win, Graywullf," he agreed.

Luke snorted derisively. He squeezed through the door. "Who ever said we're the good guys?"

It was a pleasant evening. Crickets sang among the rocks off the shoulder of the road. An occasional night bird called. The whole World just felt *different*. After an hour of walking, headlights appeared on the road behind them.

"Be ready," Lynch warned.

The headlights belonged to a pickup truck driven by a sunburned, old rancher wearing a sweat stained hat. The skin of his face resembled tanned leather. He pulled to a stop next to them.

"Goin' into town?" he asked.

"I reckon," Lynch replied.

The old rancher sized them up. "Hop in the back."

The three climbed in the back of the truck. Jacob crouched with one hand on the side rail, ready to leap out at a moment's notice. The old rancher took them into Hiko and dropped them off at a truck stop. Semi-trucks purred in the parking lot, parked side by side. The air smelled like fried grease and diesel fuel. Saliva spurted in Luke's mouth.

"I'm hungry," Jacob announced.

"This is… different," Lynch observed.

People came and went freely. A black and white police cruiser glided through the parking lot. The cruiser bounced to a stop and the sound of a barking dog came from within it. The back up lights came on and the lawman reversed up to the three. He emerged from the car and opened the back door. Milo, the half hound, half pit bull mix leaped out and bounded over to Lynch, his tail wagging furiously. He leaped up to place his front paws on Lynch's chest and tried to lick his face. The police officer watched with sudden interest. He shut the car off and approached the three.

"I'd like to buy you fellas a cup of coffee," he said.

"We're really not thirsty, Officer…uh…Sipowicz," Lynch began.

"You're Zeke's son," Luke interrupted. "I see him in you."

"We really need to go in and sit down," the policeman said. "And it's Sheriff Sipowicz."

"A beer or three would be nice," Lynch decided.

They all went inside and sat at a booth in the corner. Lynch slid in with his back to the wall. The waitress appeared and made a big fuss over Milo, who's tail thumped the floor. Sheriff Sipowicz ordered coffee for everyone.

"Where do I start?" the Sheriff began. "My father told me a lot. Eventually he put me in touch with Jack and Diane Parsons. It seems they all had memories that weren't really memories at all. They remembered living through things that happened in the future. The crazy thing is, *everybody's future changed*. Jack Parsons didn't get hurt playing football. He had a great college career and then went into coaching. Now he coaches the Hiko Hurricanes. They've won two state championships. Him and Diane have three kids. She's a well known author of books about the paranormal. My father, Zeke, was a deputy into his seventies. He was killed stopping a bank robbery, but he nailed three of them before they got him. And, unless I am totally crazy, you are Luke and Lynch. And I would guess that makes you Jacob."

"I'd like some fries," Lynch called to the waitress. "The biggest plate you have. Make that a basket. And chile burgers all around. On the Sheriff," he added. He saw the Sheriff staring at him. "It's no big deal. The county will pay for it. And a round of beers."

Sheriff Sipowicz made an exasperated sound. "Did you listen to anything I said?"

"Sure," Lynch replied. "But I'm really hungry."

"So you are Lynch, Luke and Jacob? The dog recognized you, that's what tipped me off. But Zeke told me you'd show up someday," the sheriff said. "Here," he reached in his uniform coat and pulled out a cell phone. "Diane took these the day you went through the gate in Area 51."

He scrolled through until he found photos of Luke and Lynch shaking Zeke's hand.

"I'll be damned," Luke said. He grinned. "That's me and Zeke. So," he mused, "Zeke died honoring the Code. Maybe we will meet again at the Feast." He turned to Lynch. "It worked."

"Looks that way," Lynch conceded. "Have you noticed anything...strange?" He asked the sheriff. "Any animal sightings, slaughtered cows, semi-trucks carried off the roadway, cities burned to the ground, entire communities attacked and eaten? Anything like that?"

"No," Sheriff Sipowicz regarded Lynch with suspicion. "Why?"

"No reason," Lynch dismissed. "It's just that, well, we may have let a full grown Dragon come through the gate from Norland."

"You did what?" the Sheriff asked.

"We don't know that," Luke said in a placating manner. "We haven't seen any evidence of the Dragon yet."

"True," Lynch admitted. "We haven't seen a single person with their entrails hanging out and we've been here a couple hours already.

But he damn sure went somewhere." He looked up quickly. "Our food's here. Let's eat."

"Where did the dog come from?" Luke asked around a mouthful of hamburger.

"He came back through the gate," Sheriff Sipowicz said. "We've had sentries posted up there since this all went down. President Benson wanted to know if anyone returned," He paused. "You didn't see any sentries?"

"Nope," Lynch replied. He suddenly felt exposed. "Let's get a round of these burgers to go," he suggested to the waitress. He watched her as she walked back to the kitchen. "Maybe I'll come back later for dessert." The waitress gave him a smile as she flipped her hair and swayed back to the kitchen.

Fifteen minutes later they walked with Sheriff Sipowicz and Milo back to the cruiser. He was very agitated about the sentries and insisted he needed to call it in. As he climbed back into the car, a shadow passed over the moon and disappeared into the night sky.

Lynch glanced up. "Here we go again," he said with a savage grin.

www.ingramcontent.com/pod-product-compliance
Lightning Source LLC
LaVergne TN
LVHW021655060526
838200LV00050B/2365